About the

Caroline Anderson's been a nurse, a secretary, a teacher, and has run her own business. Now she's settled on writing. 'I was looking for that elusive something and finally realised it was variety – now I have it in abundance. Every book brings new horizons, new friends, and in between books I juggle! My husband John and I have two beautiful daughters, Sarah and Hannah, umpteen pets, and several acres of Suffolk that nature tries to reclaim every time we turn our backs!'

Lauren Hawkeye is a writer, yoga newbie, knitting aficionado, and animal lover who lives in the shadows of the great Rocky Mountains of Alberta, Canada. She's older than she looks – really – and younger than she feels – most of the time – and she loves to explore the journeys that take women through life in her stories. Hawkeye's stories include erotic historical, steamy paranormal, and hot contemporary.

Yasmin Y. Sullivan grew up in upstate New York and St Thomas, Virgin Islands, from which her family hails. She moved to Washington, DC, to attend university and has earned degrees from Howard and Yale. As an academic writer, she has published on Douglass, Jacobs, Baldwin, Angelou, and Bullins, as well as the Negritude Movement and the Danish West Indies. She currently lives and teaches in Washington, DC, and when she is not teaching, she does creative writing and works on mosaics.

Sinfully Yours

Sinfully Yours:
The Ex

CAROLINE ANDERSON

LAUREN HAWKEYE

YASMIN Y. SULLIVAN

MILLS & BOON

First Published in Great Britain 2023
by Mills & Boon, an imprint of HarperCollins*Publishers* Ltd,
1 London Bridge Street, London, SE1 9GF

www.harpercollins.co.uk

HarperCollins*Publishers*
Macken House, 39/40 Mayor Street Upper,
Dublin 1, D01 C9W8, Ireland

Sinfully Yours: The Ex © 2023 Harlequin Enterprises ULC.

The Fiancée He Can't Forget © 2011 Caroline Anderson
Between the Lines © 2019 Lauren Hawkeye
Return to Love © 2013 Yasmin Y. DeGout

ISBN: 978-0-263-31949-1

MIX
Paper | Supporting
responsible forestry
FSC™ C007454

This book is produced from independently certified FSC™ paper
to ensure responsible forest management.

For more information visit: www.harpercollins.co.uk/green

Printed and Bound in the UK using 100% Renewable Electricity
at CPI Group (UK) Ltd, Croydon, CR0 4YY

THE FIANCÉE
HE CAN'T FORGET

CAROLINE ANDERSON

CHAPTER ONE

'ARE you OK?'

Was she?

She wasn't sure. Her heart was pounding, her legs felt like jelly and her stomach was rebelling, but it was Daisy's wedding day, so Amy dug around and dredged up some kind of a smile.

'I'm fine.'

'Sure?'

'Absolutely!' she lied, and tried to make the smile look more convincing. She didn't even need to ask how Daisy was. She was lit up from inside with a serene joy that was radiantly, blindingly obvious. Amy's smile wavered. She'd felt like that once, lifetimes ago.

She tweaked Daisy's dress for something to do and stood back. 'Are you ready?'

Her smile glowed brighter still. 'Oh, yes,' Daisy said softly. 'Do I look OK?'

Amy laughed indulgently and hugged her. 'You look stunning. Ben will be blown away.'

'I hope not, I want him here!' Daisy glanced down at Florence, fizzing silently on the end of Amy's arm, on her very best behaviour. She looked like a fairy in her pretty little dress and she was so excited Amy thought she was going to pop.

'OK, darling?' Daisy asked.

Florence nodded, her eyes like saucers, and for a second she looked so like Ben—so like Matt—that Amy's heart squeezed painfully with the ache of loss.

'Let's go then,' Daisy said, stooping to kiss her about-to-be stepdaughter, and with a quick, supportive hug for Amy that nearly unravelled her, she turned and took her father's arm.

As they gave the signal for the processional music, Amy sucked in a deep, slow breath.

You can do this, she told herself desperately. *Ignore him. Just keep your eyes on Daisy's back, and you'll be fine.*

And then with Florence at her side, she fell in behind them, her eyes glued on Daisy as they walked slowly down between the rows of guests to where Ben was waiting.

Ben, and Matt.

Don't look...

Matt's hair was slightly longer than his twin's, more tousled, the dark, silky strands so familiar that her fingers still remembered the feel of them. His back was ramrod straight, his shoulders broad, square, uncompromising.

She shouldn't have looked. She should have kept her eyes on Daisy, but they wouldn't obey her and her heart was pounding so hard she was sure he'd hear it.

Please don't turn round...

He didn't move a muscle.

He couldn't see her, but he could feel her there, getting closer. She was behind him, over his left shoulder, and there was no way he was turning round to look. Just getting through the ceremony was going to be hard enough, without making it harder by rubbing salt into the wound her presence here had ripped wide open.

Not that it had ever really healed.

Ben's hand brushed his, their fingers tangling and gripping for a second in a quick, wordless exchange.

You OK?

Sure. You?

Never better, and you're lying, but thanks for being here.

You're welcome. Wouldn't have it any other way.

Out of the corner of his eye Matt saw Daisy draw level with Ben, saw him reach out to her. He could feel their love like a halo around them, the huge depth of caring and emotion threatening to swamp him. The sort of love he'd felt for Amy...

Hang on in there. You can do it. It won't take long.

He heard Ben murmur something to Daisy, heard her murmur back, but he had no idea what they said. All his senses were trained on the woman standing behind Daisy. He could hear the rustle of her dress, feel the tension radiating off her, smell the slight drift of her achingly familiar perfume.

How could he be so aware of her? He closed his eyes, taking a moment to calm his thoughts, to settle it all down, to get the lid back on the box. There. He was fine. He could do this.

The ceremony began, and then it was his turn. All he had to do was to take the rings from his pocket and hand them over. Which meant he had to move, to turn—not far, but just far enough to see—

Amy...

The lid blew off the box with the force of an explosion, and he dropped the rings in Ben's outstretched hand and stepped sharply back to his place, his emotions reeling.

He had to concentrate on Ben and Daisy. This was their day, and he and Amy were in the past. Gone.

But not, apparently, forgotten.

Not by a long way.

The ceremony was interminable.

Her whole body was shaking and she was finding it really hard to concentrate on anything but Matt. Crazy, since she worked with Ben almost every day and they were scarily alike. The most identical of identical twins, with one huge difference—she loved Matt with all her broken, guarded heart, and today was the first time she'd had to face him in four years—

Don't go there!

She felt Florence wriggle at the end of her arm, and glanced down.

'You's squeezing me!' she whispered, and she realised she had a death grip on the little girl's hand. 'Sorry,' she mouthed, wincing, but Florence smiled up at her and patted her hand.

''S OK, Amy, I know you's scared,' she replied in a stage whisper that made several of the guests smile, and in the row beside her Amy heard Florence's mother give a quiet, despairing chuckle.

But then the ceremony was over, and Ben was kissing Daisy while everyone clapped and cheered, and Florence wriggled out of Amy's loosened grip and ran to them. Laughing, Ben scooped her up and kissed her, too, and as Amy watched Matt turned slowly towards her and their eyes met and locked.

Time stopped. She felt the room start to swim, and she dragged in a quick breath, then another. Matt frowned, then moved swiftly, his fingers gripping her elbow. 'Are you all right?' he murmured, his voice low, gruff and painfully familiar.

She swayed against him. All right? Not in a million years, but she wasn't telling him that. She straightened up.

'I'm fine. Low blood sugar,' she lied, and with a slight frown he let her go. Not that it made any difference. The skin of her arm was tingling from the touch of his fingers, her highly sensitised flesh branded by each one.

'We have to sign the register,' he said, and she nodded. They did. They should have done it years ago, but not like this. Not as witnesses...

'OK now?'

'Fine,' she said shortly, and took that vital and symbolic step away from him before she gave into the urge to turn her face into his chest and howl.

He thought it would never end.

The smiling, the greeting of old friends and family, the meeting of new people. And of course there were people there who'd known Amy. People who should have been at their wedding.

'Isn't that...?'

'Yes—small world, isn't it? She and Daisy are old friends. How are you? It's good to see you again...'

And on, and on, until he was ready to scream.

He drank rather more than was sensible, considering he had to make a speech, but every time he caught sight of Amy it was as if he'd been drenched in iced water and he felt stone cold sober. They sat down to eat at last, strung out in a line with Ben and Daisy and two sets of parents between them, and he was glad that his brother and his new sister-in-law had opted for a long top table instead of a round one.

Or maybe that was why they had, thinking ahead to this moment.

Florence was with Jane and Peter at another table, and he winked at her and she winked back, her little face screwing up as she tried to shut just one eye. It made him laugh, in an odd, detached way.

And then finally the food was eaten, the champagne glasses were filled and it was time for the speeches.

Amy didn't want to listen to his speech, but she had little choice. None, in fact, but she loved Daisy and she'd grown increasingly fond of Ben, and this was their wedding and she wanted to be here for it. And Matt wasn't going to spoil it for her, she told herself firmly as Daisy's father got to his feet.

He welcomed Ben to their family with a warmth in his voice that made Daisy cry, then Ben gave a funny, tender and rather endearing speech about Daisy and the change she'd made to his life, thanked everyone for coming to share their day, and then with a grin at Matt he said, 'Now, before I hand you over to my clone for the ritual character assassination I'm sure I've got coming, I'd like you to raise your glasses to two very special and beautiful women. One is my wife's dearest friend, Amy, and the other is my precious daughter, Florence. I know Daisy's appreciated their support and their help in giving us such a wonderful day to enjoy together. Amy particularly has worked absolutely tirelessly on the arrangements, and I think she's done a brilliant job. And Florence has painstakingly decorated and filled the little favour boxes for you all, so we hope you enjoy them. Ladies and gentlemen, the bridesmaids!'

She was grateful to little Florence, who was kneeling up on her chair giggling and attracting all the eyes in the room, because it meant fewer people were looking at her while she struggled with her prickling eyes and the rising tide of colour on her cheeks.

And then it was Matt's turn, and he was smiling engagingly at everyone as if he did this kind of thing all the time. He probably did, she thought. He'd always had a way with words.

'You'll have to forgive my deluded brother,' he began drily. 'Being the firstborn just makes him the prototype, and we all know they need refining, but I'm very pleased to be here today because after thirty-four years of arguments, black eyes, mind-blowingly foolish stunts and some underhanded, downright cheating, it's been settled. I am officially the best man, and now we can move on with our lives!'

There was a ripple of laughter round the room, but then he went on, 'On the subject of twins, we didn't get to bed very early last night. Ben, Daisy and I ended up delivering two rather special babies shortly before midnight, and I found myself wondering, will those little girls have as much fun growing up as we did? Because it wasn't all fights. I always had a friend, a playmate, someone to lean on. Someone to swap with. We did that quite a lot—in fact, Daisy, are you sure that's Ben? You wouldn't be the first person to fall for it. I think Jenny Wainwright's still confused.'

'No, I'm quite sure, he's much more good-looking!' Daisy said, laughing and hugging Ben.

It sounded silly, but Amy absolutely understood how she felt. The similarities were obvious. The differences were more subtle but they were definitely there, not only in their looks but in their characters, and her reaction to them was utterly different.

Ben could talk to her and she just heard his words. Matt talked, and her soul seemed to tune into his—but right now, she didn't need that spiritual connection that seemed to call to every cell in her body. She didn't need to feel the rich tones of his deep, warm voice swirling round her, that slight Yorkshire accent teasing at her senses, and with an effort she made herself listen to what he was saying.

She was glad she did. He was very, very funny, but also very moving. He told tales of their childhood escapades, but also their closeness, their enduring friendship, and finally he wound up, and she felt her heart hammer because she knew—she just knew—he was going to look at her and she was going to have to smile.

'Now, my job—as the best man,' he added with a grin, 'is to thank Ben for his kind remarks about Daisy's beautiful bridesmaids, and I have to say he's right, Florence is the cutest little bridesmaid I've ever seen. And as for Amy…' He turned to face her, as she'd known he would, and his smile twisted a little. 'Well, it's my duty and privilege to escort this beautiful woman for the rest of the day, so sorry, guys, you'll have to find someone else to dance with. She's all mine. There have to be some perks to the job.'

Amy tried to smile as he tilted his glass to her, drained it and sat down to cheers and applause, but it was a feeble attempt.

She was dreading the rest of the party. She would *have* to dance with him, and there was no getting out of it. As chief bridesmaid and best man, that was their role, but the irony wasn't lost on her.

As far as she was concerned, Matt wasn't the best man—he was the only man.

And when the chips were down, when she'd needed him most, he'd walked away.

'Good wedding—the hotel have looked after you well. It's a great venue.'

Ben smiled. 'Isn't it? We were really lucky to get it at such short notice. Good speech, by the way. Thank you.'

Matt frowned slightly, feeling another stab of guilt. 'Don't thank me. I wasn't there for you last time. I should have been.'

'No. You were absolutely right at the time, neither of us should have been there. I shouldn't have married Jane, and you weren't exactly in the right place to worry about me. You had enough going on with Amy. Matt, are you really OK with this?'

Matt met Ben's eyes briefly and looked away. 'Yeah, I'm fine.'

'Amy's not.'

'I know.'

'She still loves you.'

He snorted rudely and drained his glass. 'Hardly. I think she's finding it a little awkward, that's all. She'll be fine.'

Or she would as long as he kept avoiding her.

Ben made a soft, disbelieving noise and caught Daisy's eye. He nodded and looked back at Matt, his eyes seeing far too much for comfort. 'We're going to cut the cake now, and then have the first dance. And then—'

'I know.' He pretended to straighten Ben's cravat. 'Don't worry, I won't renege on my duties.'

'I wasn't suggesting you would. I was just going to say be kind to Amy.'

He looked up at Ben again, his older brother by mere moments, and laughed. 'What—like she was kind to me?'

'She was hurting.'

'And I wasn't?' He gave a harsh sigh and rammed a hand through his hair. 'Don't worry. I'll be good. You go and cut your cake and have your dance, and I'll play my part. I won't let you down.'

'It's not me I'm worried about,' Ben muttered, but Matt pushed him towards his wife and turned away. He didn't need to scan the room for Amy. His radar hadn't let him down. She was right there, by the French doors out onto the terrace, talking to two women that he didn't recognise.

One was visibly pregnant, the other had a baby in her arms, and for a moment his heart squeezed with pain. *Ahh, Amy...*

She could feel him watching her, the little hairs on the back of her neck standing to attention.

He was getting closer, she knew it. She'd managed to avoid him up to now, and she'd known it was too good to last.

'Excuse me, Amy—they're going to cut the cake and then have the first dance.'

And then it would be time for the second dance, the one she'd been dreading, and she'd have to dance with him and look—well, civilised would be a good thing to try for, she thought as she turned round to face him.

'OK. I'll come over. Give me a moment.'

She turned back to Katie and Laura, and after a second she felt him move away, and her shoulders sagged a fraction.

'Amy, are you all right, honey?' Katie asked, juggling the baby with one arm so she could hug her.

She returned the hug briefly and straightened up, easing away. 'I'm fine.'

'Well, you don't look fine,' Laura said, her eyes narrowing. 'Are you sick? You're awfully pale.'

'I'm just tired. It's been a busy week. I'd better go.'

She left them, letting out a soft sigh as she walked away. She'd never told them about Matt, and she'd asked Daisy not to discuss it. The fewer people at the wedding who knew they had history, the better. It was hard enough facing his mother, who'd given her a swift, gentle hug and patted her back as if she was soothing a child.

She'd nearly cried. She'd loved Liz. She'd been endlessly kind to her, incredibly welcoming, and she hadn't seen her since—

'Amy, we're going to— Gosh, sweetheart, are you all right?'

Daisy's face was puckered with concern, and Amy rolled her eyes.

'Daisy, don't fuss, I'm just tired. We didn't go to bed till nearly one and the cat was walking all over me all night. And we've been up for hours, if you remember.'

'I know. I just—'

'I'm fine,' she said firmly. 'Matt said you're going to cut the cake.'

'We are. Amy, are you sure you can do this? If you want to leave—'

'I don't want to leave! It's your wedding! Go and cut the cake, and we can have champagne and cake and dancing and it'll be wonderful. Now shoo.'

Amy turned her round and pushed her towards her husband, who held his hand out to her and drew her into his arms for yet another kiss.

'They do seem genuinely happy together.'

She froze. How had he crept up on her? She hadn't felt him approaching—maybe because she'd been so intensely aware of him all day that her senses were overloaded.

'They are,' she said, her voice a little ragged. 'They're wonderful together.'

'She's very fond of you.'

'It's mutual. She's lovely. She's been through a lot, and she's been a really good friend to me.'

'Which is why you're here, when you'd rather be almost anywhere else in the world.'

'Speak for yourself.'

He gave a soft huff of laughter, teasing the hair on the back of her neck. 'I was,' he answered, and despite the laugh, his voice had a hollow ring to it. 'Still, needs must. Right, here we go. I think Ben's going to make a bit of a speech to welcome the evening guests before they cut the cake.'

He was still standing behind her, slightly to one side, and she could feel his breath against her bare shoulder, feel the warmth radiating from his big, solid body.

The temptation to lean back into him—to rest her head against his cheek, to feel him curve his hand round her hip and ease her closer as he would have done before—nearly overwhelmed her. Instead, she stepped away slightly, pretending to shift so she could see them better, but in fact she could see perfectly well, and he must have realised that.

She heard him sigh, and for some crazy reason it made her feel sad. Crazy, because it had been him that had left her, walking away just when she needed him the most, so why on earth should she feel sad for him? So he was still alone, according to Ben. So what? So was she. There were worse things than being alone. At least it was safe.

'Daisy chose the music for our first dance,' Ben was saying, his smile wry. 'It has a special meaning for us. While we're dancing, I'd like you to imagine the moment we met—just about thirty seconds after the kitchen ceiling and half a bath of water came down on my head.'

And with that, they cut the cake, the lights were dimmed and the band started playing 'The First Time Ever I Saw Your Face'.

There was a ripple of laughter and applause, but then they all went quiet as Ben, still smiling, drew Daisy into his arms as if she was the most precious thing he'd ever held.

Damn, Amy thought, sniffing hard, and then a tissue arrived in her hand, on a drift of cologne that brought back so many memories she felt the tears well even faster.

'OK?'

No, she wasn't. She was far from OK, she thought crossly, and she wished everyone would stop asking her that.

'I'm fine.'

He sighed softly. 'Look, Amy, I know this is awkward, but we just have to get through it for their sakes. I don't want to do it any more than you do, but it's not for long.'

Long enough. A second in his arms would be long enough to tear her heart wide open—

The dance was over, the music moved on and without

hesitation Matt took her hand, the one with the tissue still clutched firmly in it, led her onto the dance floor and turned her into his arms.

'Just pretend you don't hate me,' he told her, with a smile that didn't reach his eyes, and she breathed in, needing oxygen, and found nothing but that cologne again.

Holding her was torture.

A duty and a privilege, as he'd said in his speech?

Or just an agonising reminder of all he'd lost?

She had one hand on his shoulder, the other cradled in his left, and his right hand was resting lightly against her waist, so he could feel the slender column of her spine beneath his splayed fingers, the shift of her ribs as she breathed, the flex of the muscles as she moved in time to the music. She felt thinner, he thought. Well, she would. The last time he'd held her, he thought with a wave of sadness, she'd been pregnant with their child.

One dance merged into another, and then another. He eased her closer, and with a sigh that seemed to shudder through her body, she rested her head on his shoulder and yielded to the gentle pressure of his hand. Her thighs brushed his, and he felt heat flicker along his veins. Oh, Amy. He'd never forgotten her, never moved on. Not really.

And as he cradled her against his chest, her pale gold hair soft under his cheek, he realised he'd been treading water for years, just waiting for the moment when he could hold her again.

He sighed, and she felt his warm breath tease her hair, sending tiny shivers running through her like fairies dancing over her skin. It made her feel light-headed again, and she stepped back.

'I need some air,' she mumbled, and tried to walk away, but her hand was still firmly wrapped in his, and he followed her, ushering her through the crowd and out of the French doors into the softly lit courtyard. Groups of people were standing around talking quietly, laughing, and she breathed in the cooler air with a sigh of relief.

'Better?'

She nodded. 'Yes. Thanks.'

'Don't thank me. You look white as a sheet. Have you eaten today?'

'We just had a meal.'

'And you hardly touched it. My guess is you didn't have lunch, either, and you probably skipped breakfast. No wonder you had low blood sugar earlier. Come on, let's go and raid the buffet. I didn't eat much, either, and I'm starving.'

He was right on all counts. She *was* hungry, and she *had* skipped lunch, but only because she'd lost her breakfast. She never could eat when she was nervous, and she'd been so, so nervous for the last few days her stomach had been in knots, and this morning it had rebelled. And that dizzy spell could well have been low blood sugar, now she came to think about it.

'It's probably not a bad idea,' she conceded, and let him lead her to the buffet table. She put a little spoonful of something on her plate, and he growled, shoved his plate in her other hand and loaded them both up.

'I can't eat all that!' she protested, but he speared her with a look from those implacable blue eyes and she gave up. He could put it on the plate. Didn't mean she had to eat it.

'I'll help you. Come on, let's find a quiet corner.'

He scooped up two sets of cutlery, put them in his

top pocket, snagged a couple of glasses of wine off a passing waiter and shepherded her across the floor and back out to the courtyard.

'OK out here, or is it too cold for you in that dress?'

'It's lovely. It's a bit warm in there.'

'Right. Here, look, there's a bench.'

He steered her towards it, handed her a glass and sat back, one ankle on the other knee and the plate balanced on his hand while he attacked the food with his fork.

He'd always eaten like that, but that was medicine for you, eating on the run. Maybe he thought they should get it over with and then he could slide off and drink with the boys. Well, if the truth be told he didn't have to hang around for her.

'You're not eating.'

'I'm too busy wondering why you don't have chronic indigestion, the speed you're shovelling that down.'

He gave a short chuckle. 'Sorry. Force of habit. And I was starving.' He put the plate down for a moment and picked up his glass. 'So, how are you, really?'

Really? She hesitated, the fork halfway to her mouth. Did he honestly want to know? Probably not.

'I'm fine.'

'How's the job?'

'OK. I like it. As with any job it has its ups and downs. Mostly ups. The hospital's a good place to work.'

'Yes, so Ben says.' He stared pensively down into his glass, swirling it slowly. 'You didn't have to leave London, you know. We were never going to bump into each other at different hospitals.'

No? She wasn't sure—not sure enough, at least, that she'd felt comfortable staying there. Up here, she'd been able to relax—until Ben had arrived. Ever since then she'd been waiting for Matt to turn up unexpectedly on the ward to visit his brother, and the monoamniotic twins they'd delivered last night had been something he'd taken a special interest in, so once Melanie Grieves had been admitted, she'd been on tenterhooks all the time. Waiting for the other shoe to drop.

Well, now it had, and it was every bit as bad as she'd expected.

'I like it here, it was a good move for me,' she said, and then changed the subject firmly. 'Who's Jenny Wainwright?'

He laughed, a soft, warm chuckle that told her a funny story was coming. 'Ben's first girlfriend. We were thirteen or so. They'd been dating for weeks, and she wouldn't let him kiss her, so I talked him into letting me take his place on the next date, to see if I had more luck.'

'And did you?'

His mouth twisted into a wry smile. 'No. Not that time. I did about two years later, though, at a party, and she told me he kissed better, so I went and practised on someone else.'

She laughed, as he'd wanted her to, but all she could think was that whoever he'd practised on had taught him well. She ought to thank her—except of course he wasn't hers to kiss any more. Regret swamped her, and as she looked across and met his eyes, she saw tenderness in them and a gentle, puzzled sadness. 'I've missed you,' he said softly, and she gulped down a sudden, convulsive little sob.

'I've missed you, too,' she admitted, her voice unsteady.

He stared at her searchingly, then glanced down. 'Are you all done with that food?'

Food? She looked at her plate. She'd eaten far more

than she'd thought she would, to her surprise, and she was feeling much better. 'Yes. Do you want the rest?'

'No, I'm fine, but I'm supposed to be entertaining you, so let's go and dance.'

Out of duty? Or because he wanted to? She hesitated for a second, then stood up, raising an eyebrow at him. Whichever, she wanted to dance with him, and she wasn't going to get another chance.

'Come on, then, if you really want to.'

Oh, yes. He wanted. He got to his feet and led her back to the dance floor.

She'd always loved dancing, and he loved dancing with her, loved the feel of her body, the lithe, supple limbs, the sleek curves, the warmth of her against him.

He didn't get to hold her, though, not at first. The tempo was fast—too fast, he decided, after a couple of dances, so he reeled her in and halved the beat, cherishing the moment because he knew it wouldn't last. How could it, with all they had behind them? But now—he had her now, in his arms, against his heart, and his body ached for her.

The tempo slowed, moving seamlessly from one unashamedly romantic, seductive number to another, until they were swaying against each other, her arms draped around his neck, his hands splayed against her back, the fingers of one hand resting lightly on the warm, soft skin above the back of her dress, the other hand lower, so all he had to do was slip it down a fraction and he could cup the firm swell of her bottom and ease her closer...

She felt his hand move, felt him draw her in so she could feel every move he made. Their legs had somehow meshed together so his thigh was between hers, nudging gently with every slight shift of his body, brushing the soft silk of her dress against her legs and driving out all her common sense.

She knew him so well, had danced with him so many times, and it was so easy to rest against him, to lay her head against his chest and listen to the deep, steady thud of his heart, to slide her fingers through his hair and sift the silky strands that she remembered so well.

Easier, still, to turn her head, to feel the graze of stubble against her temple and tilt her face towards him, to feel the soft warmth of his lips as they took hers in a tentative, questioning kiss.

I love you...

Had he said that? Had she?

She lifted her head and touched her lips to his again, and his breath seared over her skin in a shuddering sigh.

'Amy—'

'Matt...'

He lifted his head and stared down at her in the dim light on the edge of the dance floor, their eyes locked as each of them battled against the need raging within them. She could feel him fighting it, feel herself losing just as he closed his eyes and unclasped her hands from behind his neck, sliding his hand down her arm and linking their fingers as he led her off the dance floor and up the broad, sweeping staircase to the floor above in a tense, brittle silence.

They didn't speak to anyone. They passed people in the hall, people on the stairs—they didn't stop, didn't look left or right, until the door of his room was opened and closed again behind them, and then he cradled her face and stared down into her eyes once more.

Still he didn't speak, and neither did she. What was there to say? Nothing that would make any sense.

Slowly, with infinite tenderness, he touched his lips to hers again, and she whimpered softly and clutched at him, desperate for the feel of him, for his body on her, in her, surrounding and filling her.

'Please,' she whispered silently, but he heard her and took a step back, stripping without finesse, heeling off his beautiful handmade shoes, his hired suit hitting the floor and crumpling in a heap. After a brief fight with his cufflinks the shirt followed, then the boxers, the socks, and he spun her and searched blindly for the zip.

'Here.' She lifted her arm so he could find it, sucking her breath in as he tugged it down and the dress fell to the floor, puddling round her ankles and leaving her standing there in nothing but a tiny scrap of lace.

A rough groan was torn from his throat and he lifted her in his arms and lowered her carefully to the middle of the bed. Fingers shaking, he hooked his fingers into the lace at her hips, easing it away, following its path down the length of her legs with his lips, the slight roughness of his stubble grazing the sensitive skin as he inched his way to her feet, driving her to the edge.

He turned his head, looked back at her, and his eyes were black with need. She whimpered, her legs twitching under his warm, firm hands, and he moved, nudging her thighs apart, so nearly there—and then he froze, his face agonised.

'Amy, we can't—I haven't—'

'I'm on the Pill.'

The breath sighed out of him in a rush, and he gathered her into his arms, held her for a moment, and then his lips found hers again and he was there, filling her, bringing a sob of relief from her as his body slid home and she tightened around him.

'Matt…'

'Oh, God, Amy, I've missed you,' he whispered, and then he started to move, his body shaking with control until she was sick of waiting and arched under him, her hands tugging at him, begging for more.

And he gave her more, pulling out all the stops, driving her higher and higher until she came apart in his arms, her reserve splintering under the onslaught of his unleashed passion.

Then he held her, his body shuddering in release, his heart slamming against his ribs so hard he thought they'd break, until gradually it slowed and he rolled to his side, taking her with him, their bodies still locked together as the aftershocks of their lovemaking faded slowly away into the night.

CHAPTER TWO

HE MADE love to her again in the night, reaching for her in the darkness, bringing her body slowly awake with sure, gentle hands and whispered kisses. She laid her hand tenderly against his cheek, savouring the rasp of stubble against her palm, her thumb dragging softly over the firm fullness of his lower lip.

He opened his mouth, drawing her thumb inside and sucking it deeply, his tongue exploring it, his teeth nipping lightly and making the breath catch in her throat. She shifted so she could reach him, her hands running over him now, checking for changes and finding only sweet, familiar memories. He moved on, his mouth warm and moist against her skin, and she joined in, their lips tracing tender trails across each other's bodies. They were taking their time now for leisurely explorations, the darkness shielding them from emotions they couldn't bear to expose—emotions too dark, too painful to consider.

That wasn't what this night was about, Amy thought later as she lay awake beside him listening to the deep, even rhythm of his breathing. It was for old times' sake, no-longer lovers reaching out to touch fleetingly what had once been theirs to love.

She was under no illusions. After the wedding, Matt

would be going back to London, and she'd be staying here, nursing her still-broken heart but with a little
more tenderness, a little more forgiveness in her soul.
He wasn't indifferent. Clearly not. But their lives had
moved on, gone in different directions, and maybe it
was for the best.

Maybe this was the way forward, for both of them.
A little healing salve smeared gently over their wounds,
kissing each other better.

She shifted slightly, seeking the warmth of his body,
and he reached for her again in his sleep, drawing her
closer, their legs tangled, her head pillowed on his
shoulder as she slept, until the first light of dawn crept
round the edges of the curtains.

He woke her gently, his voice a soft murmur in her
ear.

'Amy?'

'Mmm.'

'Amy, it's morning.'

'Mmm.'

'You're in my room.'

'Mmm. I know.'

'Sweetheart, *everyone* will know soon.'

Her eyes flew open, and she sucked in a breath, the
night coming back to her in a flood of memory and sudden awkwardness. 'Oh, rats. Damn. Um—Matt, help
me get dressed.'

She threw the quilt off and starting searching for
her underwear. Stupid, stupid… 'Where the hell are
my pants?'

Pants? He nearly laughed. Try cobwebs.

'Take the dressing gown on the back of the door—
have you got your room key?'

'Yes, of course. It's—'

In her clutch bag, which was—somewhere. She flopped back down onto the edge of the bed, dragging the quilt back over herself to hide her body from his eyes. Pointless, after he'd explored it so thoroughly, knew it so well in any case, but she was suddenly smitten with shyness. 'It's in my clutch bag,' she admitted.

'Which is...?'

Good question. 'Downstairs?'

He groaned and rolled away from her, vanishing into the bathroom and emerging a few minutes later damp, tousled and unshaven. And stark naked, the water drops still clinging to his body gleaming in the spill of light from the bathroom door and drawing her hungry eyes. He flipped open his overnight bag, pulled out some jeans and boxers and a shirt, dressed quickly and took the room key out of the door lock.

'What's your bag look like?' he asked briskly, and she dragged her mind off his body and tried to concentrate.

'Cream satin, about so big, little bronzy chain. It's got a lipstick, a tissue and the room key in it.'

'Any ideas where?'

She shrugged. 'The edge of the dance floor? I put it down at one point.'

He left her there, hugging her knees in the middle of the bed, looking rumpled and gorgeous and filled with regret.

He knew all about that one. How could he have been so stupid?

And why was she on the Pill, for heaven's sake? Was she in a relationship? Or did she do this kind of thing all the time?

Hell, he hoped not. The thought of his Amy casually—

He swallowed hard and ran downstairs, to find that

staff were already starting the mammoth clean-up operation.

'I'm looking for a cream satin evening bag,' he told someone, and was directed to the night porter's office.

'This the one?'

He wasn't sure, so he opened it and found exactly what she'd said inside. Well, if the room key fitted...

He went to it, and it gave him immediate access. Her case was there, unopened, inside the unused room, and he carried it back to her.

'Oh, Matt, you're a star. Thank you.'

'Anything to spare a lady's blushes. I'll go to your room,' he said, 'and if anyone knocks on the door, just ignore them. It'll only be Ben or my parents, and they'll ring me if it's anything important.'

He slipped his mobile into his pocket, picked up his wallet and did the same, then gave Amy an awkward smile. 'I guess I'll see you at breakfast.'

She nodded, looking embarrassed now, her grey eyes clouded with something that could have been shame, and without dragging it out he left her there and went to the room that should have been hers, lay on the bed and let his breath out on a long, ragged sigh.

What a fool. All he'd done, all he'd proved, was that he'd never stopped loving her. Well, hell, he'd known that before. It had hardly needed underlining.

He rolled to his side, thumped the pillow into the side of his neck and tried to sleep.

How could she have been so stupid?

She'd known seeing him again would be dangerous to her, but she hadn't realised how dangerous. She pulled the hotel gown tighter round her waist and moved to the chair by the window. She had a view over the courtyard where they'd had their buffet supper, could see the bench if she craned her neck.

Sudden unexpected tears glazed her eyes, and she swiped them away and sniffed hard. She'd done some stupid things in her life, most of them with Matt, and this was just the icing on the cake.

She got up and put the little kettle on to make tea, and found her pills in her washbag and popped one out. Thank God for synthetic hormones, she thought drily as she swallowed the pill. Or maybe not, because without the medication to control her irregular periods, they would never have spent the night together.

Which would have been a *good* thing, she told herself firmly. But telling him she was on the Pill was a two-edged sword. He probably thought she was a slut.

'I don't care what he thinks, it's none of his damn business and at least I won't get pregnant again,' she said to the kettle, and made herself a cup of tea and sat cradling it and staring down into the courtyard until it was stone cold.

And then she nearly dropped it, because Matt was there, outside in the courtyard garden just below her, sitting on the bench with a cup in his hand and checking something on his phone.

He made a call, then put the cup down and walked swiftly across the courtyard out of sight. One of his patients in London needing his attention? Or Melanie Grieves, mother of the little twins they'd delivered on Friday night?

Or just coming inside to see whoever he'd spoken to—his parents, maybe?

Moments later, there was a soft knock at the door.

'Amy? It's Matt.'

She let him in reluctantly and tried to look normal and less like an awkward teenager. 'Everything OK?'

'Yes. I'm going to see Melanie Grieves. Ben asked me to keep an eye on her.'

She nodded. 'Are you coming back for breakfast and to say goodbye to everyone?'

'Yes. I don't want to be lynched. Let me take my stuff, and I'll get out of your way. Here's your room key. Hang onto mine as well for now. I'll get it off you later.' He scooped up the suit, the shirt, the underwear, throwing them in the bag any old how and zipping it, and then he hesitated. For a second she thought he was about to kiss her, but then he just picked up his bag and left without a backward glance.

Amy let out the breath she'd been holding since he'd come in, and sat down on the end of the bed. There was no point in hanging around in his room, she thought. She'd shower and dress, and go downstairs and see if anyone was around.

Unlikely. The party had gone on long after they'd left it, and everyone was probably still in bed—where she would be, in her own room, if she had a grain of sense.

Well, she'd proved beyond any reasonable doubt that she didn't, she thought, and felt the tears welling again.

Damn him. Damn him for being so—so—just so *irresistible*. Well, never again. Without his body beside her, without the feel of his warmth, the tenderness of his touch, it all seemed like a thoroughly bad idea, and she knew the aftermath of it would haunt her for ages.

Years.

Forever?

Melanie Grieves was fine.

Her wound was healing, her little twins were doing

very well and apart from a bit of pain she was over the moon. He hadn't really needed to come and see her, he'd just had enough of sitting around in the hotel beating himself up about Amy.

Not that he shouldn't be doing that. He'd been a total idiot, and she really, really didn't need him falling all over her like he had last night. And leaving the dance floor like that—God knows what everyone had thought of them. He hadn't even asked her, just dragged her up the stairs and into his room like some kind of caveman.

He growled in frustration and slammed the car door shut. He'd better go back, better show his face and try and lie his way out of it. Better still, find Amy and get their story straight before his mother got her side of it and bent his ear. She'd always taken Amy's side.

Oh, hell.

He dropped his head forwards and knocked it gently against the hard, leatherbound steering wheel. Such a fool. And his head hurt. Good. It would remind him not to drink so much in future. He'd thought he was sober enough, but obviously not. If he'd been sober—

His phone rang and he pulled it out of his pocket and stared at the screen. Ben. Damn.

He ignored it. He'd talk to Amy first—if he got to her before they did. If only he had her number. She'd probably changed it, but maybe not. He dialled it anyway as he turned into the hotel car park, and she answered on the second ring.

'Hello?'

'Amy, it's Matt. We need to talk—we will have been seen last night. Where are you now?'

'Oh, damn. In the courtyard. Bring coffee.'

Stressed as he was, he smiled at that. He found a

breakfast waitress and ordered a pot of coffee and a basket of bacon rolls, then went and found her.

She was waiting, her heart speeding up as she caught
sight of him, her nerves on edge. She couldn't believe
what she'd done, couldn't believe she was going to sit
here with him and concoct some cock-and-bull story
to tell his family. Her friends. Oh, lord...

'How's Mel?' she asked, sticking to something safe.

'Fine. The babies are both doing well.'

'Good. Ben and Daisy'll be pleased.'

Silence. Of course there was, she thought. What was
there to say, for heaven's sake? *Thank you for the best
sex I've had in over four years? Not to say the only...?*

'Any sign of the others?' he asked after the silence
had stretched out into the hereafter, and she shook her
head.

'No. I put my bag in the car. Here's your room key.
So—what's the story?'

'We wanted to talk?'

'We didn't talk, Matt,' she reminded him bluntly.

Pity they hadn't, she thought for the thousandth time.
If they'd talked, they might have had more sense.

'You were feeling sick?' he suggested.

'What—from all that champagne?'

'It's not impossible.'

'I had less than you.'

'I think it's probably fair to say we both had more
than was sensible,' he said drily, and she had to agree,
but not out loud. She wasn't feeling that magnanimous.

'Maybe nobody noticed?' she said without any real
conviction, and he gave a short, disbelieving laugh.

'Dream on, Amy. I dragged you off the dance floor
and up the stairs in full view of everyone. I think someone will have noticed.'

She groaned and put her face in her hands, and then he started to laugh again, a soft, despairing sound that made her lift her head and meet his eyes. 'What?'

'I have some vague recollection of passing my parents in the hall.'

She groaned again. It just got better and better.

'Maybe you thought I needed to lie down?' she suggested wildly. 'Perhaps I'd told you I was feeling rough? It's not so unlikely, and it's beginning to look like the best option.'

'We could always tell them the truth.'

If we knew what it was, she thought, but the waitress arrived then with the tray of coffee and bacon rolls, and she seized one and sank her teeth into it and groaned. 'Oh, good choice,' she mumbled, and he laughed.

'Our default hangover food,' he said, bringing the memories crashing back. 'Want some ketchup?'

'That's disgusting,' she said, watching him squirt a dollop into his bacon roll and then demolish it in three bites before reaching for another. The times they'd done that, woken up on the morning after the night before and he'd cooked her bacon rolls and made her coffee.

He'd done that after their first night together, she remembered. And when she'd come out of hospital after—

She put the roll down and reached for her coffee, her appetite evaporating.

'So when are you off?' she asked.

'Tuesday morning,' he said, surprising her. 'Things are quiet at work at the moment, so I said I'd keep an eye on Mel till Ben and Daisy get back. They're only away for two nights.'

'Are you staying here?'

'No. I'm going back to Ben's.'

She nodded. It made sense, but she wasn't thrilled.

She'd be tripping over him in the hospital at random times, bumping into him at Daisy's house when she went to feed Tabitha—because if he was next door at Ben's, there was no way she was going to stay there, as she'd half thought she might, to keep the cat company.

Or moving in and renting it as they'd suggested, come to that. Not after last night's folly. The last thing she wanted was to be bumping into Ben's brother every time he came up to visit them.

Daisy had stayed in her own house adjoining Ben's until the wedding because of Florence, but she'd be moving into his half when they came back, and they'd offered her Daisy's house. They wanted a tenant they could trust, and her lease was coming up for renewal, and it was a lot nicer than her flat for all sorts of reasons.

It had off-road parking, a garden, a lovely conservatory—and the best neighbours in the world. She'd been debating whether to take it, because of the danger of bumping into Matt who was bound to be coming back and forth to visit them, but after this—well, how could she relax?

She couldn't. It would have been bad enough before.

'Why don't we just tell them to mind their own business?' she suggested at last. 'It really is nothing to do with them if we chose to—'

She broke off, and he raised a brow thoughtfully.

'Chose to—?'

But his phone rang, and he scanned the screen and answered it, pulling a face.

'Hi, Ben.'

'Is that a private party over there, or can we join you?'

He looked up, and saw his brother and brand-new

sister-in-law standing in the doorway watching them across the courtyard.

Amy followed the direction of his eyes, and sighed.

'Stand by to be grilled like a kipper,' she muttered, and stood up to hug Daisy. 'Well, good morning. How's the head?'

Daisy smiled smugly, looking very pleased with herself. 'Clear as a bell. In case you didn't notice, I wasn't drinking.'

Amy frowned, then looked from one to the other and felt the bottom fall out of her stomach. Ben's eyes were shining, and there was a smile he couldn't quite hide. 'Oh—that's wonderful,' she said softly, and then to her utter humiliation her eyes welled over. She hugged Daisy hard, then turned to Ben—just in time to see Matt release him with a look in his eyes she hadn't seen since—

'Congratulations, that's amazing,' he said gruffly, and gathered Daisy up and hugged her, too, his expression carefully veiled now.

Except that Amy could still see it, lingering in the back of his eyes, a fleeting echo of a grief once so raw it had torn them apart.

'So, when's it due?' he asked, going through the motions. Not that he wasn't interested, but today of all days…

'The tenth of May. It's very, very early on,' Daisy said wryly. 'I did the test this morning.'

'Right after she threw up.'

Matt gave a soft huff of sympathetic laughter. 'Poor Daisy. It passes, I'm reliably informed by my patients.' *That's right, keep it impersonal…*

'It's a good sign,' Amy said, her voice slightly strained to his ears. 'Means the pregnancy's secure.'

Unlike hers. Oh, God, beam me up...

'Changing the subject, it's none of my business, but—' Ben began, but Matt knew exactly where this was going and cut him off.

'You're right, it's not. We needed to talk, there were a lot of people about. Amy slept in my room, and I went to hers.'

At a quarter to six this morning, but they didn't need to know that, and he was darned sure they wouldn't have been up and about that early. But someone was.

'Yeah, Mum said she saw you coming out of your room and going to another one at some ungodly hour.'

Damn. Of all the people...

'I went to get my phone so I could ring the hospital,' he lied, but he'd never been able to lie convincingly to Ben, and as their eyes met he saw Ben clock the lie and yet say nothing.

As he'd said himself, it was none of his business, and he obviously realised he'd overstepped the mark. He'd back him up, though, if their mother said any more, of that Matt was sure. 'So how is Mel?' Ben asked, moving smoothly on, and Matt let out a slight sigh of relief.

'Fine. They're all fine. I've been in to see them, and they're all doing really well. She was keen to hear all about the wedding. I promised I'd take her some cake—unless you want to do it when you come back?'

'No, you go for it. I'm glad she's well. Thanks for going in.'

'My pleasure. Did you order coffee or do you want me to do it?'

Daisy pulled a face. 'Can we have something less smelly, and something to eat? I really don't think I can wait till breakfast.'

'Sure. I'll order decaf tea. What about bacon rolls?'

'Oh, yes-s-s-s!' she said fervently. 'Amazing! Matt, you're a genius.'

He smiled, glancing across at Amy and sensing, rather than seeing, the sadness that lingered in her. She was smiling at Daisy, but underneath it all was grief, no longer raw and untamed, maybe, but there for all that.

Would it ever get easier? Ever truly go away?

He hoped so, but he was very much afraid that he was wrong.

'Well, hello, Mummy Grieves! Are you up for visitors?'

'Oh, yes! Hello, Amy, how are you? How was the wedding? Did Daisy look beautiful?'

'Utterly gorgeous, but I bet she wasn't as gorgeous as your little girls. Aren't you going to introduce me?'

'Of course. I hope you don't mind, but we've called them Daisy and Amy, because you two have been so kind and we really love the names.'

'Oh, that's so sweet of you, thank you,' Amy said, her eyes filling. In a rare complication, the twins had shared the same amniotic sac, and the danger of their cords tangling had meant Mel had been monitored as an inpatient for several weeks, and she and Daisy had got to know Mel very well. And this... She blinked hard and sniffed, and Mel hugged her.

'Thank *you*,' she corrected. 'So, this is Amy. Want a cuddle?'

'I'd better not—infection risk,' she lied. That was why she'd gone on her way in, so her clothes were clean, but the last thing she wanted was to hold them. Delivering babies was one thing. Going out of her way to cuddle them—well, she just didn't.

She admired them both, though, Amy first, then Daisy, their perfect little features so very alike and yet slightly different. 'Can you tell them apart yet?' she asked Mel, and she smiled and nodded.

'Oh, yes. I could see the differences straight away. Adrian can't always, but he'll learn, I expect. And Mr Walker and his brother—they're very alike, too, aren't they, but I can tell the difference. There's just something.'

Amy swallowed. Oh, yes. Ben didn't have the ability to turn her into a total basket case just by walking into the room, and just to prove it, Matt strolled in then and she felt her stomach drop to the floor and her heart lurch.

'Talk of the Devil,' she said brightly, and saying goodbye to Mel, she slipped past him, trying not to breath in the faint, lingering scent of soap and cologne, but it drifted after her on the air.

Just one more day. He'll be gone tomorrow.

It couldn't come soon enough...

He found her, the next day, working in the ward office filling out patient records on the computer.

'I'm off,' he said, and she looked up and wondered why, when she'd been so keen to see him go, she should feel a pang of sadness that she was losing him.

Ridiculous. She wasn't losing him, he wasn't hers! And anyway, since the wedding they'd hardly seen each other. But that didn't mean they hadn't both been painfully, desperately aware. Yet he hadn't once, in all that time, suggested they repeat the folly of Saturday night—

'Got time for a coffee?'

She glanced up at the clock. Actually, she had plenty of time. There was nothing going on, for once, and although no doubt now she'd thought that all hell would break loose, for the minute, anyway, it was quiet.

Did she *want* to make time for a coffee? Totally different question.

'I can spare five minutes,' she said, logging off the computer and sliding back her chair.

He ushered her through the door first, his hand resting lightly on the small of her back, and she felt the warmth, the security of it all the way through to her bones. Except it was a false sense of security.

'We ought to talk,' he said quietly, once they were seated in the café.

She stirred her coffee, chasing the froth round the top, frowning at it as if it held the answers. 'Is there anything to say?'

He laughed, a short, harsh sound that cut the air. 'Amy, we spent the *night* together,' he said—unnecessarily, since she'd hardly forgotten.

'For old times' sake,' she pointed out. 'That was all.'

'Was it? Was it really?'

'Yes. It really was.'

He stared at her, searching her eyes for the longest moment, and then the expression in them was carefully banked and he looked away. 'OK. If that's what you want.'

It wasn't. She wanted *him*, but she couldn't trust him, because when her world had disintegrated and she'd needed him more than she'd ever needed anybody in her life, he'd turned his back on her.

She wasn't going through that again, not for him, not for anybody.

'It is what I want,' she lied. 'It didn't work, Matt, and there's no use harking back to it. We need to let it go.'

His eyes speared her. 'Have you?'

Let it go? *Let her baby go?*

She sucked in a breath and looked away.

'I didn't think so,' he said softly. 'Well, if it helps you any, neither have I. And I haven't forgotten you, Amy.'

She closed her eyes, wishing he would go, wishing he could stay. She heard the scrape of a chair, felt the touch of his hand on her shoulder.

'You know where I am if you change your mind.'

'I won't,' she vowed. She couldn't. She didn't dare. She simply wasn't strong enough to survive a second time.

He bent, tipped her head back with his fingers and dropped the gentlest, sweetest, saddest kiss on her lips.

'Goodbye, Amy. Take care of yourself.'

And then he was gone, walking swiftly away, leaving her there alone in the middle of the crowded café. She wanted to get up, to run after him, to yell at him to stop, she was sorry, she didn't mean it, please stay. But she didn't.

Somehow, just barely, she managed to stop herself, and no doubt one day she'd be grateful for that.

But right now, she felt as if she'd just thrown away her last chance at happiness, and all she wanted to do was cry.

CHAPTER THREE

IT TOOK her weeks to work out what was going on.

Weeks in which Matt was in her head morning, noon and night. She kept telling herself she'd done the right thing, that not seeing him again was sensible, but it wasn't easy to convince herself. Not easy at all, and Daisy and Ben being so blissfully happy didn't help.

She ached for him so much it was physical, but she'd done the right thing, sending him away. She had. She couldn't rely on him, couldn't trust him again with her heart. And she was genuinely relieved when her period came right on cue, because although she might want *him*, the thought of going through another pregnancy terrified her, and for the first time since the wedding she felt herself letting go of an inner tension she hadn't even been aware of.

She could move on now. They'd said their goodbyes, and it was done.

Finished.

The autumn came and went, and December arrived with a vengeance. It rained, and when it wasn't raining, it was sleeting, and then it dried up and didn't thaw for days. And her boiler broke down in her flat.

Marvellous, she thought. Just what she needed. She

contacted her landlord, but it would be three weeks before it could be replaced—more, maybe, because plumbers were rushed off their feet after the freeze— and so she gave in to Ben and Daisy's gentle nagging, and moved into Daisy's house just ten days before Christmas.

'It's only temporary, till my boiler's fixed,' she told them firmly, but they just smiled and nodded and refused to take any rent on the grounds that it was better for the house to be occupied.

Then Daisy had her twenty-week scan, and of course she asked to see the photo. What else could she do? And she thought she'd be fine, she saw them all the time in her work, but it really got to her. Because of the link to Matt? She had no idea, but it haunted her that day and the next, popping up in every quiet moment and bringing with it a rush of grief that threatened to undermine her. She and Matt had been so happy, so deliriously overjoyed back then. And then, so shortly before her scan was due—

A laugh jerked her out of her thoughts, a laugh so like Matt's that it could so easily have been him, and she felt her heart squeeze. Stupid. She *knew* it was Ben. She heard him laugh all the time. And every time, she felt pain like a solid ball wedged in her chest.

She *missed* him. So, so much.

'Oh, Amy, great, I was hoping I'd find you here. New admission—thirty-four weeks, slight show last night, mild contractions which could just be Braxton Hicks'. Have you got time to admit her for me, please? She's just moved to the area last week, so we haven't seen her before but she's got her hand-held notes.'

She swiped the tears from her cheeks surreptitiously while she pretended to stifle a yawn. 'Sure. I could do with a break from this tedious admin. I'll just log off and I'll be with you. What's her name?'

'Helen Kendall. She's in the assessment room.'

Amy found her sitting on the edge of the chair looking worried and guilty, and she introduced herself.

'I'm so sorry to just come in,' Helen said, 'but I was worried because I've been really overdoing it with the move and I'm just so *tired*,' she blurted out, and then she started to cry.

'Oh, Helen,' Amy said, sitting down next to her and rubbing her back soothingly. 'You're exhausted—come on, let's get you into a gown and into bed, and let us take care of you.'

'It's all my fault, I shouldn't have let him talk me into it, we should have waited and now the baby's going to be too early,' she sobbed. Oh, she could understand the guilt all too well, but thirty-four weeks wasn't too early. Not like eighteen weeks…

'It's not your fault,' she said with a calm she didn't feel, 'and thirty-four weeks is quite manageable if it comes to that. It may well not. Come on, chin up, and let's find out what's going on.'

She handed Helen a gown, then left her alone for a few minutes to change and do a urine sample while she took the time to get her emotions back in order. What was the *matter* with her? She didn't think about her baby at all, normally. It was seeing that picture of Daisy's baby, and thinking about Matt again—always Matt.

She pulled herself together and went back to Helen.

This was her first pregnancy, it had been utterly straightforward and uncomplicated to this point, and there was no reason to suspect that anything would go wrong even if she did give birth early. The baby was moving normally, its heartbeat was loud and strong, and Helen relaxed visibly when she heard it.

'Oh, that's so reassuring,' she said, her eyes filling, and she was still caressing her bump with a gentle, contented smile on her face when Ben arrived.

'OK, Helen, let's have a look at this baby and see how we're doing,' he said, and Amy watched the monitor.

The baby was a good size for her dates, there was no thinning of Helen's uterus as yet, and her contractions might well stop at this point, if she was lucky. Not everyone was.

She sucked in a breath and stepped back, and Ben glanced up at her and frowned.

'You OK?'

'Just giving you a bit more room,' she lied.

He grunted. It was a sound she understood. Matt used to do the same thing when he knew she was lying. Maybe they were more alike than she'd realised.

'Right, Helen, I'm happy with that. We'll monitor you, but I'm pretty sure they're just Braxton Hicks' and this will all settle down. We'll give you drugs to halt it if we can and steroids to mature the baby's lungs just to be on the safe side, and then if it's all stable and there's no change overnight, you can go home tomorrow.'

She swallowed. 'That's so reassuring. Thanks. I feel an idiot now, but I didn't know what to do.'

'Don't worry, you've done the right thing coming in,' Amy assured her. 'Why don't you try and have a sleep? I might have to disturb you from time to time, but I think a rest will do you good.'

She followed Ben out into the corridor. 'Any special instructions?'

'Yes. Come for dinner. Daisy's worried about you— she thinks the scan upset you.'

She forced a smile. 'Don't be silly, of course it didn't.'

That grunt again. 'Humour her, Amy, for my sake if nothing else. You know what she's like when she's got a bee in her bonnet about something. So—seven o'clock all right?'

She wasn't going to get out of it without a fuss, Amy realised, so she gave in. 'Seven will be fine. I'll see you there—and I'll keep you up to speed with Helen in the meantime.'

She picked up some flowers for Daisy from the supermarket on her way home. And it really did feel like home, she thought as she showered and dressed.

Odd, how easily she'd settled into the little house, but she'd been lucky it had been available. Or maybe they'd deliberately kept it that way? She had a feeling they weren't exactly busting a gut to get a tenant and she wouldn't have put it past them to have caused the jinx in her boiler, but not even Daisy could make something rust through with the sheer force of her will.

It was a pity it was only temporary, but with their baby coming—well, thrilled though she was for them, it would be hard enough seeing Ben at work strutting around and showing off photos, without having it rammed down her throat at home.

At seven o'clock on the dot, she went out of the front door, stepped over the little low iron fence between the front gardens and rang their doorbell, and Daisy opened it instantly.

'Oh, flowers, thank you! Oh, you shouldn't,' Daisy said, hugging her as she stepped inside. 'I'm *so* glad you've come. I really thought I'd upset you…'

Her eyes were filling, and Amy sighed and hugged her back. 'Don't be silly. It was lovely seeing the picture and I'm really glad everything's all right.' She eased away and sniffed the air. 'Gosh, something smells wonderful. I've been starving recently. I think it's the cold, but I'm going to have to stop it. People keep bringing chocolates in.'

'Oh, tell me about it!' Daisy laughed. 'Come on through. Ben's cooking up a storm in the kitchen. He says it's a warming winter casserole, but all I know is it's taking a long time!'

It was delicious, and she would have eaten more, but her jeans were too tight and they were putting pressure on her bladder. That would teach her to stuff the patients' chocolates, she thought.

They cleared the table, and she excused herself and went up to the bathroom, but then had to hunt for toilet paper in the little cupboard under the sink.

A box fell out onto the floor, a slim rectangular box. She picked it up to put it back, and then stopped.

A pregnancy test, one of a twin pack…

Everything seemed to slow down for a moment, and then her heart lurched and started to race.

No. Don't be silly. You can't be.

Or could she? She'd thought her jeans were tight because she'd been such a pig recently, but she was feeling bloated—and her period was overdue. Only by a day, but the others…

'Amy? I've just remembered the loo paper's run out. I've got some here, I meant to bring it up.'

She opened the door, the pregnancy test in her hand, and Daisy stared down at it, her jaw dropping.

'Amy?' she murmured.

'I—um—I was looking for loo paper, and it fell out, and—Daisy, what if I'm…?'

She looked into Daisy's worried eyes, unable to say the word, but it hung there in the air between them.

'What makes you think you could be? I thought you were on the Pill? I mean, surely you've had periods?'

'Yes.' Yes, of course she had. Thank God. She leant against the wall, weak with relief. She'd just overeaten.

'And you weren't ill, were you, before the wedding?'

Ill? Alarm bells began to ring again. Not *ill*, exactly, but thinking back she'd been sick in the morning with the thought of seeing Matt, and her stomach had played up all the previous week with nerves. And it was only a low-dose pill, so timing was crucial if you were using it for contraception—which she wasn't, so maybe she'd just taken it for granted. What if...?

'I can't be, Daisy, it was only one night, and I've had three periods...' She trailed off.

Scant ones. Lighter than normal. Shorter—and this one was late.

Oh, how could she have been so dense? The signs were all there.

'Just use the pregnancy test,' Daisy offered tentatively, putting it back in her hand. 'It's going begging, and it would answer the question.'

Did she want it answered? The wedding was months ago, so she'd be almost 16 weeks—four weeks behind Daisy. Only two weeks to...

She felt bile rising in her throat again, and swallowed hard. 'Um...'

'Go on. I'll wait outside.'

She left the door open a crack, and the moment the loo flushed, she was back in there, holding Amy's hand while they stared at the little window. One line—then the other. Clear as a bell.

Amy sat down on the floor as if her strings had been

cut, just as Ben appeared in the doorway behind Daisy. 'Are you girls OK?' he asked, looking from one to the other, and then he glanced down and saw the pregnancy test in Amy's lifeless hand, and she saw the penny drop.

'Oh, Amy,' he said softly, and as she stared at him blankly, the reality of her situation sank in and she began to shake.

'Ben, I can't—I can't do this again,' she said, her voice shuddering as fear engulfed her. 'Tell me I don't have to do this again! I can't—I'm so scared. No, please, no, not again, I can't…'

'Amy, shhh, it's OK,' Daisy said, gathering her up in her arms and rocking her against her chest. 'Hush now, sweetheart, it's all right, we'll take care of you. Don't be scared, it'll be all right.'

But it wasn't all right, and it wouldn't be, not ever again, she thought hysterically. She could hear herself gibbering, feel the panic and terror clawing at her, and underneath it, below it all, the agonising grief for the baby she'd loved and lost, too small to have any hope of surviving, and yet so much loved, so infinitely precious, so perfect—so agonisingly, dreadfully missed.

Her empty arms ached to hold him, her soul wept for his loss. Every Christmas, every birthday, every anniversary of the miscarriage—each one branded on her heart.

She couldn't bear it if it happened again…

They ended up in a row propped against the bathroom wall, her in the middle, Ben on one side, Daisy on the other, both of them holding her as she tried so very hard to push it all back down where it belonged.

And finally it was back there, safely locked away in the deepest recesses of her broken heart, and she could breathe again. Just about.

Ben let her go and shifted so he could see her face. 'Do you want me to help you tell him?' he asked, and she felt her eyes widen in shock.

Matt! Matt, who'd withdrawn into himself and isolated her in her grief, and then left her to deal with the loss of their baby alone. She hadn't even given him a thought, but—

'No! No, you can't!' she said frantically, clutching at Ben. 'I don't want him to know!'

Ben frowned. 'Well, of course he has to know, Amy, it's his baby. He needs to know—and you'll need him with you for all sorts of reasons. He should take some responsibility for this. He should have known better than to get you pregnant. I could kill him.'

She shook her head and drew her legs up, hugging her knees. 'No. Ben, I was on the Pill, I told him that. It's not his fault—not his responsibility. And I don't need him. I won't rely on him ever again, I can't. If anything goes wrong…'

'It won't.'

'It might! Ben, please! He can't deal with it, and I can't cope with all that again. I'd rather do it alone. You mustn't tell him. Please, Ben, promise me you won't tell him.'

Ben closed his eyes and let his breath out on a harsh sigh. For an age he said nothing, then he opened his eyes again and nodded. 'OK. I don't agree with you, and I think he should know, but I won't tell him yet—but you *have* to tell him at some point, Amy. He has the right to know—and the sooner the better.'

She opened her mouth to argue, but then shut it. She had the pregnancy to get through yet, and that was by no means a foregone conclusion.

'I'll tell him when it's over,' she said woodenly. 'Either way.'

'Amy, just because you've lost a baby in the past doesn't mean you're going to lose this one,' Ben said firmly, but he didn't understand. He hadn't been there, and even if he had...

'You can't say that. We didn't know why it happened, it could have been anything,' she told him, not sure what Matt had told him but needing to explain, to him and to Daisy, too, because she'd never really told her what had happened. 'I was eighteen weeks pregnant, I was fit and well, there was no bleeding, no pain, nothing, and the baby was...'

She shut her eyes tight. Perfect. Beautiful. And just too small, too frail, too unready for the world. She couldn't say it, couldn't let herself picture him, couldn't go back there.

As if he understood, Ben took her hands in his and held them firmly. 'We'll look after you. I'll get your old notes sent, and we'll make sure you're OK. We'll watch you like a hawk.'

'I was in Harrogate,' she said, her voice clogged with tears. 'With Matt—planning the wedding...'

He nodded. 'I know. Don't worry, Amy. We'll take care of you—but there's one condition.'

'I *can't* tell him yet!'

'It's not that, it's about you. You stay next door, so we can look after you properly and be there for you, or I *will* tell him. That's the deal,' he said flatly, and she looked into his eyes—Matt's eyes—and gave in. There was no arguing with the Walker men when they had that look in their eyes. And anyway, the last thing she wanted was to be alone in this, whatever she might have said.

'OK,' she agreed shakily. 'And I will tell him, but in my own way, in my own time. He'll smother me, and I can't cope with it yet. I just need to get through the next few weeks.'

Just until the baby was viable.

She couldn't say the words, but they understood, and Ben hugged her briefly and pulled her to her feet.

'I'll let you tell him. And I'll look after you. We'll look after you. It'll be OK.'

She smiled at him, feeling some of the terror dissipating in the friendly face of their support. She wasn't alone. And Ben and Daisy wouldn't desert her. So maybe she could do this, after all...

'So how are things?'

'Oh, you know how it is,' Ben said. 'How about you?'

Matt frowned. His brother sounded evasive. Odd, in only a handful of words over the telephone, but there was something there, something guarded. Something he wasn't telling him.

'Ditto. How's Daisy?'

'Better. Growing,' he said. 'She's finally stopped being sick and she's looking well. We did her twenty-week scan and everything's fine.'

'And Amy?' he asked carefully, and there was a pause.

'Amy's fine,' Ben replied, and he definitely sounded guarded now. So it wasn't that Ben was walking round him on eggshells because of Daisy being pregnant. It was Amy who was the problem.

'She—uh—she didn't want to see me again,' he admitted softly.

Matt heard Ben let out a soft sigh. 'Yeah. Well, she doesn't seem to have changed her mind. I'm sorry.'

Well, that was him told. He swallowed hard, staring sightlessly out of his sitting room window at the bleak winter garden of his small mews cottage. It had taken a bit of winding himself up to ask after her, and he wished he hadn't bothered.

Hell, he should just forget about her and move on, as she'd said, but...

'Look af—' His voice cracked a little, and he cleared his throat. 'Look after her for me.'

'We are. She's moved in next door, actually, into Daisy's house. Her boiler broke and it seemed to make sense.'

He had the totally irrational urge to jump in the car and come up and visit them. She'd be next door, just through the wall, and if he listened he'd hear her moving around—

Idiot. 'Give her my love,' he said gruffly. 'And Daisy and Florence. I'll try and see you sometime in the next couple of weeks. What are you doing over Christmas?'

'I don't know. I had thought we might go to Yorkshire, but I'm working. What about you?'

'I'm working Christmas Day and Boxing Day,' he said, and had a sudden longing for his mother's home cooking and his father's quiet, sage advice. But in the absence of that... 'Look, I've got to go, but I might try and get up between Christmas and New Year. Maybe on the twenty-seventh.'

'That'd be good. Let's see how it goes.'

'OK. You take care.'

'And you.'

He ended the call and watched a blackbird scratching in the fallen leaves under the bird feeder. Winter was setting in, the nights cold and frosty, even here in London.

He turned the television on and put his feet up, but he couldn't rest. Talking about Amy had unsettled him, and he'd suggested going up there—to see her?

Idiot. Idiot! It had taken him weeks to get over seeing her last time, so why on earth did he think it would be a good idea to go up to Yoxburgh in the hope of seeing her again?

He must be nuts. What the hell did he hope to achieve?

Maybe she's pregnant.

He stamped on that one hard. If she was pregnant, she would have told him weeks ago. Or Ben would. Yeah, Ben definitely would. Anyway, she was on the Pill, and she'd probably moved on, got herself another lover. He ignored the burn of acid at the thought. Maybe he should do the same, he told himself firmly. There was a new midwife who'd been flirting with him the past few weeks. He could take her out for dinner, see where it went.

But she's not Amy.

'You've lost Amy, get over it,' he growled. He had work he could do at the hospital, and anything was better than sitting here going over this again and again and again, so he turned the television off again, pulled on his coat and headed out of the door.

'Matt sends you his love.'

Amy felt herself stiffen. 'You didn't tell him?'

'No, of course I didn't tell him. I promised you I wouldn't.'

She let her breath out, and asked the question she'd been longing to ask. 'How is he?'

'OK, I think. We didn't talk for long. He asked how you were.'

'And what did you say?'

He smiled wryly. 'I told him you were fine and didn't want to see him again.'

It wasn't quite true. She'd been thinking about little else for the past two days, but he was right, she didn't want to see him again at the moment, because if she did, she'd have to tell him, and then...

'We were talking about Christmas,' Ben went on. 'We're both working on Christmas Day and we've got Florence on Boxing Day, but he might come up afterwards. What are you doing?'

He might come up afterwards...

'I haven't decided. They want me to work, so I'll probably do the day shift—'

'So spend Christmas night with us,' Daisy urged. 'We'll have a great time.'

It was tempting, but she shook her head. 'You want to be on your own—it's the last time you'll be able to. I'll be fine, really. Christmas Day is usually a lovely shift.'

And it would stop her worrying about her baby.

Ben scanned her the next day. They'd gone down to the big scanner in a quiet moment, and for the first time she actually acknowledged her baby's existence, dared to think about it, to see it as a real baby.

She watched the beating heart, saw the little arms and legs flailing around wildly, counted hands and feet, saw the fine, delicate column of its spine, the bridge of its nose, the placenta firmly fixed near the top of her uterus.

My baby, she thought, reaching out her hand and touching the image tenderly, and through her tears, she smiled at it and fell in love.

She pressed her hand to her mouth and closed her eyes as Ben turned off the scanner. 'Thank you,' she murmured.

'My pleasure,' he said, his voice roughened, and she realised he was moved, too, because this was his brother's baby, and he must have felt the loss of their first one keenly for Matt.

'Did you take a photo?' she asked, not sure she could bear to look at it. She still had the photo—

'Of course I did. I took one for us, as well, and one for Matt. To give him later,' he added hastily when she frowned.

She nodded. 'Thank you,' she said again, and took the tissue from him to wipe the gloop off her tummy. She'd started to show already, she realised. No wonder her jeans were tight.

Just eleven more days to go…

'You aren't going to lose this baby, Amy,' Ben said firmly, as if he'd read her mind. 'I'm not going to let you.'

'You may not be able to stop it.'

'I'd like to scan your cervix weekly from now on. Matt seemed to think—'

'Have you been talking to him?' she asked, horrified, but he shook his head.

'No. No, of course not. I promised I wouldn't. This was years ago, the only time we've talked about it. It was right after you lost the baby, and he was distraught. He thought it was your cervix. He was talking about monitoring you much more closely for the next pregnancy.'

She swung her legs down off the edge of the couch and stood up, straightening her clothes automatically. 'What next pregnancy?' she asked—fairly ridiculously, under the circumstances, she thought with a touch of hysteria, but if it hadn't been for the wedding she wouldn't have seen him again. 'He walked away, Ben. I told him I couldn't cope, that I needed time to get over it, and he walked away. He almost seemed relieved.'

'Amy, you're wrong,' he said, frowning, but she knew she wasn't. He'd been cold, remote. He'd hardly talked to her. He'd grieved for the baby, but he hadn't been able to support her, and he had rebuffed any attempt by her to support him.

'Ben, drop it. Please. You weren't there, you didn't see him. You can monitor me as closely as you like, but if it's all the same with you I'll take it one day at a time. I refuse to get my hopes up.'

'Because you feel guilty?'

She stared at him. Did she? Was that the reason she'd been so slow to realise that she was pregnant, and so reluctant to recognise this child? Because she didn't feel she deserved it? Because she'd gone for that walk with Matt the day before, and got overtired and then—?

'Ben, can we leave this?' she asked a little desperately, shutting the memories away before they could swamp her.

'Sure. I'm sorry. Here, your photo.' He handed her the little image in its white card mount, and she slipped it into her bag.

'I'd better get back to work. And—thank you, Ben. I really do appreciate all you're doing for me.'

'Don't mention it.'

She was doing fine.

There was nothing—nothing at all, from any test or examination—to indicate that she might lose this baby. Just as there hadn't been last time.

She put it out of her mind, and carried on as if nothing was any different. Apart from taking the usual precautions and supplements, she carried on as normal and tried not to think about it—or Matt—too much.

She worked the day shift on Christmas Day, and in the end she went round to Ben and Daisy's in the evening, just to eat. She didn't stay long, though. Daisy was looking tired, and it was their last Christmas alone together, so she left them to it after they'd eaten, and went home and thought about Matt.

Was he alone? It was all right for her, she'd had a great day at work, and she'd had a lovely dinner with Ben and Daisy. But Matt—who did he have?

She could phone him. Say Happy Christmas, and tell him he was going to be a father.

No. It was still too early, but she would tell him soon. She would.

CHAPTER FOUR

HE STOOD on the pavement outside, staring at the front door of Daisy's house and fighting indecision.

Amy was in. He could see the light from the kitchen shining down the hall, and he saw a shadow move across as if she'd walked into the dining room. She wasn't expecting him—none of them were, and he could see from the lack of lights that Ben and Daisy were out. So—to knock, or not to knock?

Instinct told him he wouldn't be welcome. Need told him to knock on the door anyway, to give her the benefit of the doubt, to try again, just one more time, to see if he could convince her to give their relationship another go.

He still hesitated, then with a sharp shake of his head, he walked firmly up the path and rapped on the door.

'Amy, it's Matt.'

Why had he done that? If he'd kept quiet, she would have come to the door, but instead there was silence. He resisted the urge to bend down and peer through the letter box. She was entitled to ignore him if she wanted to, and anyway there was a holly wreath hanging over it and it would probably stab him in the eye.

But she didn't ignore him. The porch light came on,

and he heard footsteps and the door swung inwards to reveal her standing there unsmiling.

'Hello, Matt,' she said quietly, and his heart turned over.

She looked—gorgeous. Her grey eyes were wary, her fair hair scrunched back in a ponytail as if she'd only just finished work and she was dressed in some shapeless rag of a jumper, but she looked warm and cosy and very, very dear, and he wanted to haul her into his arms and hold her.

As if she knew it, she hugged her arms defensively, so he forced himself to make do with a smile. 'Hi, there. Happy Christmas—or should that be Happy New Year?'

She ignored both. 'I didn't think Ben and Daisy were expecting you,' she said, her voice a little tight. 'You hadn't rung to confirm.'

'No. It was only tentative—a spur-of-the-moment thing.' Very spur of the moment. Two hours ago he'd been sitting in his house staring at the bird feeder and trying to talk himself out of it. He probably should have done.

'Oh. Well, they're out.'

'Will they be long?' Hell, they were talking like strangers.

'I don't know—why don't you come in? You can't stand out there for hours.'

'Will they be hours?' he asked, following her down the hall and eyeing her bottom thoughtfully. Had she put on a little weight? He thought so. It suited her.

'I don't know. Possibly. They're looking at baby stuff in the sales.'

Why had she said that? Why bring it up? She could have kicked herself, because absolutely the *last* thing she wanted to talk about with Matt was babies, although she knew that conversation was coming sometime soon.

'I was just making tea. Do you want some?'

'Yeah, that would be good. Thank you.'

So formal. So polite and distant. If he had any idea...

'You look well.'

She felt heat climb her cheeks. 'I am well.' *Very well, and pregnant with your child.* 'Have you eaten?'

'Yes—I had lunch, but don't mind me if you haven't.'

The stilted conversation was going to make her scream, but what was the alternative? *'Oh, incidentally, while I think of it, I'm having your baby'* didn't seem quite the right opener!

And anyway, she wasn't past the danger point yet. A few more days, maybe weeks—perhaps then.

She set a mug of tea down in front of him at the table, and finished making herself a sandwich. She was still starving, still eating anything she could lay her hands on—

'I thought you hated peanut butter?'

Damn. Trust him to notice. The only time she'd eaten it had been when she was pregnant, and any second now he'd guess.

'It goes in phases,' she said truthfully, and sat in a chair across the table and up from him, so she didn't have to look straight at him, didn't have to meet those searching blue eyes and risk blurting out the truth.

He gave a soft sigh and leant back. 'I'm sorry, I should have called you, but I thought you'd probably tell me to go to hell.'

'So why come?'

His smile was wry and rather sad. 'Why do you think, Amy?' he asked softly, and she swallowed.

'I don't— Matt, I told you before...'

He sighed softly. 'I know. That night was just for old times' sake. Laying our love to rest, I guess. I'd hoped it might turn out to be more than that. Might still turn out to be more.'

Oh, so much more. You have no idea.

'Matt, we've talked about this. We clearly didn't have what it takes, and if—'

She broke off, wary of straying into dangerous territory, but Matt had no such fear.

'If you hadn't got pregnant, our relationship would have fizzled out?'

Fizzled out? She'd said she couldn't cope with the wedding so soon after she'd lost her baby, and he'd heaved a sigh of relief and cancelled their entire relationship, so—yes, clearly he would have lost interest sooner or later, if he hadn't already done so.

She shrugged, and he shook his head slowly and gave a rueful smile.

'OK. I get that you think that, even if I don't agree, but—you seemed keen enough at the wedding, so what changed?'

What changed? *What changed?* She nearly laughed out loud at that. 'At the wedding I'd had a bit too much to drink,' she said bluntly, 'or I wouldn't have done anything so stupid. I would have thought better of it.'

'I've thought about very little since,' he said softly, and her heart contracted.

Oh, Matt.

She opened her mouth to tell him, but bottled out and changed the subject, asking instead how his parents were.

He gave a knowing little smile and let it go. 'Fine. They've got snow up there at the moment, but they're OK, they've got plenty of food in and Dad can still get to the farms for emergencies, but it's supposed to be thawing this week.'

Oh, for God's sake, just tell her you love her! Tell her you want her! Tell her you want to try again, and this time you'll make it work. She's said we didn't have what it takes, but does anybody? For what happened to us, does anybody have what it takes?

He was opening his mouth when there was a sharp knock on the door. She got up and opened it, and he heard her murmur his name as Ben strode in.

'You were going to phone!' he said, hugging him and slapping his back. 'Come on, let's get you out of Amy's hair and you can give me a hand to unload the car. Daisy's been shopping with a vengeance.'

Maybe he didn't want to go? Maybe Amy was happy with him there? Maybe he hadn't finished what he'd come for?

But then he looked at her, composed, controlled but not exactly overjoyed, and he let out his breath on a quiet sigh and moved towards the door.

'Sure. Thanks for the tea, Amy. It was good to see you again.'

She smiled, but it didn't reach her eyes. 'Happy New Year, Matt.'

And she shut the door gently but firmly behind them, and went back to the table, her hands shaking.

She had to tell him sometime. Why not now? Why on earth hadn't she taken the opportunity?

She sighed. She knew why—knew that until this week was over, at least, she couldn't share it with him, but she would tell him. Ben was right, he needed to know, and she wanted their child to have him in its life. He was a good man, and he'd be a wonderful father.

What she couldn't deal with again, if anything went wrong, was his grief on top of her own.

No. Better not to have told him yet—and Ben had promised not to. She just hoped she could rely on him.

He was there until the following evening, and she spent as much time as possible at the hospital.

It wasn't hard. They were busy and short-staffed, and delighted to have her.

She'd put herself down for the night shift on New Year's Eve—better to keep busy, because she was eighteen weeks on that day, and if she hadn't been busy she would have gone out of her mind.

Her phone beeped a couple of times—Happy New Year messages from people, she thought, but she was too busy to check it, so she carried on filling in the notes and went back to her mums to check on them.

But when her night shift finished and she went home in the cold, bright crisp air of the morning, she finally checked her phone and found a text from a friend and a voicemail message.

From Matt.

'Hi, Amy, it's Matt. Sorry to miss you, I expect you're working. I just wanted to say Happy New Year, and it was good to see you again the other day. I'm sorry it was so brief. Maybe next time…' There was a pause, then he added, 'Well, you know where I am if you want me.'

If she wanted him?

She sat down on the sofa in her sitting room, and played his hesitant, reluctant message again and again and again.

Of course she wanted him. She wanted him so much it was unbearable, today of all days, the exact stage to the day that she'd lost their first baby. She laid her hand over the tidy little bump—hardly a bump at all. If you didn't know, you wouldn't guess, but assuming it made it, and it was a big assumption, this baby was going to cause havoc in her life.

And in Matt's.

She had to tell him. Ben was right, she couldn't just keep relying on them, and he had the right to know about his child. She took the two-week-old scan photo out of her bag and stared at it, tracing the tiny face with her finger. It would be bigger now. As big as Samuel...

Lord, even the name hurt. She sucked in a breath, the images crowding in on her—the midwife's eyes so full of compassion as she wrapped his tiny body in a blanket and placed it in Matt's arms. The tears in his eyes, the searing agony she could see in every line of his body as he stared down at his son.

He'd lifted the baby to his lips, kissed his tiny head, shuddered with grief. It had broken him—broken both of them—and their relationship, like their son, had been too fragile, too young to survive.

She almost rang him. Her finger hovered over the call button, but then she turned the phone off and told herself to stop being so ridiculous. She'd decided not to tell him until after the twenty-week scan. Maybe longer. Maybe not until it was viable. He'd been so gutted last time, so deeply distressed, that he'd been unreachable, and she knew—she just *knew*—he'd be a nightmare if she told him. He'd probably have her admitted so he could scan her three times a day, but she wasn't having any of it. It was utterly unnecessary, and thinking about it all the time just made it all so much worse.

So she didn't ring him, and then she was past the time of the miscarriage, into the nineteenth week. Then the twentieth, and the big scan, which she could hardly bear to look at she was so nervous.

But it was normal, and it looked much more like a baby now, every feature clearly defined. It was sucking its thumb, and Amy felt a huge tug of love towards this tiny, vulnerable child—Matt's child. 'Do you want to know what it is?' the ultrasonographer asked her, but she shook her head.

'No.' Knowing would make it harder to remain detached, and she'd been careful not to look—but the baby was moving vigorously, and she could feel it all the time now, so real, so alive, so very, very strong that finally, at last, she began to allow a tiny glimmer of hope to emerge.

Was it possible that this baby would be all right?

She wanted to share it, to tell everyone in the world, but she was still a little afraid she might jinx it, so she took the photo home, propped it up on the bedside table next to her so she could see it when she woke, and fell asleep with a smile on her face and her hand curved protectively over her child…

She went shopping the following week with Daisy, and she talked Amy into getting some pretty clothes.

'You can't just wear scrubs and jog bottoms and baggy jumpers for the rest of your pregnancy,' she scolded, and handed her all sorts of things, all of which Amy thought made her look shockingly pregnant.

Shockingly, because she'd still not really taken it on board. It was still too early, the baby wasn't yet viable, and she felt a little quiver of nerves.

'Daisy, I really don't think—'

'No. Don't think. You think altogether too much. You're fine, Amy. You're well. Everything's OK.'

'I was well last time,' she said woodenly, and Daisy dropped the clothes she was carrying and hugged her.

'Oh, sweetheart, you'll be fine. Come on, Ben says everything's looking really good. It's time to be happy.'

Happy? Maybe, she thought, as Daisy took her to a café and plied her with hot chocolate and common sense, and gradually she relaxed. She was being silly. She could buy a few clothes—just enough. That wasn't tempting fate, was it? And her bras *were* strangling her. They finished their hot chocolate and went back to the shops.

And gradually, as the weeks passed and she got nearer to her due date, she began to dare to believe it might all be all right. She was beginning to feel excited, to look forward to the birth—except, of course, she'd be alone.

Unless she told Matt.

She felt her stomach knot at the thought. It was the beginning of April and Daisy had just started her maternity leave, five weeks before her baby was due, and nine weeks before Amy's. Gosh, 31 weeks, Amy thought, stunned, and bit her lip. There was no excuse now not to tell him and she was being unfair. He'd need time to get his head round it, and he was going to give her hell for keeping it quiet, but it had gone on for so long now that she wasn't sure how to broach the subject.

The baby was kicking her vigorously all night now. She'd never felt Samuel move—well, maybe a flutter, just before the end, but not like this, not so you could see it from the outside.

Matt would love to feel it…

Oh, how to tell him? Because she knew she had to, knew he had a right to know, and she was sharing the things she should have been sharing with him with Ben and Daisy, so much so that it was unfair.

Just how unfair was brought home to her two weeks later, when she was in their nursery looking at all the baby things and she'd jokingly talked about Ben delivering her and asked Daisy if she could borrow him. They exchanged a glance, and Ben sighed softly. 'Amy, I'm not my brother,' he said, his voice gentle. 'I'm happy to help, you know that, but it isn't me you need, and I can't take his place. And it isn't fair of you to ask me to. It isn't fair on any of us, especially not Matt.'

She felt hot colour flood her face, and turned blindly and went out of the room, stumbling downstairs and out into the garden. She hadn't thought of it from his side, but of course it was an imposition, and she'd been thoughtless, taken Ben and Daisy for granted, cheated Matt—but—

'Amy, wait!'

He stopped her just before she went through the gate in the fence, his hand on her arm gentle but firm.

'Amy. Please don't walk away. I don't mean to hurt you, but it's not my baby, sweetheart. Your baby needs its proper father—and he needs to know.'

She nodded, scrubbing away the tears. 'You're right. I know you're right. I'll do it soon, I promise. I'm just being silly. I just don't know how...'

'Do you want me to help you?'

She shook her head. 'No. I'll do it. I'll call him.'

'Promise me?'

She nodded, swallowing a sob. 'I promise.'

She escaped then, and let herself into her house and cried her heart out in the conservatory where they couldn't hear her through the wall.

She was mortified, but more than that, she was

afraid. She'd been leaning on Ben, she realised, not only because he was Matt's twin, but because he was reliable and kind and generous and decent, and because he'd let her.

And all the time it had been Matt she'd wanted, Matt she'd needed, Matt she still needed and always would. But this baby was going to make life so complicated, and it dawned on her in a moment of clarity that she'd been stalling because the status quo was far easier to deal with than the reality of sharing a child with a man who didn't really love her, even if he liked to think he might.

And that, she realised at last, was at the heart of her reluctance. They'd had a great time together at first, and the sex had always been brilliant, but Matt didn't love her, not enough to cope with the worst things life could thrust at them, and she didn't want him doing what he'd done before and offering to marry her just because they were having a child.

No, that was wrong, they'd already talked about marriage last time, made half-plans for the future. He hadn't officially proposed, but they were heading that way, drifting into it, and she wondered if they would have drifted all the way to a wedding if she hadn't got pregnant. But she had, of course, because they'd been careless with contraception on the grounds that it wouldn't have been a disaster if she'd got pregnant, at the time they'd both been anticipating a future together

Except it had been—a disaster that had left shockwaves still rippling around her life now over four years later.

She went round to see Daisy the following day and apologised for being an idiot, and they both ended up in tears. She talked about Matt, about how she felt, and then looked at all the stuff in the nursery and felt utterly overwhelmed.

She was having this baby in just seven weeks, maybe less, and she'd been so busy fretting about Matt she'd done nothing to prepare for it. 'I need to go and buy some basics,' she said to Daisy, and she rolled her eyes.

'Finally! Otherwise you know what'll happen, you'll have it two weeks early and you'll have no baby stuff at all!'

She was wrong. It wasn't Amy who had her baby two weeks early, it was Daisy herself.

She'd come into the hospital on Wednesday morning to see them all because she was bored and restless and sick of housework, and she was sitting in the office chatting to Amy in a quiet moment when her eyes widened and then squeezed tight shut.

Then she gave an exasperated sigh. 'Oh, I can't believe I've been so *stupid*! I had backache all day yesterday, but I've been cleaning. The kitchen was absolutely pigging, and—Amy, this isn't funny, stop laughing at me and get Ben!'

'Get Ben why?' Ben asked, walking in, and then he looked at Daisy and his jaw dropped.

'What's the matter?' Amy teased with a grin. 'Never seen a woman in labour before?'

It was a textbook labour, if a little fast, and Amy made it quite clear to Ben that she was in control.

'You're on paternity leave as of now, so don't even think about interfering,' she told him as she checked Daisy between contractions. Her body was doing a wonderful job, and Amy was happy to let nature take its course.

It was just another delivery, her professional mask was in place, and she was doing fine until the baby was born, but once she'd lifted their son and laid him on Daisy's chest against her heart, she let Ben take over.

It was Ben who told her it was a boy, Ben who covered him with a warmed towel as Daisy said hello to their little son, Ben who cleared his mouth of mucus with a gentle finger and stimulated that first, heart-warming cry, because Amy was transfixed, her eyes flooded with tears, her whole body quivering.

She wanted Matt with her when she gave birth in a few weeks, Matt to take their baby from the midwife and lay him—her?—on her chest, and gaze down at them both with love and wonder in his eyes. If only things were different...

But they weren't different, they were what they were, and she'd be alone, not only for the delivery but for the whole business of motherhood, and her confidence suddenly deserted her.

I can't do it alone! I can't be that strong. I'm not that brave. Matt, why can't you love me enough? I need you—

No, she didn't! She stopped herself in her tracks, and took a long, slow, steadying breath. She was getting way ahead of herself. One day at a time, she reminded herself. She was getting through her pregnancy like that. She could get through motherhood in the same way. The last thing she needed was a man who didn't love her enough to ride out the hard times, who when the crunch came would walk away, however much he might think he wanted her.

And right now, Daisy and Ben and their new little son were her priority.

'Let's give them a minute,' she said to Sue, the midwife assisting her, and stripping off her gloves, she turned and walked blindly out of the door and down the corridor to the stairwell.

Nobody would find her there. She could hide here for a minute, get herself together. Think about what Ben had said.

Should Matt be there with her when she gave birth? Even if they weren't together?

Yes, if it was like this, but if anything went wrong...

He'd been there last time, distant and unreachable, his eyes filled with pain. She couldn't cope with that again, couldn't handle his pain as well as her own. The last thing she needed during her labour was a man she couldn't rely on if anything went wrong, a man who couldn't talk about his feelings or hers.

But she needed him...

No! No, she didn't! She was made of sterner stuff than that, and she could cope alone. She could. She knew all the midwives here, she'd have plenty of support during her labour. She didn't need Matt.

She got to her feet and went back to them, to find Ben sitting in the chair cuddling his tiny son with a tender smile on his face that wasn't going to fade any time soon.

Lucky little boy, she thought. So, so lucky. Her baby would have a father who loved him like that, she knew, but it wouldn't have two parents sharing its life on a daily basis, supporting each other through thick and thin.

Her hand slid down over her baby in an unconscious caress. If only...

She helped Ben get the house ready after her shift finished at three.

He was bringing Daisy and Thomas home that evening, and they were almost done.

'Gosh, I've never seen it so clean and tidy,' she said with a laugh, and he just rolled his eyes and sighed.

'Silly girl. I should have smelled a rat when I got home last night and found the place sparkling. I can't believe I was so dense.' He gave the quilt cover one last tug into place, straightened up and met Amy's eyes.

'Matt should be with you when you have the baby, Amy. Labour can be a tough and lonely place. You're going to need support.'

'Ben, it's OK,' she said softly. 'I'll be all right.'

'And what about Matt? What about my brother, Amy? He lost a baby too, you know. He needs this to put things right for him, to balance the books a bit. You can't deny him the experience of seeing his child born. This is going to happen. You can't keep ignoring it.'

She swallowed and nodded. 'No. You're right, I know you're right. I'll discuss it with him when I tell him— just maybe not tonight. You'll want to talk to him tonight, tell him your news. There are things we'll need to sort out anyway, and I've only got five weeks to go. Nothing's going to go wrong now.'

Oh, foolish, foolish words.

She woke on Friday morning with a slight headache, and went downstairs and poured herself a tall glass of fruit juice and iced water, and sat in the conservatory listening to the birds.

Gosh, her head was thumping, she thought, and went and had a shower, washed her hair and let it air dry while she had another drink.

She must be dehydrated. Too busy yesterday to drink much. Too busy, and too stressed because Matt was coming up for the weekend and she was going to tell him. She'd tried to phone him last night from the hospital but she hadn't got hold of him, and she would have tried again when she got home, but she'd worked till nine and she'd been too tired, and today she was starting at seven. She'd try again this afternoon, before he left London—not that it seemed right to do it like that, over the phone, but she couldn't exactly do it face to face. He didn't need to be an obstetrician to work it out, so there'd be no subtlety, no putting it gently.

No 'You remember that night you made love to me, and I told you it was all right because I was on the Pill? Well, there's something I need to tell you.' Nothing so easy as that—although, to be fair, it couldn't be easier than just opening the door to him. That would be pretty straightforward, she thought with a wry grimace.

She dressed for work, wriggling her feet into her shoes and sighing because even they were getting tighter. Everything was, but it was pointless buying things at this stage.

It was ludicrously busy at work, of course, and she began to think she ought to consider taking maternity leave sooner than she'd allowed.

She had two more weeks to go, come Monday, and she was working today and tomorrow. Just as well, since Matt was going to be around, although she'd have to talk to him face to face in the end.

She found time for lunch somewhere between one and two—a quick sandwich eaten on the run, which gave her vicious indigestion, but she needed something in her stomach so she could take some paracetamol for her headache.

She sat down in the office for a moment and eased her shoes off. Pregnancy was the pits, she decided, and vowed to be nicer to her mums when they complained about it in future. Really, men didn't know how lucky they were—and that's if they were even there!

No. She mustn't be unfair. She hadn't given Matt the chance to be there.

'Amy, can you come? I've got a mum about to deliver.'

'Sure.'

She squirmed her feet back into her shoes, winced and followed Angie, one of the other midwives, down the corridor to the delivery room. Roll on nine o'clock, she thought. Why on earth had she agreed to do a double shift? It was a good job Ben wasn't here to see her, or Daisy. They'd skin her, but there hadn't been anyone else available at the last minute and at least it would mean she'd be out when Matt arrived.

Any other day, she thought, and tried to smile brightly at their patient. 'Hiya, I'm Amy,' she said, and threw herself into the fray.

Matt's car was outside, and just the thought that he was there made her heart pound, her throat dry and her chest ache.

She hadn't been able to ring him that afternoon. Should she ring him tonight?

No. Tonight should be for Ben and Daisy, for him to meet his little nephew, although judging by the sounds coming through their front door, Thomas was well and truly met.

She could just picture him holding the tiny baby in those big, capable hands.

She closed her eyes to shut out the image and squeezed them tight shut. Oh, they ached. Everything ached. Her head, her eyes, her feet...

She looked down, and blinked. Her feet were swollen. Not just the normal swollen feet of pregnancy, but a more sinister kind of swollen. And her fingers felt tight, and her head was splitting. She could feel her heartbeat in her eyeballs, even, and as she mentally listed the symptoms, she closed her eyes and leant against her front door, stunned.

Pre-eclampsia? Just like that? But she'd been fine up to now. Ben had been monitoring her minute by minute until Thomas had been born, but that was only two days ago, and she'd had no symptoms at all.

Except the headache this morning, and the tight shoes and clothes, and the epigastric pain she'd put down to indigestion—

Lord, she felt dreadful.

Matt. I need Matt.

She could hear voices through their front door, and the baby was quiet now. If she called out— Oh, her head ached so much, and she moaned. It was so far to the door...

She stepped over the little fence, arm outstretched towards the bellpush, but then she stumbled and half fell, half slid down the door with a little yelp. Oh, her head. She heard a voice, heard running footsteps, then felt the door open as she slid sideways across the step and came to rest.

There was a startled exclamation, and gentle hands touched her face.

Matt...!

CHAPTER FIVE

'WHAT was that?'

Ben frowned at him. 'I don't know. Amy? Are you all right?' he called, and there was a muffled cry and a crash against the door.

'What the hell—?' Matt thrust his nephew at Daisy and ran down the hall, turning the door handle and then catching the door as it was forced inwards.

'Matt, she's…' Ben began, as the door swung open and Amy tumbled over at his feet.

He knelt beside her, cupping her face in his hand and turning her towards him so he could check her pupils.

The doctor in him was registering her symptoms. The man was in shock, and deeply, furiously angry, because Amy was pregnant, and none of them had told him—unless it wasn't his?

'It's yours,' he heard Ben say, but he didn't answer. He was too damned angry with him and too worried about Amy to deal with that now, and the fear just ramped up a notch.

'Amy? Amy, it's Matt, talk to me!' he said urgently, his eyes scanning her. How the hell had she got like this? Her feet were swollen, her face was puffy, her eyes—her eyes were opening, searching for him.

'Matt.' She lifted her hand and rested it against his

cheek, and worry flickered in her eyes. 'I've been try-ing to phone you. I've got something I have to tell you.'

He laid his hand over hers and squeezed it. 'It's OK, sweetheart. Don't talk now.'

'But I have to. I have to tell you—'

'Amy, it's all right, I know about the baby. You just close your eyes and rest, let me look after you.'

Her fingers fluttered against his cheek, and he pressed his lips to her palm and folded her hand over to keep it safe. It made her smile, a weak, fragile smile that tore his heart wide open. 'I'm so glad you're here...'

'Me too,' he said softly, his voice choked, and turned his head. 'She's about to fit, we need an ambulance,' he snapped at Ben, but he'd gone and Daisy, standing there with Thomas in her arms and shock in her eyes, answered him.

'He's getting the car—he said there wasn't time for an ambulance. I'll get the emergency team to meet you there.'

'We'll need a theatre.'

'I know. Ben's outside with the car. You need to go.'

They did. She was barely conscious now, her eyes rolling back in her head, and he felt sick with fear. He scooped her up, ran down the path and got into the back of the car behind Ben, Amy on his lap.

Please be all right. Please let the baby be all right. Don't let it happen again. I can't do this again. Amy can't do this again. Please be all right...

They screeched into the hospital, pulled up outside Maternity and left the car there with the doors hang-ing open. Ben threw the keys at the reception clerk and asked her to deal with it, and a waiting team took over.

Matt dumped her on the trolley and they had her in the lift and on oxygen instantly, a line was going in each hand and an infusion of magnesium sulphate was started while they were still on the move.

'I'm scrubbing,' he said, and earned himself a hard stare.

'No way. By all means get gowned up, but I'm doing this, not you,' Ben said flatly, and filled the team in. 'Pre-eclampsia, sudden onset, partial loss of consciousness, she hasn't fitted as far as we know but she might have done,' he told them, but they were already on it, primed by Daisy, and as Ben went to scrub they were preparing her for surgery.

There was no job for Matt, so he stepped back out of the way. Someone fed his arms into a gown and tied it up, put a cap on his head, a mask over his face, and he stood there, his heart in his mouth, and watched as his brother brought his son into the world.

A boy. A perfect, beautiful boy, but still and silent, his body blue, his chest unmoving.

Please, no, not again...!

Matt was frozen to the spot, his eyes fixed on the little chest, begging it to move.

'Come on, baby,' the midwife was saying, sucking his mouth out, rubbing his back, flicking his feet. 'Come on, you can do it.'

When the cry came, he thought his legs would give way under him. He dragged in a huge breath, then another, and pressed his fist to his mouth to keep in the sob.

'Go and meet your baby,' Ben said gently, and he went over on legs that were not quite steady and reached out a finger and touched his baby's hand. Tiny, transparent pink fingers clenched around his fingertip, and another sob wrestled free from his chest.

He stroked the fingers, oh, so gently with his thumb,

afraid for the fragile, friable skin, but he was past that stage. Thirty-five weeks was OK. He'd be OK. The relief, for a child he didn't even know he was having until half an hour ago, was enormous.

It had plagued him, all the what ifs, the regrets that not once but twice he'd let her send him away without putting up a fight, the hope that she might contact him and tell him she was pregnant that had flickered and then died. He'd even seen her at Christmas, thought she looked well, had even put on a little weight, for heaven's sake, and all the time...

He turned his head. 'How is she?' he asked hoarsely.

'Stable. We'll know more when she comes round. The neurologist is coming to have a look at her and we're moving her to Maternity HDU.'

He swallowed the fear and turned back to his son.

'Hello, my little man,' he murmured softly, his hands trembling but his voice gentle with reassurance. 'Your mummy's not very well, but she'll be OK, and so will you. Daddy's here now and I'm going nowhere,' he promised.

'Want to hold him?' the midwife asked gently.

He nodded, and she wrapped him in a soft cotton blanket and placed him in Matt's arms. 'He needs to go to SCBU for a while, just to make sure he's OK and his lungs are coping, but he's looking good so far. He's 2.1 kilos. That's a good weight for a preemie—over four and a half pounds.'

He nodded. He could feel him, knew he was a good size, but that wasn't what he was seeing.

He was seeing another child in his arms, far smaller, too small to make it in this world, a child he'd never had the chance to love. His heart ached with the love he'd never been able to give, would never be able to give that child, and now he had another child, a child whose mother might not recover from this. God, how much more—?

Ben appeared at his side, and he felt an arm around his shoulders. 'He's going to be all right, Matt,' he said softly, and there was a catch in his voice.

He nodded. 'He is. Ben, how did she get like this?'

'I have no idea. I've had her under a microscope, and I'll be going over her notes again with a fine-toothed comb, to see if there's anything I've missed, but she hasn't even had high blood pressure.'

'What is it now?'

'Two thirty-five over 170.'

'*What*?' He felt his legs buckle slightly and jammed his knees back hard. That was high. Too high. Ludicrously high. She could still fit, still end up with brain damage—

'Don't go there, Matt. She's in good hands.'

He nodded, handed the baby back to the midwife and turned to watch Amy being wheeled out of Theatre. 'I need to be with her.'

'Yes, you do. I'm sorry. If I hadn't been off on paternity leave for the past two days, I would have spotted this coming on. Someone's just told me she did a double shift today, and she was supposed to be working tomorrow.'

'That's crazy!' he said under his breath. 'What the hell was she thinking about? Or was she keeping out of my way?'

'I don't know,' Ben said heavily. 'She wasn't booked to do the double shift. I think they were short-staffed, but if I'd been here I wouldn't have let her do it.'

The anger, so carefully banked, broke free again. 'Nor would I, but I didn't get that choice, did I? Why didn't any of you tell me she was pregnant? How could you *keep* that from me? For God's sake, Ben, I'm your *brother*!'

They were following the trolley, and Ben paused and met his eyes. 'You think I don't know that? I've been trying to get her to tell you since the day she found out.'

'*You* could have told me.'

'No. I promised her I wouldn't. I said I'd look after her.'

He made a harsh sound in his throat. 'If you'd told me, I would have been looking after her, and this wouldn't have happened.'

'Oh, for God's sake, man, if you're that bothered, why did you let her go in the first place? And it wasn't me who got her pregnant,' Ben snapped impatiently, and with a rough sigh he stalked off after the trolley, leaving Matt to follow or not.

He followed, his thoughts reeling, and they walked the rest of the way in an uncomfortable silence.

She fitted in the night, and Matt stood at the end of the bed with his heart in his mouth while all hell broke loose and drugs were pumped into her and the team struggled to control her blood pressure.

He clenched his fists and forced himself to keep out of it, to let them do their jobs, but in fairness they were doing exactly what he would have done if he'd been in charge, so he watched the monitor, and he waited, and finally it started to come down as her kidneys kicked in again, and he watched the numbers on the monitor drop gradually to sensible levels.

He felt his own blood pressure slowly return to something in the normal range, and then once he could get near her again he sagged back into the chair beside the bed and took her puffy, bloated hand in his. He stroked the back of it gently with his thumb, the rhythm soothing him, the contact with her warmth giving him hope.

She'd survived, and she was breathing. For now, that was all he could think about. All he could let himself think about.

'It's OK, Amy,' he murmured, trying to inject some conviction into his voice. 'You'll be all right, my love. Just hang in there. I'm right here, and I'm not leaving. You'll be OK, don't worry. The baby's fine. He's going to be fine, and so are you...'

His voice cracked, and he broke off, dragging in a deep breath and staring up at the ceiling.

Who was he trying to convince? Her, or himself? Empty words, the sort of platitudes he heard desperate relatives telling their loved ones all the time in the face of insurmountable odds.

Were they insurmountable? He forced himself to be realistic. He treated women with pre-eclampsia all the time, and usually it was fine, but rarely—very rarely— it came on so fast, like Amy's, that it caught them by surprise, and then it could spiral out of control with shocking speed. Sometimes there were no symptoms at all, the woman went straight into eclampsia and began fitting, and then the symptoms might follow later.

The outcome then was dependent on many factors— what had caused the fit, what damage it had done, how bad the multi-system failure was—and it was impossible to second-guess it.

She might have had a stroke, or got irreversible kidney or liver damage, he thought, and stopped himself running through the list. He didn't need to borrow trouble. Time would tell, and until then he'd look on the bright side. She was alive. She was breathing for herself, her kidneys were starting to work again, her blood results were in the manageable range and he just had to wait. It often got worse before it got better. He knew that.

The time, though, seemed to stand still, punctuated only by the regular visits of the nursing and medical staff every few minutes until it all became a blur.

Underneath the worry for Amy, though, concern for the baby was nagging at him incessantly. All the staff were busy, but even so they'd given him a couple of reassuring updates. It wasn't the same as seeing him, though. He wanted to watch over him as he was watching over Amy, to will him to live, to tell him he loved him.

But Amy needed him more, so he sat there feeling torn in half, part of him desperate to go and see his tiny son, the other, bigger part unable to drag himself away from Amy's bedside until he was entirely confident of her recovery.

Then Ben came in, at some ungodly hour of the morning, and stood behind him, hands on his shoulders, the weight so reassuring, anchoring him, somehow.

'How is she?' he asked softly.

Matt shook his head.

'I don't know. She fitted. They couldn't get her blood pressure down for a while. It's down now, it's looking better but she's sedated at the moment. We've just got to wait.'

He felt Ben's hand squeeze his shoulder. 'I'm sorry.'

'Don't be,' he said, his voice clogged. 'It wasn't your fault, you weren't even supposed to be working. I was just stressed and I shouldn't have taken it out on you. I know it happens.'

'I'm still sorry. I should have made sure someone kept an eye on her. I should have done it myself.'

'No. If she was fine, you couldn't have foreseen this, and you know how quickly it can happen, and she's a midwife. She should have recognised the signs. As you say, it must have been really sudden.' He put his hand over Ben's and gripped it, leaning back against him, taking strength from his brother while he voiced his fears. 'What am I going to do if she's not all right?' he asked unevenly, and he felt Ben's hand tighten.

'She'll be all right. Have faith.'

He dropped his hand abruptly. 'Sorry. I don't have faith any longer. I used it all up last time.'

'This isn't like that.'

'No. No, it isn't. This time I've got the baby, and I might lose the woman I love. I don't know which is worse.'

'You won't lose her.'

'There's more than one way to lose someone, Ben. She might have brain damage.'

'She's responding to pain.'

'Earthworms respond to pain,' he said bluntly, and Ben sighed softly, letting go of his shoulders and moving away slightly, leaving him in a vacuum.

'Have you had a break yet? Gone for a walk, stretched your legs? Eaten anything?'

He shook his head. 'I don't want anything—except to know how the baby is.'

'He's doing well. I rang from home, and they said he's fine, he's breathing on his own and looking good. They've put a tube in and given him some colostrum from the milk bank and they're happy with him.'

He nodded, his eyes fixed on Amy, and felt a little more of the tension ease. He glanced at the clock, then up at his brother with a frown. 'It's the middle of the night. You should be with Daisy. She's only just given birth.'

'She's fine, and I've got my mobile. I promised I wouldn't be long, but I couldn't sleep, so I thought I'd come back and see how it was going, make sure you were OK. Get you to eat something, maybe.'

'I'm not hungry.'

'Come and see the baby, at least, then, to put your mind at rest. Amy's stable, and we won't be far away. They'll ring me if they want us.'

How did he know that only seeing him with his own eyes would be good enough?

Stupid question. His brother knew everything about him. He got to his feet, stiff and aching from the hard plastic chair, and walked the short distance to SCBU.

The last time he'd been in here was to see the Grieves twins, back in September. Now it was the end of April, and he was here to see his own child, experiencing at first hand the hope and fear felt by the parents of a pre-mature baby.

He washed his hands thoroughly, doused them in alcohol gel and introduced himself to the staff.

The neonatal unit manager, Rachel, remembered him from September, and she smiled at him encouragingly. 'He's doing really well. Come and say hello,' she said, and led him over to the clear plastic crib.

Ben had left him to it, giving him space. He wasn't sure he wanted it, but he was talking to a woman in a dressing gown sitting tearfully by a crib, and he glanced across and winked at Matt.

You can do it. Go and say hello to your son.

He nodded, and took the last few steps to the side of the crib. He was used to seeing babies in them, but not *his* baby, and he blew his breath out slowly at the impact. He seemed so small, so vulnerable, so incredibly fragile.

It was quite irrational. As a twin specialist he was used to delivering babies much smaller than him, sometimes as much as nine weeks younger, on the very edge of viability, but age wasn't everything and their baby wasn't out of the woods yet, he knew.

'Hi, little guy,' he said softly, and threading his hands through the ports, he cradled his sleeping son's head tenderly with one hand, the other cupping the tiny, wrinkly little feet. They fascinated him. The toes were so tiny, the nails perfectly formed, the skinny little legs so frail and yet so strong.

He looked like Ben and Daisy's Thomas, he thought. Not surprisingly, since half their DNA pool was identical. They were practically half-brothers, he realised, and smiled. They'd grow up together, be friends. That was good.

He studied the tiny nose with its pinpoint white spots on the skin, the creased-up little eyes tight shut, the mouth working slightly. There was a tube up his nose taped to his cheek, and a clip on his finger leading to the monitor, but he didn't need to look at it. He watched the scrawny, ribby little chest going up and down, up and down as he breathed unaided, and felt more of the tension leave him.

He was a tiny, living miracle, and Matt swallowed a huge lump in his throat as he stared down at the sleeping baby.

'He's doing really well,' Rachel said matter-of-factly. 'We put the tube in to get his feeding off to a good start, because he's a little light for his dates, but he's great. Just a bit skinny, really.'

Matt nodded. He was. At a guess her placenta had been failing for a couple of weeks, and although he was a good size, he was still slightly behind what he should have been. Whatever, he'd catch up quickly enough now, and he was clearly in good hands.

'He's looking good,' Ben said quietly from beside him, and he nodded again. It seemed easier than talking, while his throat was clogged with emotion and his chest didn't seem to be working properly.

He eased away from the crib with a shaky sigh and, asking Rachel to keep in touch, he headed out of the unit with Ben.

'How about coming down to the canteen?'

'I want to get back to Amy,' he said, even though he could murder a drink, now he thought about it.

'Can I get you anything, then? Tea, coffee, bacon roll?'

'Coffee and a bacon roll would be good,' he said, but when it came he could hardly eat it. Sitting there outside the high dependency unit and fretting about Amy did nothing for the appetite, he discovered, and the bacon roll only brought back memories—the morning after the wedding, when he'd spent the night with her, trying to convey with actions rather than words how much he loved her; the mornings they'd woken in his London apartment and she'd snuggled up to him and told him she was hungry and he'd left her there, warm and sleepy, and made her breakfast.

They'd been halcyon days, but they'd ended abruptly when she'd lost Samuel.

Odd. He always thought of him as Samuel, although they'd never talked about it since that awful day. They'd talked about names before, argued endlessly about girls' names but agreed instantly on Sam.

He tipped his head back with a sigh, resting it against the wall behind the hard plastic chair in the waiting area outside the HDU. Ben had brought the bacon roll and coffee up to him and then gone back to Daisy and their own tiny baby, and now he sat there, staring at the roll in his hand while he remembered the past and wondered what the future held.

Once, it had seemed so bright, so cut and dried and full of joy. Now, over four years later, Amy was lying there motionless, possibly brain injured, their newborn son was in SCBU, and Matt had no idea what lay ahead for the three of them.

He swallowed the last of the cold coffee, threw the roll into the bin and went back to Amy's side. Could the sheer force of his willpower pull her through? He didn't know, but he'd give it a damn good try.

He picked up her lifeless hand, and stopped. Was he clutching at straws, or was it less swollen? He looked at it thoughtfully, wondering if he was imagining it. No. He didn't think so. It *was* improving, slowly. *She* was improving.

Shaking with relief, knowing it was still early days, trying to find a balance between sheer blind optimism and drenching fear, he cradled the hand in his, pressed it to his cheek and closed his eyes.

She was floating.

No, not floating. Drowning. Drowning in thick, sticky fog and awash with pain.

There were noises—bleeps and tweets, hisses and sighs. People talking, alarms going off, laughter in the distance.

Hospital? It sounded like the hospital. Smelt like the

hospital. But she was lying down, floating on the fog—
or water? Drowning again. It felt like water—

She coughed, and felt her hand squeezed. Odd.
Someone was there, holding it. Talking to her in a soothing voice.

Matt? He was saying something about a baby, over
and over. 'The baby's all right…he's going to be all
right—'

But her baby was—

She felt herself recoil from the pain. It hurt too much
to think, to work it all out. She tried to open her eyes,
to argue, but it was too bright, too difficult, so she shut
them again and let the fog close over her…

'She woke for a moment. She coughed, and she tried
to open her eyes.'

'OK, well, that's good. Let's have a look. Amy? Amy,
wake up, please, open your eyes. Come on.'

The doctor squeezed her ear, pressing his nail into
the lobe, and she moaned slightly but she didn't open
her eyes or react in any other way.

He checked her reflexes, scanned the monitor, listened to her chest, checked her notes for urine output
and fluid balance, and nodded.

'She's shifting a lot of fluid, which is good. Have
you noticed any change?'

'Her hand's thinner.'

He picked it up, pressed it, nodded again, had a look
at her incision and covered her, but not before Matt had
seen it. He smiled. It was neat. Very neat, for all the
hurry. Ben had done a good job. She wouldn't have un-
sightly scars to trouble her.

'I gather the baby's doing well.'

'Yes, he is. I went to see him. He's beautiful. Amazing. Really strong.'

'Well, she's resting now if you want to go and see him again. I don't think she's about to wake up.'

He nodded. It wasn't what he wanted to hear. He wanted to be told she was lightening, that any minute now she'd drift out of the fog and open her eyes and smile, but he knew it was a vain hope.

Nevertheless, he took the advice and went to see their baby, and as he walked in, he was assailed by fear. He was exhausted, worried sick and for the first time understanding just what all the parents of sick and preterm babies went through.

And it wasn't great.

The shifts had changed, of course, and Rachel wasn't there, but there was another nurse who he'd met before, in September, and she greeted him with a smile. 'Matt, come and see him, he's doing really well. Do you want to hold him?'

He nodded. 'Could I?'

'Of course.' She sat him down, lifted the baby out of the crib and placed him carefully in Matt's arms. Well, hands, really. He was too tiny for arms. With his head in the crook of his arm, his little feet barely reached Matt's wrist, and those skinny, naked feet got to him again. He bent his wrist up and cupped them in his hand, keeping them warm, feeling them flex and wriggle a little as he snuggled them.

He pressed a fingertip to the baby's open palm, and his hand closed, gripping him fiercely. It made him smile. So did the enormous yawn, and then to his delight the baby opened his eyes and stared straight up at him.

'Hello, my gorgeous boy,' he said softly, and then he

lost eye contact because his own flooded with a whole range of emotions too huge, too tumultuous to analyse. He sniffed hard, and found a tissue in his hand.

'Thought I might find you here.'

'Are you checking up on me?' he asked gruffly, and Ben dropped into a chair beside him with an understanding smile.

'No, checking up on your son. Daisy wants to see photos, if that's OK?'

'Of course it is. I've been thinking about that. I took one on my phone and sent it to Mum and Dad, but it's not the same.'

'No. I've got my camera, I'll take some and print them. Does he have a name yet, by the way?'

He shook his head. 'I thought you might be able to tell me. I have no idea what Amy was thinking. Not Samuel...' His voice cracked, and he broke off, squeezing his eyes shut and breathing slowly.

Ben squeezed his shoulder, and gave him a moment before going on. 'She'd talked about Joshua—Josh. But Daisy said she thought Amy was going to ask you about names.'

'She *was* going to tell me about him, then?'

'Oh, God, yes! She said she'd tell you when—'

'What?' he asked, when Ben broke off. 'When what?'

He sighed. 'She said she'd tell you when it was over, one way or the other. That was right at the beginning, when she first found out. She was sixteen weeks pregnant, and I don't think she expected to get this far.'

'I wish you'd been able to tell me.'

'I wish I could have done. I so nearly did, so many times.'

The nurse came back. 'Want to try feeding him? We

gave him a bottle an hour ago, and he took a few mils. You could have a go, if you like?'

He took the bottle—a tiny little thing, with not much more than a few spoonfuls in it—and brushed the teat against the baby's cheek. He turned his head towards it, the reflex working perfectly, and Matt slipped the teat between his tiny rosebud lips.

He swallowed reflexively, and then again, and again, and in the end he took most of the small feed while Ben took photos.

How could something so simple be so momentous? The satisfaction was out of all proportion to the task, and Matt grinned victoriously and felt like Superman.

'You need to burp him,' Ben said, pointing the camera at him, and he laughed.

'What, and bring it all up again?'

'That's the way it is. Fairly crazy system but it sort of works.'

Matt shifted the baby so he was against his shoulder, resting on a clean blanket the nurse had draped over him. 'So how's my nephew doing?' he asked as he rubbed the little back gently.

'Really well. He's terrific. Daisy's in her element. Feeding's going really well, and she's feeling stronger by the hour, and it's good.'

'Does he sleep?'

Ben's smile was wry. 'I have no idea what he did last night. I was either here or out for the count. But Daisy was still smiling this morning.'

'That's a good sign.'

The nurse reappeared and asked Ben to have a word with the lady he'd seen in here before, then she turned to him with a smile. 'All gone? Brilliant. Has he burped?'

'Yup.'

'Nappy?'

He laughed quietly. 'I'll give it a go, now my brother's not here taking photos to taunt me with, but don't abandon me. I might stick it on the wrong way up.'

He didn't. He wiped the funny, skinny, wrinkly little bottom dry, got the nappy back onto him without sticking the tabs on his skin or cutting off his circulation or leaving massive gaps, and, feeling ridiculously pleased with himself, he went with Ben to see how Amy was doing.

There was still no change, so after talking to the staff so Ben could catch up on her general progress, they went for a coffee and something to eat, just because he knew he had to keep his strength up, but the moment it was finished he was twitching.

'I need to get back to her,' he said, and draining his coffee, he pushed the chair back and stood up.

'Want company?'

He shook his head. 'Not really. Do you mind? It's good to touch base and I really appreciate your support, but—I just want to talk to her, say all the things I've never said.'

Ben's hand gripped his shoulder. 'You go for it,' he said softly, and with a gentle smile, he left him to make his own way back. 'I'll bring you the photos. Keep in touch,' he called, turning as he walked away, and Matt nodded.

He would. Just as soon as there was anything to say...

He was there again.

She could hear him talking, his voice soft, wrapping round her and cradling her in a soft cocoon. She couldn't hear the words. Not really, not well enough to make them out, but it was lovely to hear his voice.

She tried to move, and felt a searing pain low down on her abdomen, and she gasped, the blissful cocoon vanishing. It hurt—everything hurt, and someone was holding her, gripping her hands.

'Amy? Amy, it's Matt. It's OK. You're safe, and the baby's safe. He's doing well. It's OK, my darling. You're all right. You're much better and you're going to be OK now.'

She lay still, sifting through the words with her fuddled brain, trying to claw through the fog. Something was wrong. Something...

The baby's safe...he's doing well...

But he wasn't. He wasn't safe at all! Why was Matt telling her that? He knew she'd lost him, he knew that, so why was he lying to her?

She heard a strange noise, like someone crying, a long, long way away, and then the fog closed over her again...

'She woke up. I was telling her everything was all right, and she started crying, and then she was gone again.'

'Don't worry. She could just be in pain,' the doctor said, and he stepped outside for a minute to stretch his legs and give them room to get to her. God, he needed Ben, but he couldn't ask.

He went back inside. They were nearly finished. They'd topped up her pain relief and checked her thoroughly. She was coming up now, hovering just under the surface of consciousness, and he was feeling sick with dread. This was the time he'd find out just how bad she was, how much brain damage she might have sustained during the fit, or in fact before it, causing it.

A part of him didn't want to know, but the other part,

the part that still, incredibly, dared to believe, wanted her to wake.

And then finally, what seemed like hours later, when he was getting desperate, she opened her eyes.

'Amy? Amy, it's Matt.'

His face swam, coming briefly into focus. So it *was* him there with her. She'd thought so. Emotion threatened to choke her, and as if he knew that he leant forwards, gripping her hand.

'How are you feeling?'

'Sore,' she said hoarsely, answering the question because it was easier than thinking about why he was there by her side in hospital. 'My head's sore. And—everywhere, really. Why do I feel like this?'

'You went into pre-eclampsia, and you had a fit,' he told her gently, her hand wrapped firmly in his. 'Ben had to deliver the baby, but he's OK. He's doing really well.'

She shook her head, slowly at first, then more urgently, because he was wrong and she had to tell him. 'No. Ben wasn't there.'

'Yes, he was. He delivered you, Amy. We found you on the floor.'

Yes. She remembered the floor. Remembered crumpling to the floor, someone coming to her, lifting her up, calling Matt. Telling him she was losing the baby...

She closed her eyes against the images, but they followed her, tearing her apart. 'I lost him. I'm sorry...'

'No, Amy.' He was insistent, confusing her. 'Amy, he's fine. He's going to be fine. He's all right.'

'No,' she whispered. 'No. I've lost him. I saw him, Matt! I saw him! Why are you lying to me?' she asked frantically, feeling panic and the raw, awful pain of loss sweeping over her and deluging her with emotion. She brushed his hands away, desperate to be rid of the feel of him, hanging onto her and lying, lying.

'Don't lie to me! He's dead—you know he's dead!'

He had her hands again, his grip inescapable, still lying to her. 'Amy, no! Listen, please listen, you're confused, I'm not lying to you, he's alive.'

'Stop it! Don't lie to me! Stop it!' she screamed, pressing her hands to her ears to block out the sound of his voice, but she could still hear him, over and over again, lying to her, the sound ringing in her head and driving her mad with grief.

'He's alive...alive...alive...'

'No-o-o-o—! Go away! I hate you! Leave me alone, don't do this.'

'Shh, Amy, it's all right, hush now, go back to sleep,' a firm, gentle voice told her. 'It's all right. Easy now.'

'Ben?' she whispered, her voice slurring. She struggled to get the words out, but they wouldn't come. 'Ben, he's lying, get him away from me! Get him away.'

'Hush, Amy, it's OK. He's gone. You go to sleep. Everything's all right.'

She wanted to argue, to tell him it wasn't all right. It was really important to tell them, but she felt herself sliding back down, felt the pain slip away as the fog wrapped her again in gentle, mindless oblivion...

Ben caught up with him in the loo off the corridor. The door was hanging open as he'd left it, and he was shaking.

He felt a gentle hand on his back. 'You all right?' Ben asked softly, and Matt straightened and leant back against the wall, shuddering.

'Ben, I can't take it. I can't do this.'

Ben shoved a tissue into his hand. 'Yes, you can. She'll be all right. She's just confused, but it'll pass. It's the sedation and the pressure on her brain from the fluid, not to mention the other drugs, the painkillers, the magnesium sulphate.' Matt lifted a hand to ward off the words, and Ben flushed the loo. 'Wash your face and hands, and come and sit down and talk this through with me. You know what's going on. She's having flash-backs, but she'll come out of it.'

'Will she? I'm not so sure,' he said, and swallowed hard as bile rose in his throat again.

'I'm sure. Come on. Sort yourself out and we'll go for a walk. You could use some fresh air.'

Fresh air? He could think of plenty of things he needed. Fresh air wasn't one of them. What he needed was a miracle, but in the absence of that, his brother's support was the next best thing.

He washed his face and hands, took a long, deep breath and went.

CHAPTER SIX

IT WAS quiet when she woke again.

Quiet, and calm.

Well, calm for the hospital, anyway. There were still the bleeps and tweets and hissings of the machines, the ringing phones in the distance, the sound of hurrying feet, someone talking, but there was a quietness about it.

Night-time, she realised.

She opened her eyes and looked around, slightly stunned. HDU? Wow. She was hooked up to all sorts of things, and Matt was asleep in the chair beside her, his top half slumped on the bottom of the bed, his head resting on one arm and the other hand lying loosely on hers. She couldn't see his face, it was hidden by a fold in the bedcover, but she knew it was him.

She thought he'd been there all the time—had a feeling she'd heard his voice in the distance. Oh. So hard. She blinked to clear her vision, to clear her mind, but it felt like glue.

She tried moving—carefully, just a little, because she was feeling sore. Something momentous had happened, but she couldn't remember what.

Samuel, her mind said, but she knew that was wrong. Samuel was years ago, and she could feel the sadness for him, the ache that never left her, but stronger now for some reason, and tinged with fear.

She eased her hand away from Matt's and felt her tummy. Soft, flabby—and tender, low down. A—dressing? A post-op dressing?

A section? Why had she had a section? Oh, think! she told herself. There was something there, just hovering out of reach, and she tried again.

Yes. She'd had a headache. It was a dreadful headache. She'd had it all day, getting worse, but when she'd got home it was awful. And then—

'Oh!'

Her soft gasp jerked Matt awake, and he sat up with a grunt, grabbing his neck and rubbing it, his head rotating, easing out the kinks. His smile was tired and—wary? 'Amy. You're awake. Are you OK?'

She nodded. He looked awful. He hadn't shaved, his clothes were crumpled and his eyes were red-rimmed. From exhaustion? Or crying? He'd looked like this before...

'Matt, what happened?' she asked, not sure if she wanted to know the answer. His face...

'You had pre-eclampsia,' he said carefully. 'Do you remember that?'

She nodded slowly, trying to think, trying to suppress the niggle of fear. 'Yes. Sort of. I had a dreadful headache. Were you there? I've got this vague recollection of you carrying me...'

His face crumpled for a moment, so she thought something terrible had happened. He looked so drained, and she felt her heart rate start to pick up. The baby...

'Yes, I was there. I'd come up to see Ben and Daisy's baby for the weekend. We heard you at the door, and when I opened it you'd collapsed on the floor. That was when I carried you. We brought you to the hospital.'

He waited, and she thought about it. Yes, she remembered that—not the hospital, but before then, his face looming over her, his arms round her, making her feel safe. And Ben and Daisy's baby. Of course. She'd delivered Thomas—when? Recently. Very recently. But—

'I had a section,' she said, not daring to ask and yet she could hear his voice in her head, saying he was all right, it was OK, the baby was fine. But there was something else, about him lying to her, some little niggle…

He smiled, his eyes lighting with a tender joy. 'Yes. We had a boy, Amy,' he told her, his voice shaking slightly. 'He's fine. He's a little small, but he's doing really well, he's a proper fighter. Ben took some photos for you.'

He held them out to her, and she saw a baby almost lost in Matt's arms. There was a clip on his finger, and leads trailing from his tiny chest, and the nappy seemed to drown him, but he looked pink and well and—alive?

She sucked in a breath, and then another, hardly daring to believe it as the hope turned to joy. 'Is he—is that really…?'

'It's our baby, Amy,' he said softly, his eyes bright. 'He's in SCBU and he's doing really well.'

He showed her another photo, a close-up just of the baby, and she traced the features with her finger, wondering at them. Amazing. So, so amazing…

'Can I see him? I want to see him. Can you take me?'

He shook his head. 'You can't leave the ward yet, sweetheart. You're still on the magnesium sulphate infusion, and you've been really ill.'

'I want to see him. I want to hold him,' she said, and she started to cry, because she'd been so afraid for so long, and there was still something there, something lurking in the fringes of the fog behind her, something terrifying that she didn't understand. 'Please let me hold him.'

'OK, OK, sweetheart, don't cry, I'll go and get him. I'll bring him to you.' She felt him gather her up in his arms, his face next to hers, the stubble rough and oddly reassuring against her cheek. 'Hush now,' he murmured gently. 'Come on, lie back and rest. It's all right. Just relax—'

His voice cracked, and she wanted to cry again, but for him this time. He'd had no warning of this. She'd been going to tell him, to explain, but she'd run out of time, and for him to find her like that—

'It's OK, Matt, I'm all right,' she said, reassuring him hastily. 'I'm fine. Please, just bring him to me. Let me see him. I need to see him with my own eyes. I need to know he's all right.'

'He's all right, I promise you, Amy, and I'm not lying. I'll get him—give me five minutes. I'll get someone to come and see you while I fetch him.'

He hesitated, then carefully, as if he was afraid to hurt her, he lifted her hand to his lips and pressed a gentle kiss to her palm, then folded her fingers over it to keep it safe while he was gone.

Her eyes flooded with tears. He'd always done that, right since their first date. The last time he'd done it was after Samuel died…

'Amy, it's good to see you awake. How are you?'

She blinked away the tears and smiled up at the nurse who was both friend and colleague in another life. 'I don't know, Kate. OK, I think. My head hurts, and my tummy's sore, but—Matt's gone to get the baby…?' she said, ending it almost as a question, but Kate smiled widely.

'Yes, he has. We can't let you off the ward yet, not till your magnesium sulphate infusion's finished, but he can come to you for a little while. You'll feel so much better when you've had a cuddle. Let's get you a little wash and sit you up. You'll feel better when you've cleaned your teeth, too.'

She'd feel better when she'd seen her baby, Amy thought, but she let Kate help her up, let her wash her and comb her hair, and she cleaned her teeth—Kate was right, it did feel better when her teeth were clean—and then she was ready, her heart pounding, every second an hour as she waited to hold her little son for the first time.

'He's gorgeous,' Kate said, smiling and tidying up. 'Ben's been in flashing photos of both of them, and he's just like their baby. Smaller, of course, but lovely. So cute. Oh, look, here he comes, the little man!'

Matt was trundling the clear plastic crib, and Amy scooted up the bed a bit more, Kate helping her and tutting and rearranging her pillows, and with a crooked smile Matt lifted his tiny, precious cargo out of the crib and laid him in her waiting arms.

Gosh, he was so small! He weighed next to nothing, his feet hardly reaching her hand, his little head perfectly round, but he was breathing, his chest moving, one arm flailing in his sleep.

She lifted him to her face, kissed him, inhaled the scent of his skin and felt calm steal over her. This was her child, here in her arms where he belonged, alive and well and safe. The last cobwebs of her nightmare were torn aside as she looked at him, taking in each feature, watching his little mouth working, his eyelids flicker as he screwed up his button nose, and she laughed softly in delight.

'He's so tiny!' she breathed, staring down at him in wonder. She took his hand, and the fingers closed on her thumb, bringing a huge lump to her throat, but then his eyes opened and locked with hers, and she felt everything right itself, the agonising suspense of the last six months wiped out in a moment. 'Hello, baby,' she said softly, her voice rising naturally to a pitch he could hear. 'Oh, aren't you so beautiful? My gorgeous, gorgeous boy...'

'He's due a feed,' Matt said softly, after a moment. 'They've given me a bottle for you to give him, if you want to.'

She felt shocked. 'A bottle?'

'Of breast milk, from the bank. Just until you're well enough, and because he's suffered a setback with the pre-eclampsia, so he needs to catch up. But if you want to try...'

She did. She desperately wanted to feel him against her skin, to touch him, nurse him, hold him.

They pulled the screens round her, and Kate eased the gown off her shoulders and then put the baby back into her arms. He was only wearing a nappy, and she felt his skin against her breasts, so soft, so thin it was almost transparent.

'He's too sleepy.'

'No, he's not. His mouth's working, look. He'll wake up if you stroke your nipple against his cheek.'

Oh, genius child! He knew exactly what to do. She touched his soft, delicate cheek with her nipple, and he turned his head, rosebud lips open, and as she'd done countless times with other mothers, she pressed the baby's head against the breast and he latched on. And just like that, he was suckling.

Relief poured through her, because so often if babies suffered a setback at this stage and had to be bottle fed for the first days or weeks, it could become almost impossible to establish breast feeding. Not so with her baby, she thought with a flurry of maternal pride.

'He's amazing,' she said contentedly. 'So clever.'

'He is,' Matt agreed, tucking a blanket gently round them to keep him warm. 'He's incredible. So are you.' He stared down at them both, at the little jaws working hard, the milk-beaded lips around her nipple, her finger firmly held by the tiny hand of this miracle that was their child.

It had taken them twenty-seven hours, but finally, mother and son were getting acquainted, her crisis had passed and they could look to the future—a brighter future than he'd dared to imagine.

Where it would take them, though, he still had no idea…

Amy didn't quite know what to do with Matt.

He'd taken the baby back to the neonatal unit after she'd finished feeding him, and once he'd changed his nappy and he was settled, he came back to see her.

She was lying down again, exhausted with emotion and effort, and the first thing he did was stick up the photos of the baby on the side of her locker right in front of her, so she could see them.

'OK now?' he asked gently, and she nodded tiredly.

'I'm fine. Bit sore. I could do with going to sleep, and you look as if you could, too. Why don't you go back to Ben and Daisy's and get your head down? Or mine,' she added, and then wondered if that was really such a good idea, but he latched onto it instantly.

'That might be better. They're getting little enough sleep as it is. I think Thomas has his own idea of a schedule and I don't think night-time features yet.'

She smiled at that. 'Babies don't do schedules—well, not at three days old or whatever he is now.'

'Day three today, which started about half an hour ago. It's just after midnight on Sunday. You had the baby on Friday night.'

She frowned. 'So long ago? How long was I out?'

'A long time. Over twenty-four hours.'

She reached out her hand, and he took it, his fingers wrapping firmly round hers and squeezing gently. 'That must have been awful for you,' she murmured, and his mouth twitched into a fleeting smile.

'I don't think you were enjoying it much either.'

She frowned again. 'No.'

'You're OK now, and so's he. And you're right, I could do with getting my head down. It's been a tough week at work and I haven't had any sleep to speak of since Thursday morning.'

He got to his feet, and hesitated. 'Are you sure you're all right if I leave you?'

'Absolutely sure,' she promised, really tired now. 'I need to sleep, too. My head's killing me.'

'It'll be better soon. Give it another few hours. You sleep well, and I'll see you in the morning. Get them to call my mobile if there's anything you want—anything at all.'

And as if he knew the only thing she really wanted was a hug, he leant over and gave her one, a gentle squeeze as his stubble brushed her cheek and he dropped a feather-light kiss on the corner of her mouth.

'Sleep tight,' he murmured, and kissing her hand again, he folded up her fingers and left her alone with her thoughts.

When he got back to the hospital in the morning, it was to find that Amy had been moved out of HDU into a single room on the postnatal ward, and he went to find her.

'Hi there,' he said, tapping on the door and pushing it open with a smile. 'How are you?'

'Much better. My hands and feet feel as if they might be mine again, and my headache's easing.' She frowned, and tipped her head on one side, eyeing him searchingly. 'Just how bad was it, Matt? Nobody seems to want to tell me and the consultant's not around, conveniently.'

'No. Well, I think Ben's sort of overseeing your care.'

'You mean you aren't?' she asked, only half joking.

Curiously, he hadn't felt the need to interfere, and he told her so. 'I think it's because I was keeping a pretty close eye on what was going on, and they were doing what I would have done, so there was no need.'

'You haven't answered the first question,' she pointed out, and he grunted softly and sat down on the chair beside her.

'You—uh—you fitted. In HDU, after the delivery.'

Amy was stunned. 'I fitted?' she said, thinking that it explained a lot about her headache. 'So what was my blood pressure?'

'At its highest? It went up to 240 over 180.'

She felt her jaw drop, and she shut her mouth and swallowed. Hard. 'Wow.'

'Do you know what it is now?'

She shook her head, and he checked on the chart in the rack by the door. 'One-sixty over 80. Still high, but coming down well. What's your baseline?'

'One-twenty over 70. I can't believe that. That's shocking!'

'Yes. It wasn't great,' he said drily.

'Were you there?'

He nodded. 'I was, pretty much all the time. Ben dragged me away for a few minutes a couple of times in the first twenty-four hours, but mostly I was there, and—well, it wasn't great spectator sport, let's put it like that. I'd rather be on the other side organising the treatment any day.'

She looked down, fiddling with the edge of the sheet. 'There's something I can't— Did we have a row? It's really foggy, I'm not sure if I dreamed it or what, but— did I accuse you of lying to me?'

His eyebrows scrunched up slightly, and he gave a reluctant nod. 'Yes. Yes, you did, but—'

'About the baby?'

'You were drugged up to the eyeballs, Amy. You didn't know what was going on.'

'I thought he was dead, didn't I?' she said slowly, sifting through the snippets of memory lurking in the fog, and then she looked up and met his eyes. 'I thought it was—last time,' she said softly. 'Didn't I?'

He nodded slowly, his eyes pained. 'Yes. You muddled them up, and thought I was lying when I said he was all right.'

Her eyes filled with tears, and she looked away. 'It still seems wrong that this baby's OK and—' She broke off, then carried on, 'We need a name for him. We can't just keep calling him the baby.'

'Daisy said you liked Joshua.'

'I do, but I wanted to ask you. He's your baby, too. Do you like it?'

'It's fine—yes, I do. It's a good name.' He hesitated,

not sure how to say this, how it would land. 'I thought—maybe we could call him Joshua Samuel.'

Her breath caught on a tiny sob. 'That's lovely,' she said, and biting her lip, she turned away.

Joshua Samuel. Both her boys.

Oh, lord.

She started to cry, broken, hiccupping little sobs, and found herself cradled tenderly against a broad, firm chest. 'I miss him,' she wept, and she felt him tense under her hands.

'I know, sweetheart, I know,' he murmured gruffly. 'I miss him, too.'

'Why did he have to die?' she asked, sniffing back the tears and pulling away. Her hands scrubbed at her face, swiping the tears aside, but fresh ones took their place and he reached for a tissue and handed it to her.

'I don't know. We'll never know. There didn't seem to be anything wrong with him, or you. It was just one of those things.'

'We went for a walk—the day before. A long one.'

'Yes. We did. But we often walked, Amy. It was what we did. We walked miles all the time, so it was nothing new. And you know that. You can't blame yourself, it wasn't your fault, or anything you or anybody else did. I braked sharply in the car on the way home, on the motorway. It could have been that, but it's unlikely. It was just one of those unexplained tragedies that happen in obstetrics. You know we don't have the answer to all of them. Sometimes things just happen.'

She nodded, and looked up at the clock on the wall. 'I need to feed him. They said if he's gained weight, I can have him with me here, and then we can go home together in a few days. They're really pleased with him.'

'Good.' His smile was wry. 'I'm really pleased with

him, too. I would have liked to have been here with you, to have known you were pregnant, to have shared it.'

She swallowed the guilt. It was too late to do anything about it, but even if she could, she wouldn't have told him until after 26 weeks, at least. 'I'm sorry. I just—'

'Couldn't let yourself believe it would be all right?'

Her smile was sad. 'Something like that,' she admitted.

'So what do we do now, Amy?' he asked, his voice soft. 'What happens next?'

The real question was too hard to answer, so she didn't even try.

'Now, we feed the baby,' she said, and started the slow and uncomfortable process of getting out of bed.

She had a rest later, and Ben came in and they went outside in the grounds with a coffee.

'So what happens now?' Ben asked quietly, echoing his own words to Amy, and Matt felt himself frown.

'I don't know. It all depends on Amy, on what she feels about my involvement.'

'Are you taking paternity leave?'

He gave a short huff of laughter. 'I have no idea. I haven't really had time to consider it. It's not a good time at work, but then it never is, is it? I've got some twins I don't really want to delegate—I need to be backwards and forwards. But if Amy will let me, I want to be around, and I'm certainly going to be part of his life.'

'I didn't doubt it for a moment,' Ben said drily. 'I just wonder if Amy's thought it through, or if she never let herself get that far. She hasn't bought any baby equipment according to Daisy. Not so much as a nappy.'

He frowned again. She really had been blanking it

out. He wondered why. Was it simply because she didn't think it would be all right? Or was it because she'd never really grieved for Samuel and hadn't moved on? Their relationship had fallen apart so soon after she lost him that Matt had no idea how she'd dealt with it. Now, he was beginning to wonder if she'd dealt with it at all.

He wasn't sure how well he'd dealt with it—not well at the time, certainly, and the thought of his first son left a hollow ache in his chest even now. But this was Joshua's time, he told himself firmly, and wondered how much of him he'd see, in reality.

Should he take paternity leave? Instinct said yes, but Amy might have other ideas. He'd talk to her about it, but he'd certainly investigate the possibility.

They kept her in for the rest of the week, and it felt like the busiest week of his life.

He had twins he was monitoring at the unit in London, and his specialist registrar called on Monday night to say they were concerned, so he drove down, weighed up all the results, added in his gut feeling and delivered them at four in the morning, then went into his office and cleared his outstanding paperwork. By the time HR were in at nine, he'd delegated responsibility for his cases, divvied them out according to severity, written a short—very short—list of patients he insisted on seeing himself, and was ready to go back.

The time he'd been away had enabled him to make one decision, at least. He phoned HR, told them he was taking paternity leave, notified them of the cover arrangements he'd put in place, and after a short detour to his house to pack some things, he was back in Suffolk by Amy's side before lunch.

'Gosh, you look tired.'

He laughed softly. 'Yeah. Been a bit busy. Some twins decided they'd had enough.'

'In London?'

He nodded. 'They were only twenty-seven weeks, but they were already struggling and they hadn't grown for five days. They're OK, but they were tiny.'

'They would be,' she said softly. 'Heavens. And I'm worried about our Josh.'

'Are you?' he asked instantly, and she shook her head.

'No. Not any more. Sorry, that was a bad choice of words. It's just that I mostly deliver babies that are term, and anything as small as those twins must be...'

Brings back Samuel, he thought, understanding instantly, and he wondered how she did her job, how she coped with stillbirths and labours so early that the babies couldn't be viable. By blanking it out? Well, it worked for him. More or less.

'How's the feeding going?' he asked, sticking to a safe topic, and her face softened into a smile.

'Great. He's doing really well. I think they're going to say we can go home in a day or two.' The smile faded, and she bit her lip.

'What?' he said quietly.

'I've been a bit silly,' she admitted. It was easy to say it, now he was all right, but before—well it had been hard to plan ahead. 'I haven't bought anything for him. No clothes, nappies, cot—nothing. I was going to do it as soon as I started maternity leave.' If she'd got that far. Well, she certainly had now, she thought wryly. 'I wonder how long things take to come if you order them over the internet. Sometimes it's quite quick.'

'Or you could write me a list. I'll just get the basic

stuff in ready for you to bring him home, and you can have all the fun of the cute, pretty stuff with Daisy once you're a bit stronger.'

It was so tempting. Just hand it all over to him and sit back and concentrate on Joshua. Which of course was what she should be doing, she realised. 'Would you mind? And it really needn't be a lot. I'll move some money into your bank account—'

'I hardly think it's necessary for you to refund me for basic purchases I make for my own child,' he said with that quiet implacability she was beginning to re-alise she couldn't argue with. Well, not and win, any-way. Pointless trying, so she vowed to keep the list as short as possible and do the bulk of the shopping once he'd gone back. He couldn't take much longer off work, surely?

'Incidentally, I'm on paternity leave,' he told her, as if he'd read her mind. 'Except for a few days here and there. I still need to go back a couple of days a week and I'm on standby for emergencies in my trickier cases, but otherwise I'll be here, giving you a hand until you're back on your feet.'

He wasn't asking, she noticed, and she wondered if she ought to mind, but in fact it was a relief. She'd been dreading going home, having to cope alone or, her re-luctant alternative in an emergency, troubling Ben and Daisy.

She was sure they wouldn't mind. They'd been bril-liant. Daisy had been in twice, Ben was always popping in because, like Matt, there were cases he didn't feel he could hand over, but they had their own new baby to worry about, and she didn't want to get in the way of that joyful time.

And now, she wouldn't have to, because she'd have the baby's father there staking his claim—

No! Stop it! Of course he has rights, and you want him to be there for your baby!

'If you're sure you can spare the time, that would be really helpful for a few days,' she said.

A few days.

He'd had in mind a lifetime, but after the road they'd travelled in the last four years, he'd settle for a few days as an opener.

'Let's write your list,' he said, pulling out his phone. It doubled as a notebook, so he keyed in the items as she thought of them, and when she was done he closed it and put it back in his pocket.

'I think it's time for a cuddle,' he said, standing up and peeling back the little blanket carefully, and sliding his hands under him he picked Joshua up without disturbing him at all.

She watched him, loving the sure, confident way he handled his son, knowing he was safe. She'd always loved watching him with babies. When she'd first worked with him, six years ago, she'd known he'd be good with his own. That had been one of the hardest things about losing Samuel—watching Matt holding him, the gentleness of his hands as he'd cradled the much-too-tiny baby, kissed him, before laying him tenderly on the white cloth, covering him...

She'd never seen him cry for Samuel, but she'd heard him. She'd envied him, because she hadn't been able to, not then, not for a long time.

But now—now he was holding Joshua, and his hands were just as gentle, just as sure, and the love in his eyes was just as certain.

If only he loved her. If only she could trust that love.

No. She wanted him in Josh's life, and she could trust him with her son without a doubt. She just wasn't sure she could trust him with herself.

CHAPTER SEVEN

HE WENT back to see her that evening, and found several of her colleagues standing around her, laughing and talking.

The moment he walked in, however, they stopped dead, smiled at him and left. 'Don't mind me,' he said, holding up his hands, but they went anyway, and he shook his head, slightly bemused, and sat down next to Amy.

'Was it something I said?'

'No, of course not. They're just—they don't really know what to say to you.'

'Hello would be a good start,' he said drily, and she chuckled, but then she pulled a face.

'One of the advantages of giving birth in your workplace is that you get spoilt to bits, but the disadvantage is that they think of you as public property, and there's only been one question on all their minds since they realised I was pregnant, and they've just found out the answer's you. That's why they can't talk to you. I think they feel a bit awkward, with you being Ben's brother.'

He was puzzled. 'Didn't they know I was the father?'

'No, of course not. I hadn't said anything about you, and I actively discouraged curious questions, but I suppose now I'm on the mend, and the baby's all right, they've stopped worrying about us and I can just *hear* the cogs turning. You know what hospitals are like.'

'You don't think they'd worked it out before?'

She shrugged. 'Maybe. Several of them were there for the evening do at the wedding, so it's quite possible someone saw us together and worked it out. Nobody really seems surprised, I guess.'

'No. I imagine they just want to know all the gory details.'

'Well, they aren't getting them from me,' she said firmly. 'I hate being the object of curiosity.'

'Yeah, me too. How's Josh?'

'OK. He's under the UV light. I thought he was looking a bit jaundiced when I changed his nappy, so they called the paediatrician. I thought they would have told you.'

'They did. It's quite common, nothing to worry about.'

He didn't know why he was reassuring her, except that she looked a little glum, and she tried to smile.

'I know that,' she said. 'It just seems odd without him here.'

'It's not for long.'

'I know.'

He frowned. There was something in her voice, something that didn't feel quite right, and he got up and went over to her, perching on the edge of the bed and looking down at her searchingly.

'Hey, what's up?' he asked softly, brushing her cheek with his knuckles, and just like that tears slid down her cheek.

'Oh, Amy,' he murmured, and easing her into his arms, he cradled her against his shoulder and rocked her gently. 'What's up, sweetheart? Are you worried about him? You don't need to be.'

She shook her head. 'No. I just miss him being here. It scares me,' she said, hiccupping on a sob. 'I don't like it when I can't see him, and I need to feed him, and my milk's come in and I feel as if I've got rocks on my chest and everything hurts—'

She broke off, sobbing in earnest now, and he shushed her gently and smoothed her hair.

'You've got the four-day blues, ' he said tenderly. 'All those hormones sloshing around. It'll soon pass. Do you want to go down there and feed him?'

She sniffed and nodded, and he got off the bed and handed her a hot, wrung-out face flannel to wipe away her tears, and then he helped her out of bed and walked her down to the neonatal unit. She was steady on her feet now, but he walked with his arm round her—just in case there was anyone there left in any doubt that he was Josh's father and definitely in the picture—and he handed Josh to her and sat beside her while she was feeding him.

'Ow, they're too full, it hurts,' she said, her eyes welling again, and he gave her another hug.

'It'll soon be easier. Give it a minute and you'll be fine, and it'll get better. You'd rather it was this way than you didn't have enough.'

'Do you have to be right about everything?' she sniped tearfully, and he blew out his breath slowly and took his arm away.

'Sorry. I was only trying to help.'

'Well, don't. I know all that. I don't need to be told—'

She broke off, knowing full well she was being unreasonable, but…

'Do you want me to go home?' he asked quietly, and

she thought, *Home? As in your home, in London, or my home?* The answer was the same, whatever. She shook her head.

'No. I'm sorry, I'm just tired,' she said. 'Tired and fed up and I want to go home myself.'

He gave a short sigh and put his arm round her again. To hell with it. She needed comforting, and he was right here, and the person who arguably should be doing it. Who else, for heaven's sake?

'You can come home soon,' he murmured soothingly. 'You could come home tonight, if you wanted. You're well enough. It's only the feeding, and you could spend the days here and stay at home for the nights. You could express the milk—'

She shook her head. 'I can't leave him, Matt. I can't leave my baby all night. I can't...'

Poor Amy. She'd been on an emotional rollercoaster for the last few months, and it wasn't over yet, he knew. They had so many unresolved issues, and if nothing else, they had to build a working relationship for the future.

'Stay, then, but I think you should restrict your visitors. They're wearing you out.'

She sighed and leant into him, her head finding its natural resting place on his shoulder. 'But they're lovely to me,' she said wearily. 'They've brought all sorts of presents, and they make me laugh and they're so kind, really.'

'I know they are, but you're tired, Amy. You need some rest. Come on, let me take him and deal with him now, and you go back to bed and get some rest.'

She nodded, and he took Josh, resting him against his shoulder where Amy's head had just been. He was getting good at winding him—he'd been practising on

Thomas in between times, and he'd got it down to a fine art now.

He put him back under the UV light with his eye-shade on, changed his nappy and left him to sleep. He fussed for a moment and then settled, and Matt went back to Amy and found her curled on her side in the bed, clutching a handful of tissues and sniffing.

'Can I have a cuddle?' she asked tearfully, so he tipped the blinds in the door, turned down the lights and lay down beside her, easing her into his arms.

'You've really been through the mill, haven't you?' he murmured, holding her close, and she sniffed again and burrowed closer. 'It's OK, I've got you. You're all right,' he said softly, and gradually the little shuddering sobs died away, and he felt her body relax, her breathing slowing as she slid into sleep.

He stayed there for an hour, until there was a quiet tap on the door and it opened to reveal Rachel, the nurse from SCBU.

'How is she?'

'Asleep,' he mouthed. 'Problem?'

'He's brought up his feed and he's hungry again. Shall I bring him to her, just for a minute? Don't move her. She's been a bit weepy today. I think she missed you while you were away.'

Had she? He woke her gently. 'Sweetheart, the baby needs feeding again, but you don't have to move. Rachel's bringing him.'

She made a sleepy little sound of protest, opened her eyes and breathed in shakily. 'Oh, I'm so tired, Matt. I can't do this.'

'Yes, you can. Just feed him. All you have to do is sit there. We'll do the rest.'

She let him help her up against the pillows, and

stared at him searchingly. 'Why are you doing all of this for me?' she asked, sounding genuinely perplexed, and he gave a soft laugh.

'Because I love you—both of you,' he replied, as if it was obvious, and then Rachel came in and there wasn't time to say any more.

But it stayed with her all night, the words keeping her company every time she woke to feed the baby or go to the loo or just to turn over, and although she wasn't sure if she could trust them, still they comforted her.

It might be true, she thought. Or at least, if he hung around long enough, maybe it would become true. People did learn to love each other, given time.

One day at a time, she told herself, just as she had through her pregnancy. One day at a time...

She went home with Joshua two days later.

Her blood pressure was much closer to normal, her hands and feet and face were her own again, and his jaundice had cleared up, so they were to be allowed out, and it couldn't come soon enough for her.

Matt came to fetch her, armed with a couple of bags. He was a few minutes late, but he'd been busy, he said. On the phone, probably, she thought, sorting out one of his cases in London, but he produced some clothes for her and the baby.

'They'll probably drown him,' he said, 'but they were supposed to be for babies of his weight.'

He looked out of his depth—strangely, for a man so at home with babies, but they were usually either still tucked up inside their mothers or slippery and screaming when he handled them, so all things considered he was doing well, and she smiled at him.

'I'm sure they'll be fine. Better too big than too small.'

'They won't be too small,' he assured her.

They weren't. She had to turn back the cuffs, and when he bent his legs his little feet disappeared, but he'd soon grow out of the first size. They always did.

'He looks really cute,' she said, smiling at Josh. 'Don't you, my gorgeous?'

The baby stared at her with startlingly blue eyes, so thoughtful.

'I wonder what he makes of us?' Matt said softly.

'I don't know. I wonder if he knows I'm his mother?'

'Of course he does. He'll know your voice.'

It was a lovely thought. She'd said as much to many mums over the years, but this time it was her baby, and she was the mother, and the thought was curiously centring.

'Right, all set?'

She nodded. 'I've packed my things—oh, Matt, we'll need a car seat! I didn't even think of it!'

'All done,' he said calmly. 'It's in the car.'

She had a committee to see her off. 'Isn't anybody in labour?' she asked wryly, as one by one they all hugged her and said goodbye.

'Go on, off you go, and keep in touch,' said Rosie, one of the midwives, hugging her again, and Matt closed the car door, got into the front and drove her home.

Bliss, she thought as he pulled up in the car port at the back and helped her out. She could sit in the garden and listen to the birds, and spend time in the conservatory soaking up the sun with Josh at her side.

They went through the conservatory into the kitchen, and she walked slowly in and looked around. In the middle of the dining table was a huge bunch of flowers in a tall vase, and they stopped her in her tracks.

'Oh, they're lovely! Who are they from?'

He put the baby seat and her bags down on the floor and gave her a wry smile. 'Me—just to welcome you home.'

'Oh, Matt—thank you. Thank you for everything...'

She hugged him, letting her head rest against his chest for a few moments, but it wasn't fair to hold him at arm's length for months and then lean on him when it suited her, so she straightened up and moved away, walking slowly through her house, touching it as if she was making sure it was still here, grounding herself.

'I bought a few things for the baby,' he said. 'They're upstairs.'

She made her way up there, and found Matt had made himself thoroughly at home.

She'd seen his laptop in the sitting room as she'd put her head in, and his wash things were in the bathroom, set out neatly on the window sill above the basin, and he'd taken over the back bedroom.

He obviously meant what he'd said about being around for her, she realised, and the implications of sharing her house with him, even in the short term, began to dawn on her.

She went into her bedroom, and found he'd changed the sheets on her bed—or someone had. Daisy? Surely not, so soon after having Thomas, but maybe she'd just suggested it and supervised. Daisy had got good at supervising towards the end of her pregnancy, she thought with a smile.

Whatever, it meant she was coming home to clean, crisp linen on the bed, and she had a sudden longing to climb into it and sleep for hours.

And then she looked beyond the bed, and spotted the pretty Moses basket draped with white embroidered cotton by the far side.

'Oh, Matt!' She trailed her fingers lightly over it, and her eyes filled. 'This is lovely—really pretty. Thank you. And all these clothes!' She stared at the little pile of baby clothes and accessories on the chest of drawers, touching them as if she didn't quite believe they were real. She'd put it off for so long, been so afraid to take this pregnancy for granted, and he'd just calmly come in right at the end and picked up all the pieces. He didn't need to do that, and she'd had no right to ask…

She felt a tear spill over and trickle down her cheek, and she brushed it away. 'Thank you so much.'

'Don't be silly, it's nothing. I didn't get many clothes. I didn't want to overdo it and you're bound to be deluged with presents, so they're only the basic vests and sleep suits and things to start him off, but he'll have grown out of them in five minutes anyway.'

She nodded. She had already been given some clothes, cute little things for him to grow into, and she knew he was right. 'They're just perfect. Thank you, you haven't overdone it at all, it's just what I would have got if I'd been a bit more proactive.'

He gave her a wry smile. 'I can quite see why you weren't, it's a bit overwhelming in there, isn't it? And as for the pram business,' he went on, rolling his eyes, 'I spent an hour in there being given a guided tour of how they fold and what clips on what and how they come apart and turn round and zip together, and some have pram inserts and car seats and face this way or that—by the time she'd finished I was utterly confused, so I just bought a seat and a base to put in my car for today, and whatever else you want you'll have to sort out yourself because frankly I think it's going to be down to personal choice and what you need it for, and I have *no* idea where you would even start!'

She bit her lip, picturing him in a sea of dismantled pushchairs, and she just wanted to hug him. Or laugh.

She ended up doing both, and he wrapped his arms round her and hugged her back, and for a moment they just stood there in each other's arms and held each other.

She could have stayed there forever, but that really wasn't wise or practical, so she let him go and stepped back, before she got too used to it, and looked at the Moses basket again.

'This is so pretty.'

'It won't last long, he'll outgrow it in a few months. I nearly got a crib, but I thought you could carry this downstairs and put him out in the garden in it, or in the conservatory, or in the sitting room in the evening, even take him round to see Daisy—it seemed to have all sorts of possibilities that the crib just didn't, and it doesn't stop you having a crib later, or even now if you wanted to. You could just use it downstairs. And, yeah, I thought it looked the part,' he added with a wry grin.

His talk of taking it downstairs held huge appeal. 'Can we take it downstairs and put him in it now? It's such a lovely day, and I've really missed the sunshine, being trapped in the hospital. It would be lovely to sit in the conservatory with the doors open and just enjoy the fresh air, really.'

'Sure. It's easy.' He looked pleased, as if he was glad his idea had met with her approval, and he lifted the basket, folded the stand and carried them both down.

She followed him more slowly, still a little tender, and by the time she'd taken Joshua out of the car seat and followed Matt through to the conservatory he was setting it up.

'Here, out of the sun?' he asked, and she nodded.

'That's lovely. Thank you.'

She laid the baby in it, and he stretched and yawned, his little arms flopped up by his head, the hat askew. 'He looks pretty chilled,' she said with a smile, and Matt laughed.

'Daddy's boy,' he said with a ridiculously proud grin. 'I always used to lie like that, if the photos can be believed. Cup of tea?'

'Oh, that would be brilliant.' She sat down on the chair carefully, her stitches pulling a little, and watched her baby sleeping. It was turning into her favourite occupation, she thought with a smile.

'Better now?'

He was lounging in the doorway, arms folded, one leg crossed over the other, looking utterly at home, and she realised it would be only too easy to get used to having him around.

'So much better,' she said, her words heartfelt. 'Matt, I'm so grateful to you for all you've done this last week. You just dropped everything, and I never expected you to—

'You didn't offer me the chance to discuss what I wanted to do, what role I wanted in your lives,' he pointed out gently, trying to keep the simmering anger under control. Now wasn't the time. 'I would have been here for you all along, Amy, if you'd given me the chance, but you always did like to go it alone.'

She looked down at her hands. 'Not really. I just didn't know how to deal with it—after the night of Ben and Daisy's wedding it all seemed so complicated.'

Oh, yes. He was with her on that. 'I wish I'd known.

I would never have left you alone to cope, and you shouldn't have allowed me to.'

'You didn't leave me alone to cope, I sent you away.'

He gave a wry laugh. 'Yeah, you're good at that, aren't you?'

She frowned at him, puzzled. 'What do you mean?'

'When you were ill—out of it, really, and you thought it was Samuel, not Josh—you told me to go away then.'

She bit her lip; her memories of that time were so patchy and veiled in layers of what seemed like fog, but through it all she knew he'd been there, and she wasn't sure she could have coped without him.

'I didn't mean it. I was so confused. I'm glad you didn't, I didn't really want you to go.'

'Didn't you? It sounded like it. You sounded desperate, Amy. And I've heard you saying it before, don't forget, when things were about as bad as they could be. I left you alone then, too, and I shouldn't have done.'

She swallowed. 'I didn't mean it then, either. Not really, not in that way. I just couldn't cope with your grief as well as mine, and the thought of a wedding so soon after we'd lost him—I just couldn't handle it. How could we have a party then, Matt? It felt so wrong. And if we'd known each other well enough, if we'd really known each other, we could have dealt with it, but we didn't, we retreated into our grief and took the easy way out.'

'Easy?'

She tried to smile. 'No, not easy. Nothing about it was easy, but it was easier than talking to a stranger about something I couldn't even bring myself to think about. And you were a stranger, relatively. We'd only worked in the same department for less than a year before I got pregnant, and we were hardly ever on the same shift or working together because I was on the midwifery-led unit and you were in the high risk unit. We hardly ever met up at work, and because we were working shifts we didn't always see each other at night, either, so even when we were living together we were like ships in the night. It was no wonder we struggled to communicate when we were grieving.'

It was true, he thought. They'd thought they'd known each other, they'd certainly wanted each other and talked about getting married, but they *had* been relative strangers, and yet they'd been expected to cope with the loss of their baby. No wonder it had all fallen apart for them. But now...

'Can we start again?' he said quietly, and she looked up at him, propping up the doorframe and looking rugged and kind and troubled, and she felt a flicker of apprehension.

If she said yes, if she let him back into her life, she'd run the risk of losing him again.

And if she didn't, she realised, she'd lose him now.

She took a deep breath.

'We can try,' she said carefully, and something flared in his eyes, something he quickly banked. 'I'm sorry I didn't tell you I was pregnant, but I was so afraid things would go wrong again.'

'Yeah. Ben said you had no confidence in your pregnancy.'

'Would you have done, in my shoes?'

He smiled wryly. 'Probably not. In my own shoes, had I known, had you told me, I like to think I'd have been rational about it.'

'Are you saying I was irrational?' she asked with an edge to her voice, and he sighed and crouched down beside her.

'No, Amy, I'm not saying that at all. Your reaction was perfectly natural and understandable, but maybe if I'd been with you I could have helped to reassure you.'

'And if it had happened again? If we'd lost Josh?'

His eyes flicked to the baby, and a spasm of pain showed on his face.

'No. I didn't think so. We didn't cope with this before, Matt, and there was nothing to suggest we'd cope with it any better a second time.'

He nodded. 'I'm sorry. I'm not very good at sharing my feelings.'

She laughed at that, a sad little hiccup of laughter that twisted his heart, and he straightened up and moved away, giving them both space. This wasn't going to be as easy as he'd imagined, he realised. No dropping seamlessly back into their old relationship, as if they'd just cut out the last five years and joined the ends together.

'About the next few weeks,' he said, getting back to practicalities because it was far easier than pursuing the other topic. 'I don't want to overcrowd you, and I don't want you to feel abandoned, either. I have to go back to London on Monday for a couple of days, and then I'll be back, and we can see how it goes. I'll try and give you space, and help with Joshua, and if it all gets too much you can kick me out and I can go and see Ben and Daisy and Thomas, or I can go back to London for the night and give you room. We'll play it by ear. Deal?'

She searched his eyes, and found only sincerity and a genuine desire to make this work. The rest could wait.

'Deal,' she said, and she smiled. 'Can we have that tea now? I'm parched.'

* * *

Ben and Daisy came round a little later, bearing plates of food and bottles of sparkling water.

'Just because we ought to have something fizzy to wet the babies' heads, and half of us can't drink,' Daisy explained, hugging Amy and bending over Josh and making besotted noises.

'He's so tiny! He's like a mini-Thomas! Oh, I want a cuddle. Hurry up and wake up!'

'No! He's only just gone back to sleep!' Amy said sternly. 'You leave him alone this minute and come and tell me all about Thomas. I feel dreadful abandoning you just after you had him.'

'Oh, Amy.'

She hugged her, told Ben to open the fizzy water and Matt to find glasses, and Amy sat there and cuddled Thomas and wondered how much better it could get.

Two days ago, she'd been in the depths of despair. Now, she was back home, her closest, dearest friends were with her, and she and Matt were going to see if they could make their relationship work.

That still filled her with a certain amount of trepidation, but she knew half of the butterflies were excitement at the prospect, and she tried to forget about it, to put it on one side and concentrate on enjoying the moment.

One day at a time, she told herself yet again, and took a glass of fizzy water from Ben and they toasted the babies. And as she lifted her glass, she met Matt's eyes over the top of it and he winked at her, and she thought, *It's going to be all right. We can do this. We can.*

'That was my parents. They send their love.'

Ben and Daisy had gone home with Thomas and

she'd just settled Josh in his crib when Matt came back into the sitting room, slipping his phone into his pocket. She'd heard it ring, and she frowned at what he said. 'They know you're with me?'

'Well, of course they do. Why wouldn't they?'

Why not, indeed? 'Have you told them about the baby?'

He gave a soft, disbelieving laugh. 'Amy, I've just become a father. Of *course* I've told them. I told them days ago.'

Well, of course he had. How stupid of her. They were a very close family, and Ben had just had a baby, too, which they would have been eagerly anticipating, and so they would all have been on the phone frequently. He was lucky to have them. So lucky...

He sat down on the sofa opposite her and searched her eyes. 'Amy, I know you've lost both of your parents, but have you told any members of your family?' he asked gently, and she shook her head.

'Not yet. I didn't want any of them to come over and have hysterics when they saw me, I just didn't need it. It's not as if I ever see my aunt or my cousins. I thought it would be better to tell them when it was all settling down and we knew the baby was all right.'

Not to mention her, he thought, because he'd had a few hours there where having hysterics wouldn't have been out of the way. 'You have a point. You looked pretty rough at first.'

She laughed, to his surprise. '*I* looked rough? Did you not look in a mirror?'

He smiled acknowledgement. 'Touché,' he said. 'I needed a few hours' sleep and a shave, but you—Amy, you worried me.' His smile faded as he remembered the sheer blind terror that had gripped him when he'd thought she might die.

'Was it really that bad? That close?'

He nodded, and swallowed hard. 'Yes, it was really that close, my love. You scared me half to death. I thought I was going to lose you.'

No wonder she'd been so out of it, she thought. She hadn't realised it had been that bad—although if she'd been thinking clearly she would have worked it out for herself from the state of him and the time that had elapsed and how high her blood pressure had risen.

'Oh, Matt,' she said softly, and he got up and came over to her and sat beside her, tucking his arm round her and dropping a light kiss on her hair.

'It's OK. It's over now, and you're getting better. I'm sorry, I shouldn't have told you. I didn't want to worry you.'

'You didn't—not for me. I know I was in good hands. You and Ben wouldn't have let anything happen to me.'

They might not have had any choice, of course. They both knew that, but by tacit agreement the subject was dropped. Joshua was asleep, Matt had put soft music on and she rested her head against his shoulder and let herself enjoy the moment.

CHAPTER EIGHT

JOSH woke at three.

Amy had fed him at eleven, and Matt had changed his nappy, put him in a clean sleepsuit and tucked him up next to her bed in the Moses basket while she'd used the bathroom.

And now he was awake again.

Prising his eyes open, Matt threw off the quilt and went into Amy's room. She was just stirring, about to get out of bed, but she looked sore and uncomfortable, and he tutted and eased her legs back up onto the bed and handed her the baby, tucking a stray lock of hair behind her ear with gentle fingers.

'You feed him, I'll get you a drink. Do you want decaf tea or herbal something, or just cold water?'

She gazed at him a little blankly. 'Tea?' she said hopefully, after a moment. 'Tea would be fabulous if you can be bothered, but you don't have to—'

'Don't argue, Amy. You've had far too much your own way. Now it's my turn to do the worrying.'

He left her alone with the baby, and she stared down at him while he suckled, his eyes firmly fixed on her in the dim light from the landing, his tiny hand splayed across her breast. She slid her thumb under it and it closed around her, and she stroked the back of his hand with her fingers, smiling down at him in wonder.

She was getting used to him now, getting used to how small he was and yet how determined and how very, very good at getting his way.

Just like his father, she thought wryly, and looked up as Matt came into the room and put the tea down on her bedside table.

He hovered for a moment, another cup in his hand, and she sensed he was waiting for the invitation, so she shifted her feet across and patted the edge of the bed. 'Stay,' she said softly, and he smiled, a fleeting quirk of his lips, and sat down at the end of the bed, watching her thoughtfully.

'How's the feeding going?'

'Well. Considering the start he had, he's amazing.'

She tucked her little finger in the corner of his mouth and eased him off, then held him out to Matt.

'Here you are, little one, go to Daddy. Want to wind him? Since you're so good at it,' she added with a smile, so he put his tea down and took the baby, and she shuffled up the bed a bit more and drank her own tea while he walked up and down, rubbing the baby's back. And as he walked, she watched him longingly.

He was dressed—if you could call it that—in soft jersey boxers, and the baby was propped against his bare shoulder, looking impossibly tiny against that broad chest. One large hand was holding him in place, the other stroking his back gently, and the tenderness of the gesture brought tears to her eyes. 'That's my little lager lout,' he said proudly as the baby burped, and she chuckled and blinked the tears away.

Matt turned and caught her eye, still smiling, and then he surprised her.

'Thank you,' he said, serious now, the smile gone, and she frowned at him in confusion.

'For what?'

'For having him? For going through all that alone, when you must have been so frightened. For mistakenly, misguidedly trying to spare me if things had gone wrong again. But not thank you for keeping me out of the loop, because I would have been here for you all along, Amy, if you'd only given me the chance.'

She felt another stab of guilt, but she'd done it for the best reasons and there was no point going over it again. 'Don't be daft, you work in London, you would have just been down there worrying and bullying Ben for hourly updates.'

He smiled wryly and brought the baby back to her side.

'You might be right, but you still should have told me.' The smile faded, and he gave a heavy sigh and ran his hand through his hair, spiking it wildly. He looked tousled and sexy and unbearably dear to her, and she took Josh from him and settled him at the other breast, suddenly self-conscious under his searching gaze.

Not because of the feeding, but because her hair must be all over the place, she had dark bags under her eyes and her tummy still looked like a bag of jelly.

But he didn't look as if he cared. He didn't look as if he was seeing any of that. Instead he gave a fleeting frown, picked up the cups and headed for the door.

'Call me when you're done, I'll change him and put him down for you,' he said, and left her alone.

He took the cups down to the kitchen, put them in the dishwasher and rested his head against the wall cupboard above it, his hands braced on the edge of the worktop.

He wanted her. Not like that, not at the moment, because she was still recovering from the eclampsia and the surgery. But he was overcome with longing—the longing to get into bed beside her and ease her into his arms and hold her, just hold her while she slept. He'd held her last night, on the sofa, her head on his shoulder and her soft breath teasing his chest in the open neck of his shirt.

It had felt so good to have her in his arms again, so right. But there was still a gulf between them, a wariness on both sides because of all the heartache and grief they'd shared and yet not really shared—and they still hadn't.

They had a long way to go before they could pick up the threads of their old life together, and he knew that, but he was impatient. They had so much going for them, and so much depended on the success of their relationship.

Not least the happiness and well-being of their son.

He heard the boards creak, and with a heavy sigh he pushed away from the worktop and headed upstairs. This he could do. The rest—the rest would come.

They just had to give it time.

Daisy took her stitches out on Saturday morning, which made her a lot more comfortable.

Matt had offered, but somehow it seemed extraordinarily intimate, and Ben was hardly any better, even if he'd put them there after the section and had a professional interest in his handiwork. She still felt uncomfortable about it, so Daisy did it for her, and then they had coffee together in the garden with the babies at their sides. And for the first time in years she felt like a normal woman again, doing the things that normal women did instead of standing on the outside looking in.

There was still a core of pain inside her for the loss of Samuel, and she supposed there always would be, but that was fine. She wouldn't have it any other way. He was still her son, always would be, and she was entitled to her grief.

Thomas started to fuss, so Daisy took him home and Amy left Matt with Josh in his Moses basket and went upstairs and had a look through the things Matt had bought—on her instructions. It seemed she hadn't been thinking quite as clearly as she'd imagined, because it had soon became obvious that the list she'd given him had some vital elements missing.

One of the most important, as Matt had pointed out, was a pram. She was still feeling tender, still walking carefully, but it was a beautiful day, and it would have been a good day for taking him out for a little stroll to the park nearby, only they didn't have a pram.

She. She didn't have a pram. They weren't a 'they' yet and might not ever be, so she'd be crazy to let herself start thinking like that.

There were also other things—very personal things—that she needed, and there was no way she was asking him, obstetrician or not! And it wasn't fair to keep asking Daisy...

He appeared in the doorway, tapping lightly and sticking his head round. 'Somebody needs his mum,' he began, and then took one look at her and said, 'What's the matter?'

'What makes you think something's the matter?' she asked, taking the baby from him, and he laughed.

'The look on your face? You're like an open book, Amy. So come on, let's have it.'

'I need to go shopping.'

His eyebrows shot up. 'Shopping?'

'For baby stuff. I was thinking, it would be nice to go out for a walk with the baby, but we don't have a pram.'

He rolled his eyes and sat down on the bed, sprawling back against the pillows as if he belonged there. Sadly not...

'You're going to take me pram shopping, aren't you?' he said faintly, and she started to laugh.

'You great big wuss, you can cope with it!'

'Twice? Dear God. I tell you, I shall have a lot more respect for women in future!' He tipped his head on one side and his face gentled. 'Are you sure you're up to it?' he asked softly. 'It's only been eight days.'

'I think so. I'll be careful.'

'Too right you'll be careful. I'll make sure of it. So when do you want to go?'

She sighed. 'I'd say as soon as I've fed him, but that seems to be pretty unreliable as an indicator of how long we've got before he wants more.'

'He's hungry. He's catching up.'

'Well, at least he eats like you and doesn't pick at his food!' she teased. 'Head down, get on with it, get it over.'

He smiled. 'It's only because I've spent so many years in hospitals and if you want hot food you have to grab the chance. So, if you feed him now and I make us something to eat while you do that, and then we make a dash for it as soon as he's done, we've probably got long enough to get part-way through the first pram demonstration—'

She threw a pillow at him, which was silly because it hurt her incision, but it was satisfying.

He caught it, put it down and shook his head.

'Steady, now. No pillow fights.'

Her breath hitched. They'd had a pillow fight once, and she'd lost—if you could call it that. She'd ended up under him, pinned to the bed by his long, solid leg across her, her hands manacled above her head by his firm, strong fingers, and he'd slowly and thoroughly plundered her body.

Matt watched her from the bed, his heart thudding slowly, the memory that was written clearly across her face still fresh in his mind. He'd held her down, and slowly and thoroughly explored every inch of her, and she'd loved every second of it—

Josh began to cry in earnest, yanking him back to reality, and he got off the bed and headed for the door. 'Why don't you feed him and I'll make you a drink and something to eat, and then we can go.'

He left her to it, getting out before he said or did something inappropriate, and as he reached the bottom of the stairs he heard her door close softly. He let his breath out, went into the kitchen and put the kettle on, and stared blankly into the fridge.

They needed a supermarket shop—and he needed an urgent appointment with a psychiatrist. Thinking about Amy lying naked beneath him was hardly the most sensible or intelligent thing for him to focus on at the moment—or ever, possibly.

He made some sandwiches—cheese and pickle, because that was about all there was and she could do with the calcium—and then carried them up to her.

He'd seen her breastfeeding loads of times, but suddenly—because of the pillow fight remark?—it took on a whole new dimension. He put the plate and cup down on the bedside table next to her and left her to it, taking his out into the conservatory so he could try to focus on something other than Amy and her body.

The pram shopping was every bit as mind-boggling and confusing as it had been the first time, but Amy took it in her stride. It seemed to make sense to her—women, he thought, must be hard-wired to that kind of stuff—and within an hour she'd chosen a travel system that seemed to do everything except fold itself.

And it had a baby seat that used the same base he had for his car, which meant greater flexibility. Excellent. It would be delivered on Monday morning, and all they needed now were the other things on her list, so she sent him off with Josh to browse.

'I need some things for me,' she said, colouring slightly in an endearing way that made him want to smile. He restrained himself until he'd turned away, just nodded and left her to it, the baby seat hanging from his hand. He was getting used to it, to the looks they were getting, the oohs and aahs because Josh was so tiny—and such a beautiful baby. Or was that just paternal pride? He looked down and met those staggering blue eyes staring up at him, and beamed. Nah. He was gorgeous. The pride was justified.

He glanced back and saw her examining a nursing bra, and he closed his eyes and tried not to think about her body. Inappropriate. Concentrate.

He took Josh to look at cots instead—travel cots, for starters, so they could take him down to London with them and stay in his house there on occasions. He hadn't discussed it with Amy, but he knew it was a possibility, so he found the same assistant who'd been so helpful over the buggy and was talked through the folding cots.

And it dawned on him very rapidly that this baby, tiny though he might be, was going to make a significant difference to his life. Starting with his car.

He sighed. He'd only had it four months, but it simply wouldn't fit all the paraphernalia of a baby on the move.

He glanced across at the underwear department and spotted her at the till. Good, because they had a lot to do. Or he did. Starting with the joys of the supermarket, and leading on to a little light surfing of estate cars on the internet.

His phone beeped at him, and he slid it out of his pocket and frowned at the screen. It was a text from Ben, telling him that their parents were coming down tomorrow for a flying visit. He blew out his breath, estate cars forgotten. He'd thought they were leaving it till next weekend, but apparently not. He glanced across at Amy again. He wasn't sure if she was up to such an emotional and stressful day. Not yet, but if they were coming down especially...

And then just to complicate it even further, Josh started to cry. He swung the baby seat by the handle, long slow swings to rock him off again, but he wasn't having any and Matt gave in.

'Come along, little man, let's go and find your mummy,' he said, and headed towards the tills.

She heard them coming, the new-baby cry going straight to her breasts and making them prickle. Damn. She'd forgotten breast pads. 'Over there,' the assistant said, and she grabbed a box and put it on the pile.

'I've just had a text from my parents,' he said as he arrived from her side, and she felt a sudden flurry of nerves. She hadn't seen them since Ben and Daisy's wedding, she hadn't spoken to them yet, and she wasn't at all sure she could cope with it.

'Where are they staying? You're in my spare room and Ben and Daisy have got Florence for the weekend.'

'I don't know that they are. I think it's a flying visit, because they have to have someone to look after the dogs. I think they were talking about coming down to see Thomas next weekend, but they've obviously just brought it forwards.'

'I didn't even know it was on the cards,' she pointed out, and he smiled wryly.

'Nor did I, really. Mum just sprang it on me. It'll be OK, though, I'll get some biscuits or something while I'm at the supermarket and you can just sit there and drink tea and let them admire him. They're thrilled, Amy, really thrilled, and you won't have to do anything.'

Was that what he thought? That she was worried about having to do things? She wasn't, not at all, but apart from a brief hug and a fleeting exchange at the wedding, the last conversation she'd had with his mother had been after she'd lost Samuel, and for all his reassurance that they were thrilled, she wondered if it would be a little awkward because she'd kept Josh a secret.

Oh, this was so hard! She thanked the assistant, scooped up her shopping and headed for the door, Matt at her side with the now-screaming baby. She fed him in the back of the car, sitting in the car park, and then they drove straight home and he dropped her off with Josh and went shopping, leaving her alone.

It was the first time he'd left her since she'd come out of hospital, she realised, except for odd trips to the corner shop, and she was glad to have a little peace and quiet.

Not that he was noisy, exactly, but having him there

was just—disturbing? As if there was an electric current running through her all the time, making her tingle.

She changed Josh's nappy, and the baby, full and contented, didn't even stir as she put him in the Moses basket. And the bed looked so inviting. Could she snatch half an hour?

Sure she could. Why not?

She slipped off her shoes, climbed onto the bed fully clothed and fell straight asleep.

The house was in silence when he got back. He'd put the car in the car port at the back, and carried the shopping through to the kitchen via the conservatory, so he hadn't used the front door, which was right under her bedroom.

Maybe she hadn't heard him come in—and maybe she was resting?

He crept upstairs as quietly as he could and stuck his head round the door, to find her lying curled on the bed, fast asleep, the baby flat out in the Moses basket next to her. It made him smile, but it brought a lump to his throat as well.

How was it possible to love someone so small so very, very much? And so soon? Or still to love a woman for all these years, even though she'd made it clear she didn't want to spend her life with him? Or hadn't. Maybe now it would be different, but maybe only because of Josh.

Maybe if she changed her mind now, it would be for practical reasons, perhaps the same reasons she'd agreed to marry him last time? And as soon as that reason had no longer existed, she'd called off the wedding.

She surely wouldn't have done that if she'd loved him.

He backed out of the room and went downstairs, his

heart suddenly heavy. He'd managed to convince himself that it was going to be wonderful, but now he felt a flicker of doubt.

Well, more than a flicker. Oh, hell.

He needed to *do* something, something concrete rather than wandering around on a knife edge. If the garden hadn't been largely paved, he'd go and dig it or mow the lawn or something, but there was nothing to do.

But there was something he could do, something he needed to do, no matter what happened with him and Amy, because he had a son, regardless, and that was already making its impact felt.

He'd put the kettle on already, so he made himself tea, went out into the conservatory with his laptop and started researching estate cars.

They heard his parents arrive the next day—the sound of the doorbell ringing faintly in the distance, the cries of delight as they went through to the garden and found Daisy there with the baby.

She met Matt's eyes, and he smiled reassuringly and gave her hand a quick squeeze.

'It'll be fine,' he promised her.

It was. He gave them twenty minutes, then got to his feet and headed for the garden, dropping a fleeting kiss on her head in passing. She could see him as he stuck his head over the fence and grinned. 'Permission to come aboard?' he asked, and Ben opened the gate in the fence to let him through.

She could hear them laughing, hear the warmth of their greeting from her seat in the conservatory, and her palms felt suddenly prickly with nerves. She hoped—

she desperately hoped—that they wouldn't come as a tribe, all the Walker clan in force to overwhelm her.

She should have known Liz, of all people, would have had more common sense. Matt's mother slipped quietly through the gate on her own, came into the conservatory and bent to gather Amy into her arms for a motherly hug.

'Oh, it's so good to see you,' she said softly, then let her go and sat beside her, holding her hand. 'How are you? Matthew said you'd had a dreadful time.'

She gave a quiet laugh. 'Apparently. I don't really remember very much about it.'

Liz smiled. 'Lucky you, from what I gather. You had both my boys worried there. And are you OK now?'

She nodded. 'I think so. Getting there.'

'And the baby?'

'Pick him up, see for yourself. He's about to wake up anyway.'

'Sure?'

She smiled, feeling herself relax. Liz was a midwife, too, and she knew she could trust her absolutely with her precious son. 'Sure,' she echoed, and Liz turned back the little cover and pressed her fingers to her lips, her eyes flooding.

'Oh, he's so tiny! Oh, bless his little heart, what a beautiful baby. Oh, Amy. You must be overjoyed.'

She nodded, but then for some inexplicable reason she started to cry, and Liz crouched beside her, rubbing her back and making soothing noises.

'Oh, sweetheart,' she murmured. 'It must have been so scary for you on your own—you're a silly girl, you should have told us, we could have looked after you. I could have come down.'

She sniffed and stared at her, the tears welling again at her kindness. 'Why would you do that?'

'Oh, poppet, do you need to ask? You were going to be my daughter, and I've never forgotten you. I've worried about you all these years, and I worried about you at the wedding, too. I could see how strong the pull was between you—and to be honest I never believed that cock-and-bull story of Matthew's about getting something from his room. A blind man could have seen the way it was with you that night, and it was only going to end one way. It was what might happen afterwards that worried me most, because I thought it had the capacity to hurt you both dreadfully, and I wasn't sure who I was most worried about, you or him.'

'Why would you worry about me? He's your son.'

'Because you left so much unfinished business between you,' she said quietly. 'So much sorrow and pain. And I don't know about you, but I don't think Matthew's ever really dealt with it.'

She nodded. 'I think you're right. I don't think either of us have really dealt with it.'

'You need to. And Joshua will help you—he'll help to heal you.'

'He already is,' she said, her eyes going automatically to her little son. His legs were starting to go, his arms flailing, and any moment now he'd begin to wail. 'I think he needs a cuddle with his grannie,' she said softly, and Liz got to her feet again and picked him up, crooning to him as she cradled him in her arms and introduced herself to him.

'Oh, he's so like Matthew.'

'Not Ben?'

She laughed. 'Not so much, no. They were different, even at Josh's age—but only I could see it. He lies in the same way, with his arms flung up. Ben never did that.'

He started to grizzle and turn his head towards her, and Liz smiled and held him out to her. 'Yours, I think,' she said, and handed him over. 'That's the wonderful thing about being a grandmother, so I'm told. You just hand them back when they need attention.'

Why on earth had she worried?

They were lovely. The visit was only short, and they all ended up having lunch under the tree in Ben and Daisy's garden, the two proud grandparents cuddling the babies in turn while Amy sat with Daisy and enjoyed the luxury of being redundant for a few hours.

Florence was there, too, pushing her own 'baby' round in its buggy, and she announced that Mummy was having a new baby for her, so she'd have two brothers soon. She seemed utterly delighted at the idea, and she was sweet with the babies, and with Daisy.

And there it was again, the knowledge that Samuel was missing from the scene. He would have been a little older than Florence, and Amy could imagine them playing, the four children growing up together. But it would never be...

'What's up?'

Matt's voice was soft in her ear, and she turned her head and found him crouched behind her, her eyes searching. 'Nothing,' she lied, but his smile told her he knew she was lying.

'Can I get you anything?'

She shook her head. 'Actually, I think I might have a lie down. I'm feeling tired.'

He laughed softly. 'Me, too. These ruptured nights are a bit wearing.'

'Ruptured?' she said with a smile, and he smiled back and leant over and kissed her cheek.

'You know what I mean,' he said, and straightened up. 'I'll take him, Dad. I think he probably needs feeding, and Amy's ready for a rest, so we'll leave you to it. Thanks for coming, it's been lovely to see you.'

'Come up soon,' his mother said, and he nodded, but he wasn't making any promises. It all depended on Amy, and Harrogate—well, Harrogate held all manner of memories.

They were hugged and kissed, and then they made their escape. And somehow, after she'd fed him and Matt had put him back in the Moses basket in the bedroom, he ended up lying down on the bed next to her, the soft sound of his breathing somehow soothing.

'I'm glad they came,' she murmured. 'It was so nice to see them again. Your mother was lovely to me.'

He turned his head. 'Why wouldn't she be?'

'No reason. She's been worried about me, apparently.'

'Of course she has. We all have.'

'She's worried about you, too.'

He sighed. 'She's got a point, Amy. We're both in limbo, have been for years.'

He turned so he was facing her, lying on his side just inches away, his head propped on his hand. 'Why don't you come back with me to London tomorrow for a couple of days? I only have to pop into the hospital for a short while, and you could sit in my garden and watch the birds while I'm out, and then we can take Josh for a walk in the park.'

She frowned. 'You don't have a garden.'

'Yes, I do—I don't live in the flat any more. I thought

you realised that. I moved to a mews cottage just a few doors from Rob.'

That surprised her. They'd often visited his friend, and she'd always said how much she loved his house. It wasn't large, but it had a garage and a garden, unusually for London, and the little cobbled lane that ran between two streets was filled with flowers and potted plants outside the houses.

They'd even talked about moving there, but then she'd lost the baby and everything had stopped.

Except he'd done it, anyway, bought one of the houses and was living their dream alone.

Why?

Because it had made economic sense, or because he hadn't been able to let the dream go?

Only one way to find out.

'That sounds lovely,' she said, feeling—excited? Maybe. She hadn't felt excited about anything in this way for years, and she smiled at him. 'Really lovely. How did you know I had cabin fever?'

He smiled back and reached out a hand, touching her face. It was the lightest touch, the merest whisper of his fingers over her cheek, but it set all her senses on fire, and for a breathless, endless moment she was frozen there, eyes locked with his, her entire body motionless.

And then he dropped his hand and rolled off the bed.

'I'll leave you to rest. I've got things to do. Give me a call if you need anything.'

Only you, she thought, but she said nothing.

It was too soon, and this time, she was going to make absolutely sure of what she was doing before she committed herself to Matt again.

CHAPTER NINE

THEY left for London after the travel system was delivered.

Matt spent an hour trying to work out how to put it all together, then eventually, temper fraying, managed to get the frame and the carrycot into the boot of his car. There was no room for their luggage except on the back seat beside the baby, and he frowned at it.

There was nowhere else he could put it, so he made sure there was nothing heavy loose in the cabin, squashed their bags behind the seats and resolved to get an estate car at the first possible opportunity.

Tomorrow would be good.

Then as soon as he was fed and changed, they strapped Josh into the car seat and set off.

'It's like going on an expedition to the Antarctic,' he grumbled, sounding so exasperated and confused that Amy laughed.

He shot her a dirty look, sighed and then joined in, his bad mood evaporating rapidly. Why would he be grumpy? The woman he loved was in the seat beside him, his baby son was in the back, and they were going to see the house where he hoped—please God not in vain—that they'd live together.

No. He wasn't grumpy. He was just driving the

wrong car. Easily fixable. The accommodation issue was far harder, and he ran his eye mentally over the house. Was it clean? Tidy? He'd issued the invitation without a thought, but he couldn't remember how he'd left it and his cleaner came in once a fortnight. Had she been?

No idea. The days since Josh had burst into his life had blurred together so he didn't have a clue where he was any more. With Josh and Amy, he told himself. That was the only thing that mattered. The state of the house was irrelevant.

The house was lovely.

It was just a few doors from Rob's, and it was bigger, the one they'd often talked about because it looked tatty and run-down and in need of love.

Well, not any more. It looked immaculate, the sash windows all renovated, by the look of it, the brass on the front door gleaming, and she couldn't wait to see what he'd done to it, especially the garden. It had had the most amazing wisteria, she remembered, sprawling all over the garden. Had he been able to save it? He pressed a button on his key fob and the roller-shutter on his garage door slid quietly up out of the way, and he drove in and cut the engine.

'Home,' he said with satisfaction, and she felt a strange and disorientating sense of loss. How odd. She had a home. Except of course it wasn't hers, not really. She was only living there on a temporary basis, on Ben's insistence, but now that Matt was back in her life, there was no need for that.

'What's up?'

She opened her mouth to tell him, and thought better

of it. 'Nothing,' she said. 'It's the house we used to talk about. You didn't tell me that. It took me by surprise.'

'It didn't look like a very nice surprise,' he said quietly, and she realised he sounded—what? Disappointed?

'It's a lovely surprise,' she assured him. 'I can't wait to see it.'

'I can't guarantee what it's like, it might be a tip,' he warned, unclipping Josh's seat and heading for a door. 'Come on in.'

It was beautiful. They went straight into the kitchen, a light and airy room with doors out into the garden. There was a sofa at one end, and a television, and she guessed he used this room more than any other. She could see why, with the garden just there, and it looked lovely. Far less overgrown, of course, but lush and inviting, a real oasis in the middle of the city. It was a little smaller than Daisy's, and the painted brick walls that surrounded it gave it a delightfully secret feel.

He opened the doors and they went out, and she could hear birds singing and smell the most heavenly scent— from the old wisteria scrambling up the back wall of the house.

'You saved it!'

His mouth twisted into a smile, and he reached out a hand and touched her cheek. 'I had to keep it after everything you'd said about it. It reminded me of you.'

What could she say to that? Nothing. She was picking her way through a minefield again, and she felt suddenly slightly nervous. 'Can I see the rest?'

'Sure.'

He left the doors open, and they went past a cloakroom and upstairs to the hall. The front door came in there, accessed from the mews by old stone steps that she'd noticed were covered in pots, and off the front of the hall was a study, and behind it a sitting room.

'You haven't got a dining room,' she said, and he gave a wry smile.

'I don't really need one. I've got a breakfast bar, and I eat there. I don't really entertain like that. Come and see the bedrooms.'

She followed him up and found three rooms, two small ones over the front, and a larger one, obviously his, next to the bathroom at the back.

'It's lovely, Matt. Really, really nice. I love the colours.'

'Yes, they're your sort of colours,' he said softly, and she noticed he wasn't smiling. Why? And why put it like that, as if he'd chosen the colours because she'd like them—unless...?

'I'm glad you like it. I was sort of hoping that maybe one day you might—' He broke off, shrugged and turned away, heading back down the stairs. 'Tea?'

'Sounds lovely.' *Might what?* She followed him thoughtfully.

'Why don't you have a potter round the kitchen and make us some tea while I bring in all the luggage?' he suggested, putting Josh down on the floor by the sofa, and she filled the kettle and searched through the cupboards.

It was logically organised, as she might have expected from Matt. Mugs over the kettle, tea and coffee beside them in the next cupboard, cutlery in the drawer underneath.

Nice mugs, she thought. Plain white bone china. She looked around, frowning slightly. The kitchen was the sort of kitchen she'd fantasised about, a hand-built painted Shaker kitchen, with granite worktops and in-

tegrated appliances. The garden was heavy with the
scent of the wisteria she'd said she loved. Everything
about it—*everything*—was how she would have done
it.

Had he done it for her? she wondered, and she felt
her eyes fill with tears.

'You haven't got very far with the tea.'

She switched the kettle on to boil again and reached
for the mugs. 'When did you buy the house?' she
asked,turning to look at him, and he went still.

'Um—it came on the market just after…'

'After we lost Samuel,' she finished for him softly.

He nodded. 'I thought…' He shook his head. 'It
doesn't matter.'

'I think it does. I think it matters a lot.'

He let his breath out very slowly, and turned to face
her, his eyes wary and yet revealing. 'I hoped—one
day—that you might come back to me. That we might
live here, together, as we'd talked about. Build a new
life, start again. Then I realised it wasn't going to happen, but I finished it anyway, because it was handy for
the hospital and—well, I loved it.'

She didn't know what to say, because it hadn't been
an invitation, as such, more a statement of why and how
he'd done it. And she wasn't sure if it was still current,
if the hope was still alive. And if it was, she wasn't sure
what her answer would be, so she just nodded slowly,
and turned her back on him and made the tea, and by
the time she'd finished, he'd found some biscuits and
taken Josh out into the garden so they could sit near the
wisteria and soak up the last of the sunshine.

The subject was dropped, and he talked instead about
work, about the people she'd known and what they were
doing, that Rob was married now and had a child, a lit-

tle girl of one, and another on the way, and how Tina, one of the other midwives, had finally convinced her registrar boyfriend to marry her—lightweight gossip that distracted her from the delicate subject of their relationship.

Then Josh woke, starving hungry and indignant, and she fed him, the sudden blissful silence broken only by the twittering of the birds and the muted hum of the traffic in the distance.

'I need to do some work,' Matt said suddenly, getting up. 'Make yourself at home. I'll be down in a while.'

She nodded, but he'd already gone, heading upstairs to his study, no doubt, and leaving her alone to ponder on his motivation and what, if anything, this new information might mean to her.

He stood upstairs at the sitting room window, staring down at her and wondering why he'd brought her here.

He'd been longing to, for years now, but at least before he couldn't actually picture her here. Now, though, her image would be everywhere, her presence almost tangible in every room. If this didn't work out...

It had to work out. There was no acceptable alternative—at least not to him. Not one he could live with.

He dialled the hospital number and asked them to page his registrar and get him to call him, then he stood there staring broodingly down at her until the phone rang. Only then did he take his eyes off her, go into the study, shut the door and concentrate on work. At least that was something he had some control over.

They stayed in London for two days, and for Amy they were idyllic.

She spent a lot of time in the garden with Josh, and

when Matt was there they walked to the little park just two streets away. It had a playground for little children, and she found herself imagining bringing Josh here when he was older.

Which was silly, because she lived in Suffolk, not London. It was where her job was, and just because Matt had hoped she'd come back to him five years ago didn't mean they were going to make it work now.

Which meant Matt would be bringing Josh here on his own at the weekends, she realised, and felt suddenly incredibly sad.

He'd been taking photos of her with the baby in the park, sitting under the trees and strolling with the buggy, and she took the camera from him and photographed them together, the two men in her life—except Matt might not be.

There was still a wariness about him, a distance from her, and she wasn't sure why it was. Protecting himself from further hurt? She could understand that, but the image of him playing here alone with his son was too awful to contemplate.

Going back to Yoxburgh was strange, and not necessarily in a good way.

They quickly settled, though, and Matt went back to London in the middle of Saturday night because they'd had a multiple pregnancy admitted and the staff were worried about the babies.

He came back on Tuesday, having delivered the triplets, and he was sombre.

'We lost one,' he told her, when she asked, and she wished she hadn't—which was ridiculous, because she worked as a midwife, she knew these things happened.

But he looked gutted, and for the first time really she

wondered how *he* dealt with stillbirth, not from the patients' viewpoint but his own.

'I'm sorry,' she said, hugging him, and he held her close for a moment, his head rested against hers, drawing strength from her. God, he needed her. He'd missed her, the last few days interminable without her and Josh, and sad though he was, it was good to be home.

Home? he thought. This wasn't home! This was Amy's home, and he had to remember that. He was getting too comfortable. Too settled.

And in too deep.

They went backwards and forwards between London and Yoxburgh for the next three weeks, the journey being made much easier by the fact that he'd changed his car for an estate version, so at least she knew he was serious about being a hands-on father. Very hands on. He got up in the night almost without fail and made her tea, staying to chat while she fed Josh and then change him and settle him again, and when she was exhausted he sent her back to bed in the day and did everything except the breast feeds. And gradually she grew stronger and fitter, her incision felt almost normal and she started talking about going back to work.

Matt was astounded. 'You can't! How can you do that? You've been ill—you've had a section!'

'Matt, I'm fine! I'm all right now, and I have no choice. If I don't work, I've got no way of paying my living expenses.'

'I'll pay you maintenance.'

'Why should you?'

'Because he's my son?'

She shook her head. 'That's different, but I need to

earn a living for me. I don't need maintenance from you for that, I can cope on my salary—'

'Only because Ben and Daisy aren't charging you the proper rent for this house.'

She stared at him, stunned. 'Matt, they won't take it! I've offered, but they won't take any more.'

'Only because they know you haven't got it, and that's unfair, Amy, it's taking advantage of their friendship and good nature, and it's costing them hundreds of pounds every month.'

She felt her mouth hanging open, and shut it. Of course it was—she knew that, but she'd avoided thinking about it. Now he'd brought it so forcibly to her attention, she was gutted. They'd seemed to want her there so much—and because she'd needed the house, she hadn't challenged it hard enough, she'd taken their argument about being choosy about their tenant at face value.

'They said they wanted me,' she said, shocked, and he shrugged.

'They do, and they can have you. They can have you, Amy, but at the proper rent, and I'll pay you maintenance so you can afford to live here. But what about Josh? You haven't answered that one yet. What'll happen to him when you go back to work?'

'I'll put him in the crèche.'

'Have you booked? Because places are usually tight, and it's tricky with shift work. And childcare is hideously expensive. Are you sure you can afford it? Have you looked into the costs?'

No, of course she hadn't. She hadn't done any of it because she hadn't dared to believe it would be all right, and now she felt sick with worry and shame and guilt towards Ben and Daisy. She bit her lip, and he shook his head and sighed.

'Amy, do you *really* want to go back to work so soon? Or is this a purely economic decision? Because if it is, you don't have to work if you don't want to. I can afford to support you, but I want to be part of his life, and part of yours. And if you moved back to London, we could do all of that. It would be amazing. You've said you like my house, and we could live there and you could be at home with him and enjoy his babyhood, and I'd get to see him growing up.'

It was the obvious answer, of course. If she lived with him, it would cost him hardly anything to support her, and he'd be with his son. But how much of it was to do with her and how much he loved her?

Because he'd never said those words, in all these weeks of talking and getting to know each other again. Never once had he said he loved her, or tried in any way to touch her, kiss her, hold her in anything other than a supportive way.

And she realised she had no idea at all where she stood.

'What happens when something goes wrong, Matt? If I leave behind my job, my home, my friends—I'd have to start again. I've done that once. Believe me, I don't want to do it again.'

'What makes you think anything would go wrong?'

'Experience,' she said quietly, and to her relief Josh woke at that moment and she had a legitimate excuse to leave the room.

He didn't say any more about it that day, and the following day he left her in Suffolk and went back to London on his own. Maybe, he thought, it was time to let her cope alone for a while, ease himself out of her life and let her see what it was like.

He was helping her with all nappy changing and bathing, he did all the shopping, all the housework, he watered the garden and weeded the flowerbeds and washed her car and cleaned the windows—mostly to fill the time between feeds because he didn't trust himself not to rush her if he was alone with her. She'd been so ill, was still getting over major surgery, whatever she might say to the contrary, and the last thing she needed was him coming on to her.

So he took himself off out of her life, and rattled round his house alone and missed her every single minute he wasn't at work.

And then he got to work one morning and checked the calendar.

It was the date they'd lost Samuel, he realised with shock. He'd never forgotten it before, never overlooked it. He was always in Harrogate on that day, always took flowers to the cemetery, but this time he had Amy to think about, and maybe it was time they confronted this issue together, today of all days.

He cleared his workload, delegated his clinics and left London, arriving back at Amy's house in Yoxburgh without warning and finding her sitting in the conservatory in tears. He'd let himself in with his keys, and he wondered if he should have done or if she minded.

'Hey,' he said softly, crouching down and touching her face with a gentle hand. 'It's OK, I'm here now.'

'I'm all right,' she lied, and he knew she wasn't, because her face was blotched and tearstained and her eyes were swollen and she was in a sea of soggy tissues.

He knew just how she felt. He'd done the same thing every year, but this year he'd been more worried about her, and he scooped her up and carried her into the sitting room and cradled her on his lap as she cried.

Then finally she sniffed to halt and tried to sit up, but he wouldn't let her, just held her against his chest and she gave in and rested her head on his shoulder and laid her hand over his heart.

Could she feel that it was broken?

She looked up at him, and with a soft sigh she wiped away his tears. 'When is it going to end?'

He kissed her gently, his lips tasting the salt of her tears, and he sighed quietly.

'I don't know. I don't know if it'll ever truly go.'

She closed her eyes, and the welling tears slid down her cheeks, breaking his heart still further. 'I just wish I had somewhere to go—a focus for my grief. Somewhere I could go and remember him, once in a while. All I've got is the scan photo and my armband from the hospital. Nothing else.'

'There is something else,' he said softly, kicking himself for never thinking of it, never telling her, never sharing their grief. If only he'd known how she felt, if only he'd thought about it. 'I asked the hospital to arrange his cremation, and I went to the…' He couldn't say funeral. 'To the service,' he went on, after a moment. 'The hospital chaplain said a few words, and they scattered his ashes in the garden there. I go every year and put flowers in the garden, but they wrote his name in the Book of Remembrance, and I'm sure you can view it. I'm so sorry, I should have told you, but I'd just put it out of my mind.'

She stared at him blankly. 'There's a book with his name in it? Can we see it?'

He nodded. 'I think so. I'm pretty sure you can. I'll have to phone, but I think so.'

'Phone them now. Please, Matt, phone them now! It's only eleven o'clock. Maybe we could go today.'

He used his phone to find the number, and rang. Half an hour later they were heading north on their way to Yorkshire, the baby fed, Amy's clothes packed haphazardly, but that wasn't what mattered. What mattered was that they were together, today, and anything else was irrelevant.

The book was open at the date, and she ran her finger down the page and found the entry.

Samuel Radcliffe Walker, beloved son of Amy and Matthew. Always in our hearts.

The words swam in front of her eyes, and she sagged against Matt, his arm firmly around her, supporting her. Joshua was on his chest in a baby sling, fast asleep against his father's heart, next to the cherished memory of their other son, and she laid her hand against the baby's back, making the connection.

'I thought he'd been forgotten,' she whispered.

His arm tightened slightly, and she felt his lips brush her hair. 'No. No, Amy, he'll never be forgotten. He'll always be our first son.'

She nodded, her finger tracing the words once more, and then she nodded again and turned away.

'Thank you—thank you so much,' she said to the kindly man who'd shown them the book. He was hovering quietly behind them, giving them space, and Matt shook his hand and thanked him, and led her back outside into the sunshine.

'Where are his ashes?' she asked unsteadily, and Matt showed her the place. He'd never seen the book, but every year he'd brought beautiful cottage garden flowers from a lady who sold them from a little barrow outside her cottage just down the road—real flowers, not a stiff arrangement of scentless hothouse blooms.

They'd bought some on the way here today, and Amy kissed them, then laid them on the grass, taking a moment to remember him and say goodbye, then she straightened up and snuggled against Matt's side, his arm automatically going around her holding her close. He pressed his lips to her hair, and she rested her head against his shoulder as they stood for a moment staring at them, and then she sighed and turned away and they strolled quietly along the paths in the sunshine, arms around each other, hanging on.

They found a bench and sat down, by tacit agreement, not quite ready to leave just yet.

'Are you all right?' he asked softly.

'Mmm. You?'

He smiled wryly. 'I'll do.'

'Thank you—for bringing me here, for coming to see me. I'm not normally that bad. It seemed worse this year, somehow.'

'Mmm. Maybe it's having Josh. It sort of underlines what we've lost,' he said, his voice unsteady, and she nodded.

'I'm so glad we came. I feel so much better now—as if I've done something I've been waiting all these years to do. And I'm glad you were there for his funeral. How did you do that?' she asked, bewildered. 'I wouldn't have been strong enough. How did you cope?'

He gave a hollow little laugh. 'I didn't really. Mum offered to come, but I wanted to do it alone. I didn't want anyone seeing me like that. I was in denial, and if nobody saw me, I could pretend it wasn't happening.'

'That was why I ran away to India,' she admitted. 'So nobody I knew would see me as I fell apart.'

'You were in India?'

'Yes. I went backpacking on my own. Probably not the most sensible thing, but while I was there I spent a couple of weeks living on the fringe of a village where the child mortality rate was dreadful, so it put it in perspective.'

'I'll bet. Amy, I had no idea. I thought you were somewhere in London, one of the other hospitals. I didn't try to find out, either. I thought, if you didn't want me, there was no point in pursuing it.'

She turned and looked at him, seeing the pain in his eyes, and she shook her head slowly. 'It wasn't that I didn't want you, it was that I felt you didn't want me.'

He gave a soft grunt of laughter. 'Oh, I wanted you, Amy. I've never stopped wanting you. I just didn't know how to talk to you, how to deal with it. Mum suggested bereavement counselling, but I turned it down flat because I didn't want to be made to think about it.' He touched her face, his fingers gentle, and his eyes were filled with sorrow.

'I let you down. I'm sorry.'

'I let you down, too. I should have stayed in England, talked to you instead of letting you shut yourself away. I never wanted to end our relationship, Matt, I just couldn't cope with the idea of a party. That great big wedding, with all our family and friends all gathered there just weeks after we'd lost him—it seemed wrong, somehow. It would have been wrong.'

He nodded. 'It would, but I wasn't sure then if it would ever be right, or if we'd lost each other as well along the way. And then you disappeared off the face of the earth, and I bought the house, in case you changed your mind and decided you wanted me after all, but you never did. You'd handed in your notice, and you were gone.'

'You could have found me. I'm a registered midwife, you could have tracked me down.'

He smiled. 'Probably not legally, but I wasn't sure I wanted to. You knew where I was. I thought, when you were ready, you'd come back to me, but you never did, and I gave up hope.'

'And then Ben met Daisy, and there you were again in my life,' she said softly. 'And now we have another son.'

'We do, and I have a feeling he has rising damp,' he said with a smile.

She laughed quietly and felt the edge of his little shorts. 'Oops. I think you might be right.'

'Can you cope with my parents?' he asked, his eyes concerned, and she smiled and nodded.

'Yes. Yes, I can cope with them. I'd love to see them. Can they cope with us, though?'

'I'm sure they can.'

They were overjoyed to see them.

There were more tears, and tea, and lots of hugs, and then they offered to babysit so Matt could take Amy out for dinner.

'Go and have a quiet meal somewhere by yourselves. We can cope. You can express some milk and we can feed him if he wakes.'

'We haven't got any bottles,' Amy said, but Liz had an answer.

'Ben and Daisy have been up here and they brought a steriliser and some bottles with them so we could look after Thomas. Now what else are you going to come up with as an excuse?' she teased, and Amy laughed.

'Nothing. Thank you. Dinner out with Matt would be lovely.'

'In which case, if you'll excuse me, I have a phone call to make,' Matt said, and he dropped a kiss in Amy's palm, closed her fingers over it to keep it safe and with a little wink he walked out with a spring in his stride she hadn't seen for years.

'Right. Let's get these bottles sterilised,' Liz said. 'I don't want you two having any excuses for coming home early.'

CHAPTER TEN

'Which rooms do you want us to have?'

His mother searched his eyes, and he lifted his shoulders in an almost invisible shrug, but she understood, it seemed, because she just smiled.

'Yours and Ben's are already made up, and the crib's in Ben's already.'

He nodded. They had a communicating door, which would mean he could help Amy with Josh in the night—and if things went the way he hoped, they'd only need his room.

He took the luggage up, opened the windows and stood staring out over the familiar countryside and breathing in the glorious fresh air. He loved London, loved his job, but it was good to come home.

'Matt?'

He turned and smiled at Amy. 'Hi. I've put your things in Ben's room with Josh's. There's a changing mat in there, and the crib, which might make life easier.'

She looked at the crib, rocking it gently with one finger, memories washing over her. It was one of two that Matt's father had made for their boys, and Liz had shown them to her when she'd been pregnant with Samuel. 'The baby will be able to sleep in one when you come and stay,' she'd said, only Samuel had never needed a crib, and now his brother and his cousin would be sleeping in them.

She waited for the wave of pain, but there was only a gentle sorrow, a quiet acceptance that this was the way things were, and now she could move on, with Josh—and Matt?

She felt a tingle of anticipation, and turned to find him standing in the doorway, watching her.

'OK?'

She nodded. 'Yes. So—where are we going for dinner?'

He smiled. 'A place Ben recommended. It's—um—it's quite smart,' he said, 'but you're about the same size as Mum. I wonder if she's got anything you could borrow?'

She looked down at her baggy jersey dress and leggings, soft and comfortable and easy to wear, but not exactly smart dining. 'Let's hope so or you might be cancelling the reservation!' she said lightly, and went to find Liz.

'Oh, gosh—right. Um—come and see. I'm sure I've got something.'

She had. A lovely black lace dress, soft and stretchy and elegant, and although her tummy was still a little bigger than she would have liked, the dress fitted beautifully and she wasn't ashamed in any way of her post-pregnancy figure.

'It's lovely, Liz. Are you sure?'

'Of course I'm sure. How about a little pashmina? I've got one that I wear with it to keep the chill off, and it might get cold later.'

She borrowed them both, but stuck to her little flat black pumps. They had sparkly gems on the toe and they fitted, more to the point.

She showered and then tipped out her bag, hunting through the things she'd thrown into it in haste on the way up, and then wailed.

'What's up?'

Matt appeared in the doorway, and she pulled the borrowed dressing gown tighter round her. 'No knickers.'

'Ah.' He disappeared, and came back a moment later dangling a scrap of cream lace from one finger.

She frowned and snatched them from his fingertip. 'They're mine!'

'Yup. I must have scooped them up with the suit and things the morning after the wedding. I didn't exactly pack carefully.'

'No.' He hadn't. He scooped everything up and shoved it in the bag, and she hadn't been able to find the tiny lace shorts. 'So what are they doing here?'

'They were in my case—in the pocket. I found them and washed them—I meant to give them back to you ages ago, but I shoved them in the case and just forgot. You talking about it reminded me.'

'Thanks. They'll go a treat with the nursing bra.'

He started to laugh, and then he pulled her into his arms and hugged her close, pressing a kiss to her forehead. 'You're gorgeous, Amy. You don't need sexy underwear to turn me on.'

And just like that, with those few words, her body came alive in his arms. Her breath caught in her throat, her heart speeded up, and she took a shaky step back and met his eyes. 'Shoo,' she said, more firmly than she felt. 'I need to feed Josh and express some more milk before we go, and I don't need an audience. If you want to do something useful, you can make me a cup of tea.'

He went, humming softly as he walked away, and she

shut the door and put on the little shorts. They looked all right, she thought, even though she'd gained a little weight. She'd been too thin at the wedding—worrying about seeing him again.

Now, she couldn't wait to be alone with him, and she put on the borrowed makeup—a touch of concealer over the bags under her eyes from the disturbed nights, a streak of eyeshadow over her lids, a flick of mascara. Nothing more. She'd eat the lipstick off in moments, and anyway Matt didn't like kissing lipstick, and she really, really hoped he'd end up kissing her goodnight.

At the very least...

'Mr Walker! Welcome back, sir.'

Matt smiled. 'Sorry—wrong Mr Walker. You're thinking of my twin brother,' he explained with a grin. 'I'm not two-timing Daisy.'

'My apologies, sir—I must say I'm relieved to hear it.' The maitre d' beamed and showed them to their table, set in a quiet alcove. 'I've put you at their favourite table. He caused quite a stir in here the night he proposed to Mrs Walker. How are they?'

'Very well. They had a boy.'

'Ah. I wondered. Well, please give them our congratulations. May I get you a drink?'

'Yes—thank you. Could we have sparkling water?'

'Of course.'

He faded away, and Amy smiled. 'Don't you ever get sick of that happening?'

He grinned. 'No, not really. I'm used to it. It's a bit more complicated when we're working together. We used to wear colour-coded scrubs and shirts to give the staff a clue, but the patients found it confusing.'

'I've never found it confusing.'

'That's because you love me,' he said, and then let his breath out on a sigh and smiled wryly. 'Sorry. Ignore me.'

It was on the tip of her tongue to say yes, he was right, but she didn't, and a waiter appeared with their sparkling water and menus, and they ordered their food. Eventually.

'I can't decide,' she'd said, and he grinned.

'Neither can I. Let's share, then we can have two dishes from each course.'

So they did, swapping plates halfway through, or a little more than half in Matt's case because he was bigger than her and it was only fair, but the food was gorgeous and she was reluctant to let it go.

'I want everything,' she said, and he just laughed and swapped the plates.

'We'll come again,' he said, and she felt a little flutter in her chest.

'Yes, let's.' She looked away to break the tension, and scanned the room with her eyes. 'It's lovely in here, a real find. I can see why Ben and Daisy like it so much.'

'Yes, so can I.'

She sighed softly, her face thoughtful. 'It's so nice being alone with you like this. It seems forever since we did it.'

'It is. The last time we had dinner together was before Samuel.'

She smiled sadly, twisting his heart. 'And all I wanted was peanut butter.'

He nodded. 'I've thought about that. I should have realised at Christmas when you were eating that sandwich.'

'I should have told you. I wanted to, but I was blocking it out, too afraid of what might come out if I let go, and I wanted to protect you, just in case.'

His hand found hers lying on the table, his thumb tracing circles on the soft skin. 'I didn't need protecting, Amy,' he said softly. 'I just needed to share it with you, whatever it was. Promise me you'll never do that again, whatever happens, whatever you're worried about, whatever you're afraid of. Tell me the truth. And I'll do the same. We need to learn to open up to each other, to talk about the things that really matter. And it won't always be easy. It never is, but we have to.'

She nodded. 'I agree.' She hesitated for a moment, then took the first step on that road. 'Can I ask you something about the house?'

He gave a slightly puzzled frown. 'Sure. What about it?'

'Why did you do it like that?'

'Like what?'

'All of it—the kitchen I'd said I liked, the colours, the granite—you even kept the wisteria, and a lawn. We'd talked about needing a lawn for children to play on, although you'd talked about having a modern low-maintenance garden.'

'It is low maintenance. It's mostly paved, and I found I wanted a piece of lawn—just a little bit of home, I suppose,' he said, but then remembered what he'd said about telling the truth, and he smiled wryly. 'And I suppose I hoped that you'd come back to me, that one day we might have another child to play on the lawn. And yeah, I did the kitchen for you, and painted it all for you in your favourite colours. I told you that.'

'But you didn't really say why.'

'For you. I did all of it for you. I wanted you back, Amy, and I still do. I've told you that.'

'You said you wanted me to come and live with you with Josh. I thought—'

She broke off, and he prompted her. 'You thought...?'

'I thought you wanted Josh with you, and it was the easiest way. And the cheapest, if you were talking about paying my rent so I didn't have to worry about money. It would be cheaper and easier and more convenient to have me with you.'

'And you really thought that was why I wanted you to come back to me?' he asked, genuinely shocked. His hand tightened on hers. 'Oh, Amy. I didn't even give the money a thought. I just—it seemed a way to convince you to come back to me. It was nothing to do with Josh, nothing at all. Of course I want to be near him, but I would have moved, would have found a way like Ben did to be near Florence. But I want *you*, Amy. I love you, I always have, I always will, and I don't want to be without you. Josh is amazing, and having him in my life is wonderful, but the thought of my life without you in it is untenable.'

'Really?' She stared at him for ages, and then her eyes filled. 'Oh, Matt. I love you, too. I thought you didn't love me, I thought losing Samuel gave you a way out of a relationship that you hadn't asked for and came to realise you didn't want.'

'Of course I wanted it! Why would I want a way out, Amy? I love you. I'll always love you. I thought four years would be enough to get over you, but I realised at the wedding that I wasn't over you at all, I'd just been marking time.'

'Me, too.' Her smile was gentle, her eyes filled with tears, and suddenly he wanted to be alone with her—completely alone, so he could hold her, touch her, love her.

And lovely though the restaurant was, he'd had enough of it. He glanced up and caught the waiter's eye, and asked for the bill.

'Is everything all right, sir?' he asked worriedly, and Matt smiled.

'Everything's fine. Thank you.'

'Matt?'

He stroked her wrist with his thumb again, tracing the pulse point, feeling it leap. 'I just want to be alone with you,' he said a little gruffly, and her eyes widened slightly. And then she smiled, and ran the tip of her tongue lightly over her lips. He groaned softly and closed his eyes.

'Stop it,' he murmured, as the waiter came back with the bill and the card machine. He didn't even glance at the bill, just keyed in his PIN and left a couple of notes on the table as he ushered Amy out.

They walked to the car in silence, hand in hand, and he drove home as fast as was sensible.

The house was quiet when they got in, a note on the kitchen table. 'All well. Josh is in with us. Sleep well.'

He met her eyes, slid his fingers through hers and led her upstairs to his room. There wasn't a sound in the house except the ticking of the clock, and he closed the door of his room and turned to Amy in the moonlight.

'Come here,' he said gruffly, and wrapped her in his arms, his mouth coming down on hers tentatively, searchingly. He hadn't kissed her since the wedding, not like this, and he wasn't entirely sure of how she'd react. It was still only weeks since Josh's birth, and although she seemed well...

He needn't have worried. She slid her arms around his neck, leant into him and kissed him back with the pent-up longing of all those years without him, and with a groan of satisfaction he let instinct guide him and plundered her mouth with his.

She stopped him after a moment, easing away and looking up at him regretfully. 'Matt, we can't. What if I get pregnant?'

He smiled. 'Don't worry. My brother's a good boy scout. I checked his bedside locker. They've just been to stay.'

'And?'

'And I may have raided it.'

She smiled back, her lips parting on a soft laugh and her eyes creasing. 'Well done,' she said, and went back into his arms.

'So how do you feel about coming back to London to live with me?'

She was propped up against the headboard feeding Joshua, Matt beside her with his arm around her shoulders, and she turned her head and met his eyes.

'It sounds lovely. I'll miss being near Ben and Daisy, but it's not far from them, we can see them often.'

'We can. They're talking of selling both houses and buying something bigger, so we'll be able to go and stay, and I'm sure we can squeeze them in here. And if you really want to work, I'm sure we can find room in the department for another midwife for a few shifts a week—especially if her name's Mrs Walker.'

She went still and searched his eyes. He was smiling, but his eyes were serious and thoughtful. 'I might want to keep my maiden name,' she said, fishing hard because she wasn't quite sure, and the smile spread to his eyes.

'They'll all gossip about us.'

'How will they know?'

'Because I can't keep my hands off you?' he murmured, and she laughed softly.

'Really, Mr Walker, that's so unprofessional.'

'I like to keep tabs on my staff.'

'Well, just make sure you're only keeping those sort of tabs on one member of staff, please,' she scolded, and he chuckled and hugged her closer.

'Absolutely. So—is that a yes?'

'Was that a proposal?'

He smiled wryly. 'I've already asked you once. And I haven't got a ring to give you.'

'I've still got the one you gave me. It's in my jewellery box, with Samuel's scan photo.'

His lips parted, and he let his breath out slowly and hugged her. 'Oh, sweetheart. I thought you would have sold it.'

'Why would I do that?'

He shrugged. 'To fund your trip to India?'

She smiled sadly. 'I could never have sold it, and I didn't need much money in India. All I did was walk along beaches and sleep under the stars and think.'

'On your own? That doesn't sound very safe.'

'I didn't care about safe, Matt, and it didn't cost a lot which was good, because I didn't have much. But I would never have sold your ring. It would be like selling part of myself.'

He picked up her hand, stroking her ring finger softly, his heart pounding. 'Will you wear it for me again?'

'You could ask me again, just so I know you mean it.'

'I just did, and you know I mean it, Amy,' he said, and then gave a rueful laugh and gave up. He wasn't going to get away with it, obviously, but he wasn't going down on one knee. That would mean letting her go and he didn't plan on doing that any time soon, so he shifted so he was facing her, still holding her hand, his eyes locked with hers.

'I love you, my darling, and I want to spend my life with you, and with Josh and any other children that might come along in due course, and I want to grow old with you, so you can trim the hair in my ears and buy me new slippers for Christmas and remind me of where I've left my glasses. So will you marry me? Share your life with me? I'll put your tights on for you when you can't bend over any more, and I promise I won't steal your false teeth.'

She started to laugh, but then her eyes filled with tears and she rested her head on his shoulder and sighed. 'That sounds lovely. So lovely.'

'Even the false teeth and the hair in my ears?' he laughed.

'I'll buy you one of those gadgets. And that's a yes, by the way. I'd love to marry you, as soon as you like, but—can we have a quiet wedding? Just family and a few friends.'

'Sure. Where?'

'Here? In the church where we were going to get married before? And maybe—if we got married on a Saturday, perhaps we could have Josh christened there on the Sunday, while the others are around?'

'That sounds lovely,' he said softly. 'In fact, if you want, maybe the vicar could say a few words before the service, to remember Samuel.'

Her eyes flooded with tears. 'Oh, yes. Oh, Matt, that would be—'

She broke off and he hugged her. 'Shh. Don't cry any more, my love. It's going to be all right.'

'Yes. Yes, it is.' She looked down at Josh, fast asleep at her breast, and smiled tenderly.

'It's all going to be all right.'

The wedding took place in September, on the anniversary weekend of Ben and Daisy's wedding, in the family's little parish church outside Harrogate. It was decorated with flowers from the lady who'd sold them the posy they'd taken to the cemetery, and it looked lovely.

So did Amy.

She was wearing a simple, elegant cream dress—not a wedding dress, because she'd refused to go down that route, and he hadn't wanted to argue with her. Not about their wedding. All he was doing this time was listening. And when he saw her as she walked towards him on his father's arm, carrying a posy of those lovely, natural flowers, Matt thought he'd never seen anyone more beautiful.

It was a short service, but heartfelt, and afterwards they took everyone to the restaurant for a meal to celebrate.

The staff had opened the restaurant specially for the afternoon, and it was a meal to remember. They pulled out all the stops, and the food was amazing, but there were not supposed to be any speeches. Matt said he wasn't going to give Ben a chance to get back at him, but there was some good-natured rivalry and a lot of love, and in the end Ben had his way.

'I don't have a lot to say,' he began, which made Matt laugh so hard he had tears running down his face, but

Ben waited him out with a patient smile, and then he started again.

'I just wanted to say how much this means to all of us, to see the two of you together again. I'm not going to make any cruel jokes about what a lousy brother you've been, because you haven't. You've supported me through some pretty tough times, and I wish I could have done more for you, but I don't suppose anyone could. However, I can take credit for bringing you to-gether again a year ago tomorrow, even if you didn't appreciate it at the time, and the consequences are de-lightful!'

At that point Josh gave a shrill squeal and banged his rattle on the table in front of Liz, and everyone laughed.

'So, no bad jokes, just a few words to wish you well, and to say how glad we all are that this day has come for you at last. Ladies and gentlemen, can we please raise our glasses to Matt and Amy!'

'Matt and Amy!' they chorused, and Matt leant over and planted a lingering kiss on her lips. It was full of promise, and the smile in his eyes warmed her to the bottom of her heart.

They went back to the farmhouse for the night. As usual they were in Matt's room with Josh, with Ben and Daisy next door with Thomas, and Amy lay there in Matt's arms in blissful contentment.

'All right, my darling?' he murmured, and she made a soft sound of agreement and snuggled closer.

'It was a lovely day.'

'It was. You looked beautiful in that dress.'

She tipped her head and searched his eyes in the moonlight. 'It was only a simple little shift dress.'

'It was elegant and understated, and you looked amazing.'

She smiled. 'Thank you. You looked pretty amazing yourself, and Josh was so good. I was sure he'd scream all through the service.'

She saw his lips twitch. 'He's probably saving that for tomorrow, for the vicar.'

He wasn't. Josh and his cousin Thomas were both as good as gold for their christening, and the vicar remarked on how alike they were.

'It'll be hard to tell the difference between these two,' he said with a smile as he handed Josh back to Amy.

'No, it won't,' they all chorused, and then laughed. He was right, they were very alike, but there were differences, more so than between Ben and Matt, and to their parents and grandparents the differences were obvious.

They filed out into the sunshine, and Matt and Amy hung back behind the others for a moment, Josh squirming in Matt's arms.

'OK?'

She nodded. 'It was lovely. Just right.'

It had been. Before the ceremony, the vicar who'd married them had asked for a few moments of silence while they remembered Samuel.

They hadn't cried. Their tears had been shed, their love was stronger, and they were looking forward to their future together. It might not be untroubled, but it would be shared every step of the way, and whatever happened, they would always know that they were truly loved.

What more could they possibly ask for?

'Come on, you two, or we'll eat all the cake!' Ben yelled, and Matt laughed.

'He's not joking. Come on.'

And putting his arm round Amy and drawing her in close to his side, he walked her out of the churchyard with a smile...

* * * * *

BETWEEN THE LINES

LAUREN HAWKEYE

To Patience, for her patience

CHAPTER ONE

Then

HE ALWAYS GOT what he wanted...except when it came to this woman.

Theo Lawrence groaned with something akin to pain as she arched her hips into him, her soft, heated flesh rubbing against his aching cock. He fisted his hands in the front of her thin, ribbed tank top, yanking the fabric up to expose her small breasts, the nipples rosy red from his fingers.

"Don't stop." Pressing her lips into the corded muscle of his neck, Jo Marchande dug her fingers into his shoulders until it hurt, sparking deeper need to life inside him. All the while, her hips rocked restlessly, teasing the rock-solid erection that was straining at the stiff denim of his jeans. "Please don't stop."

"You're killing me." He didn't want to stop—oh fuck, how he didn't want to stop. He'd never loved anyone in his life the way he loved her, and not being able to be inside her was exquisite agony.

The one decent thing he'd done in his life, however, was to keep his hands off his underage girlfriend. He loved her—loved her family—far too much than to disrespect them by taking her before she could possibly be ready.

It was the hardest thing he'd ever done. Especially when she was dead set on making him change his mind.

"You don't have to hold back." Hand sliding down between them, she rubbed her palm over his arousal. His erection jerked in response, angry at being confined to its denim prison. "You know you don't. I want this. Want you."

"Not while you're still seventeen." His words were strained. He tugged her shirt higher still, and she took the opportunity to rub her breasts against his chest, heating his skin to a feverish pitch. "It's not right."

"You're only two years older than me." Her voice was stubborn. This was nothing new—his girl was nothing if not determined. Single-minded. He admired it in every aspect of her life.

Except for this one.

"And two years won't be a big deal when you're

eighteen," Theo growled against the top of her head. He inhaled the scent of her shampoo, straight spicy mint, something he'd never be able to smell again in his life without being aroused. "Tomorrow. We can wait one more day."

In Massachusetts, the age of consent was sixteen. It damn near killed him to do it, but he was making them wait until eighteen. It just seemed like the right thing to do.

"No." That stubborn streak in her voice thickened, and she dipped a finger inside his waistband. She swiped over the swollen head of his cock, and he groaned when a droplet of liquid leaked out in response.

"Jo." Drawing on every last ounce of strength that he had, he forced himself to take a deep breath, pulling back and putting a single precious inch of strength between them. It wasn't much, but it allowed him to inhale without the smell of her skin sinking into the very cells of his being. "It's not happening. You know me well enough to know that I don't change my mind."

"I'm not asking you to." He looked down into her face, the one he'd known since they were kids. Mischief was sparkling in her storm-gray eyes, bubbling up through the thick haze of lust.

"You're going to have to use smaller words." Dipping his head, he pressed a soft kiss to her forehead, then trailed his lips down over her cheek-bone. "All of my blood has flooded south of my brain. Far south."

She laughed breathlessly, and he felt the exhalation, warm as it teased over his chest. "I'm not asking you to change your mind. But I *am* asking you to…to fuck me."

His mouth went instantly dry, his cock surging forward, cheering at her words. Her dirty words, her innocent tone belying them, were rapidly bringing him to the absolute edge of no return.

"I'm not sure you know what it does to me, hearing that sweet little mouth of yours talking about such filthy things." Releasing her tank top with one hand, he dragged it up, up until he could rub his thumb over her kiss-swollen lips. In response, she swiped her tongue over it, then sucked it into her mouth, showing what she wanted to do to another part of him.

What they both wanted her to do.

"I'm going to do more than talk about it," she insisted. Slowly, slowly, she started to work at his belt, the sound of metal on metal one of the most erotic things he'd ever heard. "Haven't you figured it out yet?"

"Jojo," he exhaled, running the tip of his tongue over the seam of her lips. She parted them beneath him, and he licked inside. "No more teasing. What are you talking about?"

"I'm not seventeen anymore." She grinned up at him triumphantly. Blood suffused her pale, creamy skin, camouflaging the golden freckles that he knew were there. "It's after midnight, Theo. And I know exactly what I want for my birthday."

Holy shit. Releasing her long enough to look at his watch, he watched as the numbers turned over from 12:02 to 12:03.

She was right. She was eighteen now. And with that knowledge, his noble intentions melted like sugar in a hot pan, becoming something even better.

He growled in response. He'd made it. And now there was nothing holding him back from sinking between those pale, pretty thighs that had taunted him for so incredibly long.

"Put your arms around my neck," he demanded. She cried out when he palmed her ass, lifting her so that she could wrap her legs around his waist. Again, the heat of her sweet core taunted his cock, but it was different now.

Now it just spurred him on because finally, *finally*, he could touch her the way they'd both wanted him to for the last year—the longest year of his life.

"I can't believe we're finally doing this," she

gasped as he carried her to the foot of the bed. Sliding her down his body, he set her down on her feet, then again fisted his hands in the front of her thin cotton tank top.

"I can." He grinned wickedly as he tugged. Jo exhaled harshly as her shirt ripped down the front. For a split second he felt bad—he'd ruined her shirt, and her family didn't have a lot of money.

But when she looked up at him, there was no judgment in her eyes, just raw need.

He'd buy her a new shirt—he'd buy her anything she wanted, if she'd let him. Heaven knew he could afford it. Right now, though, the last thing he wanted was for her to start thinking about the differences between their lives—the one point of contention between them.

Right now he didn't want her thinking of anything. He just wanted her to feel.

"Hold still." He whispered the words into her ear, savored the resultant shiver. She was nervous, and he didn't mind that.

By the time they were done, she'd be too lost in sensation to worry about anything.

He palmed her breasts, running his thumbs roughly over her distended nipples. She rarely wore a bra. She claimed that her breasts were too small to need the support. He didn't care what size they were, because to him they were just perfect.

And the lack of bra gave him easier access to heaven. Who would complain about that?

Her breath hitched when his fingers worked at the button of her low-slung jeans. The denim was worn, the fastening giving way easily. Hooking his thumbs in the waistband, he worked the garment down her slim hips until it fell to the floor. She was left in nothing but a pair of flimsy blue cotton briefs, hardly a barrier to the sweet heat between her legs.

"Lie down on the bed." She did as he told her, scooting back until her head was cushioned on the pillows of his bed. Her slim, pale figure stood out in stark contrast to the deep sapphire-blue of his linen duvet, and he knew that he'd never look at his bed the same way again.

He watched as she propped herself up on her elbows, her avid stare fixed on him. Her lips, swollen from his kisses, parted unconsciously as he undid the buttons on his expensive dress shirt, leaving it hanging open as he pulled his leather belt from his jeans. He was so hard that it was nearly painful, and yet he savored the bite of discomfort before popping the button and allowing the heavy length of his cock to breathe, his swollen length clearly outlined against his underwear.

"Oh." On the bed, Jo's entire body flushed. She ran her tongue over her lips, and he barely suppressed a groan as he imagined those lips swallowing him deep.

"You've felt me before." He'd stuck to his rule, no sex until she was eighteen, but that didn't mean they hadn't touched. But this was the first time she'd seen him naked, and he felt a strange surge of pride at her hungry gaze.

He wasn't a virgin, but nothing turned him on like knowing that she'd chosen him to introduce her to this kind of pleasure. It was a heavy responsibility, but he knew he was up to the task.

"I know," she whispered, her words rasping against the still air of his room. "But I've never really thought about…you know…how it's going to fit."

Theo closed his eyes, his head falling back. What had he done in his life to deserve her?

He hadn't done anything, but he wasn't that noble.

"It'll fit," he promised, shoving his jeans down his hips. He stepped out when they fell to the floor, then rubbed a hand over his erection, which tented the front of his black briefs.

Jo groaned, shifting restlessly on the bed. The sight of her arousal dampening the tender skin of her inner thighs was nearly his undoing.

Quickly, he shed his shirt, then let his briefs fall to the floor. He stood before her naked, and though he wanted to pounce on her and bury his face between her thighs, he forced himself to hold still, letting her look her fill.

He knew what she saw when those inquisitive gray eyes looked him over. He was tall, a good half a foot taller than her five foot six. He was also more than a little vain, and he started every day in the gym on the third floor of the house he shared with his father. He may not have had the drive for school or business that his dad had hoped to see in his offspring, but he never missed a session with his weights.

Because of that, his body was chiseled and solid as a rock, and he'd shared that body with more than a few girls before he'd finally convinced Jo to date him. He knew that girls liked his abs, his cock, and even the fact that his skin was dark gold and his hair nearly black, his coloring thanks to the Brazilian mother who had died when he was a baby.

Yeah, he knew he was a good-looking guy. And that plus his family money meant that he'd never been hard up for someone to warm his bed.

But he'd never, ever wanted anything more than what he had right now—Jo Marchande in his bed, wanting him.

He had to make this good.

"Spread your legs." He clasped her ankles in long fingers, rubbing his thumb over the tender skin at the inside of each. She shuddered, then gasped when he tugged, pulling her to the edge of the bed. Kneeling on the plush carpet that covered his bedroom floor, he hooked her legs over each of his shoulders, opening her wide. Exposing that part of her that he craved.

"Theo… I've never…" Jo squirmed, her heels digging into his back. "I don't know how to do this."

"You don't have to do anything except take what I give you." Beneath his avid stare, the thin cotton of those panties grew wet. He traced it with a finger, circling the hard bud of her clit, and she shuddered in response.

He pressed his lips to the supple skin on the inside of her thigh, just above the curve of her knee. Her quick exhale told him that she was trying desperately to hold her breath. That she was nervous.

Knowing that the nerves would only help to heighten her pleasure, he slid his lips up only the barest inch, determined to draw out the sensations for her. She shifted, and he could feel her heat, smell her arousal.

Trailing his lips farther up her thigh, he teased them both by trailing his tongue over the crease that divided her leg from her abdomen. She jerked beneath his mouth with a breathless laugh.

"Liked that, did you?" He repeated the motion,

and she groaned. He slid his mouth up even more, closer to his goal, savoring the salt on her skin.

"Theo," she breathed as he brushed his lips over the soaked fabric of her panties. "Oh God. I can't—"

"Oh yes, you can." He flicked his tongue over the cotton, and her hips lifted off the bed.

"I've waited so long for this." Nuzzling his nose against her heat, he hooked his fingers into the waistband of her simple underwear. Not wanting to take the time to pull them all the way off, he pulled hard and grinned when they ripped, allowing him to toss them aside.

She didn't give him hell for destroying a second item of her clothing, just rocked from side to side on the cool sheets of his bed. He took a moment to simply look at the glistening pink of her center, hot and wet and all for him.

Jo groaned. This was the only time she got quiet, his girl—when she was aroused. It made him want to drive her so crazy that she got loud again.

It made him want to make her scream his name.

Inhaling her scent, which reminded him of some kind of exotic cinnamon, he leaned forward and swiped his tongue through her folds.

"Oh my God," she breathed, arching up off the bed. He licked again, and she tried to close her legs against the onslaught of sensation, but he was there, the width of his shoulders holding her wide-open.

With long, slow swipes of his tongue, he licked her from bottom to top, brushing the flat of his tongue over the hard nub of her clit every time. She tasted so sweet, and he wanted more.

Using his thumbs, he parted her lips, focusing his attention on the swollen bud. Her heels began to drum into his back, her breath coming in gasps.

"Theo. I can't. It's too much." He could tell that her arousal was spiking hard and high. She didn't have much experience—hell, *any* experience—and he knew that it wouldn't take much to send her over.

That was good. He was going to make her come now, and then again. He was going to make sure that she was so ready for him that when it came to the part that might hurt, she would simply melt around him like ice cream left in the hot, hot sun.

CHAPTER TWO

"THAT'S IT, BABY GIRL." Using one finger, he traced around her slick opening, barely dipping inside. She groaned, arching her back, pressing herself against his mouth greedily. "Let go. I've got you."

"Theo!" She bucked against his mouth as he increased the flicks of his tongue against her clit. Her thighs started to shake, and then her entire body tightened as her pleasure overtook her.

He buried his face between her legs as she came, kissing her now with broad swipes of his tongue. Her words were unintelligible, and when he looked up the slim column of her body, he saw her face flushed the prettiest shade of pink, her eyes closed, her mouth parted for the breathy little pants she didn't seem able to help.

Before the waves stopped battering at her, he pressed a kiss to her inner thigh, then gently moved her legs from where they were clenched around his ears. She lay panting on the bed as he crawled up beside her, placing one hand on the dip of her impossibly slender waist.

He watched as she opened her eyes, fascinated by the glints of auburn in the mink-colored lengths of her lashes. Beneath them, those stormy gray eyes were glittering with need, and he knew, he just knew, that his dirty girl already wanted more.

"Did you like that?" He brushed his lips over the shell of her ear, nipping at the lobe. She nodded frantically but remained silent.

Squeezing her hip, he splayed his palm over the flat, quivering plane of her belly.

"What was that?" Chuckling as she garbled something in response, he slid his hand down, dipping between her legs. "I didn't understand. I guess I'll just have to check for myself."

Her hands fisted in the quilt as he used his fingers to do what his tongue just had. Pinching her clit lightly, quickly, he waited until she moaned, then slid a finger into her waiting heat.

She was wet, and tight, and if she felt like fucking heaven on his finger, then what would she feel like around his cock?

"More," Jo whispered, and he realized that she'd gone still. She was waiting, he realized, for it to hurt.

He didn't want it to hurt.

"Are you sure?" She nodded, so he worked his finger out slowly, then in and then out.

She hissed when he added a second, scissoring them the slightest bit to stretch her. He kept his gaze on her face, searching for any sign of discomfort. Instead, he saw raw, unadulterated need.

He would make this good for her.

Returning his attention to her clit, he caught it between his fingers and rubbed. Wetness slicked her folds, and within moments another keening cry slipped from between those pretty lips. He let her ride the wave of her second orgasm before reaching over her to his mahogany bedside table, removing a small foil packet from the drawer.

Her eyes widened a bit when she saw what he'd retrieved, and he watched the slim column of her throat as she swallowed thickly.

"Are you sure about this?" It just might kill him to stop right now, with her taste on his lips and her slickness on his fingers, but he would. He'd do pretty much anything for her.

"Don't you dare stop!" Rising up on her elbows, Jo caught his chin in her fingers and pulled him down for a kiss. She sucked in a surprised breath, and he knew that she was tasting herself on his lips.

The greedy noise that slipped from her mouth was the hottest fucking thing he'd ever heard.

With hands that were far less steady than any

other time he'd done this, he tore open the foil packet. Her curious eyes watched avidly as he removed the ring of latex, smoothing the sheath down over the length of his erection.

He hissed when she reached down and danced her fingers over his cock. God, he'd dreamed of this, of her hand on him, stroking him just like this.

Pleasure began to gather all the way down in the soles of his feet, and he jerked back with a rueful laugh.

"Did I do something wrong?" She sat up, eyebrows raised in alarm.

"Not at all." Catching her hand in his—the one that had just been stroking him—he pressed his lips to it in a kiss. "It was a little too good, actually."

"Oh." She drew out the word, understanding dawning. "Duly noted."

She smirked. What choice did he have but to kiss her?

They fell back down to the bed, the covers tangling around them. Rolling on top of her, he braced his weight on his arms on either side of her head, looking down into that face that he knew like he knew his own.

Jo Marchande wasn't classically pretty. Her face was a bit too square, her features too angular. Her milky-white skin stayed pale year-round, except for the times she got so absorbed in a book she was reading out in the sun that she didn't realize she was burning. The smattering of golden freckles stayed year-round, too, and he took a moment now to brush a kiss over them on each cheek.

It was her eyes that made people look at her twice. They were huge, a stunning gray that shifted with her mood, surrounded by lashes that she never bothered to tint with mascara. She never bothered with makeup at all, something he loved because it was so different from all of the other women he knew.

Her hair spread out around her head on the pillow as she returned his gaze steadily, the chestnut color adding warmth to that pale skin. No, she wasn't classically beautiful, but he wouldn't have changed a damn thing.

She was his.

"I love you." The words slipped from his lips before he could even think about what he was saying. Her mouth parted in surprise, but then he was burying his face in that long mane of hair, tucking his hand between her legs. She rocked up against him as he tested one more time that she was ready.

His fingers came away soaked.

"Theo, I—" The words got caught in her throat as he reached between them and lined the head of his cock up with the sweet, sweet heat of her center.

She gasped as he slid just the head of his erection into her slickness. He sank his teeth into his lower lip as nerves fired to life. It was everything he could do to hold still, letting her adjust to the feeling of him inside her.

He wasn't expecting her to grab onto his hips and rock herself up.

"Fuck," he cursed as he slid deeper into her soaking-wet channel. He wanted so badly to be in deep, to claim her from the inside out, but when the head of his cock met resistance, he had to force himself to still.

His limbs shaking with the exertion of holding back, he pressed his damp forehead against hers, looking right into her eyes. Their breath mingled, fanning out over their faces, and he kissed her again, their first kiss with him inside her.

"Are you ready?" He rocked back and forth the slightest bit, testing. She whimpered, but it was a sound of pleasure, not of pain.

"Hurry up." Her voice was greedy, her fingers eager as they dug into his ass. She pulled him closer, and he resisted for just one more minute before he pressed forward, the cock that was swollen past the point of pain pushing deeper.

Beneath him she winced, sinking her teeth

into her lower lip. He automatically stilled, but she urged him on with an impatient hiss.

Her body resisted him, clenching tightly until finally something gave way, allowing him to slide home. He grunted as he sheathed himself fully inside her, the sensation causing his eyes to roll back in his head.

"Holy shit," Jo whispered beneath him, looking up at him with eyes that were bright.

"It will only hurt for a minute. I promise." Theo rocked inside her, just a bit to test, and she moaned.

"It hurts, but not the kind you mean." Her hands moved from his ass to his hips, and she shifted impatiently beneath him. "It hurts because I don't even know what this is, but I want it so bad. Please, Theo. Please. *Move.*"

The last strings of his self-control snapped. With small rocking motions, he pulled back, then worked his way back in. He'd never had anything so tight, so hot around his cock, and if he wasn't careful, he was going to lose it before he could make her feel good again.

She wouldn't let him be careful. She rocked beneath him, urging him to go faster and faster. Her tight sheath was swollen, pulling him back in again and again. The pleasure rose hot and fast, and sweat beaded on his forehead as he strained to hold back.

Slipping one hand between their bodies, he located her clit and focused his attention on it. At the same time, he dipped his head and sucked one of her puckered nipples into his mouth.

Beneath him she went taut as a bow. Her cleft tightened as her eyes went wild with pleasure yet again, and he felt his own release start, fire licking along every inch of his skin. Closing his eyes, he finally allowed himself to let go, to let himself revel in the fact that Jo Marchande, the strong, proud girl that he'd loved since the day they met, had given herself to him.

After, he pressed a kiss to her brow. Pulling out, he disposed of the condom, then slid back into the bed, tucking them both under his soft, expensive sheets. She was already drowsy when he tugged her against him, fitting his chest to her back.

"You okay?" He tucked a ribbon of hair behind her ear. She sighed, a small murmur of contentment that made his stomach do a small flip.

How was it possible that she was his? He'd never done anything to deserve having someone so wonderful in his life.

According to his father, he was lazy. He had no drive, no direction, no purpose in life. He was squandering the opportunities that he had. This, of course, was in direct contrast to Theodore Lawrence Sr., who owned a huge import-export company. His mother, famous in her native Brazil before her death, had been a world-renowned concert pianist.

He'd never live up to either of them, so he didn't bother to try. He knew what he was worth, and it wasn't much. So the fact that Jo Marchande, the woman who had imprinted herself into his very DNA, had deemed him worthy?

It wasn't something that he would ever take for granted.

"I've never been better." Casting a sleepy smile over her shoulder at him, she snuggled back into his arms. "Can I stay?"

His heart skipped a beat, sending his pulse skittering to catch up.

"You can stay." If he had his way, she'd stay forever.

"You just couldn't control yourself, could you?"

Theo stiffened, a steel rod snapping into place in his spine. Slowly, he turned, doing his best to look nonchalant as he leaned back against the endless expanse of marble countertop in the rarely used kitchen of the house he shared with his father.

"What am I lacking control in this time, exactly?" His voice was cold when he spoke, every trace of the warmth he'd had for Jo frozen into daggers of ice, meant to maim or at the very least protect. "You have such a long list, you'll forgive me for not immediately understanding what it is that you're referring to, this time."

"You know exactly." His father stepped out of the shadows and into the dim kitchen, leaning against the breakfast bar, his stance mirroring Theo's own. He lifted his heavy crystal snifter of expensive scotch for a small sip. His gaze slid over the matching one in his son's hand, but as per usual, he said nothing about the fact that Theo was drinking, even though he wasn't yet twenty-one.

Theo knew that, at the end of the day, Theodore Sr. just didn't care.

"I assume you're referring to Jo." The words were sour in his mouth. He hated even saying her name right now, not wanting to cast shadows on something that, to him, was so perfect. So theirs.

"Of course I'm referring to Jo." His father's voice was layered heavily with impatience. "They are family friends. They are our neighbors. They are good people."

Theo said nothing. What was there to say?

"You have nothing to offer any of them," his father continued. The utter contempt in his voice was clear. "You've disappointed me time and again, Theodore, but I thought that you at least had the morals to stay away from those girls. Shame on you."

It shouldn't have hurt, but it did. Theo took a hefty swallow of his drink, focusing on the fire that it left as it traveled down to his gut. Taking a moment to study his father—the man he'd come from—he wondered how a person could seem to detest someone who had come from them so very much.

Ha. Why was he even questioning that? He knew exactly what his father saw—he saw his lost wife. Theo had inherited his golden skin, his exotic features, his glossy black hair, even the charm that he used regularly, from his mother.

Theo knew that, if given a choice, his father would rather have his mother here in his place.

"Did you hear what I said, boy?" Theodore Sr. set his glass down on the polished countertop with a sharp crack. The hand not holding Theo's own glass fisted in the thick velvet of his robe, kneading at it like a stress ball.

"Jo and I have been dating for over a year." Theo tried to rein in his temper. "It's not like I plan on sleeping with her and leaving the next day."

"You shouldn't be sleeping with her at all," his father snorted with derision, shaking his head. "What if you got her pregnant? You really think you could make a go of it? You'd run right out the door, and then where would she be?"

Theo expected nothing less from his dad, but

hearing the harsh words was still a lash from a whip. *He* knew he'd do no such thing, but hearing out loud what his own flesh and blood really thought of him reminded him of the worst hangover he'd ever had. Try as he might, he just couldn't ever outrun the nagging pain.

"Have a nice night, Dad." Draining the last of his scotch in one giant swallow, he left the kitchen through the servants' door, preferring the longer route back to his room to going anywhere near his father.

The conversation they'd just had was nothing new. Often he was able to completely deflect the criticism, keeping the barbs from landing and piercing his skin.

Tonight, though? Some of those words had landed.

He loved Jo more than anything. But what if his father was right?

CHAPTER THREE

"Happy birthday, dear Joooo, happy birthday to you."

"Cake! Gimme." Standing up in her seat, Jo reached for the tower of cupcakes that Mamesie had so painstakingly arranged on the antique silver platter. Grabbing the one with the most frosting, she sank her teeth into the decadent chocolate cake, shuddering with pleasure when the sweetness of the icing hit her tongue.

"I'm hurt." Warm breath misted over her ear, and she made a sound low in her throat. "I thought I was the only one who could pull that sound out of you. Yet here you are, cheating on me with a cupcake."

"Sorry, babe." Turning in his arms, she tuned out the chatter of her mother and three sisters as she focused in on Theo. Thinking about what they'd done last night had a fizzy feeling bubbling up inside her, making her feel like she'd drunk a giant glass of champagne too fast. "The cupcake offers instant gratification. Unlike someone I can think of, who made me wait an entire year."

"It was worth waiting for, though, wasn't it?" His voice was a low rumble against her ear. And even though she was still sore, she felt molten heat gather between her thighs. "At least, you seemed to think so this morning when you were moaning my name."

She uttered another small moan at that. Putting space between them before she shoved the cupcakes off the table and pulled him down for another round, she tucked another bite of cupcake in her mouth as a distraction.

"I know you're trying to change the topic, but I don't think it's working the way you hoped." Jo sucked in a sharp breath as Theo's stare tracked the way her tongue was licking sprinkles off the top of the cupcake. "I can think of a lot of places that would look awfully pretty with a bit of white icing on them."

"Stop it!" Elbowing him, Jo took another deliberate step away, conscious of the fact that her family was right there. But when she looked around, Mamesie had gone into the kitchen for plates, and her sisters Beth and Amy were fully occupied by their own pieces of cake, still being young enough to have their attention fully commanded by the promise of sugar.

Her older sister, Meg, though, cast her a wink before handing her a napkin. Even if she hadn't heard what was said, it was obvious that she knew that something had changed with her little sister. In response, Jo felt her cheeks heat.

"I need to use the bathroom." Giving Theo's hand a little squeeze, she swallowed the last bite of her cupcake and excused herself. She headed upstairs to the bathroom she shared with Amy rather than the small powder room on the main floor.

She splashed icy-cold water on her face, which felt good but did nothing to fade the flush on her cheeks. How was it possible that she wanted Theo again already? Did that *wanting* ever stop?

Wanting to give her telltale blush time to fade before she returned downstairs—Mamesie was no idiot, but Jo still wasn't keen on the idea of flaunting her newfound sexuality in front of her mother—Jo wandered down the hall to her bedroom. Her laptop sat open on the slab of plywood and two sawhorses she used as a desk, flashing a retro screen saver of different shapes made of neon lines, undulating around the screen. Yellow legal pads clumped in haphazard piles around the computer, most covered in her messy scrawl.

The keyboard beckoned. She still had a thousand words to go on her latest story. It was just a little article for the local paper, something she submitted every couple of weeks, but for every article that they published, she received a check for a hundred dollars. It wasn't much, but she loved the process of sealing that check in the crisp white envelope, of feeding it into the bank machine to deposit it into her account.

Mamesie had raised her, Meg, Beth and Amy by herself, and while they certainly no longer had access to some of the finer things that they'd had when her dad had been alive, she knew that Mamesie would never accept money from her girls—not unless the situation were truly dire. So Jo tucked away what she could. She didn't dare to dream too big, but maybe one day she could take some journalism courses. Learn a way to apply her writing to a career, when she'd saved enough.

She reread what she'd written earlier while she waited for her body to calm the hell down. Pulling out the creaky desk chair that she was pretty sure bore a permanent imprint of her butt, she rolled up to her laptop and started clicking through.

"What are you doing up here?" She had no idea how long it had been when Theo spoke from the doorway, scaring the shit out of her. She jolted, her elbow sliding over the keys of her keyboard.

Swearing, she hurriedly pressed the back arrows to restore her work.

"I came up to cool off a bit after you got me all hot and bothered," she replied, her gaze veering back to her screen. She was almost at the end. She was pretty sure she only needed a couple more sentences, and they were right there, fresh in her head…

"It's your birthday party." Theo frowned at her computer as he entered her room, closing the door behind him with the heel of his shoe—his fancy, hand-tooled, Italian leather shoe. Jo didn't pay any attention to fashion, none at all, but her sister Meg did, and she was forever sighing over the gorgeous things that the Lawrences had.

Things the Lawrences had. Things the Marchandes did not. Neither family talked about it, but the difference in their positions in life was always there, the elephant in any room in which members of both families had gathered.

At least, it was always there for Jo. It hadn't been, not always—back when her dad had been alive, they'd enjoyed a lot of the same privileges that the Lawrences had. She knew that Theo and his dad couldn't have cared less that there was now a class difference between their families, but it also meant that when it came to certain things, like money, Theo especially just didn't understand.

"Are you working?" Hastily Jo tried to close out of her document, but when she looked up and saw the puzzled expression on his face, she knew that he'd seen. "Why are you hiding up here working when everyone is downstairs waiting for you?"

"I told you. I came up here to cool off a bit." She could hear the defensiveness in her voice and pulled in a deep breath. "I read a few lines of my article and got sucked in."

"Well, come back down." He reached for her hand. "It's present time. Amy's about to pee herself, she's so excited."

Jo started to rise, but something about the way he was being so insistent had her hackles rising. Lowering herself back to her chair, she crossed her arms over her chest, the movement stiff. "Tell them I'll be down in ten minutes. I just have a few more lines to finish."

"Forget the lines, babe." Theo's smile was charming, deadly when he aimed it at you, but Jo had known him long enough that she could steel herself against it—well, sometimes. "It's your birthday. Finish them another time."

"I can't." Her eyes narrowed—why was he pushing? "My deadline is tonight. I should have handed the piece in already."

"Does it really matter?" Clearly confused, Theo waved a sure hand through the air—the lord in his manor. "Blow off the deadline. I don't see what the big deal is."

"The big deal is that they're counting on me to hand the piece in. If I don't, they have to scramble to find something else for that spot." Jo's voice was incredulous—why was this so hard for Theo to understand? "And also, if I don't hand the article in, I don't get paid."

"They pay you peanuts. What's the point?" Theo reached for her hands again, and this time instead of just avoiding him, she swatted them away. Rising from her chair, she stood to face him, clenched fists growing sweaty at her sides.

"A hundred dollars is not peanuts." Her voice was shaking. Damn it, Theo knew—he *knew*— that this job was important to her. "I'm saving it for school, and you know it."

"Well, a hundred dollars isn't anything to me." He shrugged dismissively, and Jo felt the bottom drop out of her stomach. "Just…please. Just forget about the article. I'll give you the hundred dollars, okay? Just please come back downstairs so that I can give you your birthday present."

For a long moment she was speechless. She actually kind of felt like throwing up.

She and Theo had their differences, but she *loved* him. She'd given him her body. Her heart.

And here he was pushing her to forget something that meant the world to her, just so he could get his way right now.

"You think I'm going to take money from you?" Horrified, Jo rubbed her hands over the hips of her jeans, trying to ease the clamminess. "After what we just did last night, how do you think that makes me feel?"

Understanding dawned on his face—at least, the tiniest inkling of it. "No, no. Jo, Jojo, that's not what the money is for. Please—"

"No, of course it's not." Damn it, she was shouting. This was nothing new for her, not with her temper, but she couldn't ever remember feeling exactly like this, sickness mixed in with the growing rage. "The money is so that I will ignore what I have repeatedly told you that I want right now, on my own damn birthday, and so that I will go do what you want. Lord Lawrence gets his way yet again."

"Don't call me that." A dangerous spark flickered through Theo's eyes. Lord Lawrence was what they'd all called him when he'd been younger and acting like a bit of a brat. "You know I fucking hate that."

"Sucks, doesn't it," Jo taunted, finding a sick pleasure in getting some kind of reaction out of him. "When someone ignores what you've repeatedly said you want so that they can do what they want instead."

"Wait a minute." Theo suddenly stood up ram-rod straight. He scrubbed his hands over his face before looking back at Jo. "You're not talking about last night. Please tell me you're not talking about last night."

"Jesus Christ, Theo." An inarticulate scream burst from her throat. "No, I'm not fucking talk-ing about last night. If I hadn't wanted your hands on me, you would have bloody well known it."

"Right. I know," he replied hastily, his rest-less hands now moving to rake through his hair. "You're just so mad. And if we're just talking about the article…"

If we're just talking about the article, then I don't know what the hell you're so worked up about.

Her mouth, the mouth she'd used all over his body not twenty-four hours earlier, fell open with disbelief. Theo's indifference to the gifts he'd been given had been a bone of contention between them before, but it had been…a small bone. A fish bone. Something that a sweet smile from him could help send into the garbage disposal.

This? This was a dinosaur drumstick, too big to be ground down in the kitchen sink.

"Look, I shouldn't have done that." Theo spoke

hastily, trying to smooth over what he'd said. "That was wrong. Let's not fight on your birthday."

"Are you saying that because you're actually sorry?" Resentment was bitter on her tongue. "Or are you saying it so that you get your way?"

She watched, almost as if she'd stepped outside herself, as temper flared in those caramel-colored eyes. Copper fire—that was what it looked like.

"Why are you acting this way?" He bit his words out the way he always did when he was angry, as though it took more effort to form them. "I just wanted to spend your birthday with you."

"That's not an answer." He growled in response, actually fucking growled, and took a step toward her. She held up both hands and thought she might even have hissed. They'd been reduced to animals in their fury, and she was really fucking tempted to bite him.

And not in a fun way.

"Get out of my room." Her voice was shaking. As she pointed at the door, she noticed that her hand was, too.

"What?" Incredulity lent an almost comical cast to his face. "Are you fucking serious right now?"

"I said get *out*!" she screamed, her voice echoing off the small confines of her room. Theo reeled back as if she'd slapped him, and her palm itched to do just that. He must have read the desire in her eyes, on her face, because his face reddened, the effect of his own temper, but he took a step back. With one last look, he spun on the heel of his ridiculously expensive shoes and stormed out of her room, slamming the door behind him. Minutes later, Jo felt the frame of the house shake as he slammed the front door as well. Crossing to her window, she hugged her arms to her chest and watched as Theo's tall, lanky figure strode across the lawn, climbing over the short fence that separated their properties, his movements jerky.

He would drink now, she knew that absolutely. He'd pull one of his dad's priceless bottles of scotch from the ornate liquor cabinet and numb everything he felt with the gilded liquid. He would retreat into a sullen cocoon, erecting the barriers that were his first line of defense.

He'd never erected those same barriers against her, but she knew him inside and out. And knowing him as she did, she saw with sudden, startling clarity that he truly wouldn't understand why she'd responded the way she had. Why she hadn't been able to just jump onboard Theo's Fun Train… because to him, responsibility didn't exist.

Knowing him the way she did, she wondered why she only now understood that this particular quirk of his meant that they were never, ever going to be able to work.

Acid churned in her belly as she sank down to the floor. It rose to her throat when Beth, the sister she was closest to, cracked open the door and stuck her head in, and she couldn't reply.

"We heard you guys yelling." Her sister's bright blue eyes were wide, meaning that she was as shocked by the argument as Jo was. "Are you okay?"

Jo looked up at her younger sister, the one she most often confided in, and felt the first small crack reverberate through her heart. Wordlessly, she held Beth's gaze and shook her head, just the smallest bit.

And when Beth crossed the room, sank to the floor beside her and wrapped Jo in her skinny tween arms, Jo burst into tears.

And that pissed her off, too.

CHAPTER FOUR

Then

THEO LAY SPRAWLED in the massive leather chaise that occupied the corner of his bedroom at one… or was it two in the morning? He lifted the bottle of scotch that he'd brazenly lifted from his dad's supply, squinting as he tried to discern just how much he'd had to drink.

He was pretty sure that the bottle had been full—a brand-new one, in fact. After the first couple of shots from a heavy crystal tumbler, though, he'd decided to forgo the glass and swig straight from the bottle. And then he'd spilled some on the floor in the hallway, leaving a sticky lake of amber liquid for the cleaners to find in the morning.

So basically…he had no idea. He knew he'd drunk a lot, but it wasn't having the effect he'd hoped for. The buzz he was chasing kept dancing just out of reach, and instead the alcohol was filling him with lead, weighing him down until he thought he might never move again.

"Why do you do this to yourself?"

He didn't have to move to know that Jo was standing in the doorway of his room. He caught a whiff of spicy cinnamon, heard her quiet sigh as she entered, closing the door behind her.

He remained motionless, listening as she moved around his room. She straightened his sheets, probably pulling down his covers for him. He tracked her footsteps to his bathroom, heard the tap and knew that she was getting him water and aspirin. Finally she closed the space between them, reaching out for the bottle he still held.

Because he was in the mood to be a dick, he held tight. He heard a grim hum from her lips, and then she smacked the bottom of the bottle, twisting it over in his grip and upending the contents onto his lap.

"Fucking hell, Jo!" Shocked into motion, he scrambled upright. A tight smirk of satisfaction was on that fascinating face of hers, and she simply stood back, arms crossed over her chest as he reached for the closest thing he could find, a sweatshirt, to mop up the liquid on his lap.

"I'm going to bed," he informed her. She didn't

move. He wasn't surprised. Damn it, what the hell was going on with her? All he'd wanted to do was make sure that she enjoyed her birthday. She didn't have to write those freaking articles. She'd just turned eighteen today—no one expected her to contribute. And if she was worried about money, he had plenty, and he was happy to share. So what the fuck was the problem?

"Theo." Her voice was a sigh again. He glared up at her as she pulled his footstool closer to his chair, lowering her small frame to a perch. "We need to talk."

He was just drunk enough that talking seemed like a horrible idea. As he looked at her sitting there, her pert, perfect breasts clearly outlined in the flimsy blouse that he knew Meg had made her wear for her party, he thought of something that sounded like a lot more fun than talking.

"C'mere." He gestured, overshooting and making his arm swing wildly. "I still need to give you your birthday kiss."

She closed her eyes, muttered something beneath her breath and then pinned him with thunder in those storm-gray eyes. "It's not sexy time, Theo. Sexy time is not on the menu anytime in the near future. Just sit up and answer something for me."

Theo rather thought that he could convince her on the sexy-time front if she gave it a fair shot, but the clipped quality of her voice finally sank through the scotch-soaked folds of his brain. Warily, he scooted to the edge of his seat, bracing his elbows on his knees and trying to look like he was sober.

From the grimace she made when she caught a whiff of his breath, he knew he wasn't fooling her. Sighing, he scrubbed a hand over his face, then gave her his full attention. "What do you need to say, Jojo?"

Her question was like a punch in the kidneys. "What are your plans, Theo?" He waited for her to elaborate, but she just waited for his response, her entire frame unnaturally still.

"You mean like…my plans for you?" Anxiety pitched his words higher than usual. He loved her, but wasn't it a little…soon…to have that talk?

"You are such a jackass," she muttered. He scowled, opening his mouth to reply, but she forged on. "No. Not your plans for us. Which, incidentally, would be *our* plans, but whatever."

His brain wasn't moving quite fast enough to keep up with that train, but he put all his energy into focusing so that he could catch her next sentence.

"I'm talking about you. Your plans for your own life. What are you doing with it? What do you even *want*?"

"I—" He paused, unable to verbalize the tangle in his head. "I don't—what do you mean?"

She studied him, the sharpening of her features making her appear faintly birdlike. Not like a sweet bird, though, he thought grumpily, like a canary or something. No, she was putting him more in mind of a raven, or a crow, maybe a hawk—something gorgeous and wild and more than a little bit dangerous.

"What I mean, Theo, is that you have so many opportunities. *So many.* More than anyone I know." When he didn't respond, she threw up her hands. "What I *mean* is…do you see yourself going into business with your father? You could, you know. He'd love that."

"Not bloody likely," Theo muttered, thinking of the nasty little altercation he'd had with Theodore Sr. last night.

Jo ignored him, plowing on. "What about school, then? You can afford to go anywhere. *Anywhere.* Doesn't that excite you, even a little bit?"

"Don't be stupid. There isn't a school in the world that would take me with my SAT scores." Theo snorted with disgust, making sure Jo didn't know that disgust was actually with himself. "College isn't an option."

"That's ridiculous." The glare she shot him was

like a laser beam, slicing right through to his core. "You can retake those any time you want."

"I can retake them, but I won't be any smarter." Shrugging as if he didn't care, he took another large swig from the scotch bottle. When he swallowed, the alcohol felt like acid in his gut, eating away at him from the inside out.

Jo threw her hands up in frustration. "You won't get any smarter if you won't freaking *try*, Theo. It's called studying. The people who get good SAT scores do it."

"Why are you on my case like this?" He couldn't handle even one more of her biting observations, because each one was like the lash of a whip, slicing away another sliver of his defenses. Soon he'd be left open, raw and bleeding, all of his insecurities out for her to see.

No one was allowed that close. Not even Jo.

"I'm on your case because I don't understand what's going through your thick skull." Her temper was up now, and so was her voice. "You have opportunities that some people only dream of, and you're throwing them all away because…what? You're just going to lounge around and drive your dad crazy forever?"

Theo stilled. "My dad treats me like shit. Since my mom died, he can't even look at me. You know that."

"You don't treat him any better!" Jo's harsh words reverberated off the walls of the room. "You might not get along, but he's still trying to help you make something of your life, and you thwart him at every turn!"

Theo had known that Jo had a temper since the second day of their acquaintance, when they'd gotten into a fight during an impromptu softball game and she'd accidentally beaned him with the bat when she'd thrown it in a rage. His anger management wasn't much better, though, and she'd just stuck a crowbar into his most tender parts and cranked it.

He fisted his hands at his sides, blood rushing to his head so fast that he felt dizzy.

"Thwart? Who actually says that in conversation?" he sneered, his words aimed to pierce her delicate skin. "I get it now. It's not that you *care*, that you're *worried* about me. It's that I have chances you don't, and it's driving you crazy!"

Jo's mouth fell open in disbelief, and her eyes were wild. "I've known you were a lazy prick with entitlement issues since the day we met, but stupid me, I thought you'd grown up a bit. But you never will, will you? You'll never figure out what you're going to do with your life, because you don't want to do anything!"

She sucked in a big breath before continuing.

"Your mom is the one who died, Theo! Not you! So why the fuck do you keep acting like you went with her?"

Theo couldn't think past the roaring in his ears. Grabbing her by the shoulders, he fought the urge to give her a shake. He'd never hit a woman in his life, and he didn't intend to start, but Josephine Marchande sorely tempted him to.

He growled, an unintelligible sound low in his throat. He had so much to say, to try to make her understand, but the words were stuck in his suddenly dry throat, choking him. He needed an outlet for the rage, the confusion, even the hurt that was storming through him, and Jo was safe. She'd always been safe.

Instead of shaking her stupid, he tugged her against him, crushing her lips against his. She shoved at his shoulder seconds before he felt a hint of the tension leave her body, her lips softening beneath his.

And then a stabbing pain as she sank those razor-sharp little teeth of hers into his lower lip.

"Motherfuck—" He reared back, clapping a hand to his injured lip. It came away bloody, but before he could utter another word, Jo followed the bite with a straight shot to his solar plexus.

His breath escaped his body in one giant cloud. Wheezing, he doubled over, sinking back into his chair, one arm around his stomach, the other pressed to his lip.

"What the actual fuck, Jo?" If she'd wanted to stop him in his tracks, she'd done it—he couldn't believe she'd hit him. He'd have been proud of her right hook if he didn't think there was a distinct possibility that he was going to vomit all over her bare feet. "What was that for?"

"Are you serious right now?" She laughed, but the sound was dry and harsh. "I can barely look at you right now, so you sure as fuck don't get to touch me."

"What?" He tried to focus on her face, but his head was spinning. "Jo. What?"

She sucked a breath in through her nose before jamming a finger right in front of his face. "You don't touch me unless I want to be touched. And you sure as hell don't try to kiss me when you're breaking my heart."

He watched, at a complete loss for words as she stepped back, putting some much-needed space between them. Crossing her arms over her chest, she started to shake, and when she looked back at him, her eyes were shiny and red, though not a single tear actually spilled.

Without another word, she turned and made her way to the door. She didn't slam it, didn't even close it—just left it hanging partway open like a wound that needed stitches but couldn't be closed.

He should call out. Go after her.

He couldn't. Wouldn't.

She'd cut him open, flayed his flesh, and he didn't know how to fix it. Didn't know if he could.

Instead, he sat motionless in his chair until the sun came up, warring with himself. He was furious with Jo, with his dad, with his dead mom, with himself. He was absolutely, utterly incapable of dealing with any of it.

When pale golden light began to filter through the paned glass of his window, he stood. Strode to his closet. Opened the small safe inside it, retrieving his passport, birth certificate and the stacks of cash that he kept just for the hell of it. Pulling a supple, chocolate-brown leather trench coat from his closet, he stuffed the retrieved items into the pockets and threw the coat over his shoulders.

By the time the sun was fully up, shining fat and high in the sky, Theo was gone.

CHAPTER FIVE

Now

THE NUMBER ONE question in my in-box? The biggest thing that readers want to know? It's how much of what I report on is something that I actually do. Yes, you filthy-minded little freaks want to know all the dirty details, and I know why...because if I've tried it, then you're not so weird if you do, too.

If you're waiting with bated breath for me to answer, you're going to have to keep on waiting. Why? Because I think that if you want to let your freak flag fly, you should find the guts to hoist it yourself. Color it with your own kinks, and don't be afraid to invite a partner...or three.

Now keep reading as I chat with Emma Muse, a cam girl with over six hundred thousand Instagram followers, about why so many women are

choosing to pleasure themselves on camera for
money, and why she thinks it's a viable career—
not to mention fun!
   Sluttily yours,
   Jojo Kink

Exhaling hugely, Jo sat back in her rickety desk
chair. Lacing her fingers together, she twisted
them outward, extending her arms and arching her
back in a giant stretch. She'd only been working
on this post for a couple of hours, but she'd been
so into it that she hadn't been paying attention to
her posture, and as the minutes had ticked by, she
hunched up tighter with every word that she typed.

Scrolling back up, she reread the introduction
and couldn't quite hold back her grin. The post was
good, and she wasn't one for false modesty, especially when she was alone in her bedroom with no
one to see her crow over it.

She knew that she could write. She'd been doing
it steadily for pay for years, which was a pretty
good sign that she wasn't a complete hack. But
after a seemingly endless period of churning out
things that other people wanted, writing about
something that interested *her* felt like she'd grown
a pair of giant, feathery wings.

Reading the post through one more time, she

made a few small edits before copying the text to her blog site, Jojo Kink. As it uploaded, she opened her blog's email in-box, scanning through the messages and the alerts of comments on her blog, which ranged from rapturous praise to things like *Die in hell, skank.*

Skank. Ha. If only they knew.

Checking the box that would allow her to delete everything with one click, she emptied her in-box, then blinked at the single message that slid in right after. Marked urgent, it carried the subject Job Opportunity.

"Oh, I just bet." She rolled her eyes and almost deleted this one, too. She received "job offers" every week, and most of them were invitations to meet up with very gracious gentlemen who were interested in letting her blow them. She mostly ignored them, but once in a while she skimmed over one of these fascinating missives and her temper— her Achilles' heel—would get the better of her. It never failed to amaze her how many men couldn't understand that no woman on this earth wanted an unsolicited dick pic. Actually, most didn't want a dick pic, period, but pointing that out usually just resulted in a flurry of them.

She was in the mood to argue, though, so she opened the email, bracing herself for a veiny close-up. She was surprised that, instead of an image of throbbing male genitalia, the email contained an actual message, complete with a website link.

To Ms. Kink,

My name is John Brooke; I'm a freelance business mentor currently working with the dating app Crossing Lines. We at Crossing Lines would like to meet with you to discuss the possibility of writing some blog posts for our site. We love your voice and think that you are just what we need to appeal to the female demographic.

    We would love to hear back from you, at your earliest convenience.

Sincerely,

John Brooke and the Crossing Lines team

"Say what?" Jo sat up straight as hummingbirds of excitement flocked through her veins. Clicking on the site link, she found herself staring at a logo that she actually knew. Crossing Lines had been everywhere lately—she was pretty sure her youngest sister, Amy, actually had a profile on it. Their advertising was slick—they clearly had a lot of money behind them.

    And they wanted *her*? How the hell had they found her blog, anyway? Her blog had decent traffic, but she was a medium-size fish in a gigantic pond.

"Who the hell cares?" She wasn't an idiot. This was huge. Palms suddenly slick with sweat, she scrambled to reply. John Brooke, whoever he was, must have still been in his email, because he came back again almost instantly, asking her if she had time to meet the next morning. When she agreed, he gave her an address close to the financial district in downtown Boston and told her they looked forward to meeting with her. She didn't have a clue who else was included in the *they*, but the thrill fizzing through her wouldn't let her care.

Shoving back from her desk, she closed her eyes and savored the moment. She could hear music coming from Beth's room, some kind of weird electro-pop that she normally couldn't stand, but right now it was perfect, and she did a little walk-dance of joy around her cramped room to the beat.

She'd been writing for years. *Years*. She'd started with the local paper, and her secret dream had been to go to journalism school. When her sister Beth had gotten sick, though, and the family had started to drown in debt, she switched tracks. Words were her skill set, so she searched out the best way to make quick cash from them. Her ghostwriting gigs—writing stories to spec for other people—had been what allowed them to stay in their grand old historic home, but she'd always felt like she lost a bit of herself when she signed away the rights to something that had come from within her.

Now Beth had hooked up with Ford, and while at first Jo had been certain he'd been using her little sister as a stroll through a kinky park, she now had to admit that he'd saved their asses, for no reason other than his love for Beth. His idea to build a small boutique hotel on part of their massive property had led to a source of viable income for their family, which meant that Jo could finally, finally, write whatever the hell she wanted.

She'd been surprised at how much she'd enjoyed ghostwriting erotic stories, and that was what had led to the idea for Jojo Kink. Researching and interviewing people about freaky sexual topics threw in that love of journalism and, it turned out, was just *fun*.

But writing for a big company didn't mean that she couldn't still blog—at least she hoped it didn't. And writing for a big company meant money. She brought in a bit through ads on her site, but a regular paycheck…

She couldn't even imagine what she'd do with that. She'd never had one.

Thinking of the hotel reminded her that Ford had organized a sneak-peek open house for

Marchande Boutique for that evening…and it was in just over an hour.

"Shit." Breathing a bit heavily from her dancing, she looked around the room, a bit lost.

Dressing up? She hated it.

Socializing with human beings who weren't part of her social circle? She hated it even more. There was a reason that she chose to make a living from behind a computer screen.

If she tried to stay home, though, her sisters would drag her bodily from her room, and experience had taught her that Amy went for the hair, the bitch. Sighing as though the world was ending, which the stone in her gut told her it was, she shuffled across her room to her tiny closet.

She hoped that Ford would be okay with ripped jeans and a T-shirt, because that was all that she owned.

"Aah!" Opening her closet, she ducked when something flew through the air. Batting at her head as though something might be nestled in her hair, she exhaled on a laugh when she realized that the flying object had been something swooshing on a hanger—a dress. No wonder she hadn't expected it.

A dress. *What the hell?*

Scowling, she unhooked the hanger from her closet door. A note fluttered to the floor as she did.

Jo,
No, you can't wear jeans to the open house.
Wear this instead.
Meg
(PS: Matching shoes are under your bed.)

"Shit." Jo groaned out loud. She did not wear dresses. In fact, she mostly wore men's clothing. She was used to people wondering if she was a lesbian—the way she dressed, the way she carried herself, the lack of any long-term relationship seemed to invite the question. She'd even wondered herself for a while if the lack of sexual interest she'd had in men since Theo was because she wasn't attracted to them as a species.

One female fling later and she'd discovered that that wasn't right, either. She was who she was—not a lesbian, not a boy trapped in a girl body. She was just Jo, and she was far happier when she dressed how she wanted, behaved how she wanted, dated—or didn't—who she wanted.

She thought her sisters understood that, and she felt her infamous temper rise as she examined the offensive garment.

The fabric was actually quite nice—some kind of heavy, silky stuff, none of that wispy, flirty fabric that always made her feel like she was half naked. The top part had a halter neck, which she liked, and though the back dipped lower than she was comfortable with, she actually quite liked the fact that the tattoo on her back—a stunning phoenix inked by her sister Amy—would be shown off.

That left the skirt part, which she didn't think she could get past—except that when she examined it, it wasn't a skirt at all, but rather shorts. Meg had gotten her what she supposed would be called a romper, and the relief was like chugging icy lemonade on a scorching-hot day.

A quick glance under the bed showed that her older sister had had enough sense not to get her high heels, either—the shoes Meg had chosen were flat, gladiator-type sandals, with straps that wound up her calves. She could deal with that.

After slithering into the simple garment and struggling with but ultimately conquering the shoes, she looked in the mirror and thought that maybe, this time, Meg had known what she was talking about. Jo didn't feel like she was playing dress-up, she was fairly comfortable and she wasn't wearing jeans—everybody won.

Flicking a glance at the time on her phone, she saw that she only had five minutes to get across the grounds to the hotel. With any luck, her sisters had already left, and no one would try to attack her with lipstick or a hair straightener.

"Slayyyyy." Giving one last look in the mirror,

she tried out the word that Amy used whenever she was trying to tell someone that they were looking hot. She placed a hand on her hip and tried out a seductive, come-hither expression before bursting out laughing.

Ironic for someone with a blog called Jojo Kink, she thought as she clattered down the stairs and out the front door, that its owner wasn't the least bit, and had never been, sexy.

CHAPTER SIX

"IT'S JUST LIP GLOSS," Meg insisted as she aimed the wand from a glossy tube of red goop at Jo's face.

"I don't want it!" Ducking, Jo tried to avoid the lip gloss, and Meg missed, swabbing Jo's cheek instead.

"Now look what you did," Meg sighed as Jo scowled. Leaning in, she rubbed at the red stuff on Jo's cheek and then, lightning quick, swabbed a matching stripe on the other cheek. "There. It'll work as blush. Now you at least look like you've seen the sun sometime in the last decade."

"For fuck's sake, Meg." Holding up her hands to fend off another attack, Jo took a giant step back, putting space between herself and her fashion-loving older sister. "I'm wearing the outfit. Isn't that enough?"

"The blush looks good," Meg continued as if

she hadn't heard Jo speak, "but you'd look even better if you'd just let me comb your hair."

"Don't touch it," Jo warned, backing up yet again. She'd kept her formerly long, chestnut waves in a sleek bob since she'd hit her twenties, the only reason being that, in her opinion, she never needed to do anything to it—it always looked the same. "Seriously, Meg. The energy it takes me to fend you off is the energy I should be using to smile at strangers without baring my teeth."

"Fine," her sister huffed, turning her attention to her own reflection. As usual, she looked like an Instagram post—something Jo knew she could never achieve, even if the thought of spending several hours on her hair and makeup didn't make her want to stab herself in the eye.

"You look good enough for both of us," Jo insisted, herding her sister to the door of the funky little bathroom in the lobby of the hotel. There was a fireplace and a lounge chair inside the room, which puzzled her—why would anyone want to hang out in the bathroom?—but she supposed that Ford knew what he was doing. Actually, maybe she'd sit in that chair and hide here for the rest of the evening…

Before the door closed behind Meg, though, she turned and grabbed Jo's hand, tugging her back into the lobby. Snagging a fresh glass of sparkling wine from a passing waiter in what looked like a vintage tux, she pressed it into Jo's hand, then gestured around the room.

"Chug that, then go mingle," she ordered, straightening her sequined, spaghetti-strapped sheath. "Ford said we had to. You don't want to disappoint Beth."

Damn it. Meg knew that Beth was Jo's kryptonite—the sister she'd always been closest to, the sister she still was terrified of losing if her illness came back.

Yeah, she'd do anything for Beth—even mingle.

Pasting what she suspected was a terrifying smile on her face, she shuffled a few awkward steps farther into the room. Chugging down her sparkling wine so fast that it burned, she grabbed a second glass as a prop while she stood awkwardly, shifting her weight from foot to foot.

"You look like you could use some company." Jo looked up as a man sidled up next to her. He smiled, revealing toothpaste-commercial teeth, and she cocked her head, taking him in.

He was good-looking, she supposed. Objectively, he was tall and well built, with the kind of body that wore a suit well. His features were distinct, with high cheekbones and a strong jaw. He even had a dimple in his chin.

"Are you all right?" His blinding smile faltered,

and she realized that she'd left the silence run on too long as she studied him. She had a bad habit of doing this, losing track of the conversation as she scrutinized a potential partner, wondering what the hell was wrong with her when she inevitably wasn't interested.

Again.

"I'm fine, thank you." She smiled politely, sipping at her wine. "Why are you here?"

Her potential suitor blinked, and Jo winced. Man, she sucked at small talk. "What I mean is, what brings you to this event?" There. That sounded fancy enough.

"I'm one of Ford's friends from back home." He sipped his own wine, looking at her over the edge. "I'm barking up the wrong tree here, aren't I?"

"Pardon?" Jo blinked, even as his meaning flooded through her. She could have recited his next words along with him.

"You're not interested." He smiled at her, though he seemed slightly puzzled by her reaction. At least he hadn't said *You're not interested in men*, which was what she'd been expecting.

"Sorry." She shook her head and offered what she hoped was a winsome smile. "Better luck elsewhere."

He was clearly startled by her response, but then she was gone, scurrying across the lobby floor as fast as she could in her slightly slippery shoes. She gulped at her wine, leaving the empty glass on a table as she headed unerringly for the wide, stone-tiled stairs, desperate to get away.

She wasn't good with words in person. She was socially awkward to the extreme. And Dimples had picked up on her one insecurity, the one thing that she just couldn't figure out about herself—no, she wasn't interested. Not in him, not in any man. Hell, not in any woman, either.

She hadn't been since Theo. She'd tried, and sometimes she managed a mild affection, but attraction? Sexual arousal?

Forget it. That was why she'd fallen in love with her blog—it was an outlet, a place for her to explore her sexuality in a place where her own biology had failed her.

She could rage against it, she supposed, as she reached the upper floor and sighed with relief at the sudden muting of the party noise, the voices. But what was the point?

Footsteps sounded on the staircase behind her, along with the hushed murmur of voices. Shit. Her encounter with Dimples had drained her—she just couldn't handle interacting with even one more person.

Desperate, she tried the handle of the closest

door. It opened, and she wasn't going to question it. She hurriedly ducked inside.

The heavy door swung shut behind her, enclosing her in a dim, quiet space. She ran a hand over the wall, searching for the light switch, then decided to leave the room in the dark. The lack of stimulus after the sensory assault of the party was soothing.

She'd recharge here then go downstairs and force herself to mingle for twenty more minutes—long enough to say that she'd given it a go.

Then she'd go home, put on her jeans and tank top and return to the cocoon of blissful aloneness.

The doorknob turned. A feminine giggle shattered the womblike tranquility, followed by a deeper voice that was undeniably male.

She had no idea why she ducked into the closet—maybe just the urge to not have to interact with even one more person. She stood in the small space, behind the half-opened door, fisting sweaty palms as the people entered the room, letting the heavy door fall closed behind them with what sounded like an ominous click.

"How much have you had to drink?" The man's voice made her straighten, like she was in school and her knuckles had been slapped with a ruler.

"Not so much that I don't know what I'm doing." The woman giggled, a bubbly, breathless sound.

Jo squinted across the room. It was dark in the room, more shadows than light, but she could see shapes, outlines.

She could certainly hear, and knew that the metallic rasp couldn't be anything but the lowering of a zipper.

"This wasn't what I had in mind when I invited you to this party as my date," the man said, his voice wry. The woman shushed him. Jo's eyes were gradually adjusting to the dark, and she watched the woman drop to her knees in front of the door the man was leaning against.

The woman inhaled sharply, and the man exhaled slowly, a circular dance. Jo fought to hold her own breath, lest she give herself away.

Why, oh why, had she ducked into the closet? It was past the point where she could announce her presence. *Oh, pardon me, I'll just look the other way if you don't mind letting me through.*

"Chill out," the woman said, voice exasperated. "This doesn't mean anything, okay? I'm your assistant, and I'm supposed to make your life easier. I don't know why you're all keyed up tonight, but let me take the edge off. It's nothing we haven't done before."

The man said nothing, did nothing for a long moment. Then a low rumble of pleasure escaped his throat, followed by the wet sound of mouth on skin, sounds that screamed sex.

Close your eyes, Jo. Close them now.

A rustle of movement, then a groan as the man tangled his hands in the woman's hair. That groan should have been a sound of surrender, the man acquiescing to the woman's desire to please him, but somehow he still sounded like he was the one in control.

Jo shifted in her hiding place as something dark and wild tangled in her belly. She found herself rubbing her thighs together against the sudden ache. It took her brain a few moments to catch up.

Was she actually *aroused* by this? By hiding in the closet, watching a woman she didn't know suck on a strange man's cock? How could that be, when nothing had turned her crank in the years since Theo had left—absolutely nothing?

She swallowed, hard, pressing her forehead to the cool plaster of the wall. Watching this when they didn't know she was here was so, so wrong. But this was the first hint of arousal she'd felt in so long—she knew she wasn't going anywhere.

Taking another quiet breath, she focused in. The woman's mouth made obscene sucking noises as she worked on the man, but she wasn't what held Jo's attention, though she supposed that the woman's inherent enjoyment in the action of pleasuring the stranger was erotic. No, it was him, something about the man. About the way he looked downward, attention focused on the point of contact. And something else about him—the outline of an imposing body, the unapologetic way he held himself, as if he deserved to be serviced.

Like he was doing the woman a favor by letting her place her mouth on his cock. He almost seemed impatient.

How strange.

Jo watched, now entranced, as the woman seemed to redouble her efforts. The sounds she was making said that servicing the man was pleasurable for her as well. How could that be?

Her attention was caught on him as he sucked in a breath that sounded pained, his focus sharpening. Sliding his hands through her hair, he caught the woman's face in his palms. The thin, inky darkness seemed to thicken, to throb along with the pulse between Jo's legs.

"Pull off," he growled, and the woman did with a sound so wet it was obscene. She hummed, low and satisfied, like she'd just indulged in some delicious treat, and a jolt of hunger struck Jo.

She sighed, just the quietest of sounds, but it was enough to be heard. The man's head snapped up, his head orienting right in Jo's direction, even as he exhaled harshly, thrusting into the woman's cupped hands.

Oh shit. Had he heard her? Could he see her? Did he know she was there? Spell broken, Jo pulled back farther into the closet. A single bead of icy sweat rolled down her spine.

"See? I told you you'd feel better," the woman purred, satisfaction thick in her voice. This puzzled Jo as well.

The man had come. The woman had not. Why, then, did the woman seem so pleased?

The man simply grunted. The unfamiliar slickness between Jo's thighs and the buzzing in her head, the flush of her skin begged her to step from the closet, to get one more look at the shadowy figure who'd brought her senses to life. That, though, would be pure insanity, so she forced herself to stay crouched in her hiding place, her pulse thrumming through her veins.

She listened, trying to slow her breath, as the man zipped himself up. Listened as the pair exited the room, the door closing heavily behind them, and then listened to the silence left in the room as she absorbed the fact that she was alone.

"Jesus." Cautiously, Jo pushed off the wall, stepping softly onto the thick, luxe carpeting of the hotel room. Part of her thought—hoped?— wildly that the man might still be here. He was gone, though—of course he was gone. She was left alone with the vague sense that it had all been a very dirty dream.

And, of course, that suddenly pressing need to fill the aching space between her legs. That was new. Actually, it was old—so old it was new again.

Throwing her head back, she huffed out a laugh at her own expense. She was a disaster.

Against her hip, her phone buzzed. Since the romper had no pockets and no back, the only place she'd been able to tuck her phone was under the elastic waist of her panties. She pulled it out, frowning when she saw a message from Beth.

Ford says he's sorry. He didn't know.

Well, that was clear as mud. Shrugging it off, Jo replaced her phone, took a cleansing breath and left the room. She held her breath as she walked down the empty, elegant hall, still half expecting to see the couple who had just awakened her slumbering carnal appetite.

She didn't see them. Of course she didn't, and even if she had, how would she have known?

What is wrong with me?

Descending the ornate staircase, Jo made a beeline for the bar. She both needed and, she thought, deserved a drink—something a little stronger than the cheerful glasses of sparkling wine that were still being circled.

Standing on her toes, she leaned against the polished dark wood of the lobby bar, trying to catch the bartender's attention. The gray-haired, heavily mustached server didn't even spare her a glance.

Meg was way better at this. Then again, Jo thought as she looked down at her rather flat chest, Meg had a little more to work with.

"Scotch on the rocks with a twist." The voice came from behind her. Jo turned as irritation snaked over her skin—she was here first, and also, that was her drink.

Slapping a palm down on the counter, she angled her chin up as she pivoted on her fancy sandals. "Back of the line, buddy."

"I've been lots of things to you, Jo, but *buddy* was never one of them."

Jo whipped her head the rest of the way around so quickly that she felt a pinch in her neck. A roaring sound filled her ears as she found herself staring at a wide, hard chest, then up to broad shoulders. Tequila-gold skin started at the neck, covering chiseled features that were set off with night-black hair and eyes just as dark.

"Hi, Jo."

Her mouth fell open. She must have looked like she'd gone simple, staring up at him like she'd never seen a man before. Though it was true enough that she hadn't seen this particular man for quite some time—years, in fact.

"Theo," she managed, her tongue thick and cottony in her mouth. She'd always known he would come back, had known it right down to the marrow of her bones. And yet of all the ways she'd imagined that the reentry of Theo Lawrence into her life would go—and she'd dreamed up plenty—she'd never expected that she'd actually manage to smile and be charming. To hide her innate social awkwardness and show only what she wanted of herself, the way so many women seemed able to do.

After all, this was the man who'd been like a part of her family. Who'd spent holidays with her family, who'd been her first kiss, her first love.

Her first experience with the kind of pain that could tear a person in two.

Drawing on every ounce of strength she had inside her, she turned back to the bar. She couldn't deal with this without some liquid courage.

When Theo snagged the drink from the bartender's hand, she felt anger whip through her. When he handed her the heavy tumbler, ice clinking merrily against the glass walls, the anger evaporated into a dense cloud of confusion.

"Scotch on the rocks with a twist, right?" He studied her with those coal-dark eyes, the ones that still haunted her dreams. "You never could stomach the hard stuff without a little ice."

The rage winked back to life. "Do you really think that remembering what I drink will make up for ditching out on life?"

His smile dimmed, and Jo cursed internally. Damn it. *Damn it*. After that, how could she smile and pretend that she was doing just fine?

"So that's how it's going to be." He smiled at her, but the press of his lips was tight. Still, she was distracted by it—the way that full, beautiful mouth moved. She'd always thought of his mouth as his Latin-lover lips, inherited as they'd been from his gorgeous Latina mother.

Well, she could look, but she was no longer interested in his lips, gorgeous or otherwise. Since she'd already blown the cool card, this was where she should scream. She should rage, pummel his chest with her fists. Flood the lobby of the hotel with angry tears.

At eighteen, she would have. She still had a temper, but she was also no longer that young—or that innocent. It took enormous effort to reseal the bottle that contained everything she felt and had felt for Theo Lawrence, but she did it, shoving the cork back in until she could get somewhere alone, a safe place for that bottle to explode.

Instead, she took a deep swallow of the drink

he'd pressed into her hand, even though she resented that he'd been the one to procure it. Then she finally managed that civil smile, though it felt like pushing through a thick wall of cement.

"You look well, Theo." There, that was normal. No hint of weirdness there. "What brings you back to Boston?"

For just the merest blink of an eye, she thought she saw something like confusion flicker through his stare. Then it was gone, and she was sure that she'd imagined it, because he turned the charm back on—and he still had plenty—showing her a flash of teeth against that delicious skin.

"Business." He didn't elaborate; she didn't ask. "And you're still writing."

It wasn't a question, and she resented the hell out of what he hadn't said with that, with the drink. "You don't know me anymore, Theo. Don't presume that you do."

"I suppose that's true." She didn't miss the hint of danger that snaked its way into his voice—he never had enjoyed being told that he was wrong. "For instance, I never would have pictured you as a voyeur."

Time crashed to a standstill. Jo's fingers, suddenly sweaty, slipped on her drink, which would have crashed to the ground if Theo hadn't caught it, setting it back down on the bar.

"What did you say?" she finally gasped, her pulse stuttering before starting to throb double time. Her mouth was dry—she wanted her drink but didn't trust herself to pick it up.

"I think you heard me," he replied mildly, gesturing to the bartender, who brought him a glass of something that looked like club soda. In some dim recesses of her brain, Jo noted that it was odd to see him drink something nonalcoholic in a party setting, but she couldn't give the matter more than a passing thought.

"I heard you," she managed, narrowing her eyes. She tucked a strand of her loose hair behind her ear for something to do with her hands, and when his stare tracked her movement, it caused conflicting sensations to reverberate off one another inside her. "Explain."

"I know you were just in that room upstairs." The way he was looking at her was like a dare. He knew—there was no sense in denying it. He knew she'd just watched him get sucked off.

Of course, she hadn't known it was him. Though really, it seemed like some part of her had. Hadn't he always been the only person in existence able to arouse her? Just her fucking luck.

"I was already in the room when you and your little friend decided to have a private party," she replied tartly. Damn it, now she sounded like a jealous shrew when in fact she felt nothing of the sort. No, when she thought of what she'd seen, she got that sticky, sweet sensation between her thighs again—and knowing it was Theo was a new but not entirely unwelcome element. "I couldn't exactly go anywhere while your dick was in her mouth."

"I suppose not," he replied thoughtfully, looking at her over the rim of his glass. To avoid that stare, Jo looked up, down and around, but all she managed to do was note that he still wore a suit better than any man she'd ever met—and that even to her unskilled eye, the suit looked like it cost more than she made in a month. "But you didn't have to watch, either."

Jo cleared her throat. What the hell was she supposed to say to that? It was one hundred percent the truth. She'd gouge her eyeballs out with one of those little plastic cocktail swords, though, before she admitted to him what watching had done to her—for her.

"How did you know it was me?" This seemed safe enough.

His grin was both wry and the tiniest bit wolfish. Her pulse responded, even as her brain scolded it. "You still smell like cinnamon."

She'd never cared about makeup, but she'd always like to smell good, and she always had a little bottle of cinnamon essential oil on the go, ever since she was thirteen. That he remembered should maybe have been touching, but instead it brought out her caged fury yet again.

"I'm surprised you noticed it. You were a little busy." Her words were too loud, too sharp—social awkwardness was back in the room. But where lots of people would have recoiled, starting to look at her like she was a bit odd, Theo didn't even seem to notice.

Nor did he apologize, though Jo certainly didn't expect him to—not for this. But neither did she expect what he said next.

"Then I suppose my next question should be, did you like it?"

Jo barely held back a strangled sigh. He was deliberately pushing her buttons, but for the life of her, she couldn't understand why. Surely he didn't think they were just going to pick up where they'd left off? Theo was a lot of things, but he'd never been crazy.

She didn't answer. He let the silence between them stretch and thicken.

"Everything all right here?" Like a wave of fresh spring air, Beth appeared at Jo's elbow. Gratefully, Jo tore her focus away from her ex to pay attention to her sister.

Clad in a slinky little red dress, Beth looked

like she'd never been sick a day in her life. The spaghetti straps and short hemline left her many tattoos on full display. The purple streaks in her dark hair should have clashed with the deep crimson of her dress, but instead they made her look effortlessly cool.

On her other side, her fiancé, Ford Lassiter, was dressed in a suit that was probably even more expensive than Theo's. He looked like he'd stepped out of an issue of some men's business magazine. He definitely didn't look like the kind of man who would be enamored of a woman who was a walking advertisement for a tattoo parlor—namely, her sister's tattoo parlor—and yet somehow they worked.

"Theo!" Placing her hand on Jo's elbow, Beth offered up a polite smile. "It's been forever. What brings you back to Boston?"

"Business." Theo offered the same one-word explanation he'd given Jo. The smile he offered Beth was genuine, however, with none of the layers of undertones that his voice had when he spoke to Jo.

"I haven't seen you since that tournament...was it at Palm Springs? Two years ago. What are you into now?" Ford, too, seemed friendly as he offered Theo his hand, but the other man had been hanging around the Marchandes for long enough now that Jo caught the hint of stiffness in his voice.

"It's funny that you didn't mention you knew my girl's family when you accepted this invite."

"I didn't put two and two together." Theo smiled smoothly, but Jo's bullshit alarm screamed. He was lying through his teeth—but why? "I never would have imagined the girls opening a hotel on their property."

"The girls, huh?" Ford rocked back on his heels. "You must go way back."

Jo exchanged a glance with Beth as the two men puffed up like peacocks, each trying to posture their way to dominance.

"I've known the Marchandes for a long time," Theo started, and Jo had suddenly had enough of the bullshit. Holding up her hands, she waved them in the air to stop the argument in its tracks.

"Let's just cool it before we get to the point where you guys hose each other down with testosterone, okay?" Both men grunted, and Jo turned her attention to Ford. "Thanks for defending our honor and all that, big bro, but if you don't like the dude, don't invite him."

"I liked him just fine before I knew what he'd done to you," Ford muttered, "but I'd like him better back on one of the golf courses in LA, where I could go after him with a nine iron."

Beth turned away, her shoulders shaking as she tried to hold in her laugh. Her laugh died as Ford dipped his head to whisper in her ear. Jo watched as her younger sister flushed from head to toe, her posture changing just slightly as she took in whatever dirty thing Ford had just said to her.

"I might be wrong, but I think they've forgotten about us," Jo said wryly as Ford caught her sister's elbow and led her from the lobby. She felt the pang of envy reverberate around her rib cage.

She was happy for Beth. She was. But was it too much to ask that she have someone who made her feel like that, too?

"Never would have thought that sweet little Beth would hook up with Ford Lassiter." Theo took another sip of his club soda, calling Jo's attention back to him. She watched as he swallowed, cursing inwardly when she caught herself watching the lines of his throat.

Couldn't he have gone soft under that suit? Did he still have to look so damn *physical*?

"What's that supposed to mean?" Jo felt the flare of temper as a knee-jerk reaction. "You don't think one of the Marchande girls is good enough for a hotel tycoon?"

"Jo." The exasperation he managed to inflect that single syllable with was a talent of his. "I was actually referring to the fact that, according to rumor, he's a kinky fucking bastard."

"What rumors? He said you were golf buddies."

Jo glowered up at Theo. Man, he'd been gone for so long, and yet within seconds he'd managed to tap right back into that special talent he had for getting under her skin.

It was during those times, when he would put his mouth all over her body except the place she most wanted it, that made her hate the fact that he made her wait.

"Golf buddies," Theo agreed, a slight smirk curling the corners of his lips as he watched her. Heat rose into her cheeks—he knew. Damn it, he knew where her mind had gone. "And we also had some mutual friends. Friends who were into things that would shock you."

Jo's mouth went dry as Theo looked her over, top to bottom and up again. His eyes glinted with mischief, and also something darker.

"Shock me more than being trapped in a room watching you get blown by some other woman?" She found her voice and used it as a weapon. She no longer cared if she sounded jealous—she wanted an excuse to leave, leave this conversation and leave Theo, because the longer she stood here with him, the more she started to want things that she could no longer have—at least not if she was smart.

Theo. The dark. The rasp of a zipper, the wet sound of lips on skin. Without warning, Jo felt moisture surge between her legs, just from the memory.

She wasn't jealous at all. Rather, being a voyeur on that little scene had awoken something she'd thought she'd never feel again.

Theo didn't reply—he just kept on watching her with those dark eyes. And she absolutely did not have to fight back the urge to rise to her toes and trace her tongue over the golden line of his jaw.

"Fun as this has been, I'm going home." Setting her now empty glass down on the bar, she wiped her palms over her thighs to hide the fact that they were trembling. "Good night."

The way that Theo had been acting, the way he'd been flirting—for that was what it had been—Jo was surprised that he remained silent as she walked away, though she knew, just knew, that he watched her until she was out of sight. It wasn't until she was back in her own room, her back pressed flat against the door she'd just closed, that she acknowledged that she was disappointed that he'd let her just go.

"No way, Jo. Not happening." She shed her romper and the sandals as quickly as if they'd burst into flame. Pulling on white cotton panties and a worn Marilyn Manson concert tee, she exhaled with relief, as though in taking off the party clothes, she'd shed the Jo who was tempted by Theo Lawrence.

It was still there—that thing between them, that indescribable connection. Even in the dark, even not knowing who he was, he'd managed to turn her on.

"Don't be stupid," she muttered to herself as she climbed into her bed, crawling beneath the covers.

The only man who made her crave was also the man who had broken her heart. What kind of person would she be if she took him back? Not that he'd asked. Not that she would.

But as she lay there in the shadows of nighttime, listening to her sisters return from the open house, she couldn't stop shifting back and forth in her bed. If she got up and looked out the window, she could see the Lawrence house. Was he staying there? Probably not, but the thought of him being so close after so many years made her pulse race.

So she stayed in bed, but when she finally fell into a fitful sleep, she was chased by images of dark eyes, golden skin and wicked hands that woke her up from the sleep she'd been in since he'd left.

CHAPTER SEVEN

LET'S TALK ABOUT VOYEURISM. *If you're reading this blog, chances are you're a dirty birdie and you already know what it is, but for those of you who don't, it's getting hot and bothered watching someone else involved in illicit activities. Now, while this sounds like it could be a sexy good time, if you take it too far, it ventures into crime territory, so don't expect to peep into your sexy neighbor's bedroom window without consequences. But say you're at a party and you're grabbing some alone time. A couple with oral sex on their mind stumbles upon your hidey-hole, and before you can make your presence known, she's giving him a happy ending and you've been whisked along for the ride. Is this awkward, or is it hot? Is it hotter if they discover you're there?*

Food for slutty thought,
Jojo Kink

* * *

The offices for Crossing Lines took up the entire third floor of a tall office building just outside the financial district in downtown Boston. The building was sleek, the smell of latex paint still evident as Jo closed herself in the shiny silver elevator that was so eerily silent she double-checked to make sure she was actually moving.

The woman at the front desk was the type who intimidated lesser specimens without having to lift a finger. She barely even looked up as Jo crossed the plush carpeting to the massive chrome desk, clearing her throat when she arrived.

"Can I help you?" When the woman finally did look up, she flicked a glance over Jo, and though there was no visible change in her expression, Jo felt her distaste flavoring the air. Jo knew what she saw and couldn't help but squirm a bit under the assessing stare.

She'd never gone on a job interview. The position at the paper so very many years ago had been offered to her over the phone based on her work on her high school paper. When she ghosted stories for other writers, they didn't care what she looked like or how she dressed. She deliberately left images of herself off her blog.

That left today. She hadn't had time to go shopping for something more appropriate and didn't know what that was at any rate, so she'd settled on a pair of black jeans that were free of rips and tears, a black sweater from the men's department, and a clean pair of sneakers. Face-to-face with this woman, whose hair was glossy and highlighted, and who wore a white blouse without a single wrinkle, Jo knew that she'd missed the mark, but there was nothing she could do about it now.

"I have a meeting with John Brooke," she stated, drawing herself to her full, if insignificant, height, trying to look like what she was wearing was just fine. "At ten o'clock."

"I'll take you to his office." When the woman stood up, Jo noted that she was also wearing heels that added at least three inches to her height, and that her skirt came to midcalf, hugging her legs like a second skin. How did she walk?

The woman, who hadn't introduced herself, seemed equally interested in Jo, taking a long moment to look her over, her expression faintly puzzled. Maybe, Jo thought, she was wondering how security downstairs had let someone with such little fashion sense into the building.

Finally, the other woman turned and walked down the hall, gesturing for Jo to follow. Jo watched the sleek length of the woman's ponytail, thinking of the woman last night, savoring the resultant heat.

Not now, Jo!

The woman paused outside a glass door. It was cracked open, but she knocked on it smartly. A voice called out for them to enter. The woman didn't follow Jo in, just studied her intently again as she gestured her in, and Jo felt her stomach slowly roll with nerves.

"Miss Marchande?" The man who stood up from behind the desk was tall, well over six feet, and absolutely gorgeous. Light brown skin set off pale green eyes, and the short buzz of his black hair showed off the strong lines of his face. Dressed in a well-cut suit, he was, quite simply, hot. "I'm John Brooke."

His smile was friendly enough that some of Jo's nerves eased. He didn't make her feel out of place like Miss Tight Skirt had, and when he offered a large palm for her to shake, she felt some of her confidence return.

"Nice to meet you." She winced a bit as the words came out just a bit too loud, but he didn't seem to notice. Gesturing for her to sit, he checked the expensive-looking watch on his wrist. "The owner will be here momentarily. While we wait, would you like coffee? Water, tea? I can have Ava get you whatever you'd like."

Assuming that Ava was the girl at the front desk, Jo was tempted to ask for something as a petty revenge for the scrutiny. She knew she wouldn't be able to swallow a thing, though, since the news that another person would be joining them had ratcheted her anxiety back up again.

"I'm fine." Doing her best to smile like a normal human, Jo took a second look at John Brooke. He'd said in his email that he was some kind of adviser to the company, which made her think of endless travel, city to city, clandestine encounters in airport bathrooms. He looked the part—sleek and sexy.

He did nothing for her, roused nothing more than a mild appreciation for a fine-looking man.

"Sorry I'm late."

No. Oh, hell no.

Jo hadn't recognized Theo's voice last night because she hadn't heard it in so very long. Now, with it fresh in her mind, she was on her feet before he'd even cleared the doorway, his voice triggering an instant surge of adrenaline.

"Miss Marchande." He cast her a polite smile, almost as if they were truly meeting for the first time—almost. There was a glint in his eye that told her he was looking forward to seeing how this played out.

It pissed her off.

"What the hell, Theo?" Still standing, she planted her hands on her hips and stood up straight. "What are you doing?"

"Do you know each other?" John stood as well, furrowing his brow in Theo's direction. "I thought Miss Marchande was the writer of that blog you showed me."

"She is the writer of that blog," Theo replied, fully entering the room. Crossing the room, he propped a hip on the massive desk, looking like he truly didn't give a fuck about the tension brewing.

He'd never given much of a fuck about anything…anything except her. She couldn't make out what his game was here, though, and she didn't like being a pawn in it.

"Explain yourself," she demanded crisply. He gestured for her to sit, but she remained standing, refusing to do anything he told her to.

"I'm going to go," John announced, clapping his hands together as he cast Theo a stern look. "Please stop by my office after…whatever this is."

Theo acknowledged the other man with a jerk of his chin, and then John was gone. He closed the door behind him, leaving Jo alone with Theo.

Her pulse tripped, then started to beat double time.

"What are you doing, Theo?" Her voice trembled, and she told herself that it was with anger. "You had a chance to talk to me last night. You didn't have to drag me all the way here with a made-up story."

"Let me be quite clear." Theo's voice was suddenly sharp, commanding in a way that she'd never heard before. It caught her attention, and she eyed him sharply. He still lounged against the desk, but he'd straightened.

Rather than the lazy, hedonistic Theo she was acquainted with, this man looked in control. She had no idea what to make of it.

"There was no false story. I own Crossing Lines. I am looking for a unique voice to draw in new users. The offer of a job is real." His expression darkened, and he didn't hide the way his gaze swept over her small frame. "But at the same time that John and I came up with that idea, I was looking into what my ex-girlfriend was up to, since I was coming back to Boston. Imagine my surprise when I discovered that the sweet girl I'd left was the writer of a blog exploring all things kinky."

"I've never been a sweet girl." Jo made air quotes around the last two words with her fingers. "And you didn't discover that I was the writer of my blog with a simple internet search. I've made sure of that."

The corners of his lips twisted in a smile. "Touché. I may have had one of my programmers dig a little. But your secret is safe with me."

"Why offer me the job, Theo?" Jo's voice was quiet. "There are a million writers out there who could write what you want. This has messy written all over it."

He paused.

"I owe you," he finally said, tapping a finger on the desk. "Though of course, if you weren't qualified, this wouldn't even be an issue."

"You *owe* me?" Jo heard her voice echo off the high ceiling and realized she was shouting but didn't care. "Fuck that noise, Theo. You thought you'd come throw a job at your fancy new company at your hard-up ex and all would be forgiven? I don't need your charity. I don't need *you*."

That was it—she was done. Her fury at his actions overrode the very real disappointment that the job wouldn't work as she stormed toward the door.

When Theo grabbed her arm, she slapped at it with angry hands. "Stop manhandling me!"

"Then stop acting like an ass and listen." Hauling her around so that her ass was pressed against the desk, he leaned in, a hand on either side of her hips, forcing her to rear back.

She could smell him, some kind of pricey cologne that made her throat go dry. She could feel the heat of his body all along the line of her own, and damn it, that ache between her thighs decided that it would be a fine time to wake up.

It was Theo. It had always been him.

"The reason I offered you the damn job, and the reason that you're going to take it, is because we have unfinished business." He leaned in, and she felt his warm breath mist over her lips. "I didn't leave because of you, or us, and you damn well know that. And there's still something here. You can't deny that."

Opening eyes that she didn't realize she'd squeezed closed, Jo looked up at Theo, saw the glint of truth in his eyes.

Her heart felt as though he'd placed it in his fist and squeezed.

"You may not have left because of us, but you still left." She did her best to keep her voice level. "You really expect us to just pick up where we left off? Unbelievable."

She placed her hands on his chest, intending to push him away, but the feel of his body beneath her palms made her hesitate. Like a shark sensing her weakness, he closed the ribbon of space between their bodies, pressing himself against her.

"Tell me you don't want me to touch you." He touched his lips to the thin skin behind her ear, and she couldn't hold back the shudder. When her fingers dug into his chest, he slid those lips down her neck and over, measuring the beats of her heart in the hollow of her throat.

Damn it. Damn herself. She'd gone for so, so

long without feeling this heat, and now that she'd had a taste, she wanted another hit, and another after that. Would it really be so bad to just let herself go, one more time?

Slowly, giving her time to say no, he moved his hands from the desk to her hips and up, until his long fingers framed her waist. He squeezed gently, and she remembered what it was like to have him grip her like that when he was inside her.

She also remembered what it had felt like after he'd left, in the days and weeks and months when she'd missed him so much it felt as though she'd been stabbed with a ragged shard of glass. It had taken everything she had to move past that—was it worth feeling that again, in exchange for just a few moments of pleasure?

No. No, it was not.

Pulling back abruptly, she pushed him away and broke the embrace. Her breath came fast and hard as she made space between them, wiping sweaty palms on the thighs of her jeans.

"We're not doing this." If only she felt as sure as she sounded. If he so much as crooked a finger at her, she'd strip off all her clothes and lie down on the desk for him to play with. "It's not fair to ask that of me."

Theo looked as though she'd clocked him in the head. He, too, was breathing hard, and when she saw the outline of his erection pressing against those fancy suit pants, she almost gave in again.

"I have to go." Shaking her head, she blindly pushed her way out of the office, heading straight for the elevator doors. Once inside, she turned and saw the satisfied smirk on Ava's face, realizing that she must have been the woman she'd caught with Theo. She should have felt jealousy, but instead the memory sent another bolt of heat through her. So long feeling nothing, and the sudden onslaught meant she was about to self-combust. But she held firm, and as the elevator doors closed, she pressed her damp forehead to the chilly steel of the elevator wall.

What the hell was she going to do?

"Want to explain to me what that was about?"

Theo was slouched in the chair at his desk, a can of icy club soda open in front of him. He desperately wished that it was three fingers of hideously expensive scotch.

"Is this where you spank me for not telling you that I knew Jo?" he asked wryly as John came in, closing the door briskly behind him.

The other man rolled his eyes. "Don't be such a drama queen. But yes, I'd like an explanation. You're paying me a lot of money to help get this company off the ground, Theo, and I'm not interested in being blindsided with whatever shit that was that you just pulled."

Theo took a large swallow of his club soda. It was flat and tasteless—why did he drink this shit, anyway?

John remained silent. Theo knew the tactic well— he often used it himself to make the other person talk first, to establish power.

He didn't have enough energy to fight it.

"Jo was my girlfriend when I was nineteen, but I've known her family since I was a kid. We lived next door to each other."

"And what did you do to piss her off like that?"

"What makes you think I did something?"

John snorted inelegantly. Reaching across to the sleek minifridge, he pulled out a club soda for himself. He grimaced after he took a sip. "This stuff is nasty."

Theo shrugged. "I realized that I wasn't good for her, and I left."

John cocked his head, as if waiting for the rest of the story. When he realized that there wasn't any, he slammed his can down on the desk.

"Let me guess—you haven't talked to her in all this time, am I right?" Theo didn't answer, but John was already building up a head of steam. "And you lured her here with a job offer in the hopes that—what? She'd be so thrilled at your return that she'd jump right back into your arms?"

Well…yeah, that had essentially been his plan. Hearing it come from someone else, though, made Theo wince.

He hadn't thought that out very well. With Jo's legendary temper, he was lucky she hadn't pushed him through the window.

"You." John pointed a finger at him before rising to pour the rest of his club soda into a plant. "You don't approach her about the job again. I'll handle that end so that we have a hope in hell that she takes the job, assuming you haven't fucked that up beyond repair. That blog of hers is the ticket to a successful launch, Theo, and that is my very expensive, professional opinion."

Theo cast his colleague as a sidelong stare. "You done yet?"

"Not even a little," John replied cheerfully, sitting down again and bracing his elbows on his knees. "Now, as someone who is an absolute magnet for the ladies—"

Theo interrupted him with a snort before waving his hand through the air. "Sorry. Carry on, Casanova."

"As I was saying before I was so rudely interrupted, you can't just come back after something like that and expect a woman to jump for joy at your mere presence."

"Then what the hell am I supposed to do?" Theo burst out, frustrated. "She's the most difficult woman in existence, ever."

"Ah, but the greater the challenge, the sweeter the reward." John grunted when Theo furrowed his brow. "You know, for the brilliant, maverick owner of a start-up valued at over ten million dollars, you can be an idiot." Standing, he tossed the empty can into the recycling bin, then leaned over the desk to pat Theo on the shoulder.

"Woo her, my man. Woo her like you've never wooed before."

CHAPTER EIGHT

WHEN JO GOT HOME, she headed straight for the garage. The small space housed her sister Beth's mechanic shop, and the sister she was closest to could almost always be found there during work hours.

She didn't want to be alone, but she wanted someone she could be silent with.

"Beth?" She strode into the garage, throwing her arms up at the last second when she saw her sister, who was very much not alone. "Oh shit! Sorry! I'll go!"

"No, no. Stay." Beth pushed Ford away with a mock-stern stare and pulled her coveralls back up to her waist, where she tied the arms in a knot, then straightened her tank. "Mr. Handsy here was just trying to convince me to take a break, but I have too much to do."

Beth stopped when she caught sight of Jo's face.

Jo thought she'd done a pretty good job at masking what she felt, but her sister knew her well enough to know that she wasn't all right. "For you, I'll take a break. Sit."

Beth gestured to her workbench, then shot Ford a look with eyebrows raised. He took the hint, buckling up his pants as he entered the house through the door that joined the two.

"I'm not going to bug you if you're busy," Jo started, but Beth waved her off.

"You can talk while I work," she said, ducking under the hood of the car she was working on. Jo saw something spark and took a cautious step back, out of range.

"It's nothing. Really," Jo insisted, but she didn't leave, instead opening up the mini fridge that Beth kept in the corner. The door was lined with shiny glass bottles of kombucha. So gross. Jo wrinkled her nose and shifted things around, finally locating a can of Diet Coke in the back corner. She didn't love soda, but she did like having something to do with her hands.

When she closed the fridge, Beth was watching her. Her sister's skin was still flushed from what she and Ford had been doing when Jo entered the garage, and Jo felt a pang of what was undeniably loneliness.

She wanted what Beth and Ford had. Not just

the companionship, either, damn it. She wanted the lust, the can't-keep-your-hands-off-each-other headiness.

And the only person who had ever done it for her was Theo.

Fuck her life.

"I'm going to take a wild guess and assume that it's Theo who's gotten that crazy look in your eyes." Beth eyed Jo's drink, then crossed to the fridge and retrieved a kombucha for herself. Jo couldn't hold back a grimace when her sister downed half the bottle. Sure, it was supposed to be good for you, but it had little floaty things in it. Yuck.

"So, tell me." Beth gestured with her bottle. Jo squirmed. She'd come here because she'd wanted to rant to her sister, absolutely. But after seeing Beth and Ford together, she felt more like curling up into a ball in her room. Alone.

"How can you drink that?" Both Jo and Beth jumped when the door Ford had just disappeared through banged open, smacking into the unfinished drywall of the shop. "It has chunks in it."

Beth arched an eyebrow at the bottle of beer Meg carried. "But beer before noon is okay?"

"It's craft beer." Meg smiled sweetly. "Doesn't count."

Looking to Jo for support, she stopped short. "What's going on?"

"Theo," Beth supplied before Jo could answer.

"Damn it." Meg handed Jo the beer. "Want to talk about it?"

"No." Jo scowled. She'd come here wanting to talk to Beth, but now she didn't know what the hell she wanted.

"Hello?" All three sisters turned at the sound of the male voice. Jo felt awkwardness weigh down on her like wet wool as she saw John Brooke standing in the open door of the garage. His pristine suit looked completely out of place against the oil-stained walls.

"Mr. Brooke." *Shit.* Jo had no idea what the social nuances of a situation like this were. She also had no idea what the hell he was doing here.

"Miss Marchande." Sidestepping a slick of oil on the floor, John closed the distance between them, offering her a hand. "I don't feel that we had an adequate discussion of the position at Crossing Lines. I'd like to remedy that. Perhaps we can try again, tomorrow morning?"

"What?" Jo blurted, ignoring the hand that he still held out. "But didn't Theo tell you about us?"

"I don't know what you're talking about." John arched his eyebrows in a way that he suggested he didn't *want* to know, either. "If you need time to think about the offer, I can give you twenty-four hours. But I don't think you were informed of the compensation for the job, which might influence your decision."

He named a sum that made her two sisters gasp and left Jo gaping. It wasn't astronomical, but it was far more than most writers made...ever.

"Apologies—I didn't think that it might be crass to drop numbers in front of others." He looked over at her sisters as he spoke, then did a double take at Meg. She looked right back, and the smirk that curved her lips said she liked what she saw.

"Thank you," Jo said, a little too loudly, but this time her volume was on purpose. John cleared his throat and forced his attention back to her. Working on anything connected with Theo was a bad, bad idea, but she was human, and she had no money. The sum he'd named had her mind spinning wildly with possibilities.

She could maybe, possibly awaken that dream of going back to school. At the end of the day, she supposed that she was like most people—money was a powerful motivator.

"If I come in tomorrow to discuss this, will I be speaking with you?" She chose her words carefully. The last thing on earth that she wanted to do was discuss her complicated history with Theo with his business partner, so she was relieved when he simply nodded.

"Yes. I'll go over the job with you, what we hope it will bring in terms of visibility to the company." Tucking his hands into the pockets of his well-tailored trousers, he looked her in the eye. "But there will also be some input from the owner on the creative side."

"I see," she replied slowly, swallowing past a dry throat. Could she really do this? Could she work at a job where she knew she'd have to see Theo every day?

For that kind of money—life-changing money—could she not?

She could feel her sisters watching her—well, Beth was watching her. Meg was staring at John while licking her lips. She sucked in a deep breath, then nodded decisively.

"I'll see you then."

Beth jumped in place as John turned and exited the garage. Meg stared blatantly at his ass. And Jo felt as though all of the air had been sucked from her lungs.

What had she done?

Theo heard them as soon as he turned his ignition off. Taking advantage of the warmth of the early spring day, he'd taken his convertible, leaving the top down. He'd meant to pull his car into the yawning garage of the estate, which he had to do manually since he had no idea where the fob was—his dad had left an insane amount of personal things to sort through. But when he heard the feminine laughter, he was reminded of all the times he'd hung out with the Marchande girls on the very same lawn that they were on now.

Woo her like you've never wooed before.

His partner's words reverberated in his head. He wanted to balk—he was Theo Lawrence. He'd made something of himself, even though no one had ever thought he could. He could have any woman he wanted, and he frequently did. He didn't have to *woo*.

Those women weren't Jo.

"How the hell am I supposed to *woo* her?" He waited for inspiration to strike, and when it didn't, he reached for his phone. A few taps later, and his screen was filled with images of flowers, chocolates and people eating dinner with napkins in their laps.

A date. He should ask her on a date—a real one.

An unexpected pang of nerves shot through him, and he mercilessly squashed it down.

He needed to approach this like he would approach a business meeting, confident in his success.

As he strode back down the driveway, the rosebushes that had grown wild since his father's death caught his eye. Among the tangle of branches were a handful of early blooms.

He'd never given Jo flowers. What an ass he'd been.

"Ow!" The branches were thorny, but he managed to gather enough stems to make a small bouquet. Arranging them clumsily in one hand, he took a deep breath and headed for the house next door.

"It went through!" Triumphant, Meg brandished a…was that a croquet mallet? Yes, they each had one, and there were thin wire hoops set up all over the lawn.

"No good! You weren't holding your drink!" Amy pulled a fresh can of beer from a small cooler and tossed it to her eldest sister before taking a long drink from her own. "This is how you do it!"

Holding her can in one hand, Amy waved her mallet in an inelegant arc that somehow managed to connect solidly with a black ball. It flew through a wire hoop and smacked against the orange ball that Meg had just hit. "Yes! Two extra strokes for me!"

"From what I've heard, you don't need any extra strokes to get the job done." Beth grinned wickedly at her youngest sister, waving her mallet in the air like a pointer finger. "Who is it this week? Mason? Caroline?"

"A lady never kisses and tells," Amy sniffed before sending a ball through the next hoop. Jo snorted in response.

"Since when are you a lady?" She'd been lying out flat on the grass, but now she propped herself up on her elbows, shielding her eyes from the sun. He could tell the moment she spotted him, because her spine straightened, her body tense. "Oh."

"What?" Beth turned to look in the same direction. "Oh. Theo."

"Hi, Beth. Meg. Amy." He nodded at each of them in turn, suddenly feeling as though he was facing a firing squad. He'd never met an opponent he couldn't best in the boardroom, but facing these four women that he'd known a lifetime ago made him wish for a drink. "May I ask what on earth you're doing?"

"Playing beer croquet. Obviously." Amy looked him up and down. At least he was assuming it was Amy—he could see whispers of the girl she'd been in the lines of her face, but this woman had blond dreadlocks and so many tattoos that he could barely see the ivory of her skin. "Wanna join?"

"Amy!" Meg glared at her sister, gesturing toward Jo with her head in a not-at-all-subtle manner.

"What?" Amy tossed her mallet to the ground with exasperation. "We've known him forever. You can't just erase that because he went on some rich-boy rumspringa and grew up."

"That's right." The sound of his own voice surprised him—he hadn't intended to say anything. But as all four of the women looked at him curiously, he cleared his throat and continued, flying by the seat of his pants. "You can't erase it."

He focused in on Jo, offering her the bouquet he'd plucked. "Here."

The expression on her face wasn't one he'd seen before, a cross between confusion and terror. "Did you pick these?"

"I—yes." Damn it. He should have thought this through better. Gotten something made up at a fancy florist. Something spiky and tropical, with lots of wild greenery—something that suited her better than a bunch of garden roses. "I'm here to woo you."

"What?" Jo threw her hands in the air. Behind her, Meg choked on her swallow of beer, and Amy cocked her head, watching him intently. "Woo? What the hell does that mean? Who says that any-more?"

"Shush, Jo." Meg wiped the back of her hand over her mouth. "Or you won't be able to hear the wooing."

Jo growled at her sister, who smiled beatifically back at her. The fact that Jo's sisters hadn't
run him off the property with their mallets re-
stored the smidgen of confidence that had been
misplaced by doubt.

Jo hadn't told him to leave yet, and the heat of
her skin was still on his lips. She wasn't immune
to him, and her sisters hadn't chased him away. He
was going to take that and run with it.

Shutting out the other women, he crossed the
lawn to Jo. Her expression was stony, but he saw
her swallow thickly when he got close.

He held out the roses. She looked like she'd as
soon eat them as accept them, but she reached out
a wary hand.

"I want to take you on a date." She sucked in
a sharp breath, and he felt a stab of vindication.
No, she wasn't immune. "Tomorrow night. Dinner. You and me."

Jo opened her mouth but never got a chance
to speak.

"She'll go!" Meg and Amy shouted at the same
time. Jo turned to glare at them, but her gaze
stopped at his hand.

"You're bleeding."

He looked down at his hand. Multiple scratches
from the rosebush striped his skin, and a drop of
blood welled up from one. "I didn't notice."

He wiped it on the thigh of his suit pants, and Meg winced. Amy watched him thoughtfully, and Beth pretended to be busy moving clips on the hoops, though he knew that she was paying attention, too.

Jo, though, squinted at him as though trying to peer into the dark recesses of his brain to find what his motivation was. He really thought she should have known.

Her. His mind was full of her. She'd never been far from his thoughts, even when he'd tried to tell himself that choosing to locate the offices of Crossing Lines in Boston was because of the location, or when he'd dated other women—fucked other women—in a desperate attempt to wipe her out of his mind.

He'd gone to that party knowing damn well that he'd see her, but he hadn't been able to stop himself. He'd let Ava give him what she wanted—his cock in her mouth—to try to tell himself that the only reason he wanted to see Jo was to check in, to make sure with his own eyes that she was doing all right. That the job offer was really just a job offer.

And then there she'd been in the dark, watching him. Watching him and liking it. And just like that, it all came roaring back.

She looked up at him with an indecipherable glint in her eyes.

And then she nodded. "Okay."

CHAPTER NINE

"WHAT DO YOU know about Crossing Lines?"

Jo rocked back and forth a bit in her chair. Unlike the hardware store special that was at her desk at home, this one was sleek leather, softly cushioned, and had wonderful support for the achy back that Jo figured most writers probably had.

She was enjoying the chair so much that it took her a moment longer than usual to answer John's question. When he cleared his throat, she looked up, realizing that she'd taken too long.

"I looked it up," she admitted, "after you emailed me. I read the Wikipedia entry on it and took a look at the site. But I'm afraid I didn't really understand the specifics of it."

"Did you download the app?" John asked. Jo shook her head, trying to hold back her grin.

"I'm sorry. I know most people would have, but

I don't have many apps on my phone at all. I use it for email and jotting down story ideas when pen and paper isn't around. That's it."

"You don't use it as a phone?" John's expression registered horror at this, prompting Jo to laugh. He'd had to pause their meeting several times already because he'd gotten calls that he couldn't ignore.

Jo was the opposite. "Hell, no. I hate talking on the phone." She shuddered.

John stared at her, perplexed. "You're a unique woman, Jo."

"Is that bad?" She might have felt nervous, but she had a sneaking suspicion that John was one of the few people in the world who both wasn't related to her and genuinely liked her.

"Not at all. It's very refreshing." His smile was very nearly dazzling, and Jo might have thought that he was flirting—except that she knew she very much wasn't his type. Never mind that he hadn't been too subtle in checking Meg out yesterday, but she wasn't most people's type. Antisocial tomboys with tempers weren't in high demand.

"Okay. Where to start, then…" John stopped his pacing—he was constantly in motion, full of energy—and pulled a second chair up to the massive desk. "What dating sites are you on?"

Jo couldn't hold back the laugh this time. John looked at her, perplexed.

"I'm not on any dating sites." She wasn't sure how she was supposed to interpret the look that John cast her then—not quite pity, but like he couldn't figure her out.

She didn't really like it. Romance was for other people. She'd mostly accepted it, until Theo had crashed back into her life. She was the one who was friend-zoned, considered one of the guys. On the rare occasions that another person seemed interested in her, she was too awkward to figure out the interaction—and she rarely found it worth it at any rate, since none of them ever made her hot and bothered.

She wasn't about to express this to some slickly suited guy that she'd met yesterday, though, so she searched his face for a cue and decided to deflect. "I think my sister Amy is on this one, though. She's on a few."

"Amy." He rolled the name over his tongue. "Is she one of the sisters I met yesterday?"

Jo refrained—barely—from rolling her eyes. "The sister you're ever-so-delicately inquiring about is Meg. She's a caterer with small-business dreams. She tells very dirty jokes, treats thrift-store shopping like an Olympic sport, and she's single."

John blinked, then ran a hand over the buzzed ebony hair on his head. "I guess I wasn't that subtle, huh?"

"Not even a little bit." *Damn.* Should she be more formal with someone who was now her boss? She wasn't the formal type. And hadn't he said that he liked the fact that she was unique?

Theo always had.

Do not go there, Jo.

"Okay. The Wikipedia article said that Crossing Lines is revolutionary. Can you explain that to me?" She tugged on the hem of the black tunic thing that Meg had shoved at her that morning. She was wearing it with some stretchy leggings that her sister had also strongly—forcefully— recommended, but she'd ignored the ballet flats in favor of her Converse sneakers.

"Okay. I'm going to explain as though you don't know anything about dating sites, so apologies if any of this is redundant."

Jo nodded. *It won't be. I know nothing.*

"So on most dating sites—Cupid.com, PlentyOfFish, even older ones like Match.com and Lavalife—people set up a profile. They talk a little bit about themselves, about what they're looking for, and then they conduct searches for matches with their criteria. Often the sites will have algorithms that suggest profiles that members might want to check out. Following?"

"Yes." It sounded a little bit tedious to Jo. She spent enough time at her computer, and the thought of scrolling endlessly, looking for a partner, didn't appeal to her.

"What makes Crossing Lines different is that it adds back a bit of the meeting-in-person element. You know, how everyone up to our generation was stuck meeting." He grinned, tapped on the keyboard, then turned the monitor to show her the screen. "What our site does is connect you with people that you come across in real life."

"I'm not following." Wasn't that just…meeting in person?

"Bear with me." John tapped on the keyboard again, and she was surprised to see him bring up what appeared to be his own profile. "Okay. So let's say that your hot sister and I were both members of Crossing Lines."

Jo couldn't hold back the smirk.

"Then let's say we both happened to go to the same Starbucks at the same time—crossing lines, so to speak. We would each receive an alert that someone else from the app was in the vicinity. You could then check out their profile and indicate whether or not you're interested."

"Oh…" Jo cocked her head to the side. "Oh, so

that saves the nerves of approaching someone you find attractive for a date, too."

"Exactly!" John beamed at her like she'd performed a trick and earned a treat. "So then let's say your hot sister and I checked out each other's profiles and indicated that we were interested. Then I could approach her, or she could approach me, and we could set up a date."

"What if one of you didn't hear the alert?" Jo didn't hear her phone most of the time, though in her case she kept her notifications on silent deliberately, so they didn't annoy her. "Doesn't that kind of screw things up in this magical meet cute?"

"No matter when you catch the alert, you're still able to see the profile," he assured her, pointing at the screen. "So even if you check an hour, two hours later. The next day. You still might think, oh, that's the cute girl from the coffee shop. Or, oh, that guy was with his kids, but now I see that he's a single dad, so I'm going to hit him up to *install my kid's car seats*."

Jo snorted at the innuendo that John infused his last words with. Pushing back in her chair, she took a moment to let it all absorb.

"This is actually kind of brilliant." She drummed her fingers on the arm of the chair. "Who thought this up?"

"Theo did." John suddenly, deliberately, busied

himself with closing out his profile and readjusting the screen.

Yeah, Jo was pretty sure that Theo had filled him in on their history. She wondered if he also knew about the upcoming date, and what he thought about it.

She still wasn't sure what *she* thought about it. She didn't—couldn't—dwell on it right now, or she'd think herself into a spiral of doom, so she changed the subject again. She was becoming an expert at it.

"So where do I come in?" She couldn't really think what place a creative writer would have on the staff of a cutting-edge dating app. She especially couldn't imagine what her kinky sex blog could contribute to anything.

"We're still what's considered a start-up company," John explained, pushing out of his chair and starting to pace again. "We're the new kid on the block—the *weird* new kid on the block. Our business model tells us that we can be incredibly successful, but we need to find new and creative ways to bring in users. Millennials and Gen Z are statistically the most likely to give something a bit different a try, and they are also the generations that are more open to new things when it comes to sex and relationships. They're intrigued by kink, and that's where you come in."

"You don't expect me to put up a profile, do you?" Panic was a flock of tiny birds in her belly. She couldn't imagine something less appealing. "I just write about it. I don't want to get kinky with strangers."

John looked at her as though she'd grown a second head. "Of course not."

She exhaled, trying to expel those tiny birds from her system. "Sorry. Go on."

"We want you to write content for us, targeted toward millennials and Gen Z." Pulling his phone from his pocket, he glanced at the screen before returning it. "We plan to start a blog that will be advertised on the home page of the site. We'll be advertising it on Facebook, Amazon and all social media. Essentially it's to be a column about sex and dating as a member of that generation. We're a new, edgy site, and we want edgy content. Your blog stood out because you aren't afraid to go there."

"Are you sure it didn't stand out because I used to date Theo and he has some kind of guilt complex?" Jo winced as the words left her mouth, but even if it was brazen to ask, she wanted—needed—to know.

She wanted this job. She had that hit of adrenaline, cold sweat, sick-with-want kind of feeling in her gut, and that wasn't even factoring in any feelings left over between her and the boss.

Her writing was hers and hers alone. No matter how much she wanted the job, any joy from it would be tainted if Theo had only offered this out of guilt.

John stopped his pacing in front of the window, his face set in serious lines. In the pale light filtering through the thick glass, Jo noted again how classically handsome he was—and again, she felt nothing. When she looked at Theo, though, with his wild dark eyes, the skin that reminded her of caramel, the way he moved his hands when he spoke about something he was passionate about...

Her entire body clenched just thinking about him.

Damn you to hell, Theo Lawrence.

"Jo, when Theo showed me your blog, he didn't tell me anything at all about your history. I had no idea that you two had ever even been in contact, let alone...close." John tapped a finger on the glass. "I agreed that your writing was perfect. And I have to say, I'm a bit jealous—you have the most fascinating dating life. Reading about it almost makes me feel like I'm there."

If only you knew. Jo forced herself to smile, nodding along with John. If he liked her content, then she didn't think there was any reason to let him know that she had experienced precisely nothing that she'd written about on her blog...well, except for this morning's. Lack of real sex, of desire, meant that she'd filled that void in her life another way, with a fascination of all things kinky. She threw in anecdotes about her sisters, too, since they always insisted on sharing every single dirty detail of their relationships, their hookups.

But her own experiences? Her blog hadn't included a single one, because there hadn't been any—not until Theo had come back.

"So that's what you want me to write, then?" Shit...did Theo think she'd done all those things she wrote about? Not that she would be ashamed of it, she just...hadn't. It was weird that he might think she did. "What I write about on my blog?"

"Essentially, yes, with an emphasis on the dating experience posts. But—" He was cut off when a knock sounded on the door. Theo entered the room without waiting for an answer. "As I was going to say, Theo will be in momentarily with a list of ideas for topics."

"And here he is." Theo's words were light, but his gaze was a punch of pure heat when he ignored John and focused in on Jo. "Is John treating you right?"

Something about the way he asked made the question sound deliciously dirty. Jo found herself unconsciously rubbing her thighs together under the shiny surface of the desk.

"Like a lady," she retorted, casting a smile in John's direction. On anyone else the expression might have looked coquettish—on her, Jo imagined it looked pained, but it had the intended effect. Theo narrowed his eyes at his partner.

Like Jo, he'd always had a temper, often fueled by jealousy. Where that had caused them to self-combust when they were younger, now Jo tasted a hint of how that possessiveness could be...well, hot.

Moving her gaze from John to Theo, she instead found it a bit hard to breathe.

What the hell was she supposed to do with this?

John's phone rang, the no-nonsense ringtone slicing through the thick air. Without another word to the pair of them, he answered it, waving goodbye as he exited the office, closing the door firmly behind him.

They were alone, and the heaviness of Theo's gaze made Jo want to break eye contact. The thread of stubbornness that had been wrapped around her since birth refused to let her back down.

He wasn't challenged by the direct stare. If anything, he seemed amused, his lips curling into a faint smirk. Holding eye contact, he closed the distance between them, stopping when he reached the front of the desk.

Jo immediately felt the need to stand, to put them on even ground, but she knew that the movement would show how off balance he made her feel.

Why did this feel so much like war? And why did she want to wave the white flag and throw herself at that rock-solid chest?

"Since you showed up this morning, I'm assuming you've accepted the job." His posture was arrogant, as though it would never occur to him that she would say no. Looking him over, though, Jo noticed him rubbing the pads of his thumb and forefinger together at his side. It was an old tic of his, a way of releasing excess energy when he was feeling more than he wanted to be.

What was he feeling now? Lust? Guilt? What would she do if she knew?

"I haven't accepted it officially, no."

Theo said nothing, just kept watching her with that dark gaze. Damn it, he knew—he knew how much she wanted this job. Refusing it would show him how much he was affecting her.

Still looking at her, he pulled out his tablet, moving his fingers over the screen. "I just emailed you the employment agreement. There's no need to print it—it can be signed electronically. Of course, you'll want to read it all the way through, but I think you'll find that it's an extremely generous offer."

"Theo…" She closed her eyes. Why was she bothering to put up a front at all? He'd always been able to read her better than anyone, and she had no doubt that he knew exactly what she was struggling with right now. She might as well say it. "Look. I want this job. I'm still attracted to you."

She choked on the last part—that she was terrified of falling for him again, only to have him leave. There was vulnerable, and there was *vulnerable*.

"I don't understand why you can't have both."

Jo's chin snapped up. There was no disguising the desire that was thick in his voice, a sound that was imprinted onto her very DNA.

"You can review the agreement in the car." He tossed an inky-black silk scarf onto the desk in front of her, and for the first time since he'd entered the room, she noticed that he was wearing a light peacoat. "You can also look over the list of potential blog topics that I sent. I'm curious which one catches your attention first."

"The car?" Picking up the fabric, she discovered that it was a kerchief, the type an old-time movie star might have once worn to protect her hair. "Where are we going?"

"You agreed to go on a date with me." The cocky smile he shot her made her feel like she was fifteen years old again, all knobby knees and fluttery feelings for the boy next door. "It's date time."

"I agreed to go to dinner with you." She pointedly checked out the clock on the wall. "It's not even eleven in the morning."

"We'll have dinner, too. Maybe more, if you're good." Damn it. The confidence in his voice, in every line of his body, shouldn't have still been so sexy, and yet it was like his words cast out a hook that caught her and reeled her in.

"You know damn well that I've never been good, so I wouldn't get your hopes up." Even as she spoke, she found herself rising, reaching for the cardigan sweater that was part of the ensemble when Meg had dressed her up like a doll this morning.

Theo frowned when she shrugged into it. "Don't you have a heavier coat?"

"I only wear coats when it reaches minus twenty." Jo held up the kerchief thing. "What am I supposed to do with this?"

"Tie your hair back." He gestured with his hands. "Otherwise it'll get in your face."

Puzzled, Jo struggled to arrange the scarf on her

head. Breathing out on a chuckle, Theo rounded the desk, taking it from her hands.

"Like this." Turning her with the press of a hand on her lower back, he stroked his fingers through the sleek, chin-length strands of her hair. Her pulse stilled as he tucked them behind her ears, brushing over the tops of her ears.

A rough breath escaped her as he arranged the silk over her hair. When he tied it in a knot at the base of her skull, he whispered a light touch down the back of her neck, tracing a line to the top of her spine.

Just a simple touch, but she felt it over her entire body. Her breasts swelled, aching, and she arched into his hands.

"There. You're ready." Breaking the connection, Theo stepped back, put some much-needed space between them. Her heart was hammering so hard that she spoke extra loud in order to be heard over it.

"Ready for what?" And she wasn't ready. She wasn't ready at all.

He grinned, then dangled a set of car keys. "Ready for a ride in the convertible."

CHAPTER TEN

"Jo, YOU MIGHT as well relax. We're going to be in the car for a while, and you're going to get a headache if you keep clenching your jaw like that."

Theo had his eyes on the road ahead but was aware of every movement, every breath Jo made in the passenger's seat of the low-slung F-Type Jaguar.

She'd been tense since they'd left the office, navigating through the congested streets of the city and onto the interstate. He could still feel the heat of her skin, branded onto the tips of his fingers from when he'd helped her with the scarf, and he didn't think the tension was because she didn't want to be there. In fact, he knew it—he knew Jo.

He knew that breathy little sigh, the same one she'd made when he was inside her. She was tense for the same reason he was—because she still wanted him. She wanted him, and she was confused about it.

He hoped that what he'd planned for today would help her clear her mind.

"Where are we going?" She'd asked this approximately every ten minutes since they'd left Boston, making him grin. Patience had never been one of her virtues.

"You'll find out when we get there." Luckily for her, he had patience enough for the both of them. "For now, let's go over that list of article ideas. Pull it up and let's see what grabs you."

Huffing out a breath of exasperation, she wriggled her phone out of her pocket. He watched from the corner of his eye, enjoying the view of her thighs and her slim hips, wondering how on earth she'd managed to fit anything into the pocket of pants so tight.

"'Wildest one-night stands,'" she read. He expected her to make some kind of sarcastic remark—in fact, he was looking forward to it—but instead she nodded thoughtfully. "I could work with that."

What?

"What is the main purpose of Crossing Lines, as far as your marketing goes?" She sank her teeth into her lower lip, and he wanted to do that himself. "Is it for casual dating? Relationships? Or is it like that one site…what's it called? Timber?"

"Tinder." He pressed his lips together, trying not to laugh, since he could see that she was being serious. "And it's for all of the above. But the hope is that by having you blog about all kinds of interesting topics relating to sex and love, it will set us up as being more cutting-edge than our peers. More avant-garde, the ones with our finger on the pulse of what the cool kids want."

She nodded, returning to the list.

"'Sugar dating—dating on your terms.'" She cocked her head, curious. "What's that? I know I've read about that, but I'm a little unclear on the details."

"Ever heard the term *sugar daddy*?" She nodded. "There are a number of sites to connect people who are looking for that kind of situation. Sugar daddies—or mommies—who don't have the time or inclination for a relationship will post, seeking an arrangement with a sugar baby, mostly women, but there are some men now. In return for company and, most of the time, sex, the sugar daddies will fulfill wishes on the sugar baby's list—often that's someone to cover the rent, to help with student debt, to fund travel."

"So we could do an article about why it's called dating when, really, it's a form of sex work?" She chewed on her lip as she thought about it, and he fought to keep his eyes on the road against the distraction those pink lips provided.

"That could work," he said, taking a moment to look the other way, away from those sexy lips. Unfortunately, the endless field of grass didn't have much to offer that could hold his attention.

"I don't think we should do this one. It will make readers curious about these arrangement sites, driving them away from yours. We want to write about things that get them excited about exploring what they've read about, eager to meet people...but to meet people on Crossing Lines. Right?"

"I hadn't thought about that," he said, surprised. She was right, of course, and John would have likely said the same thing if he'd reviewed the list before Theo had sent it to Jo. "That's a good point."

Jo tapped a finger to her temple, grinning. "Not just air in here, my friend."

A dart of warmth—not heat, not lust, but warmth—spread in Theo's chest. This was the first genuine smile that Jo had given him since he'd returned. Something twisted in his rib cage, causing a bone-deep ache.

"'Erotic fire cupping. Naked summer pool-hopping. Marijuana lube.'" She continued reviewing the list, commenting as she went. When she was halfway through the list, she paused, letting out a sexy little sound that made his dick sit up and pay attention.

"'Sex with an ex,'" she read, setting her phone down on her thigh. "'Exploring kink with an old flame can be easier than getting dirty with someone you want to keep.'"

He said nothing. He hadn't added it to the list just to broach the topic, at least not consciously. That said, he'd wondered what she'd say about it, if anything.

With other women, he was on sure footing. He was charming, he was cocky, he was bossy and it worked—oh, how it worked.

Jo, though? Jo wasn't like any other woman he'd ever met. She saw through his charm, laughed at his cockiness, and if he was bossy, well, one nudge too many and she'd kick back like a mule. It didn't leave him with many options—at least, not ones he'd used before.

She was silent for a long moment, her thumb rubbing over the screen on her phone. He wasn't prepared when she half turned in her seat, tucking one leg up underneath her.

"What would you think about that?" she asked, curiosity thick in her words.

"What?" His fingers tightened on the steering

wheel. "Like…what do I think about that in general?"

"No." She drew the word out into three syllables. "You know what I mean. Sex. Us."

She'd managed to shock him. He'd thought that she might read that item and tuck it away in that busy brain to think about later. She might even have ignored it entirely, refusing to give him the satisfaction of letting him know that she was thinking about it.

Never in his wildest dreams—and when it came to Jo, he had a lot of dreams—had he imagined that she would come right out and ask him what he thought about them having sex.

"I think I've made it pretty obvious what I want here." He cast her a sidelong look. "That's why we're in this car, right? This is a date."

"It's a date, but I wasn't planning on sleeping with you after it," she replied archly. He made a show of wincing.

"Way to hurt a man where it counts, Jo. Right in the desperate hope."

"You've never been desperate in your life," she snorted, tapping her phone on her knee. She was quiet for a moment, and he had to claw back the urge to demand to know what was running through her head.

"I'm not saying this properly." She swallowed,

tapping her phone faster. "Look. I know that I write about a lot of…stuff. Kinky stuff. And you must think I write about it convincingly, or you wouldn't have offered me this job."

"Right." He drew out the word, his pulse picking up. She'd always been easy for him to read, but right now he truly didn't know what she was thinking.

"You're going to make me spell it out, aren't you?" She huffed out a breath, then scrubbed her hands over her face. "Look. I write about kink because I'm interested in it. But I don't…you know I don't do all of those things, right?"

Her words came out in a rush. A terrible, wild hope began to build up inside him.

"Are you saying that you want to try some of those things?" His attention had been on her since the moment he'd walked into that office, but now it was laser focused.

"Yes." His Jo had never been anything but direct, and right now, by God, he appreciated it. "But I don't… I'm not interested in exploring with most people."

"Are you saying that you're interested in exploring with me?" His hands clenched on the steering wheel.

"That's exactly what I'm saying." Turning, she looked up at him with those wide gray eyes. "But I need you to understand that that doesn't…it doesn't mean that things are the way they were before."

The tiniest dart of pain hooked itself into his chest. He'd known that she wouldn't welcome him back with open arms, but it still hadn't killed the evil that was hope.

He wasn't a man to settle for halves when he wanted the whole—he was, however, a man who'd learned that nothing was sweeter than something you'd worked for.

"So what you're saying is, you want to use me for my body and nothing else?" Her cheeks were flushed, and he knew that it wasn't from the wind as they flew down the interstate. "I'd be a very stupid man not to take you up on that offer, Jo Marchande. I like to think I'm rather clever."

"So you don't need to do stuff like…this." She gestured out the window as the Jag swung onto the exit to the town of Concord. "Planning dates. Being charming. You know."

"Baby, my charm is natural. You should know I've never been without it." He grinned at her, wiggling his eyebrows, and she giggled, a wholly un-Jo-like sound, but one he was pleased to have pulled from her. "As for the date. Just go with it. You might have been here sometime since I left, but I wanted to bring you here anyway."

"Bedford Street." Letting his GPS navigate

them through the town, he finally brought the car to a stop outside a large set of wrought-iron gates. On either side of the entrance were long, low-slung stone walls, worn with age and slicked with moss.

Jo squinted forward, reading the sign.

"Sleepy Hollow Cemetery," she read, her words tinged with confusion. He waited patiently.

Every other woman he'd dated would have been horrified to be taken to a cemetery on a date, and rightly so. But this truly was someplace he'd wanted to take her for well over a decade, and when the confusion on her face gave way to delight, he knew he'd scored a home run.

"Author's Ridge!" Shoving her phone back into the pocket of her pants, she undid her seat belt, then scrambled out of the car. "Let's go!"

High on the success of his idea, Theo followed more slowly, catching up with her as she paused to take a picture of the cemetery entrance. "How have you not been here yet?"

She shrugged, turning to get a shot from the other direction. "Well, I drive, but I don't trust my scooter to go this far. And no one I know is even the slightest bit interested in going to see graves."

"Their loss." He shrugged. He wasn't overly pumped about graveyards as a whole, but knowing how much Jo had wanted to come here made it appealing for him. Plus, he thought as he looked around, sucking in the clean air of the wide space, the freshly budding trees and the scent of spring, there were worse ways to spend an afternoon than outdoors, exploring history.

"Come on!" More animated than she'd been since he'd come back, at least to him, she grabbed a paper map from a box affixed to the gate. "Did you know that Ralph Waldo Emerson gave the dedication speech when the cemetery first opened? *And* that he's buried here?"

Theo chuckled as he followed after her. Watching Jo study the map, her brow furrowed, something settled in his chest, something that he recognized as contentment.

He'd missed this. He'd missed her. And he understood why she was wary when it came to her feelings about him, but once he'd seen her again, he'd known that this was it.

He just had to convince her that this—them—was it, too.

He enjoyed the walk through the cemetery, which reminded him of one of the gorgeous, slightly overgrown gardens that he often saw in Europe. The stones were weathered but well taken care of, and the greenery was lush and wild. It was peaceful, he realized.

One thing he'd never really had in his life was peace. It was the thing that had been lacking among the countless other luxuries he'd once taken for granted.

He caught up with her when she paused, staring with barely concealed excitement at a stone marker. "This is it. This is Author's Ridge."

He didn't entirely understand why she was so excited that she was trembling a bit. He didn't have to understand to respect it, though, so he stayed silent, his arm brushing companionably against hers as they started to weave their way among the graves.

"Henry David Thoreau." She pointed to a simple stone that, rather than being marked with the last name, displayed the first in blocky letters. "Wow."

"What's with the pencils?" Scattered among the bouquets of flowers and votive candles that showed that something noteworthy lay here were pencils—singles, bundles wrapped with ribbon, even whole boxes, the cardboard warped and faded from the sun and the rain.

"Thoreau and his father ran a big pencil company before he was a writer," she murmured, capturing the image with her phone, then consulting the map. "And just over here should be…holy crap. It's Louisa May Alcott."

"*Little Women*, right?" He followed Jo over to where she'd stopped at the base of a plain stone set into the ground. Around it were more flowers as well as a handful of apples and paper—so much paper. Dog-eared books, shiny new copies, torn book covers, what looked like art.

"That's right." Jo's voice was hushed, and he understood that this particular grave was why she'd so badly wanted to come here once upon a time. "I don't even know how many times I've read that book. I still have my first paper copy, the one I had as a kid, but it's so tattered you can't read it anymore. But I feel like… I almost feel like part of myself is in those pages, because they gave me so much growing up. That sounds stupid."

"It doesn't sound stupid at all." A lightbulb went on in his brain. "Was she what inspired you to start writing?"

"Yeah." Jo nodded, then looked up at him with a wry smile. "She wrote a classic American novel, beloved by millions. I have to wonder what she'd think about me writing a sex blog."

He grinned. "If you found so much inspiration in her, then I have to think she was pretty cool. She'd probably say that as long as you were writing what made you happy, it was all good."

The look Jo cast over her shoulder at him then was almost shy, and he felt something in the vicinity of his heart squeeze, just the littlest bit. Turning, she closed the space between them until she had just enough room to place a hand on his chest, the other behind his neck.

"No matter what else happens with us, thank you for this." Drawing up on the tips of her toes—he really had forgotten how small she was—she drew him down for a kiss. It was a sweet brush of the lips, almost chaste, but the bolt of emotion he felt as she sighed against his lips nearly set him back on his heels.

He'd thought he'd loved the girl that she once was, but he saw right now, with clarity, that what he'd felt then paled compared to the potential of what he could feel now.

He looked down into her eyes, where she was watching with curiosity and a hint of wariness. He wanted to pull off the scarf she was still wearing, to grip that sleek hair and plunder her mouth with his tongue, but he figured that was probably inappropriate when standing at the grave of her idol.

Still, the moment seemed to call for something—something to pin it in place, bookmarked for the future.

"You know why I had to go."

"Of course I know." Angling her chin up, she regarded him with those big eyes. "We fought. You realized that we didn't fit. That we never would."

"What?" His fingers squeezed her shoulders as the words hit him like a bat. "You think I left because we fought? Is that seriously what you've thought this entire time?"

The sneaky snake that was guilt coiled in his belly and settled in. He'd thought the reason for his leaving was so obvious, he hadn't left a note. Hadn't emailed. Hadn't said a damn word to anyone, not even his dad.

No one had come after him, either. Years later, that still hurt.

"That wasn't why you left?" Jo pushed lightly on his chest, enough that she could look up at him. "What on earth was your reason, then?"

"I left because you were right." He slid his hands down until he held her by her upper arms, somehow needing the connection.

"I was right?" Her brow furrowed.

"I was throwing my life away. Drinking and partying and wasting money that wasn't even mine." He rubbed his hands up and down her arms, as though to warm her, though he was the one feeling a chill. "I looked at how hard you were working to achieve your goals, you and your sisters. The way I was must have just rubbed it in your face that I was squandering what I had, and what you so badly wanted."

"That's part of it," she admitted, then to his surprise leaned forward and pressed her forehead to his chest, letting out a soft sigh.

"What was the other part?" he asked quietly.

She kept her face buried, and he liked how it felt. Finally she sighed again, then spoke.

"The other part was that I loved you." She shifted position, now pressing her cheek against him. "I loved you, and I believed that you were capable of taking over the world if you wanted to. Instead, you seemed intent on self-destruction. I couldn't just sit by and watch."

Theo opened his mouth to reply but found that he had no idea what to say to that. Most of the decisions that he'd made over the years had been pondered with Jo's voice in his ear. He'd done it with an eye to proving himself to her, even though he wasn't sure if he'd ever see her again.

He had no idea that she'd thought him capable all along.

A drop of rain splashed squarely on his nose, breaking up his thoughts. It was followed by a sprinkling of rain in Jo's hair.

"Shit." Clouds rolled in, thick as soup, and a bolt of lightning lit up the sky and made the hairs on the back of his neck stand up straight as the electricity charged the air around them. "Let's run!"

Jo squealed with laughter as he grabbed her hand, tugging her back in the direction they'd come. They were both soaking by the time they reached the car, which he'd thankfully folded up the top to.

He opened her door, helping her in, before sprinting around to the driver's side. When he was safely enclosed in the dry space, he shook like a dog, cursing as he looked down.

"Since when do you get so worked up about rain?" Peeling off the silk scarf, Jo combed her fingers through her hair, which was sleek with moisture. "I distinctly remember you once streaking down the street in it after a few too many beers with your school friends."

Theo grimaced, unbuttoning his suit jacket. "I'll go streaking anytime you want me to, baby. But I'd prefer not to ruin this suit. I was assured that it was made by blind monks on a hill somewhere, woven out of their blood and tears or some such nonsense. That's the only explanation behind the price."

He tossed his jacket behind his seat, then loosened his tie, unbuttoning the top of his shirt. Moving on to loosening his cuffs, he found Jo watching him with more than a hint of hunger on her face.

He didn't think; he just acted, placing his palm flat on the nape of her neck and hauling her against his chest. She made a muffled moan as he crushed his lips to hers, his tongue immediately tracing the seam of her mouth, demanding that she open for him.

She did, a sigh of surrender on her lips when he slipped his tongue into her mouth and tasted her. The smoky scent of cinnamon that he swore came from her very skin surrounded him, drugging him as he stroked between her lips the way he wanted to taste between her legs.

A crack of thunder so loud that the car vibrated crashed through the air, and they jolted apart, both breathing heavily. When he looked at Jo, saw her lips swollen from his kisses, her cheeks flushed with desire, it took everything he had not to haul her astride him then and there.

He didn't want their first time again to be in a cramped car outside a graveyard. No, what he wanted was to strip her naked, lay her out on his bed and do every single thing he'd ever dreamed of doing to Jo Marchande.

The way she was looking at him right now? He thought he might finally have the chance.

CHAPTER ELEVEN

THE HOUR-LONG RIDE back to Boston was quiet, the only words exchanged as they picked their way through the picnic that Theo had packed. Actually, he'd ordered it from a popular deli downtown, but he didn't see why that made any difference. She was too keyed up to eat more than a handful of grapes and a small wedge of smoked cheddar, and he liked that she seemed worked up.

"Where do you live?" As he turned down their street, he realized how little she still knew of his life in the years between. "I can't imagine you're staying at the house. It's been empty since…well, since your dad died."

"I actually am." He cast a sidelong glance at her in the growing shadows. Warmer weather was approaching, but the nights were still long and the light was already fading. He liked it—the blueberry tones of twilight seemed to wrap them in a little cocoon, where they could stay as long as they liked. "I stayed away for a while because…well, I just couldn't handle going through his things yet. Not when I know what a disappointment I was to him."

"You didn't come to his funeral." There was no judgment in her words.

"I did, actually," he admitted, pulling the Jag into the long driveway that led to the stately mansion. Jo gaped at him as he put it into Park and turned to face her.

"Why didn't I see you there?" A spark of anger licked at her words, and he knew he deserved it.

"I made sure you didn't," he replied simply, shrugging. "I wasn't ready."

"Ready for *what*, for the love of God?" She threw her hands in the air.

"I wasn't yet the person I'd gone away to become." He watched her steadily as she seemed to mull that over. He knew she had questions—she'd always displayed every single thing that she thought on her face without a filter.

"Have you been back in Boston since then?" she asked carefully.

"No." He wanted to reach for her, to touch her, but wasn't sure she'd welcome it right then. "No, I came back just for the funeral. I was in New York then. Had been for a few years. I only moved back to Boston a couple of months ago, when I opened the Crossing Lines office here. I stayed at the Boston Plaza until this week."

"Until you were ready to let me know you were back?" She seemed to chew on that. He held his breath, wondering what she was going to ask next. "Is Crossing Lines that new of a company?"

"Yes and no." He thought back, pulling up the details. "It's been in the works for a few years. I didn't want to use my dad's money for it, so I had to raise funds, which took a while. Then there was the programming, structuring the company. I didn't move the offices to Boston until we were officially open. Some of the staff came with me, which made me happy. I'm trying to instill a certain kind of corporate culture, one that treats its employees right and makes them happy, because I think that happiness will filter down to the users of the site."

"Was Ava one of the employees who moved with you?" Theo studied her face as she asked. He didn't see jealousy, but there was a hint of possessiveness that made him want to drag her into the house and claim her, caveman style.

"She was." He didn't feel guilty about anything he'd done with Ava—he assumed that Jo had had lovers over the years, as well. "But we were never together romantically. It was just sex."

Not even that great of sex, either, but he didn't think that Jo needed any details—at least, any more detail than what she'd already seen with her own eyes.

She nodded, appearing to accept that, but then pinned him with an intense look. "I don't care what you've done when we were apart. But I'm not comfortable with you being with other women while we're...while we're doing whatever we're going to do."

"Say it." He savored the spark that lit her eyes. "Say what you want me to do to you."

"I want you to fuck me." Her voice was quiet, but sure. His girl had always known what she wanted before she reached out and took it. "Only you."

Taking her chin in his hand, he tilted her head so that she was sitting up perfectly straight, his hand on her skin their only point of contact. "You don't want to see what I'd do to any other man who touches you."

"While we're together," she added, expression daring him to argue.

He smiled grimly. "We'll see."

Leaving her frowning over that, he exited the car, circling round the back so that he could open her door for her. He helped her out, hooking his suit jacket—now only slightly damp—over her to protect her from the relentless drizzle that was still coming down.

He led her through the front door, closing it behind them. The door was old, like the rest of the house made of heavy wood. The sound of it closing was satisfying, solid, and Theo again had the sense that they were being wrapped in a cocoon that was all their own.

"Do you want a refresher tour?" he asked quietly, watching as she looked around, those keen writer eyes taking in every detail. "It's been a long time."

She turned her attention from the heavy, dated crystal chandelier overhead to him, and his heart skipped a beat when he saw the decision in her eyes.

"No." She inhaled softly, pulling his suit jacket off and holding it back out to him. "I just want to see your room."

If he touched her, they wouldn't make it to his room. Hanging his jacket carelessly on the post of the banister, he followed her upstairs, stopping her when she tried to turn into his old room.

"I've moved." With a jerk of his chin, he pointed her in the direction of the master suite. "Over here."

Inside the massive room, he slid the dimmer switch on halfway—he wanted to be able to see her, every part of her. Pulling off his tie, he enjoyed watching her explore the space.

"You must have just redone this." She paused to run a finger over the headboard of his bed—a new one he'd had custom built when he'd decided to move into this house. "I can smell paint."

"It was just finished last week, actually." Kicking off his shoes, he undid a few more buttons on his shirt, noting the way her eyes tracked the movement. "Moving into my old room felt like moving into the past. But I thought it would be weird to live in here with my dad's old stuff, which was hugely dated, anyway. So I gutted this room and the master bath. Some of the crew was actually putting the finishing touches on your hotel, so I'm not surprised you didn't notice. They would have blended right in."

She appeared to chew on that as she moved to the window. Bracing her hands on the sill, she peered outside, in the direction of her house, the one that her family had been in for decades, the one he knew she'd worked herself to the bone to make sure they kept.

"You renovated these rooms." She spoke carefully, measuring each word. "Does that mean you plan on staying?"

He was taken aback by the direct question. He

knew his plans for the next few years, but beyond that…he hadn't really thought.

He couldn't help but be honest. This was Jo. He'd never lied to her, and he didn't want to make it a new habit.

"I'm here as long as it makes sense for me to be here, for the company." He took a deep breath. "I've always assumed that sooner or later I'd sell, though. That I'd take the profits from Crossing Lines and go invest in something else. Something bigger."

"Something away from Boston," she said as she stared out the window. He wanted her to turn around so that he could see her face.

"Well…probably," he agreed, raking his hand through his hair. Why did that suddenly not sound as appealing as it once had? Why was he even asking that question? He knew why. Chances were, after this he would move back to New York, or more likely, to LA. His dreams didn't start and end with Crossing Lines. And no matter what happened here between him and Jo, she would never leave Boston. Never leave her family.

He shifted uncomfortably in the silence, suddenly filled with a restlessness that made him edgy. He watched as Jo pushed away from the window, sauntering over to the bed. Her body language said that she didn't care one way or another what his answer to that question had been, and it made a thread of something darkly possessive spark to life inside him.

She perched on the edge of the bed, smoothing a hand over the steel-gray quilt. "This bed is huge. You could have an orgy in it."

"Let's save that for another night." He felt his lips form a lopsided smile as she arched an eyebrow at him, seemingly content with the subject change. "I promised you dinner."

"I'm not hungry." Rising, she crossed to him, stopping a foot away. His stare fixed on her pulse, beating rapidly beneath the glove-thin skin of her throat. He wanted to press his mouth there. Use his teeth to mark her as his own.

"What should we do, then?" Even as he spoke, he undid the last of the buttons on his shirt, letting it hang open. He enjoyed her appreciative glance. He'd always logged long hours in the gym, even as a teen, since he wasn't doing much else. But he'd thickened since then, no longer had any of the gangly limbs associated with puberty. As Jo shed her cardigan, he noted that her body had changed, too, though the differences were subtle. She'd always been petite, nearly skinny in her teens. Now she was curved in all the right places, and though her breasts were still small, they'd plumped up enough to make him think about all the dirty things he wanted to do to them.

"What should we do?" he repeated, taking her by the waist. She shivered as he drew her slowly to him, until the tips of those pretty breasts brushed against the bare skin of his chest.

"I'm cold." He didn't think she meant just physically, though her hands were chilly from the damp, the rain. "I want you to warm me up."

Heat rocketed through Theo's body. He'd been with other women, beautiful women, sexy women. Most of them had been so eager to be with him that he hadn't had to do much to charm them into his bed. He hadn't had to do much to please them there, either, since ultimately what they were after wasn't really him. No, they wanted the idea of him—the maverick rich boy, the one who turned his back on his family fortune and made his own millions. They liked the travel, the luxury, the lifestyle.

With Jo, his money had always been more of a hindrance if it was anything at all, which it often wasn't. The woman who stood before him in what he was pretty sure were clothes belonging to one of her sisters had no interest in money beyond keeping her family comfortable. She wasn't into shopping, hadn't batted an eye at his Jag. So the fact that she was here at all meant that it was because she wanted *him*. Him, Theo.

He'd never had to work so hard to get a woman into his bed. And no other woman heated his blood quite like she did.

He wanted this to be good for her, wanted her to be fully aware of who was inside her when she came on his cock.

"Strip for me." Peeling her cardigan down just enough to expose her delicate shoulders, he pressed a kiss to one then stepped back. He enjoyed the shiver that passed through it, because he knew she was thinking of what was about to happen.

"I said I was cold. How am I supposed to get warm if I take off my clothes?"

But even as she spoke, she was tugging the damp sweater down her arms and off, tossing it to the floor.

"Keep going." Wanting to see if she would buck against the command, he infused it with arrogance. His brave girl merely arched an eyebrow and slithered out of the long shirtdress thing that hid far too much of her tight little body.

"Last time we were together, I don't think you even owned a bra." He nodded at the simple, baby blue cotton that covered her chest. "This is new."

"I was a little smaller then. I didn't need one."

Rosy pink flushed the skin of her torso. "They're still not that big, but it's enough that I'd be giving everyone a show without one."

"I like it." He really did—the simple cotton held up her sweet breasts like an offering. "Take it off."

"You're probably used to seeing women in things a lot sexier than this." Flicking open the front clasp, she held the bra up by cupping her hands around her breasts. "I can get something fancier."

"Don't you dare," he ordered with enough force to make her blink up at him with surprise. "If I wanted to see other women in fancy lingerie, then that's what I'd be doing right now. But I'm here with you, so what does that tell you?"

She stared up at him almost nervously, her tongue flicking out to lick over her lips. She didn't answer.

Before she could inhale even one more time, he'd closed the space between them, threading a hand through her short, sleek hair. She gasped but arched into the touch, letting her bra fall open and down to the floor.

"I want to hear you say it," he commanded, focused on every little detail of her expression. Her pulse had quickened, her eyes were dilated and her lips had parted, making him think about how they would look wrapped around his cock. "Answer my question."

"You're here because you want me." Her voice was quiet, but her words were clear. She knew it, too—there was no point in fighting the connection that had snapped tight between them since the moment they'd met.

"I like hearing that from your mouth." Without letting go of her hair, he tugged at her leggings, yanking them down her thighs, along with a pair of briefs that matched her bra. Sliding his foot between her legs, he pushed down until she was forced to step out of them.

She gasped when he lifted her without warning, hauling her over his shoulder. "What the hell are you doing?"

"I told you to strip and you took your sweet time about it, so I decided to do it for you." Carrying her toward the bathroom, he let his palm roam over the supple planes of her ass. "Since you don't seem to take direction well, I decided that I would just take you where I wanted you, rather than wait for you to get around to it."

"Since I don't take direction well?" Her lips parted in shock as he carried her right into the massive shower that he'd had installed when he redid the bathroom. Flipping her hair out of her eyes after he set her on her feet, he saw her struggle to make sense of that play out over her face.

Her lips parted as if to ask him something, then closed again.

"Ask me," he said as he entered a series of settings on the sleek control panel built into the wall of the shower. Triple rainfalls burst down around them, steam rising hot and quick. He looked back at Jo, was entranced by the droplets of water sliding over her skin.

"Do you expect me to do what you tell me to?" Her voice was tentative. "Are you dominant? Are you into that?"

She didn't sound horrified, only curious, which raised his temperature far past the point of comfort. Shrugging out of his now soaking-wet dress shirt, he tossed it to the floor, his slacks and briefs quickly joining it.

Her stare immediately went to his erection, and even over the thunderous spray of the shower he could hear her soft moan. He'd been hard since they stepped into his bedroom, but with her eyes on his cock, he swelled even more.

"I'm not into hard-core BDSM, if that's what you're asking. I don't expect you to call me sir." He grinned down at her; she snorted in response. He grabbed her wrist, tugged her wet, naked body against his own and gave in to the urge to lick those water droplets from her neck.

"I'd rather hear you say my name when you're coming on my dick," he murmured into her ear, nipping at the lobe when she shuddered. "And like I said. I'm not dominant, but if you let me be bossy, I think you'll find that you enjoy it."

"I'm…not…the…submissive…type." She gasped, rocking into him when he trailed kisses down her neck. He laughed.

"I don't want you to be submissive. I like women who give me hell." Trailing a hand down her spine, he pressed her to him, groaned himself when his erection pressed into the lean planes of her belly.

"That's always been a special talent of mine," she gasped as he ground into her. He was surprised at how tentative she was when her hand slid lower and found him. She stroked his length, cupped his shaft as though she'd never seen a cock before.

Her next words nearly brought him to his knees. "I'm always happy to give you hell. But… I don't think I'd mind if you…told me what to do. I think I'd like to try."

"Hell, Jo." Both of his hands found her hair, smoothing through the wet ribbons of it and dragging her mouth to his. He claimed her lips, tonguing her until she was rocking against him with breathy little sighs. "If you don't like what I'm doing, you just say so in plain English. Or shake your head. Whatever. I'll stop."

She nodded breathlessly, then raised her chin defiantly. "You're talking an awful lot. Got any action to back it up with?"

With a growl that was part laughter, part pure animal lust, he cupped his hands under her ass and lifted her, carrying her to a small seat carved out of the marble wall. Placing her on it, he reached for his discarded pants, pulling his belt free from the loops.

His leather belt, his suit, they were all ruined after today. He didn't give even a single fuck. It was all going to be worth it.

Jo's eyes widened at the sight of the belt. "You're not hitting me with that thing."

Theo snorted, though he couldn't resist slapping it against his palm, just to test her reaction. "Not this time, baby. But something tells me you might like a little spanking."

"You're not—" Her words were stuck in her throat when he grabbed her hands, pressing her palms together. She watched with wide eyes as he wrapped his belt around them, securing her wrists together before sliding a finger underneath to make sure the belt wasn't too tight.

Part of him, the one that was very familiar with her temper, expected her to tell him to fuck right off if he thought he was going to tie her up. But this Jo was older, more mature and had a self-professed interest in all things kinky. This Jo made a low, breathy sound when he lifted her bound wrists and hooked them over one of the showerheads, tethering her in place.

"Oh, I like this." Stepping back, he admired his handiwork. Seated on the small bench, the position of her arms forced her to arch her back, which showed off those pretty tits. Man, he'd missed those. Cupping one in each hand, he circled his thumbs over her nipples, satisfaction coursing through him when they pebbled beneath his touch. "I can do whatever I want with you all trussed up like this, can't I? You can give me lip, but you can't do much about it."

He was testing her. If she gave him even one sign that she wasn't into it, that she was scared, he'd let her go in an instant. Instead, her body rocked forward, trying to get closer to him.

"For heaven's sake, Theo, stop messing around. Come here." Her voice was raw with need.

Letting go of one breast, he tapped a finger against her lips. "You're not the boss here, remember? You'll get my cock when I say so, and not a minute before."

She cursed, and he laughed. Sliding his hands down, he parted her thighs wide enough for him to stand between them. She gasped eagerly when the head of his shaft brushed the soft heat of her cleft, but he had other ideas.

"I wish I had another belt in here to hold you open just like this, but since I don't, we'll just have to make do." He slid a finger through her folds, her knees tightening on either side of his hips against the sudden contact.

"You're soaked." He lifted his fingers up so she could see her own moisture on them, wetter even than the water pouring down around them. When he slid those same fingers into his mouth and licked them clean, her head fell back, watching him through partially lowered lids.

"You're the only person who's ever made me that way." Her focus stayed locked on him, and he understood that she was sharing something important with him. The weight of her words hit him with the impact of a bulldozer.

He didn't deserve this, not after the way he'd left. But then, he'd never claimed to be a good man. He certainly wasn't above taking what she was offering to him.

He thought he just might die if he didn't.

"Are you warming up?" He ran a hand along her inner thigh. She melted beneath his touch, her muscles liquefying like honey in the sun. She continued to regard him with that laser-like focus, as though she was afraid he would disappear if she looked away.

"Keep looking at me like that." Moving his hands to brace them on either side of her face, he leaned in, let his cock press against her slick heat. "It makes me so fucking hard."

"Good." She gasped when he rubbed against her, her thighs clenching around his hips. "That's how I want you."

"Mmm, but this isn't about what you want. I'm bossy, remember?" Dipping his head, he laved his tongue over her nipple. "It's about what I want to give you."

"Damn it, Theo." She tugged at her bindings, cursing when they wouldn't give. "I want to touch you."

"And I want to touch you." Standing, he reached for the detachable showerhead mounted into the wall. "Guess what? I win."

So would she, though, and very soon. Adjusting the nozzle of the showerhead until the water flowed in a steady stream, but not one that would be too hard for her sensitive flesh, he aimed it between her legs. Her gasp when the water made contact sent a stream of pure desire through him.

"Jesus." She writhed on the bench, twisting against her restraints like a wild thing. Her hips bucked, and he wasn't sure if she was trying to lean into the spray or push away. Steam rolled through the shower, and he couldn't tell if the droplets of water on her skin were from the water falling around them or sweat, not even when he laid his tongue to her shoulder for a taste.

"Theo. I can't… I'm going to…" She arched like a bow as he began to move the spray in slow circles between her legs, edging around her clit but not coming in direct contact with it. Her frenzied motions brought her heat into contact with the swollen length of his dick, and he briefly closed his eyes to regain his control.

When he opened them again, he was struck by the visual that was laid out before him. Slim as an arrow, she still curved in all the places that made his mouth go dry. Her milky-white skin was a pretty shade of pink from arousal and heat. Her nipples were cherry red and their tips bunched enticingly, begging for his mouth. Her eyes were still at half-mast, glassy with lust but fixed on the visual of his cock, the water and her parted thighs.

"You surprised me," he said as he ran a finger through her folds again, letting the water beat around the touch. She gasped, groaning when he pulled away again.

"What do you mean?" She ground this out through gritted teeth. He could tell from the look on her face, the increasingly frenzied movements of her body, that the pleasure was rising high and fast inside her. He loved that he could bring her there so quickly.

Grinning wickedly, he returned his hand to her pussy. This time he tucked two fingers inside, savoring the way she clenched around him as he slid through her liquid heat. "You're completely bare. That's new."

"I…like it…that…way." He found that special place inside her, rubbed over her and watched the way her eyes blurred. "Jesus fuck, Theo. I can't take it anymore."

"You will take it, because I say so." He kept up the pressure inside her but moved the showerhead so that the spray was focused directly on her clit. She cried out, the sound echoing off the glass walls of the shower, her inner walls squeezing him so tightly it hurt.

"Come for me, Jo." He'd barely said the words when she screamed his name, her body clenching tight, her mouth open as she cried out. She rocked against him once, twice, then shuddered, every muscle melting like candle wax.

His cock actually throbbed with the need to be inside her, to claim her as his. He wasn't sure that he could keep her here once they were done, though—he thought she might go rabbiting back home to overthink what had just happened. With that in mind, he ground his teeth and called up every ounce of restraint that he possessed, not yet ready to stop playing with her.

She murmured something as he reached up and unhooked her from the showerhead, then undid the belt around her wrists. She was pliant, letting him pull her to her feet, pressing his front to her back.

She unconsciously rocked back against him, pressing her ass against his length. Grabbing his shaft at the base, he stroked it gently between her cheeks. She shuddered when it pressed against the tight rosette, and he grinned.

"Dirty girl." She murmured in agreement. When he rubbed the bar of soap over her breasts, she leaned her head back on his shoulder trustingly, and he stilled for a moment.

She might still be scarred from what he'd done, but some primal part of her, something that they'd just tapped into through their bodies, still trusted him. He would hold on to that and pray that the rest of her followed suit.

When her skin was coated with a creamy lather, he set the soap down and squirted shampoo into his hands. The crisp scent of citrus permeated the steam as he rubbed it into her hair, massaging her scalp, her neck and her shoulders.

Once he'd rinsed her clean, he watched as the sleepiness disappeared from her limbs. Turning in his arms, she cast a very obvious glance down at his red, swollen length. "I think someone is feeling deprived. I'd better take care of him."

She panted out a breath when he yanked her against his chest, hands splaying over her back so that she couldn't move away. Those watchful gray eyes focused in on him like lasers, questioning, and he slowly rubbed his erection back and forth across her soft flesh.

"You don't listen very well, baby." His cock slid between her thighs, and they clenched around its length, making him exhale sharply. "You don't get to make the rules."

CHAPTER TWELVE

SHE WAS GOING to have sex with Theo again. To-night. Soon. There was no question. After so long with numbness as her constant companion, she was overwhelmed with feeling—like steam building up in a pressure cooker, she needed to let some out before she exploded.

The orgasm that had just exploded through her body hadn't relieved the pressure, not at all. As Theo rubbed his cock against the tender skin of her inner thighs, she wondered if she was going to survive this intact, or if her entire body would self-combust the second he slid inside her.

"Put your arms around me." She did as he com-manded, her heart melting a little as he scooped her up in his arms, fireman-style. He snagged a towel the size of a lake as he carried her from the shower to the foot of the bed. When he wrapped her in it, the hem of the plush fabric fell almost to the floor. Content for the moment, she watched as he crossed to the massive fireplace, picked up a remote and set a blazing fire to life with the press of a button.

"That's quite the toy," she commented when he returned to her, rubbing the towel over her hair and then lower. She closed her eyes against the sensation when he scrubbed the fabric over her sensitive nipples and then between her legs, the nubby fabric a tease.

"I like toys." He didn't bother to dry himself off, instead tossing the towel to the ground. She felt his gaze everywhere he looked at her just as much as if he was stroking her with his hands.

What was it going to be like, this time? In the first few years after he'd left, she had a few fumbling encounters, but she always stopped it short of penetration, because why would she go there if it did nothing for her? But now, all she could think about was the one time he'd been inside her, how it had been when he'd slid his arousal right into her very core.

"Please." She didn't want to wait even a minute longer. However stupid it was, it felt like all this time she'd been waiting for him to come back— him, the only person who could make her feel good. Her entire body was restless, riding an edge of need that was almost painful in its intensity.

"Please what, Jo?" Her gaze snapped to his when she heard the need in his voice, equal to her own. How was this happening? How were they here together again? "I need to hear you say it."

Need, not want. That little distinction did something funny to her insides. She reached for him without meaning to, wrapping her arms around his waist, pressing her cheek to his heart.

"I want you," she whispered, listening to the thunder of his pulse, knowing that hers matched. "I want all of you."

"How do you want it?" His hands roamed over her back, tracing the lines of her shoulder blades, the curve of her spine.

She thought of all the filthy things she'd written about, the pictures she'd seen as she researched.

He was giving her a chance to ask for what she wanted. To explore.

Swallowing past the hard, sudden lump in her throat, she gently disentangled herself from his arms. Trying not to feel self-conscious about the fact that every inch of her naked body was on display, she knelt at the edge of the bed, angling herself away from him.

"I want it like this." She was sure that her skin

was on fire, but her voice was sure. "And I don't want you to be gentle."

The sound he made was nearly inhuman, and she felt herself grow impossibly slicker. "You can't be real. I'm imagining this."

"Not this time." Not sure what to do, she leaned forward until her hands rested on the bed, so that she was on all fours. She knew he had a full view of every intimate part of her, and knew damn well that he was looking, but knowing that sent a little thrill through her. Made her feel powerful.

"You asked for it, baby." She heard the rip of foil. Her pulse stuttered, then began to beat again, double time, as she closed her eyes and imagined him rolling the tube of latex over his cock. She nearly looked back over her shoulder, just for the visual of those sure fingers on his own erection.

Next time, she promised herself. This time she didn't want to think, because then the little voice in her head would nag, reminding her of the heartbreak she was opening herself up to here. No, she just wanted to be taken, to have all thoughts shoved from her mind so that the only thing in her existence was Theo and what he was doing to her body.

"What is that?" Something soft danced over the skin of her lower back, and she gasped.

He didn't answer, but a moment later something was placed over her eyes. He smoothed her hair back, then secured what she now knew to be the silk scarf at the back of her head.

"I don't want that busy brain of yours thinking of anything but what I'm doing to you. Understood?" She nodded, her throat suddenly so dry that she couldn't have spoken to save her life.

She didn't have to speak. Like he said, all she had to do was feel. And that's exactly what she did when he pressed the head of his cock to her aching entrance, alighting nerves that hadn't been touched in a very, very long time.

She inhaled sharply when he pushed forward. Or rather, when he tried to. Her body was as tight as it had been when she was a virgin, and it wasn't sure what to do with this intrusion, no matter how good it felt.

"How are you still so tight?" His hands gripped her hips as he stilled, only the head of his cock tucked inside her. "Am I hurting you?"

"Not hurting." Dropping down to her forearms, she tilted her hips, changing the angle. He slid in another inch, and she gasped at the friction. "I just—I haven't—"

"Jesus, Jo." He stopped again, and she felt the tension in the hands that gripped her hips. "Tell me you've been with someone else."

There was no shaming in his words, but she felt

it all the same. "I didn't—I've never wanted to." And she hadn't. Something was just different with her body, her brain.

If she didn't love the person, she wasn't interested in sex.

Oh shit.

She was still in love with Theo. In love again.

This was going to hurt.

"Baby." His voice was full of wonder. "You're a gift."

Then he reached forward, sliding his hand between her legs. Sure fingers found her clit, circling and teasing, and as she melted into the pleasure of his touch, he worked in another inch.

"That's it," he coaxed, circling her swollen nub again and again until she felt that strange tension low in her belly, that aching need for more. "Just relax. We've got all the time in the world."

Her forehead was damp with perspiration, and she pressed it to the soft cotton of his quilt. Her hips were canted, and the higher his fingers brought her, the farther he was able to slide inside her. When he pinched her swollen flesh between his forefinger and thumb, she gasped, feeling something inside her open, and he worked in the final inch. Stilling, she felt his hips resting against the curves of her ass and shifted against the unfamiliar fullness of him inside her.

"How are you doing?" His voice was strained, and she knew that the slow pace had to be killing him. He was doing it all for her. It made her a little weak in the knees.

How could she be afraid of him hurting her when he acted like this? How could she believe that he'd once again be careless with her heart?

"I'm good," she gasped, unable to keep from pushing back against him when his clever fingers worked her higher still. "So good. I think I—"

"Don't you dare come yet." Clenching her waist, he pulled back, and the slow drag of his erection over her swollen tissues had her eyes rolling back in her head. "Don't you do it."

"I don't think I can help it." That wild wave was rising inside her as he worked his way back in, swiveling his hips to get her body to let him in. She gasped when he sheathed himself to the hilt again. "I can't—I think—"

"We're going to go together." His pace quickened slowly, bringing to life nerves that she hadn't even known she had. "Hold on."

She was lost in the world he created for her. Eyes covered, she existed in the seductive dark, her fingers scrabbling to hold on to something and finding nothing, realizing that she had to let herself fall. He gripped her hips, moving in and out of her tight flesh with increasing speed, a relentless onslaught of pleasure that had them both gasping each time he bottomed out inside her.

Her knees gave out, and she fell face-first on the bed. Bracing his weight on his arms, he continued to pump. Beneath her, the cotton rubbed against her damp clit with the friction she needed to fly over the edge. She started to chant his name, trying to wait as he'd told her to, but the rocket inside her was ignited and counting down to launch.

"That's it," his voice rasped in her ear. "I want you to feel this tomorrow. Every time you take a step, every time you sit down, you're going to remember who filled you up. Yes?"

"Yes," she agreed wildly, and then she was flying. He pushed into her one final time, thrusting as he emptied himself once, twice, three times. The smell of salt and sweat hung heavily in the air as her body clenched around him, her muscles shaking as she exploded so brightly that stars danced behind her eyes.

She was aware when he pulled out of her, and when he used the towel to dry the sweat on her brow, but it was as if she was watching someone else. Surely that couldn't be her who felt so sated, so blissful. Surely that couldn't be her half draped over Theo's chest as he tucked them in and promised that he would cook her spaghetti just as soon as they could move.

That dead space inside her was alive, filled with light. And she was scared of going back to the dark.

CHAPTER THIRTEEN

I GET A lot of repeat questions in my in-box. You, my dear readers, have helped me to define some of the most common problems of our generation. The one on my mind today is, can you ever really let an ex back into your life?

Hear me out. We're all familiar with that phenomenon where our memories make things in the past seem better than they actually were. So when an ex comes back into your life, and you're consumed by that flood of emotion that inevitably shows up with it, how can you be rational? Throw sex into the game, and it's like all of your efforts to move on and heal have disappeared like a puff of smoke.

The question you ask me, time and again, is if I think a relationship can be different the second time around. Can a cheater change his stripes?

Can you find common ground when you want different things? Can people grow up, can people change? I don't have the answer to that for you. What I can tell you is what I've discovered for myself this week—even if it's scary, even if it means you might get hurt, aren't you going to be disappointed if you don't try? Now, I'm not talking getting back with someone who didn't treat you well, or taking an abuser back because he asked you nicely. But what if the reason you parted ways with someone ultimately came down to youth and stupidity? What if, as an adult, they're the best thing that ever happened to you? Will you turn them away because you never make the same mistake twice? Or will you let them back in, even knowing that you might get—probably will get—hurt again?

Is the experience worth the pain?

Thoughtfully yours,

Jojo Kink

"Hey." Jo jumped when Theo poked his head into her office. She hurriedly—and not very subtly—closed the screen of her laptop, not wanting him to see the post she was working on. When she'd sat down at her computer that morning, she'd debated which topic on Theo's list to tackle first, but ultimately, when her fingers started to fly over the keyboard, she'd found herself writing about him.

She wasn't ready for him to read it, though. She might not ever be. But it had been cathartic to get her feelings out into words.

"You left before I woke up." He studied her with those dark eyes as he entered the office that had been assigned to her, closing the door behind him. She sat up straighter when she saw the sternness on his face.

"I had to get ready for work." She cocked her head slightly but saw that he knew the truth.

"And?" He crossed his arms over his chest, his muscles pulling at the fabric of his suit. After the up-close and personal look she'd gotten at his muscles a few days earlier, it was extra distracting, because all she wanted to do was rip off his jacket and shirt and run her tongue over the bumps and ridges.

She considered pretending not to know what he was talking about, but he would see right through it. Sighing, she tucked a ribbon of hair behind her ear and leaned back in her desk chair.

"I just needed to think," she admitted, shifting restlessly in the cushioned seat.

"You couldn't think with me there?" His voice was gruff, and she saw that she'd actually wounded him, which hadn't been her intention at all.

"I'm sorry," she blurted out, rubbing her suddenly sweaty palms together. "You're—you're very distracting. I needed to think about you, but I couldn't be around you while I did."

"You needed to think about me, huh?" Crossing the room, he only stopped when he could brush against her knees as he sat. "And what conclusion did you come to?"

Her mouth was dry. She reached for her coffee cup, only to find it was empty. She replaced it on the desk, desperate for something to do with the nervous energy in her hands.

"You might hurt me again," she started, holding up a hand when thunderclouds gathered fast and thick in his eyes. "Just bite back on your temper for a second, okay? You might hurt me. I might hurt you. I feel like I still know you, the real you, but the truth is that I'm missing the details on a huge chunk of your life. I'm terrified that that's going to jump out and bite me on the ass."

"If anyone is going to bite you on the ass, it's going to be me," he promised darkly before gesturing for her to continue. "Go on."

"But…" The words stuck in her throat, nearly choking her before she forced them out. "Nobody ever made me feel the way you do. I don't think anybody else *can*. So… I want to keep exploring whatever this is. Slowly."

He lifted her out of the chair by her elbows. She sucked in a breath when he brushed his lips over hers so softly it felt like butterfly wings. "There's never been anything slow about either of us, Jo. We both jump headfirst, all or nothing. But know that when you fly off that cliff, I'll be right there beside you."

"When did you learn to be so smooth?" She huffed out a laugh, pressing her forehead against him.

"Baby, I've always been smooth." He grinned down at her, then jerked his chin at her laptop. "Now. What were you working on that you so desperately don't want me to see?"

"Nothing." The lie was automatic. Damn it, she wasn't ready for him to read those words yet. "It's nothing. It's not ready. Don't open that."

"You know that just makes me want to look even more, right?" Arching an eyebrow, he reached for the computer. She smacked his hand—and wasn't gentle about it.

"You did not just smack me." His eyes glittered, and she felt something dark come to life inside her.

"You're not going to read that. Not as long as I'm standing here." Stubbornly, she lifted her chin in the air.

"Oh really?" Bending down to her height, he brushed his lips over the shell of her ear. "I've heard that I can be very distracting."

"Damn you," she exhaled, then before she could

overthink it, she snatched up the laptop and darted to the far side of the office. Pressing herself back into the corner, she watched Theo warily as she fought to keep a grip on the computer with her slick hands.

She had no idea what the hell she thought she was doing, but when he grinned, her stomach flipped with a potent combination of nerves and excitement. The sensation only intensified as she watched him remove his suit jacket with excruciating slowness, folding it before placing it on the seat of her chair.

"What the hell are you doing?" Her pulse quickened when he loosened his tie. All the time he watched her with laser focus, and she suddenly understood what a gazelle was faced with when cornered by a lion.

"Seems to me like you want to be chased." He grinned, but there was no humor in the expression, just wicked intent. "Who am I to say no to that?"

"What?" She darted a panicked glance between him and the door, even as wetness surged between her thighs, a fresh ache blooming where she was already sore. "It's nine o'clock in the morning. Your whole staff is out there. *John* is out there!"

"If you're so concerned about where John is, maybe I should invite him in to watch," Theo commented mildly, taking a step closer. "Then you won't have to wonder."

"Oh God." He wouldn't. Would he? The dangerous look he was casting her way told her that she really had no idea what he was capable of in that moment. "The door isn't locked!"

"Guess you better hope no one comes in, then." Without warning, he leaped forward. She squealed and scuttled down the wall away from him, still clasping the laptop to her chest, though she understood it wasn't about the article anymore.

"I don't know why you think you can run." He started toward her again, but this time his steps were slow and deliberate. "Where are you going to go?"

Having lulled her with the steady moments, he sprang, catching her by the front of the silky T-shirt that she'd stolen from Meg's closet that morning. She made a wordless, choking cry when he yanked and it tore right down the front, gaping open to expose the lacy bralette that she'd liberated as well.

"If you run out of the office right now, everyone will know what we're doing." He grinned, running a steady palm down her torso, between her breasts. She was quivering with suppressed sensation. "The new girl fucking the boss. Whatever will they think?"

"No!" The laptop slipped from her hands onto the plush carpet, and she barely noticed as it bounced away. Backing up rapidly, she wasn't aware that Theo had stopped in his tracks until her ass hit the edge of her desk.

"No?" He searched her face intently, and she realized what she'd said. "Do you want to stop?"

Something delicate inside her snapped. He'd stopped. His cock was so hard that she could see its full outline, straining against the fabric of his pants, and his face was flushed with arousal, just like hers was. They were in the middle of some hot, kinky game that she didn't fully understand, and he'd just *stopped* because she'd said no, even when she hadn't really meant it.

How could she not trust this man with her heart?

"No. I mean… I don't mean no. I mean, I meant it, but not like that." Sighing with frustration, she scrubbed both hands over her face. "Is this where a safe word comes in?"

"*No* will always work with me. I'll always check in with you if you say that, okay?" The intensity he spoke with told her that he needed her to understand this. "But if you want to choose a safe word, choose it now. Make sure it's something you wouldn't normally say in conversation."

"Shower," she blurted immediately, feeling herself flush when he grinned. "That's my safe word."

"Shower. Got it." He nodded to emphasize the point, and then he unbuttoned the collar of his shirt. Her eyes fixed on the inch of golden skin it revealed, desperate to press her lips there, to gauge his pulse.

"Run."

She blinked, not sure she'd heard him correctly, but when he moved, a surge of adrenaline had her scrambling back. The corner of the desk bit into her hip as she pushed past her chair, but she didn't feel a thing besides the need to get away.

She knew she wouldn't, not in the end. It didn't stop the urge to move, move, move, move, because once he caught her, she was at his mercy.

"Might as well give up," he taunted, continuing after her with that slow, relentless pace. "You know I'm going to win."

"Not if I can help it." Bracing herself to leap back the way she'd come as soon as he got a little closer, she wasn't prepared for him to anticipate the move. He caught her around the waist, hauling her off her feet as she cried out.

"I don't care if anyone hears you," he informed her as he dragged her back to her desk, splaying her out on its surface, "but you might not like it when someone comes to investigate just why you're being so damn noisy."

"Theo," she begged, and she wasn't sure if she

was asking for him to let her go, or to touch her. Still caught up in the game, she writhed against him, forcing him to pin her arms above her head with one of his hands, to catch her lower body with a thrust of his hips. With the other, he tore at the front of her bralette, treating it to the same fate as her top.

"I told you not to buy anything fancy just for me." Cupping one of her breasts, he squeezed the mound lightly. "I told you I liked what you wore."

"That was Meg's," she spat out, still struggling. The dressy jeans that completed her outfit—also her sister's—caused delicious friction against her clit as she wriggled against where the firm pressure of his hips pinned her down, her legs dangling on either side of his hips.

"Guess I owe Meg some clothes then." He grinned, not sorry at all, as he continued to massage her breast. Her world narrowed to the point of his touch, the pleasure he was pulling out of the swollen tip of her breast. "Gonna tell her what happened to the things you borrowed?"

"Something tells me she'll know." She yelped quietly when he swatted the side of her hip.

"You're awfully mouthy for a captive." Dragging his hand roughly down her torso, he tugged at the waistband of her jeans. "I'd like to give your mouth something else to do, but I don't have enough time for that today. Guess I'll have to hope that a quick fuck will knock that sass out of you for a while."

Her mouth fell open. Never in her life had someone spoken to her like that—not even Theo when he was younger—and it shocked her to her core. It also thrilled her, that part of her that was fascinated by the new, the different.

How he managed it, she wasn't sure, but he managed to work her jeans open with one hand while she was bucking against him. Dragging them and her underwear down over her hips, he worked one of her legs free before wrapping it around his waist.

"Keep on struggling," he told her as he undid his own slacks. She found herself watching avidly as he shoved his boxer briefs down far enough to release his erection. It was thick, and long, and swollen with need, a slick of moisture already making the head shine. She marveled for a moment that she'd managed to fit that inside her. And then she just wanted it inside her again.

"I won't let you do this," she spat, fully immersed in the role she was playing. She pulled against him with renewed vigor, even managing to pull free for a split second, causing him to curse and haul her back to the edge of the desk.

"It's happening, baby." The dark intent in his

words made molten heat pool in her core. Her spine pressed into the flat surface of the desk, her breasts freed by the torn garments on her torso. Her ass was balanced on the edge of the desk, one leg still tangled in her jeans while he held the other tightly to his hip. "I'm going to let go of your hands, but there's no point in trying to get free. I'll just catch you again."

"I have to try," she said breathlessly when he released her arms. She tried to roll, but he caught her, forced her back down with a hand pressed flat on her chest. Dropping the leg he'd clutched to his hip, he lined his shaft up with her wet slit and pushed inside, the intrusion making her eyes fly wide-open.

"Fuck," she groaned, letting her head fall back to the desk. He held still for a moment, letting her adjust to his thickness just inside her, but before she could get too comfortable, he flexed his hips and drove himself home.

A wordless cry escaped her lips, her hands sliding over the slick surface of the desk as she tried to catch hold of something, anything. Finally she settled on his shirt, his tie, but instead of shoving him away as her role demanded, she pulled him down closer until he was bent overtop of her, his chest rubbing against the tips of her breasts with every movement.

"Fuck, that's good." Bracing one hand on the desk above her head, the other again finding her hip, he pulled back until he almost slid out. Her slick channel clenched around him as he drove forward again, his length dragging over sensitive flesh and igniting a level of arousal she'd never felt. "Shit. *Shit.* I'm not wearing a condom."

She growled when he pulled out, wanting him back in. Propping herself up on her elbows, she watched, fascinated, as he fumbled with his wallet, pulling out a condom and tearing into it with his teeth. Within moments he was sheathed, his wallet was on the floor and he was pushing back inside her with renewed urgency.

"How is it possible for you to feel so fucking good?" He worked in and out of her at a slow, steady pace, and she watched with fascination as beads of sweat appeared on his forehead. She was hot, too, aroused to a fever pitch as she felt the pleasure begin to gather in her core like it had the night before.

"You feel good to me, too," she admitted as she watched his cock slide in and out of her parted lips. She'd never thought about watching, but it was just about the hottest thing she'd ever seen. "I feel so much, and I don't know what to do with it."

"You don't have to do anything with it except what I tell you to." He slid back into his role, and

Jo eagerly followed. It was so easy to let go when she pretended that she had no other choice. There was no point in worrying about getting hurt if the decision was being made for her.

"And what are you telling me to do?" She couldn't resist taunting him. Reaching down between them, she grabbed his waist, holding him tightly to her as he thrust deep.

"Mouthy brat." He grinned down at her, but his eyes were starting to glaze over with what she realized meant he was edging close to his own release. Knowing that she was the one to bring him there was heady, a kind of power she could get drunk on.

"That's not an answer." Her hand slid from his waist to dig into the hard planes of his rear, and she wished she could have that view, too—what he looked like from behind as he thrust inside her, the muscles of that truly spectacular ass flexing as he moved.

"You're going to come on my cock, is what you're going to do." He increased his pace, his head falling back. Her vision started to blur as the pressure inside her coiled tighter and tighter, a spring about to snap. "And you're going to do it now."

His hand slid to the place where they were joined, and the first touch of his fingers on her clit sent her flying over the edge. She swallowed her cries as she contracted around him, senses dulled to everything but the bliss that was riding her.

He grunted as he emptied himself in her, and she found herself fascinated by watching as he was lost. Stilling himself above her, he remained as he was, fully inside her, fully connected.

Fully hers. Without thinking, she reached up to brush a lock of his inky hair back from where it stuck to the sweat on his forehead. He opened his eyes, and when he looked down at her, she felt a jolt as she wondered what he was trying to say without actually saying it.

"I still want to read what you wrote." He broke the strange tension of the moment by nodding toward where her laptop lay, discarded on the floor. "I also feel that this is a good time to remind you about respecting company property."

"Jackass." She smacked his chest lightly, struggling to sit up. "And you can read it when it's ready, which it might be if someone hadn't decided to hunt me down in my own damn office."

"Much as I'd love to spend the rest of the day inside you, I should get back to my own office." He pulled out of her slowly, holding on to the condom as he did. "I'm very busy and important, you know."

She rolled her eyes, but inside felt lightness buoying her up. She'd missed this, too, so much it had hurt—this friendship that they'd shared before everything had gone to hell. Because when he'd left, she hadn't just lost her boyfriend and her love, she'd lost the best friend she'd ever had.

"I missed this." There. She'd said it. And though a flicker of surprise crossed his face as he tied off the condom and tossed it in the trash, he nodded in agreement.

"I missed it, too." Stepping back, he slowly zipped himself back into his slacks, straightening his shirt and tightening his tie. Catching her watching, he cast her a cocky grin. "How do I look?"

"Put your jacket on, and no one will know you've spent the last half an hour abusing every human resource code you put in the contract in the first place." Sliding from the desk, she struggled to pull the snug jeans back up over her hips, then looked down at her chest in dismay. "What the hell am I supposed to do about this?"

"You wore a sweater into work this morning. I saw you." He gestured to the back of the door, where a thin cardigan hung. "Just wear it buttoned up."

"With no bra?" But she was already reaching for it. It wasn't like she had much choice.

"Never used to stop you." He smirked at her, then stared avidly as she tucked her now braless breasts beneath the thin sweater. "Just don't get too close to anyone else. Not that you'd want to after having a taste of this."

"Go!" She rolled her eyes, then pointed to the door. "My boss is a bit of a tyrant. If you're not careful, he'll literally hunt you down just to check on your work."

"Sounds like my kind of guy." Opening the door, he cast a look back over his shoulder at her. She couldn't stop the swelling of her heart as he winked at her like this had all been their dirty little secret. "Dinner tonight?"

"All right," she replied softly, thrilling to the question even as she knew she was diving off a very high, very dangerous cliff.

But oh, how she was enjoying the fall.

CHAPTER FOURTEEN

THEO FELT LIKE he'd just completed a champion workout. He was riding high on endorphins, body loose, mind sated as he all but staggered back into his office.

Hell. He'd had some good sex before. He'd had some great sex. But what had just happened with Jo was so astronomically amazing that it couldn't even be described.

They'd connected on a physical level when they were younger, for sure. He'd thought he just might die from insisting they wait until she was eighteen.

Now, though? That innocent girl he remembered was kinky as fuck, and he knew he'd never in a million years find someone who inspired the same filthy urges in him. Never find another woman who challenged him, who called him on his shit. Who got excited when he took her to a graveyard on a date, and who really could not have cared less about the number of zeroes in his bank balance.

He was in love with her. Again? Still? It didn't really matter, because the truth was there, written in the way he could still feel her hands on his skin.

He wanted to tell her. Wanted to give her that certainty that he wasn't going anywhere. That he couldn't, not without her.

Loosening his tie that had just been straightened, he sat forward in his desk chair, tapping his keyboard to wake up his computer. He'd take her out for dinner, not someplace fancy, because she wouldn't care about that. Someplace that had meaning for them.

What was the name of that little Brazilian dive they'd frequented when they were in high school? His mom had taken him there when he was little, whenever she'd been craving food from home, since she was the type to burn toast. He'd never gone there with anyone else, not even his dad— not until he'd decided to share it with Jo.

It would be the perfect place to tell her what he felt. He knew she'd catch the significance. Now if only he could remember what the hell it was called, so he could look it up and make sure it was still open.

As he typed Brazilian food restaurant Boston

into his web browser, his cell phone vibrated against his hip. John's name flashed across the screen, and Theo put it on speaker.

"What's up?" When Theo had hired the consultant to help ensure a smooth official launch of Crossing Lines, he'd somehow pictured a rich old white dude. John Brooke was rich, certainly, but he wasn't old and he wasn't white, or anything else that Theo had expected. He was, however, everything that he'd promised, and Theo knew he'd miss him when he'd finished out their contract and moved on to another business. The other man had really thrown his heart and soul into Crossing Lines and was the nearest thing that Theo had to a real friend.

"Ass into my office, Lawrence." There was barely concealed glee in the other man's voice. "I'm about to make all of your fantasies come true."

"In your dreams, Brooke." Theo started walking as he spoke. Ava looked up from her desk, arching an eyebrow at him since he was talking so loudly. He shrugged, striding down the hall to John's office, which would be empty soon enough. "You don't have the right equipment."

"I could have you if I wanted you." John held out a paper cup of coffee as Theo entered the room, grinning mockingly. He leaned back in his chair, smugness written in every line of his body.

"We'll see how I feel about you after you tell me whatever has you grinning like a freaky-ass clown." Settling himself in the chair across the desk, Theo sipped at the coffee, gagging as soon as it touched his tongue. "What the hell is this garbage?"

"I made it myself." John frowned, gesturing at the coffee machine in his office, one that looked like it belonged in Starbucks. "It's an Americano."

"It's swamp water, man." Shuddering, Theo set it down on the desk. "But it's reassuring to know that you're human, after all. Now what's up?"

John took a cautious sip of his own coffee, and Theo watched with amusement as his eyes widened. He swallowed gamely. "It's not that bad."

Theo rolled his eyes; John set the cup on the edge of his desk.

"When you hired me, you told me that your goal was to grow Crossing Lines from a highly valued start-up to a company that could sell for a minimum of fifty million, correct?" Theo nodded. "We estimated three to five years for that growth."

"I know all this, Brooke." Theo waved a hand in his air. "What's the news that makes you look like you're going to come in your pants?"

"I have far too much self-control to ever come

in my pants," the other man replied archly. "Now. What if I told you that I've found a buyer for Crossing Lines already? One willing to pay seventy-five million, not fifty, with the caveat that she take over the company now. Now, not in three to five years! I've never come across this kind of deal, man. You must shit gold."

"Every morning," Theo responded automatically, but his eyes widened as the news sank in. "Seventy-five million? Are you for real?"

"Real as rain, brother." John drummed his fingers on the desk. "She's the sister of some European prince. I guess she met her now-fiancé on Crossing Lines and fell in love with the premise. She's excited to take it in a new direction."

"A new direction?" Theo frowned, rubbing a hand over his chest. "We've barely started going in *this* direction."

John shrugged, his smile wide. "For seventy-five million, I'd say she can take it in whatever direction she wants. And here's the thing. She wants to hire you as the business head of her corporation. Interview other people with start-ups like yours, develop them under her banner."

"Really?" That was what he'd vaguely thought that he'd wind up doing eventually, but years down the line—and for his own corporation, of course. Still, excitement buzzed along his skin. It felt like validation—this was the kind of opportunity that most people only dreamed of, and it was being offered to him because he'd earned it himself. It sounded too good to be true. "I can't even wrap my head around that."

"It's the dream." John cocked his head, studying Theo's expression. "Of course, you'd probably have to leave Boston."

"What?" The airy excitement crashed to the ground, weighed down by reality. It *was* too good to be true. Because leaving Boston was the one thing he couldn't do.

His fingers reached out to grip the edge of the desk, steadying him as his world tilted.

"Well, she's from some little country I've never even heard of," John said slowly, watching Theo closely. "But she did mention something about San Francisco."

San Francisco was a million miles away.

His unease must have shown on Theo's face, because John cocked his head, looking at him with concern. "What's wrong? I thought this was what you wanted. You should be thrilled."

"It's amazing." Theo heard the hollowness in his own words. "I think I just need to let it sink in."

John smiled with relief before rising to his feet. Pitching both his coffee cup and Theo's into the trash, he leaned across the desk to clap Theo on the shoulder. "To hell with this swill. I'm going to go send Ava out for a bottle of scotch. No, I'll go myself, to that place next door. This calls for a celebration."

Theo opened his mouth to tell his colleague that he didn't drink, but the words caught in his throat. He nodded numbly as John rounded the desk and opened the door.

Jo was on the other side.

"Jo!" John was flying so high on the offer that he reached out and caught Jo in a one-arm hug. "Come on in! We'll be celebrating in a minute. Join us."

Jo arched an eyebrow at the uncharacteristic buoyancy in John before casting a vaguely amused smile Theo's way. "What are we celebrating? Must be good. He was bouncing like Tigger."

Theo blinked up at her mechanically. He should have been thrilled. This was everything he'd worked for, everything he'd dreamed of, years ahead of schedule. He'd prove to everyone, and finally to himself, that he was no longer just a trust-fund baby. He was a self-made man.

The only person he cared about proving that to was standing right in front of him.

"There's been an offer to buy the company." His words sounded like they were coming from a great distance, somewhere outside his own body. "A great offer, actually."

Jo's face lit up, and it was like she'd taken a pair of tweezers and started pinching at his heart. "That's amazing! So amazing, Theo. I'm so happy for you."

Theo's arm felt like it weighed as much as an elephant as he lifted it to rub a hand over his face. "Yeah. Plus, it came with a new job offer. One that's hard to turn down."

Jo flew at him, wrapping him in an enthusiastic hug that was completely devoid of any of the shadows of their past. He caught her around the waist, urging her back to her feet instead of hauling her into his lap like he wanted to.

She blinked, clearly startled. Wariness flickered through her eyes. "What's wrong?"

There was no good way to tell her, but he knew that she'd never tolerate him keeping something so monumental from her.

"I wouldn't be able to stay in Boston."

Jo froze. Literally just froze in place, eyes wide, an empty smile pasted on her face. She stared at him for a long moment, and he knew that she could see every ounce of the angst that he was feeling, pouring off him in waves.

"Well, of course you have to go." She clapped her hands together, as if in glee, but her voice was hollow. "This is what you wanted, even if it's a little ahead of schedule!"

"Jo." He couldn't handle it. Her voice was positively perky. The girl he'd known, the woman he knew were many things, but perky wasn't one of them. "What about us?"

"Theo." Her almost manic smile dimmed a few watts but remained pasted on her face. "We've been back together…or whatever this is…for less than a week. I'm glad we got to move past some of that old hurt, and I'm grateful for it. But there's no question that you have to take this!"

"Jo," he said again, this time more urgently. Her eyes widened, but the mask of fake happiness stayed plastered to her face. "Talk to me."

"I actually have to get back to work." She dusted her hands on the thighs of her jeans. "I just had to ask John a question about the article I'm working on, but I can ask him later. I promised him I'd have it in this afternoon, so I really do have to get back to work."

Her movements were choppy, robotic, as if controlled by someone else. And as if he didn't already feel like absolute shit, Theo realized that if he sold the company, there was no guarantee that Jo's job would still exist once the new owner had taken over.

Closing his eyes for a second, he fisted his

hands at his sides as he tried to get ahold of his options. When he opened them again, Jo was halfway through the door, her own hands balled into tight fists, too.

"Jojo." He used her old nickname without thinking. She stiffened, her shoulders hunching up around her ears. "Tell me not to go."

She didn't turn around. Theo held his breath, and he knew that he wanted her to tell him to stay more than he wanted to sell his company.

"This is the best thing that's ever happened to you." She didn't even bother to turn around, instead directing her words back over her shoulder. "And you know what, I'm really not feeling well. I promise I'll get the article in on time, but I think I need to work from home for the afternoon."

"Jo." Rising to his feet, he strode across the office after her, but she sliced a hand through the air, letting him know without a word that she wouldn't tolerate being touched.

"'Bye, Theo." And then she was gone, down the hall and into the elevator. Ava stood as Jo hurried by, clearly picking up on the waves of emotion emanating from the other woman. His assistant looked back down the hall toward him, and the pity on her face told her that she'd intuited what happened.

He didn't know what to say. He didn't know

what to do. He started down the hall after Jo, but Ava shook her head, halting him in his tracks.

"If you go tearing after her, you'll argue and one or both of you will say something that you regret." Shaking her head, she sat back down at her desk. "But honestly, Theo, I don't know what you thought you were doing with her. You're on your way up. You're a star. And she's just the girl from where you started."

Theo looked down at her, wondering how he'd ever found her attractive. How he'd ever even looked at a woman besides Jo. Still, Ava had a point. Jo needed some time to calm down.

And he needed to absorb the fact that the woman he'd planned to tell he loved had told him in no uncertain terms to go ahead and move across the country.

The elevator doors slid open, and Theo felt his heart leap into his throat. He groaned when he saw that the only occupant was John, bearing a bottle of what Theo recognized as a brand of scotch that was both hideously expensive and very old.

"Don't look so thrilled to see me," the other man said drily as he stepped off the elevator. He held up the bottle of scotch, wigging it so that the amber contents sloshed invitingly. "After all, all I've done today is earn you seventy-five million big ones."

Striding forward, John passed the bottle to

Theo, then continued down the hall. "Ava, can you grab us some glasses? Then come join us. It's time to celebrate!"

Acid churned in Theo's gut. The last thing he wanted to do was celebrate. His heart was too heavy for that. But if Jo didn't care whether he stayed or went, then what else was he going to do?

Drawing everything he felt into a tight bundle and shoving it down deep inside, he followed John down the hall. He was about to accept the deal he'd been working toward since…well, since the night of Jo's eighteenth birthday, when she'd opened his eyes to everything he'd been taking for granted.

So why did it feel like he'd lost it all?

CHAPTER FIFTEEN

THE BOTTLE OF hideously expensive scotch sat on the polished Brazilian wood coffee table. Its legs were carved with whimsical tree frogs and palm fronds, one of the pieces that his mother had once hauled into the house to counteract his father's love of everything stiff and dignified.

He would have given that entire seventy-five million dollars away on the street just to be able to talk to his mom again, right now. His relationship with his dad had deteriorated beyond the point of repair by the time his father had died, but he still believed that if his mom had been able to fight back the cancer that had killed her, they would have still been close. He would have been able to call her right now, to ask her how to fix this gigantic mess.

He couldn't do that. And so he was still eyeing the unopened bottle of scotch, its contents glimmering enticingly in the fading light streaming in through the living room window.

A drink wouldn't help him make Jo love him, but it would sure numb the misery that had weighed down his limbs so much that he wasn't sure he'd ever move again.

He leaned back on the stiff sofa, letting his head rest on the back. Closing his eyes, he fought the desire for the drink that was taunting him. He focused on slowing his breathing, on trying to find some semblance of calm. When a chime sounded, he thought that maybe he'd finally achieved some deeper state of being, though he wasn't entirely sure he believed in stuff like that.

The musical note sounded again, and he sat up stiffly, feeling like he'd been drugged. The doorbell— it was the doorbell. Woodenly, he pushed off the sofa and moved to the front door.

Jo's mother stood on the other side. Well-worn yellow oven mitts covered her hands as she clutched tightly to a large pot.

"Hello, Theodore." She smiled up at him, the fading sunlight catching in the virulently crimson strands of her hair as she held out the pot. He smelled garlic, Italian seasoning and, best of all, spicy sausage.

He knew that smell. "Italian sausage soup?" He'd eaten countless bowls of that soup on the well-worn table in the house next door. His heart contracted, and the warmth he'd been so desperately craving as he stared at the bottle of scotch gathered in his core.

"You know it." She arched an eyebrow, and he saw a hint of Jo's stubbornness play out over her finer features. "Are you going to invite me in, or do I have to be rude and invite myself?"

Choking out a laugh, he stepped back and let her in. She sailed through the door like a steamboat, heading back to the kitchen.

"I'll just get this right on the stove. You'll eat a bowl now, yes?"

He knew Jo's mother—Mamesie—well enough to know that this wasn't a question. She wanted to talk to him, and she'd decided that he could use a meal while she did.

He rubbed his stomach, which had woken up at the tantalizing scent of the comfort food. She wasn't wrong. He couldn't remember if he'd eaten lunch, and he remembered quite well that his breakfast had been derailed by sex with Jo.

Mamesie had already filled a large bowl by the time he entered the kitchen. She'd placed it on the wide marble island with a spoon and had produced a loaf of bread from the tote bag she'd had slung over her shoulder. The yeasty scent of home-baked bread made his stomach rumble as she sawed off a gigantic slice and balanced it on the edge of his bowl.

"You haven't been by to see me since you've been back," she commented mildly as she leaned over the edge of the island, across from where she'd set the soup. He winced as he slid onto one of the bar stools.

"You still don't pull punches, I see." Lifting the spoon, he trailed it through the soup, watching the red droplets as they slid off the metal.

"I'm not done." Hooking her thick-rimmed glasses into the front of her blousy shirt, she cast him a disapproving stare. "I've got one miserable girl at home. She's holed up in her room and won't talk to anyone, not even Beth."

"Shit." Theo dropped his spoon. "It's my fault, Mamesie. I'm so sorry. I didn't mean for any of this to happen."

"Are you the only person in this relationship?" she asked mildly, and he shook his hand, feeling as though she'd slapped his hand. "Then I highly doubt that it's all your fault. So why don't you tell me about it?"

He opened his mouth, then shook his head. "With all due respect, I don't think I should. Jo is your girl."

"Theo." The depth of emotion in Mamesie's voice had him looking up, startled. "Jo is my girl.

But you've been my boy, ever since the day I met you. Don't you know that by now?"

Her words were the balm he'd needed. Swallowing thickly, he forced himself to begin speaking. He found himself telling her everything, right back to the night he'd left—well, everything except the sex. There were some things a mother didn't need to know.

She nodded when he was done, and he set his spoon down. He was surprised to discover that he'd eaten all of the bread and soup, and felt a hell of a lot better for it.

"So let me get this straight." Pushing back from the island, Mamesie fixed him with a cool, pale stare. "You told Jo, before this offer came in, that this exact thing was what you dreamed of accomplishing. Then you told her that your dream had come true. And *then* you told her to be the one to tell you to stay."

"Ah…yes. That would be accurate." When it was all laid out like that, it didn't sound so great. "But I want to stay, if she'll have me."

"Do you think my daughter loves you?" There was no judgment in Mamesie's words, but the question brought Theo up short. He knew how he felt, but Jo's response earlier that day had made him question whether he'd imagined everything between them.

But…he knew he hadn't. Jo might not want to love him, but she did. They'd been apart for a long time, but he still felt he knew her heart.

He nodded.

"So she loves you. And she told you to go pursue your dream, because it's what she thinks will make you happy." Mamesie shook her head. "Gee, I wonder why that is."

Hope was a wild thing, unfurling inside him. "So what do I do?"

Unhooking her glasses again, she placed them squarely on her nose, then peered at him with the withering expression that no one mastered like a mother. "You go get her, you lunkhead. But have another bowl of soup first."

CHAPTER SIXTEEN

"You're going to have to talk about it sooner or later," Amy commented mildly. Jo peeled a slice of cucumber off her eye and glared balefully down at where her youngest sister was painting her toenails neon pink. "If you don't we're just going to keep torturing you with beauty treatments."

"There's nothing to talk about." Jo removed the second cucumber slice, tossing them both into the trash can as she struggled to sit up. Holding up a foot, she wiggled her newly polished toenails and grimaced.

"Why pink?" she asked Amy, voice sullen. "You have every color of nail polish known to man in your room, so why the hell would you choose pink for me?"

"Pink with sparkles," Amy replied cheerfully, pulling her legs up under her where she sat on Jo's bed. "And I just told you. We're torturing you with spa night until you talk to us."

"There's nothing to talk about." Jo crossed her legs as well, looking down at the floor where Meg was stirring something in a bowl. "What the hell is that?"

"It's a hair mask." Meg smiled beatifically up at her. "Egg yolk and avocado oil. And it's going on your head unless you spill."

"I just said, there's nothing to spill!" Throwing her hands into the air, she accidentally brushed one against her cheek. It came back with a smear of green slime. "Can I wash this off now?"

"Not until it's dry." Beth sat on the floor with Meg, holding a plastic shower cap. "The clay won't have pulled all the crap out of your pores until then."

"Fantastic." Jo sucked in a deep breath. Her sisters had her number—this was a form of torture unique to her, and she wasn't enjoying even a second of it. Her room smelled like flowers, the mask on her face itched and her toenails were fucking pink. More than that, she was miserable.

Had it really only been a few days since Theo had crashed back into her life? As far as her heart was concerned, he'd never left. But that was the thing, wasn't it—he was going to leave.

And if she stopped him, what the hell kind of

person would she be? Not one who wanted the best for the person she loved, that was for sure.

Her computer pinged, a notification that she had a new comment on her blog. Normally she loved checking out people's responses to what she'd written, but right now she couldn't imagine ever posting again. She couldn't imagine wanting to know anything about sex ever again, because she'd always associate the act with Theo. He was her match in every sense of the word.

She'd known he would probably go, but the pain was worse than anything she could have imagined.

"Well, then. Since you're still holding out, it's hair treatment time." Meg wiggled a paintbrush in her direction. "Come here!"

The thought of raw egg, cold and slimy on her head, was finally enough to make her crack. Scuttling back into the corner of her bed, out of Meg's reach, she growled at her sisters as a whole. "Fine! Fine! I've been sleeping with Theo. And I fucking fell in love with him again, and he's moving to San Francisco with all of the hippies, and I'm *miserable*! Is that what you wanted to hear?"

"It's what I wanted to hear." Jo shrieked as Theo stuck a leg inside her window, knocking her pen cup off her desk. Clapping a hand to her chest as he hauled himself up so that he was straddling her windowsill, she gaped at him in shock. "What the hell do you think you're doing?"

"The last big discussion we had, you climbed in my bedroom window." With a grunt, he pulled his second leg in through the window, sliding into her room. Offering a disarming grin to her sisters, he nodded. "Hi, girls. Do you mind giving us a minute?"

"Not at all." Balancing the bowl of hair gunk in one hand, Meg rose smoothly to her feet. Smirking at Jo, she waved the paintbrush around. "Should I save this for later?"

Jo bared her teeth, and Meg just laughed. Offering Beth a hand, she hauled her other sister to her feet, then nudged her to the door. "Come on Beth, Amy. You guys can argue over who gets the hair mask."

"Not on your fucking life," they said together, all three jostling their way through Jo's bedroom door. Beth was the only one who looked back over her shoulder, smiling softly at her older sister. "Don't be a total bitch, okay? You know what you want."

Then she was gone, closing the door softly behind her. Jo didn't even take offense to her parting comment, because heaven knew, she was *feeling* bitchy. Bitchy, and prickly, and spoiling for a fight.

"That's a good look for you," Theo commented

mildly as he turned to face her, arms crossed over his chest. Damn it, why did he have to look so good? Dressed in a pair of jeans that were faded in all the right places, with a navy T-shirt that stretched tight over his chest, she had to curl her fingers against the urge to reach out and touch.

Jo looked down at her torn jeans. She was only wearing a cotton sports bra on top, since she still had a thick layer of clay on her face. Her hair was scraped back from her face with a fuzzy head-band, and her toes were pink and glittered when she moved.

Well, he'd seen her looking worse. Spreading her hands wide, she shrugged. "This is who I am, Theo. What's the matter? Not fancy enough for your big new job?"

He ignored the hostility in her voice. Instead, he held out a small, tattered package wrapped in faded paper. Hesitantly, she took it, squinting to read the words printed on the wrapping. "Happy birthday? My birthday isn't for months. How quickly they forget."

Never mind Beth's gentle admonishment—she was being bitchy. She couldn't seem to help it. She was furious, not with him for pursuing his dream, but with herself for knowing that she'd never get over him.

"I'm reenacting our last night together, back

then. But backward." He stuffed his hands in his pockets, then rocked back on his heels. He was barefoot. "You climbed in my window. I'm climbing in yours. We had a fight, and I didn't give you your present. We are *not* going to have a fight now, and I'm finally giving that birthday present to you."

"This is the present you were going to give me then?" Shock crashed over her like an ice-cold wave. "You kept it all this time?"

"It was still in the drawer beside the bed in my old room when I moved back here." He grinned mischievously. "Right beside a box of condoms that are most definitely expired."

Jo rolled her eyes but couldn't stop her fingers from trembling. Why was he giving this to her now? Couldn't he just go and leave her and her broken heart alone?

"Open it," he commanded, and before she could think it through, she was tearing open the paper. Inside was a square gift box, and as she lifted the lid, her pulse started to thunder at the base of her throat.

Inside, nestled in a bed of cotton, was a gleaming white-gold pendant. She didn't wear jewelry, never had, but when she held it up closer to her eyes, she immediately understood why Theo had chosen it for her.

"These are made from antique wax seals, ones that were actually once used by someone to seal letters," he informed her, attention focused on her, laser sharp. "Your Louisa May Alcott probably used one. I didn't know that then, but I'm just trying to make you like it more now."

"I do like it," she managed to force out through her dry throat. "But—"

"In case you haven't looked that closely yet, it has two hearts on it," he interrupted, smiling innocently when she glared at him. "They're tied together with a ribbon. And it says *forever*."

Jo felt her heart crack right open. "Why the hell would you give this to me now?"

"I love you, but sometimes you need to try to see beyond that thick skull of yours." Her head snapped up, but he wasn't done. "I was going to tell you that I loved you this afternoon, before everything went to shit."

When he dropped down to one knee in front of her, Jo gasped. "What—"

"Just let me finish before you yell at me." Grabbing one of her hands, he held tight even when she tried to pull away. "Look. You walked in right after I heard that news. I hadn't even begun to digest it yet, and I needed to tell someone. You were it."

"And I still think you should go." This was

a nightmare, bringing her so close to what she wanted before cruelly tearing it away.

"I don't want to." A cry of anguish tore out of her throat, and when he tried to speak again, she shook her head.

"You can't stay because of me. You'll resent the hell out of me, and I'll wallow in guilt." She swallowed past the sting of incoming tears. "But I...fuck, I'm just going to say it. I love you, too. You can be a cocky asshole, but you're my cocky asshole. I... I'll go with you. If you want me to."

A grin as bright as sunshine spread over his face, and its light chased away some of the dread that crowded after her declaration. She absolutely would go with him, because she needed to be with him. But leaving her family would be one of the hardest things she'd ever done.

"I don't want to go." He growled overtop of her protest. "Hear me out, woman. This deal is amazing, but it's not the deal for me. I'm not ready to turn Crossing Lines over to someone else. I might not ever be. And I don't actually want to move. I've lived in lots of places, but this is the one that feels like home."

"I—what?" Jo gaped down at him as a terrible hope sprang up inside her.

"But I want to stay on one condition." Squeezing her fingers, he looked up at her, and love shone from his eyes. "I'd marry you tomorrow, but something tells me that you'll inform me that that timeline is ridiculous. So I think, in exchange for my selfless decision to stay here in Boston, that you should move in with me."

"Move in with you?" Jo couldn't keep up. Her fingers clenched around the small box that she still held. "Next door?"

"That's the idea. I know you're attached to your family home, but I've discovered that I'm kind of attached to mine, too." He cocked his head, studying her face. "I suppose I could move in here, but I think Ford might try to punch me in such close quarters, and it would be a shame to leave that giant house next door all empty. Just think, you could have an office. You could have a suite of offices."

"You sweet talker, you." Closing her eyes, she shook her head in disbelief. "I don't know what to say. I'm sorry I was such a bitch."

"It's part of your charm." He rose to his feet when she snorted. "I'm serious. I love you, Jo, every last bit of you. I wish I had a ring to put on your finger right now, but today has been a little bit busy. Tomorrow we can go pick a ring."

Unable to hold back the laughter, Jo allowed a tear to spill over. It scalded the tender skin of her cheek, allowing another to trickle down, and before she knew it she was crying full out, burying her clay-covered face in Theo's T-shirt. He didn't even complain, just pressed her against him as though he never wanted to let go.

"I don't need a ring." Her voice cracked, and she cleared her throat. Lifting her head, she grinned up at him as a content she'd never imagined she could feel flooded through her like warm sunshine. "I only need you."

"And I need you. I love you." Dipping his head, he pressed a kiss to her clay-smeared forehead, then wiped the excess off his mouth with a grin. "Come on. Let's go home."

* * * * *

RETURN TO LOVE

YASMIN Y. SULLIVAN

For my mother, father, brother and grandmother,
who have given me the richness of the human heart;
for Jennie and Tanya,
who have been my sister-friends;
and for Madeline, Freddie and William,
who have shaped my vision of love.

Chapter 1

When Regina Gibson heard the door swing open and the chime sound, she didn't glance up from the last shards of cobalt-blue tile she was fitting into place. She had them laid out in her mind, and if she looked away, the order would be lost.

She caught the coattails of a suit out of the corner of her eye and hoped he would be a paying customer.

"Let me know if you see anything," she called from the back.

It was getting on in the evening, but with the nearby restaurants still open, people wandered in now and again—once they could tell that the beaten-down corner house was now actually an art gallery and studio.

The exterior of the building hadn't been changed yet, except for a sign, but inside, they'd added installations, shelving, display cases, work spaces. They'd even added tables in the back rooms to teach classes, and they'd partitioned off the kilns.

Once the inside was in better shape, they could start work on the outside so that it didn't look like a rickety brownstone. And once they caught on, they could start the real renovations. It wasn't the perfect place yet, but it was the perfect location—right on the border of the arts and crafts district and near the Torpedo Factory Arts Center in Alexandria, Virginia.

Regina finished laying in the final pieces and cocked her head toward the back room, checking on the two kids. Kyle and Tenisha were still fixated on their little art projects. No problem there.

When she finally looked up, he was standing right in front of the table she was working at, his eyes trained on the children in the back room.

Her eyes didn't follow his gaze to the children. They were drawn to the figure in front of her. His rugged features seemed trapped and contained by his flawless business attire, but his athletic-cut suit didn't hide the rough-hewn inflections or the ridged sculpting of his body. The polish of the crisp navy cotton didn't conceal a raw, unrefined beauty in his shape. It was as if something untamed was tamped down by the elegance of professional trappings.

He had a firm, never-back-down stance that said he would be a hard adversary to rumble with in...whatever his business was. And it was business. Everything about him said that he was all business—everything from the no-nonsense cut of his suit to the angular inlay of his jawline. The smooth, dark brown skin of his face held a concentrated expression that was softened but made no less determined by the curves of thick, sensuous lips. His eyes were serious but also wistful. His eyes...

Regina flinched and sucked in a breath. She knew those eyes.

The face was older, harder, different than the face she had known before. But inside it was the prior face, and she recognized it now as if someone had just pointed it out to her. The childhood had gone out of it—the baby fat that had plumped his cheeks, the boyish grin that made his eyes sparkle. These had been replaced by the calm, jagged confidence of an adult. He would be twenty-eight now—the same as her. He even seemed taller, his shoulders broader.

Regina could barely place this new configuration with what she knew of the boy behind it. It didn't fit the idler she had known—the slacker lazing on the sofa with his buddies or running the streets with his jeans hanging halfway down his hips. The face before her didn't match the one she had known, the one skipping classes and sleeping through exams. The one who had skipped out on her.

As recognition dawned, so did Regina's rage.

What made him think he could pop in on her after all this time? No way. No how.

Growing more livid with each second, Regina shoved the plywood base of her mosaic farther onto the table, got up from her chair and walked over to the display case on which the cash register sat. This put them out of sight and out of earshot of the children.

Nigel Johns had understood to follow her across the room and now faced her across the counter. And what he faced was wrath.

"Unless you know how to turn back time or are here to tell me I've won the lottery, you better get the hell out."

Regina's voice was low, but its venom was unmistakable, and her body clenched in outrage.

His eyes now turned to her for the first time, but what she found there she couldn't decipher.

"I'm not here for any of that. I'm here for you and—"

"You're not here for me or anything else, because I don't want to have anything to do with you."

His face remained calm, and his tone remained even and commanding, which infuriated her more. He may have thought he could waltz in the door, but she would be cutting him off at every pass.

As if it would somehow explain things, he took a folded sheet of paper out of his pocket and put it down on the counter.

"This is for you—for—"

"Whatever it is, I don't want it."

When he didn't move, she snatched up the sheet of paper and unfolded it. It was a check for five thousand dollars.

"You think you can buy me?" she said, ripping up the check. "You think you have anything that I want?" She threw the pieces at his fine navy suit and watched them scatter down to the floor. "I told you before, didn't I? I don't need you. Now get the hell out."

Nigel Johns held his stance. Maybe he was waiting for her to get it off her chest and get it over with. But it wouldn't be over anytime soon.

Regina put her hands on her hips and simply glared at him. He said nothing, but he also didn't move.

"Wait," she said. "Do you have a card? I have an item that belongs to you—to your grandmother, actually—and once you have it back, I won't need to hear from you ever again."

He sighed heavily.

"This is not the way I wanted this to be, Reggie."

His voice was low, but it was deep and steady. Even that had changed. The disappointment in his tone calmed her a bit, but her position had not altered, and she held her ground.

"This is not the way it's supposed to be between us," he said.

Regina couldn't believe his audacity. Were they on the same planet? She hadn't seen him in over six years!

She threw her hands up in exasperation.

"There is no us, and there never will be again."

"Don't say that before you hear me out."

"You can't possibly have anything to say that will change my mind."

Nigel stepped around the counter, and before she knew what he was about to do, he had pulled her into his arms and was kissing her.

Startled by what was happening, Regina was momentarily unclear on how to react. Her thoughts flew out of her mind.

Something about being in the curve of these arms was familiar—the firmness of the grip about her waist, the abandon of the lips moving over hers, the heat rising up between them. But everything else seemed part of the newness of him—the way his height sent her head back, the buttons of his suit pressing against her abdomen, the boldness of his fingers along her back, sparking flames in her.

These filled her senses, and she became lost in them.

Wait. What was she doing?

Startling her again, he pulled away.

"That's the way it always was for us," he said, letting her go and stepping back.

Regina felt like she'd been caught in a lie, one he'd forced her to tell, and her anger sprang back to life. How could she let herself get caught in the moment? And how dare he put his hands on her after he had disappeared— ditching her, ditching them, ditching everything?

No way was it going to go down like that.

She stepped up to him, poking her finger against his chest and raising her head for the attack. But she didn't know what to say. Her head had not cleared; she hadn't been able to remember her logical arguments about why what had just happened didn't change anything.

Little footsteps clacked toward the front, and both of them stopped in their tracks.

Tenisha appeared, smocked in the jumbo trash bag that Regina had tied at her neck and around her waist. And thank goodness. The bag was covered from top to bottom with splotches of paint, swipes from the brushes and handprints of various sizes.

Tenisha hesitated when she saw a man there.

"Come, sweetie. What is it?" Regina coaxed, giving her full attention to the child and relieved to have a moment to collect her thoughts.

Nigel stepped back around the counter, his eyes fixed on the little girl.

Behind Tenisha trailed a path of paint that was dripping from the ceramic bisque platter she was carrying. It was shaped like a butterfly, its various quadrants plastered with pastel shades of glaze.

"I'm finished with mine. Kyle is still working on his."

"Did you get the bottom, honey?"

"Yup. Look."

She turned it over for Regina to inspect, all the while smudging little fingerprints of paint from one color to another.

Regina took her back to the table in the classroom.

"Let's just set it here to dry for a few minutes before we add a topcoat." She turned to the little boy, still vigorously applying paint to the baseball-shaped bisque platter he was working on. "How is yours going, little one?"

"Uh-huh."

Regina could see that Kyle was fully engrossed, and so she turned back to Tenisha.

"Once we add the topcoat, we can put these in the kiln and head upstairs to have something to eat. Okay?"

"Okay."

"You sit here and keep Kyle company while he finishes his. Is that okay?"

"Okay."

Regina turned and walked back to the register. Nigel had popped up thinking...whatever he was thinking, but it wasn't going to work on her.

"I've had enough, Nigel. There is no us, and there will be no us."

When the corners of his lips twisted into a smirk, Regina's temper stirred again, and she seethed. She'd wanted to be calm, but he wasn't going to let that happen.

"Get out. Get out, and don't come back here."

"Reggie, I—"

"No. Get out."

When the chime at the door sounded, neither one looked over.

"Get out," she said again.

Neither moved.

"Hey, hey. Is anything wrong here?"

Regina knew Jason's voice immediately and was relieved when he came over to stand next to her. He was over six feet four inches, and he worked out religiously. It was clear to all three that Nigel, despite his new height and weight, couldn't take Jason even if he tried. There was nothing left for him to do but withdraw.

Only he wasn't going to back down easily. He held his ground and gave a brief nod to the other man, as if sizing up his competition. Yes, he must be a formidable adversary in the business world.

"Nothing's wrong. This man is just leaving," said Regina.

Nigel didn't move right away, and when he did, it wasn't in the direction of the door. He casually searched one of his inner coat pockets and took out a silver case—a business-card holder.

"You asked if I have a card."

He took out one of the cards and stepped up to the register, handing it in her direction.

When Regina didn't move to take the card, he laid it on the counter. She glared at it as if it had leprosy and then glared at Nigel.

"I'll get that item out to you as soon as possible," she said in a professional tone, stifling her hostility.

Nigel bent his upper body toward her.

"This isn't over, Reggie."

She picked up the business card and put it in the pocket of her jeans.

"It will be soon enough."

Regina watched as Nigel slowly walked out of the studio. She was completely shaken.

Jason, holding Kyle on his hip, sat down at the workstation in the back of the shop.

"You need to talk?"

"No. Yes."

Regina walked over to the table, glancing in on Tenisha before sitting down. Tenisha was blowing on her plate to get it to dry, and Kyle squirmed down to go get his piece.

"It can wait until tomorrow."

"I got time now."

"No. Really. It will be better said tomorrow."

Kyle returned with his baseball platter. "I made this for you, Daddy."

"I can see that you did."

Jason smiled down at his son and took the plate from him before lifting him back onto his lap.

"Here," said Regina. "Let me have the platter so that I can topcoat it and get it in the kiln."

"But I made it for Daddy."

"I know, sweetie, but it's not finished yet. We want it to be hard on the outside so that you can use it. Come, let me show you."

Regina was almost finished applying the topcoat when the bell at the door chimed. He wouldn't have come back, would he? How dare he show up out of nowhere—twice?

Luckily, it was only Ellison, who had come to look for his partner and child.

"Hey. What's the deal with leaving me in the car?"

"My bad. We're in here," Jason called to him. "The pieces aren't done yet. You want to wait or come back another time?"

Before he could answer, Regina offered, "I have some lasagna upstairs. You can eat while you wait for the kiln to fire them."

"We can wait," Ellison replied, picking up Kyle.

Regina set the cones and started filling the kiln. Nigel had had the nerve to throw money at her like she could be bought.

"It's set. Let's lock the front door and head out back."

Gathering Tenisha in her arms, she climbed up the back stairs and let her down to unlock the apartment. She was glad for the company but couldn't keep her mind focused on the random conversations that popped up between them.

Keeping her hands busy wasn't a problem. She heated up and dished out the lasagna, got them all soda and bread, got the adults salad, found an animated movie that the kids could watch and ran down to check on the kiln.

Quieting her mind was another story. What had happened when he'd started to kiss her? Why hadn't she thought to push him off right away? It was because she hadn't known what he was going to do. But that would not happen again.

She heard a car pull up out back, and her pulse quickened. But it was only Tenisha's mom, as expected. *Get a grip, girl. He won't have the nerve to just show up again anytime soon, and if he does, I'll be ready for him.*

While Jason opened the door, Regina moved into the kitchen to fix another plate of lasagna. She stopped and pulled out the business card from her pocket. It was a local address. Damn.

That was okay. She had what she needed to send him the item. No use worrying about it now. In fact, she would be rid of him for good soon enough.

Chapter 2

"Get out. Get out, and don't come back here."

He knew the moment she opened her mouth that he shouldn't have gone. And though he'd taken his time leaving, it was clear that he'd been outgunned.

If he had any hope at all, it was that fraction of a second during his kiss when he felt her lips part beneath his, felt her body arch ever so slightly against his chest. But her arms never came around him, and then he saw the reason why.

He had heard the little boy call out "Daddy" and come running, wrapped in a paint-splattered garbage bag just like the little girl. It had gotten dark outside while he'd been there, so in the glass of the front door, he had been able to see over his shoulder. He could see the little boy jump into the man's arms, talking a mile a minute about whatever it was that he'd made.

He hadn't lost his stride, but his heart just about broke.

He never imagined that when he was ready, it would be too late.

"I don't need you. Now get the hell out."

Inwardly, he was shaking his head. Her hair had been longer, but still smooth and shiny, and her almond eyes had been as piercing as ever. She had been as beautiful and as sensuous as the day she had driven him away, and things could not have gone more badly.

Nigel Johns sat behind his mahogany desk with spreadsheets piled up on his right and a keyboard in front of him. Today, he was off his game. This wasn't like him, and it wasn't good.

He worked in the accounting department of an investing and accounting firm. He hadn't been there very long, but he was doing well, thanks to what he was able to do for his clients and what he'd done with his own portfolio.

"We don't need you, so just leave, and don't come back."

He hadn't expected her to fall into his arms, but he'd thought they could talk like two rational adults—now that he was an adult. But that was admitting that he hadn't been before. Well, it was true, he hadn't been. Their breakup had been his fault, and now maybe it was too late.

He'd decided to crunch numbers for the rest of the day—something simple he could do without too much thought. He always double-checked every calculation, but today he was having to triple and quadruple check because his mind just wasn't where it should be.

"I don't need you. Now get the hell out."

He should have sent her the money, laid out a plan and put the plan fully into place before entering the picture himself. If he hadn't gone there…

He wasn't getting much done. He pushed the keyboard away, shaking his head. He had clients coming in within the hour. At least their folders were ready, and the review of the accounting figures would be easy. This was a good thing, because where his head was right now didn't leave him a great deal of concentration.

"...so just leave, and don't come back."

He'd allowed himself to be chased off once. It was the last time that they'd seen each other six years ago. It was in college, and he was in her apartment. They'd been arguing more, but he didn't expect her to actually call their wedding off and cast him to the wind. She'd used the same kind of language.

"Now get the hell out."

No way was he going to be run off again. If he hadn't gone there, things might have worked out differently. But in for a penny, in for a pound. Now that he'd shown himself, he wasn't backing down, and she wasn't keeping him from his child.

Children? Was it one, or was it both of them? The girl was bigger, but then girls grew faster. Right? He wasn't sure, but he sure as hell was going to find out.

He'd only found out a few months ago that there was a child—or children. He'd been working, saving, building a life that he could offer Regina. He didn't want her to see him until he had made it—made something of himself that contradicted the waste of time he'd been in college. The news had hit him square in the gut.

"You ever see Regina? You been in touch with her since then?"

He was visiting his parents at home when he'd run into one of his college buddies—the one who used to date Regina's roommate. The question put him on guard because it pried into places he didn't want opened.

"Why do you ask?"

He wanted to skirt the issue and let it die, but his friend persisted.

"Because I need to know if you ever found out."

"Found out what?"

The silence and the cryptic way his friend was treading around the subject told him that whatever it was, it was serious.

"Found out what?"

"Look, I'm not supposed to know, but I've never stopped thinking that you should have known."

"Known what?"

"Regina was pregnant when she graduated."

"Pregnant?"

"She was pregnant, and it was yours, and that's all I know."

This was all the information he could get out of his old friend, but it sent him reeling.

Regina had called things off between them just before she graduated. They were supposed to graduate together from Howard University and then get married. Except that, by the end of senior year, he was still a year behind on his classes because he'd been partying too much.

His parents had never given up on him, even after his near-failing grade reports. When Regina put him out, he'd felt like nothing. He'd decided not to come back until he'd made something of himself, until he could show her that he could take care of things. Although he tried, he couldn't do much about that semester, and he mourned the whole summer over their breakup. But the following semester, after she'd already finished and moved on, he was back with a vengeance, determined to prove himself.

He finished his undergraduate degree in accounting and did an internship within the year. Then he went on to an MBA in accounting and finance. He couldn't get into an accelerated program because of his grade point average, but he used the two-year program to take real-estate and investment classes. He graduated at the top of his class and then sat for the CPA exam.

In a way, his goal had become money. He joined an accounting firm and used all his degrees to start amassing a bank account. Then he made a vertical move to the position he was in now so that he could move back to the DC area, where Regina still was.

But it wasn't just money; he wanted everything that came with real success, real responsibility. And he wanted to be more cultured, too. No more baggy pants, no more ghetto fashion, no more looking like the hood. Everything about his life was bent on making it, looking the part, being professional, working hard, getting it right.

She'd gone to study with some artists for a year—or so he'd heard. But other than that, she had stayed in the area after their Howard years. He didn't have many details; after a while people had finally started to get the message and had stopped telling him her activities. By the time she got back to DC after her year away, he was immersed in his own MBA program down home in South Carolina, trying to catch up. What his buddy had said fell into place. That year away would have been when she'd had their child.

Was it one child or two? Yes, he would be finding out.

He just had to get through the day. Then he had to get his game back and make it through the rest of the week. This weekend he would stake his claim.

Regina turned the car off and grabbed her purse. She'd had an errand to run for her morning office job, and then she had to drop off some of her pieces at a gallery downtown that was having a showing of local artists. By the time she got to the studio, she was running late.

She found Amelie finishing up with a customer. She had sold one of her large, bead-covered bowls and had a new beadwork project in process on the back table in the bead section.

"Sorry I'm late. I hope that means we've been doing well today."

"No problem, and yes—relatively speaking. We've sold one of yours and one of mine. Whoo-hoo."

There was no one else in the shop, so Regina started pulling out her project. "I don't know if that's anything to whoo-hoo about. But it's good. We have to get our front fixed up soon."

"I know. I registered us for the seminar you were talking about," Amelie said, "the one at the community center on starting up a small business."

"Oh, good. I've been working on our paperwork from the books I found."

And she had been. It was like having another part-time job. Regina pulled out her tiles and began setting up her workstation.

"I didn't make it to the post office today," Regina said.

"I'm going to leave early to get some of my jewelry to the consignment shop. Is there anything you want me to take to the post office for you on my way?"

"No, I haven't even wrapped the package yet. I'll get it tomorrow. You take off."

"Okay. I put out two new pieces. This one—" Amelie pointed to a necklace "—is made of yellow jasper beads with cowrie shell accents, and this one—" she pointed to a jewelry box "—is made with rose quartz and Czech glass."

"They're beautiful. You keep getting more elaborate."

"That's the point."

After Amelie left, Regina sat down to her project. She was on the sky section and needed to break some more light blue and white tiles. It was the act of hammering the pieces under a cloth that made her think of Nigel. That fraud.

She replaced the cloth and banged the center of a large blue tile, splitting it into triangles. It had been almost a week since he'd appeared out of the blue, and she'd finally stopped worrying that every stranger who turned up might be him coming back for round two.

She straightened out the cloth and went for the triangles, smashing them into small trapezoids. She would get him his item and be done with him. She had too much going on in her life that she wanted to get done. She didn't need one more thing to distract her.

Nigel checked the inside pocket of his sports suit to make sure he had everything. She wouldn't be flinging his check back at him this time. He took a breath. No need to go there yet. He hadn't gotten anything in the mail, so maybe her bark wasn't as bad as her bite.

He got out of the car and started unloading the packages from the backseat. It was after 8:00 p.m. on a Sunday, and the studio was closed, so he assumed they'd be home, tomorrow being a school day. He'd get all the packages up the back steps before ringing the buzzer.

It was beginning to get dark outside, so when she opened the door, the warm, yellow light from inside haloed behind her and made her look like an angel—his angel. She had on white leggings and a summer camisole, but the soft fabrics hugged her curves in a way that made his mouth water.

Except that her hips were deeper, she hadn't changed from the girl he loved. She had natural dimples in the curve of her cheeks so that she looked always on the verge of a smile, and her tapered waist flared out into the most luscious behind he'd ever seen. Even in the simple leggings that she had on now, she made his knees weak.

Her hair was different this time—pulled back in a pony-tail at the nape of her neck in a way that emphasized her umber eyes. The anger he saw form in her eyes at the sight of him in the doorway snapped him back to the present, to the fact that they were torn apart.

"Hello, Reggie."

"Don't hello me. What on earth are you doing at my house?"

The moment she opened her mouth, his calm was shat-tered, but he didn't show it. There was no mistaking the animosity in her voice. She didn't want him in her private space. She didn't want him anywhere near her at all.

"I still need to speak with you. Can I come in?"

"No. No, you cannot. And I don't have anything to say to you."

He didn't want to force things with her. He'd let her cut him off time and again in the studio, intentionally giving her the upper hand so that she could see that he wasn't there to threaten her. But this time, he wasn't going to back down. This time, he wasn't going to be sent away.

"Look, Reggie. You and whoever you're with will not keep me from my child. Or children. You don't have the right to do that."

"What?"

"I want to see my children. I know I haven't been there for them so far, but that will not be the case from here on out."

She sighed, and he saw some of the fight go out of her—not the rage or the anger that he saw in her eyes, but some of the fight. Her shoulders slumped, and she turned into the apartment, walking away from him.

He gathered up the packages from the stairwell and

followed her inside. She had her back to him and seemed to be staring at the wall or at nothing, so he shut the door behind them.

He had been gone a long time. He knew that. Perhaps she had to decide if he was safe or if she was willing to share their children. Or perhaps she just needed to get her mind accustomed to the idea.

He was standing in what turned out to be the dining area, with a kitchen off to the side. There was no partition separating it from the living room, where she now stood.

The first thing he saw was the art. It filled her rooms with color, and she'd even painted the chairs and cabinets and bookshelves to make them pop. All of her touches filled the room—the African masks and dolls on the walls, the embroidered cushions on the sofa, the framed paintings and mosaics covering the walls. So much claimed his eyes that he almost missed how worn down the permanent structure underneath was.

The kitchen and dining nook seemed to have come straight out of the '60s—battered wooden cabinets, ancient countertops, worn linoleum flooring—and the rest of the place didn't fare much better. Downstairs, everything that they'd added stood out as new against the old.

Her voice tore him away from his perusal.

"How did you find out?"

He put his bundles down.

"I found out from someone who's not supposed to know."

"Please tell me."

The resignation in her voice pulled at his heartstrings.

"I ran into your roommate's ex-boyfriend a few months ago. But it shouldn't have taken finding that out to make me come look for you. I just wanted to make something of myself before I did. But when I found out that you were pregnant when…when you called things off between us… Reggie, why didn't you tell me? Why did you send me away without me knowing?"

He took a step toward her, but she took a step back.

"What would you have done? You were too busy hanging with your friends and blowing off school. You might have stayed, but it would have been for the wrong reasons. And I didn't need you to make a life for…"

She shook her head, trailing off.

"But I should have known. I had a right to know. And if—"

"Let it go."

"Why didn't you tell me?"

Her jaw was set in a rigid line that told him she would not be offering any answer to that question.

"Where are they, Reggie? I want to see them. And I plan to be there for them from now on. It doesn't matter if you're with someone else. I'm still their father."

He pulled the check out of his suit pocket.

"If you don't want it, that's fine. But they deserve it. And so do you. Where are they?"

She looked at him as he put the check down on the dining table, and what he saw in her wet eyes was a combination of sadness and hate.

She turned away from him again and buried her face in her hands. When she spoke, it was through tears, but it was with rage.

"There is no they."

He didn't understand. "What?"

"Don't you get it? There is no they. There was no child."

He wondered for a split second if she had…let go of it…after they had broken apart. But then he looked at her shaking shoulders. He knew her better than to think that.

"No child?"

It started to sink in. He wasn't a father. The little boy he had seen wasn't his. Nor the little girl. His child had not made it. His heart fell. He crossed over to her but stopped just behind her without touching her, not knowing how to comfort her, not knowing if she would receive his comfort.

"There was no child," she said again, stammering. She whirled toward him, ready to strike, but didn't. She just stopped and stared at his face, her own face crumpling.

He wrapped his arms around her shoulders and drew her to him, but she wrangled against him.

"There was no child," she repeated, lashing at his chest with her fists. It was like a dam had broken, as though she couldn't stop herself once she'd started letting it out. She kept pummeling his chest with her fists as if it was his fault, or maybe because he'd been the one to make her say it, relive it. "And you weren't there."

She drew back after she said it—the truth of it all. She had tears spilling down her face, and her fists were still balled, ready to strike. Her eyes were red and wet, filled with rage and hate. And now he knew why.

Regina kept hammering at him, as if she wanted to pound him until all the hurt she had carried over the years was finally over. But when she stood back and looked up at his face, what she saw there stopped her. Nigel wondered if she could see that the disappointment in his eyes was as bottomless as her own heartbreak must have been. Nigel knew the moment that the resistance went out of her and stepped toward her, folding her in his arms again.

"When I saw the kids downstairs—"

He wanted to go on, but he couldn't control his voice.

For a while she didn't say anything but simply sobbed against his chest.

When she found her voice, it was shaky. "I was babysitting. Kyle belongs to Jason, and Tenisha to another friend.

They're not related, and they're not even the same age. Kyle is five and a half, and Tenisha is seven."

After she got the words out, she convulsed in tears again.

He just held her while she wept.

When he thought she was back in control, he ventured, "What happened…to ours?"

For a few moments, she cried harder. Then she took in a deep breath.

"I lost it. I miscarried."

She broke from him and went to the window, trying to wipe her face with her hands.

"And guess when. Guess."

Her tone was sardonic, but she was still fighting back her tears.

"On the day that would have been our wedding day," she said.

He went to her and wrapped his arms around her again, but she fought him. "No. You weren't there. You weren't there."

She hit at his shoulders with her open palms, her body racked by sobs.

He pulled her into his embrace. "I'm so sorry," he said into her hair. "I'm so sorry. Please forgive me."

"No. I won't."

"Please. I didn't know."

"You should have known. You should have been there."

"You sent me away, Reggie."

She was silent, tears still streaming down her face. He held her and rubbed her back until her body shook less. He smoothed her hair and kissed her temples until her tears abated some. He ignored her periodic attempts to rustle from his arms.

When she had stilled, he pulled her chin up to look at

her, to see that she was all right. Her eyes were red from crying, and her lips were tender from being pressed so hard together. He wanted to drain the redness from her eyes and soothe the pain out of her expression.

"I'm so sorry, Reggie, so sorry."

He folded her against his chest and ran his hand down her back. In the quiet, he could feel the way her body pressed against his in the embrace. He wanted to feel that forever. He wanted to make her his again.

This time when he pulled her face up to his, he bent down, softly kissing her lips. He wanted to turn back time, to undo the hurt he'd caused, to be there when he should have been there.

"I'm so sorry, baby."

She said nothing, but she didn't move from his arms either.

He bent his head to the side of her face and kissed her eyelid, her cheek, her earlobe. Then he cupped her head and took her mouth with his, parting her lips with his own and claiming her breath.

He felt her hands tighten around his upper arms and knew that her body was responding. He wanted to assuage the hurt inside her with his lips, pacify the anger out of her with his fingertips.

When he moved his tongue into her mouth, it opened for him, and a quiet murmur escaped into his mouth, igniting fire inside of him. She took a small step back, but he stepped with her, closing the gap between them before she could make it. He claimed her hips with his hands and pressed her against his loins. She sucked in her breath and then another murmur filled his mouth.

She put her arms around his neck, and her tongue played against his, inviting him deeper inside. He could read her desire. He had always been able to. It was clear that she was starting to want him the way he wanted her.

Nigel could sense the battle being waged inside Regina. The years of hurt and anger, of bearing the burden alone, were at odds with everything else that was happening between them. He wanted for everything else to win.

"Let me be there for you now," he whispered against her lips.

Then he reclaimed her mouth, running his hands along her back. He couldn't resist cupping her bottom and pulling her closer, and when he did, he felt a slight tilt of her hips as she drew nearer. He knew where she yearned, and he wanted to ease that need, even as his own grew hotter and less controllable with every passing minute.

He bent down farther, his mouth finding her neck, and cupped her buttocks again, lifting her body against his. When he heard her low moan against his ear, he lifted her off her feet and strode toward the back of the apartment to find her bedroom.

He expected her to stop him, but she said nothing while he eased her down on the bed and lowered himself over her, pressing his swollen groin against her sweet center. Instead, she reached for his arms and pulled him closer to her, kneading herself along his body. It had been so long for him that even this small movement sent him close to the edge, but he knew better than to let himself go. He knew that this was for her, that this was to let her know that she wasn't alone all that time, that he was still loving her. It was to calm the sore places, to hush the anger and the rage.

He looked at her tearstained face in the moonlight. He had been waiting for this for so long, so long. Her fingers at his back let him know that his wait would soon be over. But he wouldn't rush to that place. This was for her.

He settled next to her and slid his hand into her leggings.

When he found the wetness of her womanhood, his loins leapt, and he heard her moan.

Her long, sepia legs came into view as he removed her leggings, and her beautiful breasts fell into the open as he pulled the camisole over her head and undid her bra. He pulled the bow from her hair and laid her back down. He meant to take his own clothes off as well, but the sight of her pulled him back to the bed.

When he took the closest breast into his mouth, he heard her moan. He couldn't resist the feel of her nipple against his tongue, the feel of her wetness at his fingertips, the way her body writhed with his caresses. This was for her.

Before he lost control, he stood up and removed his suit, his shirt, the rest of his clothes. He found a condom and got it on quickly, returning to Regina's side on the bedspread. He kissed her, reminding himself to take it slowly. This was for her.

He ran his hand over her body, listening for the places that made her breath heavy and feeling for the places that made her body sway toward his. He kissed her neck and pulled her leg over his thigh so that he could touch her warm, wet center again, and when he did, she let out a low, guttural moan that filled his body with need. He couldn't wait any longer.

When he moved between her thighs, her legs spread for him, pressing against his hips. And when he entered her, her mouth opened beneath his, drawing him in. He pressed gently toward her center, stifling his own moan and barely able to keep control. It had always been this way for him with this woman.

She moaned as he pressed slowly inside of her. She was as tight as she had been the first time they had been together many years ago, tighter even than he remembered. Drowning in her beauty, he found her mouth and covered it again with his own. He had to remind himself to slow down, to take his time. He had been wanting this for so long, so long. But this was for her.

Chapter 3

Regina got up before the sun came up. The bed next to her was empty, but she had been wrapped in the top sheet and spread. Her body was still pleasantly tender from the activity of the night before, and she was glad to have some time to collect her thoughts before beginning her day. Even more so, she was glad to have time before facing Nigel again—time to figure out what to say, how to explain that things had gotten out of hand.

She knew she should have stopped him when he kissed her, but after the emotional roller coaster of the evening—the anger that he had come back again, the anguish over the fresh memory of the loss of their child, the unspeakable shame that she had lost it—after all of that, she needed those arms around her.

When she had looked in his face, she had finally seen someone who understood what having and then losing their child had meant to her. And for the first time, she had just let herself cry.

Someone could finally comprehend what she had been through, someone who felt the pain, as well. Maybe that was what had wrenched all of that turmoil to the top. Maybe that was what had made her vulnerable to his advances.

She should have stopped him when he ran his hand up and down her back, sending tingles through her, but right then, the wounds in her had finally found a place where they could be held, and she wasn't willing to leave that shelter. She hadn't been touched in so long. She hadn't had a place to unburden the past. That's what his hands did to her. They softened the rage; they caressed the hurt.

She should have stopped him when he carried her to her bedroom, but she hadn't been touched with understanding in so long—the kind of understanding that made her needy and wanting. Yes, by then, she wanted it as much as he did.

She should have stopped him, but it had always been this way between them.

Regina kicked off the sheets and went into the bathroom to run a bath. It wasn't her usual routine, but she had time, and it would help her calm down and think.

He was taller than he'd been before, but mostly, he was more in control, more able to take his time, more able to respond to her body rather than running along ahead of her. This made him a different lover than the one she had known.

Having him inside of her had felt just like the first time. He was slow and gentle. He filled her with his presence. At first, he had made long, slow thrusts, stroking the aches out of her and making her body arch off the bed. Then he had found her spots and made her eager, pushed her toward the edge.

He had kissed her tears, lulling her sadness away, consoling her heartbreak. But he had also run his thumbs over her breasts, lighting fire in her. Between the tenderness and the flame, she wasn't sure which was most consuming, most arousing.

When he cupped her head in his palms and kissed her, the gentleness of his kiss had alleviated her anger and healed her bruises, but his chest moving along her breasts as he plunged inside of her made her wrap her legs around him and draw him farther inside.

"Reggie, Reggie, I've missed you so much," he had murmured over and over.

His deep voice sent tingles down her back, and when he whispered it against her ear, her body had broken out in goose bumps, and an agonizing pressure built up at her center.

"Tell me what you need, baby," he had said.

She couldn't speak, and she just held on, clinging to his shoulders. She only needed.

Then he had moved his hand down between them and begun to massage her while he moved inside of her, making her moan, making her grind against him, tears streaming from the corners of her eyes. Then the first waves of climax hit her, and her body gripped his length. He groaned and thrust against her, but waited for her full release before burying his face next to hers and bucking inside of her as he rode his own wave of orgasm. When it was over, she had turned from him, and he had pulled her back against his chest, and they had slept spooned together that way.

Remembering the night sent arrows of heat through Regina's body. She was letting the memory overwhelm her, when she needed to be figuring out what to do now and where they would go from here.

Only, there was no they, and one night of passion didn't erase six years of frustration and hurt and loneliness. It didn't bring back their child or make their wedding happen. It didn't turn back time.

Nigel had woken up early, before dawn. He couldn't get back to sleep, but he didn't want to wake up Regina. He thought about it—round two—but decided he had better not. His day would have to start in a bit, and he wouldn't be able to take his time.

He just held her for a while, smiling to himself because she was back in his arms. His happiness was tainted by the fact that their child had been lost. He still needed to deal with that, and he needed to help Regina deal with it, too. He could see how much she was still hurting, and how angry she was that he hadn't been there. He could never make up for that, but he wanted to spend the rest of his life trying.

Nigel slipped out of bed just as the sun was about to come up. He washed up as best he could, dressed and went to look for something for them to eat. He didn't know whether she had to be up early on a Monday or what time the studio opened, but he knew he would wake her before he left. This way, they could have breakfast together. They could start their day and their lives together, start healing.

He found her key on the counter next to her purse and drove down the street to see if any place was open. It turned out that he could have walked, because the café on the corner already had customers. He got them bagels with cream cheese, bacon and eggs, pancakes, orange juice and coffee—more than they could eat.

When he got back, he heard her running water in the bathroom but decided not to disturb her just yet. He found a fork and sat down to his breakfast, checking out her pieces on the walls and thinking about where each one could go when they had their own place.

Nigel caught himself imagining their life together and sighed. They had a lot of talking and healing and forgiving left to do, but he was eager to begin the journey.

Regina didn't smell the bacon until she was almost finished getting dressed. Was he still there? She threw on some slacks and a top and peeked out of her bedroom.

He smiled at her from the dining table and began moving the packages he had brought the night before to clear a space for her to sit. His smile almost turned his face into the boyish one she had known before—almost. The cheeks plumped out the way they used to, but the rougher angles remained.

"I thought I smelled bacon…"

"Good morning, beautiful. You did."

"…but I knew I didn't have bacon in the house."

"No, I ran down to the corner to get us something. I hope you're hungry because I think I overdid it. Come sit."

Before she could sit down, he pulled her onto his lap and into a long hug. He kissed her cheek and her forehead. He didn't seem to notice that her body stiffened now at this touch. And before she could protest to the affection, he released her to the chair he had cleared.

She could tell that they weren't on the same page about last night. She wasn't ready to broach the issue, but she knew she had to.

"I thought you were gone," she said.

He must have read that hesitance in her voice as concern or disappointment because he slid his hand under her chin to pull her face toward his. He caressed her cheek with his thumb and said, "No, no way. You must think I'm a rat."

He let her face go and uncovered her plate and juice,

smiling at her. "I know I have a lot to make up for, a lot to prove, but I won't be running out ever again. I just went to get us some eats. I figured we needed it after last night, which was…amazing."

Regina looked at the mound of food in front of her and tried to figure out how to get them on the same page.

"I got up early and didn't want to wake you. I didn't know what time you had to be up."

"Early."

"Then eat up."

Regina heard the mirth in Nigel's tone when he mentioned last night. She read the possessiveness in Nigel's eyes when he looked at her. In contrast, she couldn't even bring herself to eat. Tired of pushing the food around on the plate, she put the fork down and just looked at it, trying to find the right words.

He came around the table and knelt down next to her chair.

"Hey, what's wrong, Reggie? I know there's hurt, but we'll face that together now." He put his arms around her and pulled her toward his chest. Regina tensed, not responding to the embrace.

"Hey, what's wrong?"

"I think we need to talk."

Nigel scooted back onto his chair. He bent toward her and covered her hand with his own. "Okay. What's going on?"

"Last night was…"

She saw his face drop, as if he could tell what was coming.

"…like it used to be between us."

"But?"

"But it's just what it was."

"Which is?"

"Something we both needed."

He let go of her hand and leaned back in his chair.

"That's not all it was, Reggie. Don't you know that?"

His voice was calm and sincere, but it had an edge that bordered on exasperation. His eyes pleaded with her to see it his way.

"That's all it can be. I don't even know you anymore."

"But that's what I want, Reggie—for us to spend the time getting to know one another again. You don't have to make any decisions now. Just give it a chance."

Regina got up and covered her plate before taking it to the fridge. She needed to be away from his eyes for a minute, to have something to do with her hands. His eyes followed her every move.

"No. We had a chance. I can't go back there. Maybe I'm just finally getting over what happened back then."

"Maybe I am, too. Maybe it's something we can do together."

She whirled around and looked right at him. "I can't just forgive you for leaving and then for not being there when I needed you."

He balled his fists and shook his head. They had finally gotten to the real issue.

"You told me to leave. You put me out. You can't put me out and then hold it against me when I go. And you didn't tell me about…the baby."

"We were engaged. I needed you to be more serious about life, especially about our life together. You weren't supposed to jump ship. You were supposed to grow up. You should have been there."

"How can—"

"Stop. I'm not going to argue with you. And that's all we can do now because we're never going to agree on it."

Regina got up from the table. This wasn't going well. They were never going to see eye to eye. She disappeared into the bedroom and returned with a small, black jewelry case.

"Here."

She handed him the case, and he opened it. It was his grandmother's wedding ring.

"I'm sorry I didn't have time to mail it."

"It wasn't just time. If it was that important, you would have mailed it. There's a reason you didn't make the time to do it."

She considered his statement. Maybe it was true. Maybe she'd dawdled because part of her wanted to keep the past alive, to have a keepsake of it.

"Maybe I wasn't ready to let it go. I am now."

"I don't want this back, Reggie. It was for you."

"It belongs in your family, Nigel, not mine."

Nigel shook his head. She knew he was fighting a losing battle over the past. Regina saw the disappointment in his face, but it had to be this way. She went back to the dining table and sat down, turning to look at him seriously.

"Now it really is over between us. There's no reason we need to have contact again."

"Reggie, this isn't what I wanted to happen. I want us to have—"

He moved to touch her, but she pulled away. His touches made her stop thinking straight, and right now, she needed all of her faculties.

"I know this seems crazy after...last night."

"Last night was something special. Don't throw it away."

"I...I'd just been holding so much in for so long. I guess

it all came out. I didn't mean for that to happen. I didn't know it would happen. I shouldn't have let it happen."

"It was meant to happen. It's always been that way between us."

She shook her head and picked up the check from last night, which was still on the table.

"And this." She ripped it up like she had the other one. "I'm doing fine on my own, and there is no…child…that you need to care for."

It was ending, really ending, and her heart had grown heavy with the reality of it, as heavy as the look on Nigel's face.

She took a teddy bear out of one of the bags on the seat next to hers. It had on a baseball jersey and a cap and had a bat sewn to its hands. It brought tears to her eyes, but she didn't let them fall.

"Reggie, we're not meant to end."

"We ended a long time ago. Over six years ago."

She turned the teddy bear around in her hand and found a string to pull to make it talk. She fingered the string but didn't pull it.

"Do you know anyone you can give these to?"

Nigel took a deep breath and looked at the bear in her hands, seeming to feel the same wistfulness she did.

"I have little cousins."

"Good."

She shook her head. There was one more thing that she wanted to say.

"Nigel, I'm sorry…it has to end this way."

But that wasn't what was on her mind. It wasn't what was in her heart. She was thinking about having lost their child, but she had no way to speak her shame.

"It shouldn't end this way. It doesn't have to."

"Yes, it does."

* * *

Nigel carried his packages back down to his car with a heavy heart. He'd almost had it all back, but now he didn't have any of it. He could have spent all day trying to convince her to give them a chance, but until she could forgive him, he knew that no effort on his part would make a difference.

He opened his trunk and put in the packages. There was no need to keep them now. There was no boy, no girl.

He would have taken the day off if she had been willing to spend it with him. Now he had an hour to get to his place, shower, shave, change clothes and get to the office. Fine.

He'd gone from ecstasy to despair in less than twenty-four hours, and now she had simply shut him down. But he wasn't going out like that. He had worked too hard to get this far. He would have to bide his time until he could come up with a new point of entry, a new way to get her to soften her heart to him. It still wasn't over, not yet.

Chapter 4

It had been two weeks since she had seen Nigel, and Regina's spirits were finally picking up after the emotional turmoil. She had her focus back, and she had an on-site installation to keep her busy.

"Are you going to take off from your morning job tomorrow to get the installation done?"

Amelie was at a workstation in the back of the studio stringing an elaborate necklace—one with rows of turquoise and cowrie shells that tapered to a long V. They didn't have any customers at the moment, so she and Regina could chat across the back of the shop.

"No, I'll still need the money," Regina said. "That's the only reason I have that secretary job to begin with—steady income until our income here gets steady. Will you be able to stay late next week so that we don't have to shut down too early?"

"Yeah, no problem. I've already covered all of my evening jewelry-making classes at the bead shop. We'll only have to close early one day."

Regina had a large order to install in a couple of weeks—a custom kitchen backsplash that she'd been working on for most of the last month. It would bring in some much-needed money, so she had to forgo her hours at the store. Half of the money that came in would be going to renovations, so it was worth losing some income at the store.

"I can't thank you enough," Regina said with a smile.

"No prob. You cover for me enough, and you're here more hours than I am anyway."

"Yes, but right now, your beadwork is bringing in more income than the mosaic pieces."

It was true. Amelie was a talented bead artist and sold beadwork supplies as well as her own pieces—mostly jewelry but also hair accents, art objects and even some clothes.

"Oh, mostly the small stuff. My biggest pieces are still sitting here."

"As are mine."

Regina made more from her installations than from the studio, but she did mosaics of just about everything one could think of. She had her standing art pieces, but she also did tables, mirrors, planters, sculptures—anything strong enough to stand a layer of tile and grout. For installations, though, she did kitchens, pools, walks, stairs and fireplaces. She'd even done a patio once.

"You know what we need?" Amelie said. "A showing."

"After we finish the renovations, we should have a real grand opening."

"And we need to change the name."

"Actually," said Regina, "we need to do that now. I've been looking into getting our website back on track, and

we should get all the updates done at the same time—
save money."

"Speaking of which, I got information about the semi-
nars at the community center you mentioned—the ones I
signed us up for."

Regina looked up from the tiles she was laying out.
"Excellent. I've been working on the paperwork, but it's
like figuring out tax forms. Why didn't they teach us this
business stuff in college?"

"At least you went to college."

"Girl, you did, too. You just took your classes in different places one by one. Then you taught yourself. I admire you for that."

Amelie looked up from her necklace and smiled.
"Thank you, sweetie. About the name, we need to get
something Black in there, let people know that there are
some sisters up in here with some culture."

"I agree with you there. I actually want to do some more
African sculptures. When the front is redone, we can put
them in the window with some of your work that has the
cowrie beads. More than half of what we do has a Black
flavor. We need to find a way to announce that."

"And we need some incense."

"No." Regina groaned and waved her hand in front of
her face. "We have enough smells in here with the paints
and the clay and your soldering and the hot glue."

"That's why we need the incense."

"No, our classes will pass out from all the fumes."

The door chime sounded as a couple came in. Amelie
winked over at Regina; it was Regina's turn to see to the
customers. She pushed her mosaic onto the table, grabbed
a wet rag to get the mastic off her hands and got up to approach the couple.

"Good afternoon. Can I help you find anything today?"

Regina showed them her various mosaic pieces and then the beadwork. They stopped for a long time in front of one of her favorite mosaics, a large piece of a woman in a sarong looking over a patio at the ocean and horizon. They seemed interested in it and took one of her business cards from the counter. They even looked over her portfolio of in-home installations, but Regina couldn't tell if they would come back.

By the time she was done, Amelie had already begun wrapping up her project and getting ready to leave for the afternoon, as usual.

Mr. Lundstrum came in just before she left.

"Regina has our rent check ready for you, Mr. Lundstrum."

"I do. It's under the register," Regina said.

Their landlord was an old man and walked with a cane. It was clear that he hadn't had the ability to look after this place for a long time. But he was pleased with the upgrades they'd made and liked having them as tenants.

"Come, my dears. I have a bit of hard news."

"What is it?" Regina asked, worried that something had happened to his wife, who was also getting on in years and was not as agile as her husband.

"Well, this won't be easy for you to hear."

He settled down in one of the chairs at Regina's worktable and sighed heavily.

"You know I've been waiting for you to come up with the down payment on this place. You had first refusal."

"Oh, no." Regina could tell what he was getting ready to say, and her heart sank.

"What? What is it?" Amelie hadn't caught the clue.

"You've taken another offer on the house, haven't you?"

"I'm sorry, dear. I just had to."

Amelie turned to Regina. "What are we going to do?"

"Mr. Lundstrum, can't you give us more time? I have an installation in a couple of weeks. That's a couple of thousand dollars. We can give you that. It's not the down payment, but…"

Regina didn't know what else to say. Thankfully, Amelie stepped in.

"We have a good portion of it saved up, and we're looking for a small-business loan now. Just a little more time is all we need."

"I'm so sorry. My granddaughter starts her junior year at American University in a couple of months, and we're strapped. Retirement and the rent on this place haven't been enough, with school bills and all. We needed somebody who could pay now."

The old man took off his glasses and wiped his eyes. His sight was going, as well.

"Gentleman in a fine suit came in willing to pay more than we're asking—pay it now, one time. Wife and I couldn't say no. Was like looking a gift horse in the mouth."

"Oh, no," said Amelie. "What do we do now?"

"Isn't there anything we can do, Mr. Lundstrum? Anything?" Regina asked.

"I'm so sorry, girls. We just had to take it. Wife wouldn't want me to tell y'all, but the savings is almost gone—with the economy and all. This way we can pay tuition and put some in the bank to replace what's gone."

Regina sighed heavily. "I understand."

"We wanted it to go to you, help y'all out. But weren't no way we could wait. Look, I know it's hard. You just forget about the rent this month and the month after that."

"We can't do that," Regina said firmly. "Can we contact him, Mr. Lundstrum—the gentleman who's buying the place? I know it's a long shot, but maybe if he hears us out, if he knows how much we've put into this place already, maybe he'll let us have it after all."

The old man patted his pockets. "I know I've seen his card. Had one of those little cases you hold business cards in. I think I gave it to the real-estate agent we got to handle the sale for us. I'll get it for you, but dear—" he looked at Regina "—don't hold out hope for that. He'll want more than you were going to pay."

"I know you're right," Regina said, "but we have to try."

"I'll bring you the information tomorrow."

"When do we have to be out?" Amelie asked.

"Six weeks from the first of next month. I wanted to give you some time to find someplace new to sell your things."

"Six weeks for upstairs, as well?" Regina asked.

"Yes, ma'am, the whole building's gone. He worked for some kind of investment firm. He'll probably turn it into another restaurant or something. Said he had someone come check it out just a couple of weeks ago."

Regina went to the cash register and returned with the rent check.

"Here is this month's rent. We wouldn't think of not paying it."

Amelie gave her a wry look but went along.

Mr. Lundstrum crumpled the check in his hand and left it on the table.

"No, dear, no. You'll need that to find another place to live in, another shop. I know I'm going back on my word to you. I told you I would wait and sell this place to you, didn't I? Give you time to fix it up a bit and get her going. Didn't I?"

Tears filled Regina's eyes and spilled down her face. Her dream for the shop was being ripped away. "Yes."

Amelie's arms went around her shoulders and the two women hugged one another.

"Don't cry," Amelie said. "You never cry. Now you'll start me crying."

But Amelie was already crying, as well.

"I gave my word," said Mr. Lundstrum. "And here I am going back on it. It's the last thing I wanted to do. And you've got only two months to figure things out and move. I'm so sorry, girls. We just had to take it. Else I don't know what we'd do for tuition next fall. But that means the least I can do is cut you some slack on the last two months of rent. I won't take it, no matter what you do."

"We appreciate it. We really do," Amelie said.

Regina pulled herself together and let out a deep sigh.

"Thank you, Mr. Lundstrum. Thank you. We understand that you would have waited for us if you could have. And we appreciate you giving us a break on the rent to help us move."

"Y'all start looking for a place right away. Won't be easy to find one in this neighborhood."

"It'll be impossible to find one here," Amelie said, but Regina gave her a look that stopped her from going on.

"We'll start looking," Regina said. "I'll let you know what we find."

After walking Mr. Lundstrum to the door, Amelie flipped the store sign to Closed and locked the door and leaned against it.

"What are we going to do?"

Regina heard the devastation in Amelie's voice.

"I don't know. I don't know. This changes our whole business plan—everything. We'll need to find a new space—"

"And it sure won't be in the art district," Amelie said.

"There isn't a vacancy anywhere around here, and if there is, we can't afford it."

"We can check, but I know you're right. That's how we ended up here."

Regina was on the verge of tears again. She looked around the shop, at all they had done already, all the money they'd invested in fixing things up. But she didn't want to give in to those tears. It wasn't hopeless; it was just overwhelming.

"We can't figure it all out right now," she said. "Let's finish the day as usual and then start to create some kind of plan tonight—when to go looking for other places, how to move things, where things can go in the meantime."

"You're right. I have to get these pieces to the consignment store and then get to my sister's shower with a present. It's too early to panic," Amelie said, but Regina could read the disappointment in her voice. "Let's talk tonight."

After Amelie left, Regina tried to carry on with her regular tasks, but her mind kept churning. If they couldn't find a place in the art district, maybe they should try to get a space downtown. But that would be way out of their price range. Their business proposal wouldn't float without a location. They even needed an address for their website.

She worked as efficiently as she could on the mosaic for the installation. All of a sudden, that project took on a whole new significance. A couple thousand dollars could make a big difference right now for her apartment search.

Of course she had some money in her savings, and she had her morning job, which could always pay rent. And her parents would always let her come back home temporarily, but she had no intention of asking them for assistance. She had to figure this out.

A man had come in offering more than the asking price

for the place. He probably knew it was worth more than Mr. Lundstrum was asking, too.

Regina's mind suddenly flew to Nigel—flashing five-thousand-dollar checks around and wearing his fancy suits. He had had a case for his business cards, and if she remembered correctly, his card said he worked at an investing firm. He was also the only one she could think of who hadn't come in shopping. Could he have been the one to make an offer on the place? Did he know that she was planning to buy it? He could see that they were trying to fix it up; he might have assumed that they were trying to get it. If it was him, she was going to be angry as a wet cat.

In fact, the more she thought about the possibility, the angrier she got. Maybe he wanted it as leverage to try to get her back. There he was thinking he could buy her again. Or it could be that he was trying to get back at her for not seeing him. Or… What else, she didn't know, but she sure as hell was going to find out.

It was three o'clock, and no customers were there. She could close the store for a couple of hours and probably not miss a sale. She called Amelie to let her know, ran upstairs for Nigel's business card and got in her car.

Chapter 5

She could tell from the outside of the building that she would feel out of place entering the investment and accounting firm of Hoffman, Johnson and Dowd, and when the elevators opened on their floor, she knew she hadn't been mistaken. They had plush beige carpets, mahogany furniture and expensive art in the lobby, and she was greeted simultaneously by two receptionists. Everything about the place was swank.

"How may I help you?" one of the receptionists asked.

"I'm here to see Nigel Johns, and no, I do not have an appointment."

"Who may I say is here?"

"Regina Gibson."

"Does he know what you're here about?"

"I believe he does."

"He has someone in his office right now, but as soon as he's free, I'll let him know. Please have a seat."

The receptionist gestured toward the waiting area, but Regina didn't feel like sitting down.

"Can I get you coffee, a soda?"

"No, thank you."

She remained standing but moved off to the side.

She spotted the door marked Nigel Johns from her spot in front of the receptionist's desk, and though she didn't have an appointment, she moved right for it when she saw it swing open. Her orange capris, African-print chemise tank and flat gold sandals may not fit in with the decor, but her anger made her more than assertive.

Just inside the door, she found Nigel hugging a tall Black woman who was holding a toddler on her hip. The little boy looked like Nigel, and Regina's temper flared even more. It would make sense that he'd fathered another child or two after leaving her, reckless as he was. And if he already had another child of his own, why would he come worry her about theirs?

He seemed surprised to see her. He must have read the anger in her gaze as jealousy because he immediately introduced his guest.

"Regina, please meet my cousin Michelle and her son, Andre. We were just saying goodbye."

Regina didn't feel like being pleasant, but she nodded at the woman and moved out of the way for them to leave. She shouldn't have let them spike her temper anyway. He had a right to his life, whatever it was. Why should she care?

Nigel stuck his head out of the door behind them to speak to one of the receptionists. "Please tell Mr. Harris that I'm running a bit late. I'll see him shortly."

He closed the door and turned to her.

"My cousin Michelle just moved to DC from down South after a vicious divorce. She needed to get away. I'm helping her out a little, just to get her on her feet. And

Andre is just a doll. I gave him some of the presents that I had for…"

He didn't know how to finish, and she wasn't interested in helping him.

"All the ones that weren't too big for him, he got."

He strolled back to his desk and perched his behind on the front side of it—all businesslike in his tailored black suit and red power tie, all innocent-looking, as if he hadn't pulled the rug out from under her.

"That's none of my business," Regina said, spitting anger.

He seemed a bit confused by her tone.

"It's been over two weeks," he said. "I thought you had written me off for good, but I'm glad to see you. You look beautiful."

She glared at him, waiting for his pleasant exterior to crack and reveal the louse he was, but he just leaned against his desk, waiting. He seemed to fit in here. His Italian watch shone above his French cuff, and his class ring glistened on his finger. She hadn't noticed it before; he must have finished school after all.

"I think you know why I'm here."

"I know why I want you to be here. But no, I don't have any idea why you're actually here. You seem angry. Have I done something? Is something wrong?"

"Nigel, stop playing. You've made a nice little niche for yourself here."

He smiled proudly at her acknowledgement, ignoring the unpleasant tone that accompanied it.

"So why are you trying to take mine away?"

He leaned forward, concerned. "What are you talking about? If anything, I wanted to make things easier for you, not take anything away."

"Well, your little ploy hasn't made it easier. You've

made it harder. Much harder. There's nowhere else in the art district that we could get for that kind of money. What are you going to do with it? Turn it—"

She had started pacing furiously, her cotton capris swishing in the hush of the office. She was trying not to let her voice escalate, but she was distraught, and she was wearying of his innocent act.

"Reggie, sit down."

He tried to put his hand on her shoulders, but she twisted free of his reach.

"Reggie, sit down, and tell me what's wrong."

His voice was low and soothing, but she wasn't about to be lulled by it, not again.

"Did you know we were going to buy it, or did you just decide to snap it up for fun?"

"Reggie, I haven't snapped anything up. Tell me what's going on. Maybe I can help."

"No, I'd say you've done enough. Wouldn't you?"

"Regina, calm down. Sit down. Talk to me. What is it that I've done?"

She stopped pacing and stood her ground to look him right in the eyes.

"Did you or didn't you buy the studio right out from underneath us?"

"Oh, no." Nigel went to her and stopped right in front of her. "I assure you that I didn't, and I didn't know about it either."

He spoke firmly, looking right at her. She scanned his face for a lie, but his features only registered sincerity. If anything, he seemed surprised by her accusation. And worse, he also seemed concerned.

She had no choice but to believe him. She finally sat down in one of the chairs facing his desk. She just sat and stared at the carpet while the anger drained out of her and realization dawned. She should have waited until to-morrow, when Mr. Lundstrum would be bringing her the information on the buyer, rather than rushing over here.

"I do purchase and resell property from time to time. But if I had purchased it, it would have been to give to you, not to take from under you."

"I don't know what I was thinking. Except there you were flashing money in my face, and then…I called things off between us."

"I'm not vindictive, Reggie."

Regina threw her hands up. "*You* I could fight. But now there must be someone else who bought the property, and there's nothing I can do."

There were tears in her eyes, but she wasn't going to let them win. The last thing she wanted was to have Nigel comfort her again. She didn't want to seem like she was overly emotional or like someone who needed a man. She'd been doing okay on her own so far without him. She stood.

"I'm sorry to have bothered you."

"Wait," he said, cornering her in front of the chair until she sat down again. Then he took the other chair. "Let's talk about this. I didn't buy it, but maybe I can help you get it back. As I said, I do invest in real estate sometimes—buy old places, fix them up, make a little money. I have some experience in this kind of thing. I can afford—"

"No, I'm sorry to waste your time."

"Why not let me try to help you?"

"I don't want to owe anything to you or anyone else. My business partner and I will figure it out."

"Why are you being so mule-headed? Maybe I can help. Think of it as repayment for—"

"There's nothing you need to repay me for."

"Then let me try to acquire it, and you can buy it from me."

"No, I'm sure the new owner has plans for it. It's a perfect location. And we weren't ready to make the purchase anyway."

She stood again, feeling small in her flat sandals and out of place next to his black suit, which dominated the posh office space.

"Please, Reggie, don't go. I might be able to help."

"I've bothered you enough. I'm sorry—for everything."

He put his hands on her shoulders to keep her from fleeing. She stared at his chest, feeling as stupid as could be. Then he cupped her chin to raise her face to his.

"It will be okay. I don't know if I can help, but I'd like to try."

She pushed his hands away and straightened. "No, I'll be fine. It was my mistake."

Head held high, she walked through the reception area as fast as her sandals would carry her.

Once outside, Regina stopped for a newspaper and went back to the studio, feeling like a fool for having barged into Nigel's office slinging accusations. To add to her embarrassment, he had been nothing but concerned and kind the whole time. Her reaction seemed so silly now. Anyone walking by could have scouted their studio and seen that it was a perfect location. And in the DC area, there were probably a thousand investors with tailored suits and business-card holders. It just so happened that Nigel Johns was the only one she knew.

And that was the other news of the day: Nigel Johns was now a well-tailored investor-accountant who worked at a top firm and was totally at home in that world. How had he gone from the brother with baggy pants to that?

Regina shifted her mosaic to the side and started looking in the paper for rental spaces where they were—near the Torpedo Factory in Alexandria, Virginia, not that far from downtown DC. There was nothing on King Street, nothing on Union Street, nothing listed for the area at all. She would have to try online later that night.

In the end, she tried to concentrate on the mosaic for the installation, but the news of losing the place still occupied the center of her mind. They were just starting out but had been knocked off their feet, and she didn't know if they could get up again.

She was also trying to pull her face out of the mud after the tantrum she'd thrown in Nigel's office. The tables seemed to have turned. She had gone from being the one telling a bumbling boy to get his act together to being the one whose life was falling apart. And it was falling apart in front of him.

Maybe that shouldn't matter, but it did. It stung like a slap to the face. And worse, she had cracked open a door that she had wanted to keep closed. Now he wanted to help. Hopefully he would remember that she didn't want and didn't need his help.

Chapter 6

Nigel pulled one of his best suits out of the closet and laid it on his bed. It had been almost a week with no sign of Regina since she'd left his office, and he was going to see if she would have a late dinner with him after closing the shop. He hadn't called because she would have said no, but he hoped that if he showed up, he could change her mind.

He needed to see how she was doing, and he wanted to talk to her more about helping her to get the property back for the studio. He had done an online search for the address and had started making calls almost as soon as she left his office, and it didn't take him long to find out who was brokering the purchase, who was buying the location and how much they were paying.

As pigheaded as she'd been at the firm, he expected to have a hard time getting her to let him help, but he was pursuing it anyway. She'd frustrated him to no end in his office, not because she'd accused him of deliberately buying it out from under her but because she wouldn't let him help.

He sprayed some cologne across his chest and pulled on one of his Italian dress shirts. She had come to the office in her casual work clothes, but she had looked amazing. Even when she was ranting at him and pacing his office, he could remember feeling her in his arms, feeling her beneath him.

She'd had on a sleeveless top, which made him want to touch her shoulders, and it was made of two layers of a sheer printed material. It would be cool in the heat, but it made him want to run his fingers over her breasts until he raised the nipples. Even more, he wanted to run his tongue along the curve of the fabric until she moaned the way she'd done that night.

He pulled on his slacks and took a belt off the hook. Even her pants, which came down just below her knees, had made him want to caress the bare curves of her calves and squeeze the rounded globes of her behind. He remembered the way she felt when he had lifted her against him, and it made his knees weak.

He slipped a tie from the rack, looped it under his collar and began tying the knot at his throat. He had been wanting her since she'd given him back his grandmother's ring, but he had stayed away. Seeing her standing in his office had been a gift that made his pulse race.

He hoped to see her tonight again, but this time just to talk, just to get her to stop being obstinate and let him help her. He wanted more, but he would have to wait for that—maybe forever.

Nigel finished dressing with a pair of silver cuff links. At his car, he checked his tie in the window before opening the door, and then he was on his way.

When he got to the studio, he saw that it was still open and parked out front.

Once he got inside, though, he saw that they were already beginning to dismantle the place. Boxes were piled up in the back room and along the back walls. Display cases had been broken down and moved to accommodate the piles of packing paper, bubble wrap and boxes that were lined along the walls and shelves. Only the finished pieces at the front of the studio were still on display.

"Hi, can I help you with anything?"

It wasn't Regina. It was a shorter woman wearing big African-print pants with braids piled high on her head.

"You weren't here when I came last time. I'm looking for Regina Gibson."

"You just missed her. She's on her way home."

"I'll head out back, then."

Nigel stopped, intrigued by the other woman and the possibility of finding out more about what was going on with the studio. He turned back.

"Are you her partner?"

"Yes, hi." She came to shake his hand. "I'm Amelie Richards. Were you looking at a particular piece? Perhaps I can help you."

"No, I'm an old friend of Reggie's. I wanted to help her look into getting this place back. I didn't know that you'd be packing up so soon."

"We tried to get it back, and Regina even talked to the man who's buying it, but it seems like a done deal."

Nigel thought he knew better but left it alone.

"Mr. Lundstrum would have waited for us if he could, but he has his own worries."

He knew that name from the research he'd done so far.

"Do you have a card?"

"Yeah, right by the register."

Nigel wandered toward the register to pick up the card. Amelie had gone back to packing beads into little plastic baggies and throwing them in a large box.

"Do you guys have any plans for what to do next?"

Amelie seemed to become lost in thought for a moment and then shook herself out of it. "We're trying just about everything we know. We're looking for other places. We're checking into consignment shops. We've ruled out anything in the immediate area being in our price range, so we're spreading our net wider. All of that to say 'we don't know.' I wish we did, but right now, it's all up in the air."

Nigel already liked Amelie. At least she would talk to him, confide in him. He had probably learned more in the last five minutes than he would get all evening with Regina.

"Why are you packing up so soon? You don't have to be out yet, do you?"

"We have a few more weeks, but we want to do most of the moving ourselves to save on the cost of movers. It means we need to start now. We'll still need movers for the heavy stuff—the tiles, the kilns."

Nigel leaned against the counter near the register.

"I'm sorry for your loss. I know it meant a lot to both of you."

"You make it sound like a person. But I guess in a way it is like that. It hasn't been easy letting it go." Amelie's eyes misted over, and for a moment, Nigel thought she might cry, but she didn't. She sighed and went back to the beads.

"Where do the boxes go from here?"

"Beadwork comes home with me. Regina has to move as well, so hers are along the back for now."

"Why not rent a storage compartment until you can move into your new place?"

"We thought of that. But we don't know how long it will

be, and we both need to keep working on our art or there won't be income coming in. And Regina has a big installation she's working on this week. I don't know how she's getting it all done."

Nigel had gotten comfortable talking to Amelie. It was nice to ask questions and actually get answers. From what she said, he knew he had to continue pursuing the possibility of getting the property back for them. More than ever, he wanted to be of help to Regina.

"Hey," she called to him, making him stir from his place against the counter. "If you want to catch Regina, you'd better get a move on."

"Okay."

"She left a little early to get ready for a hot date—finally. That one needs a life more than anyone I know."

"A date?" Nigel stiffened.

"Yeah."

"Is it that tall guy?"

"Hah. Not on your life," said Amelie. Then she laughed. He didn't get the joke. "No, this is a real date. You better run along to catch her."

"I'll do that. It was nice to meet you, Ms. Richards."

He had intended to talk to Regina about getting the property back, but now that his temper was piqued by the prospect of Regina going out on a date, he knew he should just go home. He could see her another time, talk to her another time.

Ignoring his better judgment, he headed up the back steps, taking two at a time, and rang her buzzer.

She opened the door with her back to him and one hand coiled around her hair, letting in, presumably, her date.

"I'll be ready in one minute. Sit down for a sec."

Nigel hesitated in the doorway. As she walked away, he could see that she had on a blue dress that flared around her bottom. She also had on heels, showing off her beautiful calves.

Seeing her look so beautiful made his manhood swell. Knowing that she looked so beautiful for another man spiked his temper even more. He should have turned to go right then, but he told himself that he was only there to talk to her about the property. Dinner would be out of the question now, but maybe they could set up another date. A date. The irony wasn't lost on him.

He didn't get the full effect until she came back, and he saw that her hair was wrapped upward and spilling over the top of her head and around the soft curves of her face. The blue dress didn't reveal a great deal, but it seemed to cling to the shape of her body. With her hair pulled up, he could see that she had on a pair of Amelie's beaded earrings, ones that dangled down to her collarbones and accented the shape of her neck. She was beautiful, ready to go out for the evening, and it made Nigel even angrier.

She was surprised to see him.

"I didn't know I let you in."

"You should glance through the peephole before you open the door," he said and came to stand in her dining room. "You look beautiful. Where are we going tonight?"

She seemed excited about a night on the town, and she wasn't even angry at his sudden appearance.

"I'm afraid *we're* not going anywhere. *I'm* going out. So there."

He raised his eyebrows at her unusually good mood, and she chuckled.

"Wait, let me explain. I'm in an odd mood tonight. I've been letting things get me down recently, and I've decided that I'm going to try not to do that any longer. And when do I ever get out for a night on the town? So tonight is a night off from my problems. I won't speak of them. And since I'm not talking about my problems, and you being one of my problems, you should leave."

She pointed him to the door, giving him an impish smile.

He had only intended to talk to her, but the grin on her face inflamed him. He narrowed his eyes and stepped closer to her, wondering if she would be so devilish in his arms. Before he knew he would do it, he had wrapped her in them, had lowered his face to hers and had started to kiss her.

She laughed in his mouth, and her hand came up between them, but it wasn't really a struggle. She must have expected him to let her go, but he didn't, not until her lips had softened and her palm had come to rest upon his chest.

Then he pulled his head up, but she didn't back out of the circle his arms formed around her body.

"I'm sorry, Reggie. I couldn't resist with you smiling that way."

He expected her to get all fiery, like usual, but apparently she was in a playful mood that wasn't dampened by his audacity.

"Stop now. I have someone coming."

She tapped on his chest with her hand, a signal for him to let her go.

"Are you sure you want me to let you go? You look so sexy in your high heels."

"Thank you, but yes."

"I'm not convinced."

He had only intended to talk to her, but now that she was in his arms, he wanted so much more than to talk. He leaned toward her again, taking her hand from his chest and wrapping it around his neck. She let out a startled chirp as his mouth covered hers again—this time for real, this time claiming hers for him and no one else.

He parted her lips with his own and used his tongue to find hers. With her impeding arm now around his neck, he pressed her body close to his until her chest came to rest against his blazer. He stepped even closer, until her thighs were settled against his legs. With his tongue moving deeper into her mouth, he ran his hand up and down her back, pressing her body against his.

Finally, he heard her murmur, and the sound was triumph to his ears.

He came up for air, pressing his forehead to hers and smiling. She must have seen the victory in his eyes because she swatted his arm and laughed.

"There's something between us, Reggie."

"I admit you can have an effect on me." She stepped back. "But I think that's all it is—a lingering effect from the past. Now you have to be going."

He stepped toward her again, bringing his forehead down to touch hers. He had only intended to talk to her, so maybe he should have taken her cue, but he didn't want to let go of her.

"I thought we could talk about getting this place back for you. Come to dinner with me."

"I can't. I have a date. And I've already looked into..."
She paused when he placed a soft kiss on her temple.
"...all of that."

He was right there, and he loved her. But she still insisted on going out with someone else. Jealousy flared in him again, reviving his temper. If he'd taken her cue, he'd have been on his way to his car by then. Instead, he was on his way to letting his temper get the best of him.

"So how many boyfriends do you have?"

He regretted the words as they flew out of his mouth, and he felt her stiffen in his embrace and begin to push off. He opened his arms to let her go.

"There's the tall guy who came to get his son the first night I was here. And now this is a different one."

He shouldn't have said it, but his anger spurred him on, and it was out before he could check himself. "Are any of them serious?"

"Don't you dare talk to me that way."

The fire was back in her eyes, and her shoulders were pulled back again.

"You don't know anything about my life."

"No, I guess I don't." He couldn't hold back the sarcasm, even as he wondered how things had gotten so far from his original intention.

"You're right about that. Now, it's time for you to go. I have a date."

"Well, I'll leave you to it, then."

"You're good at that. And while you're at it, do me a favor and leave me alone for good."

He knew he shouldn't, but he turned back one more time, unable to resist a final barb.

"So you really want me to leave you alone? Not like the first time when I was supposed to read your mind?"

She had gotten a light silk wrap, and she now flung it over her shoulders angrily.

"Yes. Hell, yes. Leave."

He turned and headed out the door just in time to hear another car pull up out back. Now, as he got to the bottom step, he angrily butted his shoulder against that of the guy on his way up—the date.

He was average-looking, average height, nothing special— nothing to get worked up over. Except that he had a date with Regina.

Nigel banged his car door shut, started the engine and tore a path from the studio. The high and low of the evening had him thinking that loving someone shouldn't feel

like being on a carnival ride all the time. But that was
the problem. He did love this woman, and he was jealous enough to prove it. He had taken her good mood and
turned it into ire. He had just intended to talk to her about
the property, but now they were as antagonistic as ever.
All of this gnawed at his mind while his body still wanted
to hold her.

Chapter 7

She'd had enough.

She caught sight of Nigel's antics on the bottom step and slammed the door. One moment, she was entertaining the idea of a night out on the town. The next moment, he was ruining the highest spirits she'd had since they'd gotten the devastating news about the studio.

She had just wanted a night in which she didn't have to think about all of it. And she hadn't been out with anyone in years. In fact, it was with some hesitation that she had accepted the invitation from the package carrier who made deliveries at the architectural firm where she worked in the mornings. He'd asked her out several times and seemed sweet enough. There weren't sparks, but he seemed nice enough to have a dinner with.

She'd just wanted to get out and not worry about... everything. It felt good to be dressing up and going somewhere, not with friends but with someone new, someone who suggested at least the possibility of a relationship in her life.

Even the sight of Nigel in the doorway hadn't put a damper on her humor. She shouldn't have given in to his kiss, but being dressed up made it feel like a thrill to be held. And he did always have that effect on her. Then he'd had the nerve to ask her how many boyfriends she had. She wanted to give him one swift cuff.

Regina's buzzer rang, and she wasn't sure what to do. She didn't really feel like going out anymore.

Her date seemed sweet enough, but she couldn't imagine explaining to him about this other person who'd bumped shoulders with him on her steps. In fact, she couldn't imagine telling him about her past at all. That meant she probably didn't need to go out with him. And that was probably why she hadn't been going out in general.

She was just starting to think that maybe she could start seeing someone again, but now she just wanted to curl up and sleep.

She opened the door to her date.

"Hey, there's been a bit of a hiccup."

"A hiccup?"

He had on a pair of dark slacks and a white shirt, with a vest that had phrases embroidered on it. It reminded her that she'd only seen Nigel in two- or three-piece business suits since he'd reappeared. It was nice for a change, but not nice enough to alter her decision about the evening.

"Would you mind terribly if we cancel for tonight?"

"You're all dressed. You look wonderful. Is something wrong?"

She didn't want to lie to him, but she didn't feel like getting into the real story either. She hoped something vague would suffice.

"I've just had a real letdown. I can't go out for fun tonight. I'll be heading over to a friend's place in a few minutes. Perhaps another time."

"Do you want to talk about it?" He seemed genuinely concerned.

"No. I don't. I'm sorry to send you away when we had plans, but please understand."

"I can't say I'm not disappointed."

"I was looking forward to a night out, as well." She walked him back toward the door. "I'm sorry."

"You'll let me know when we can go out again?"

"Yes, I will."

She shut the door. She could have put on a smile and gone out, but she didn't want to pretend tonight. She was still too sore to pretend. The nerve of him.

Regina changed into something more comfortable, got in her car and called Jason on her cell phone. She didn't want to stay in after getting all dressed up, even if she had changed, and she could use a friend right now. He was more than happy to have her come over.

Regina was greeted at the door by Ellison, who carried a tired Kyle on his shoulder.

"Hey, sweets." He bent down and kissed her cheek. "You're just in time to say good-night to this one."

The cranky little one said something groggily.

"I can tell. Good night, honey bunny," Regina said and kissed him on the head. "Here, let me take him. I'll help put him to bed."

"Okay," Ellison said, handing Kyle over to her. "I'll find Jay."

"I'm not lost," Jason said as he entered the room.

He bent down to hug Regina and was about to take Kyle.

"No way. I just got him away from that one. I'll help put him down."

"I'll go get the bed ready."

"Okay, have you eaten?" Jason asked.

"No, but you have. I'm okay."

"Not if you're staying over."

"Am I?"

"I'll get you home in the morning. You owe me a pow-wow," Jason said. They headed toward Kyle's room. "Do you mind eating alone? Once we get this little one down, I need to put that little one down."

Regina laughed. Ellison was almost six feet. Only Jason could call him a little one.

"Okay. But don't leave me alone too long."

"I won't."

With the three of them surrounding him, Kyle fell asleep before the story was halfway through, regardless of the fact that the three adults in the room were having a hilarious time trying to do voices for the different characters.

Ellison went up to change for bed while Jason heated up leftovers for Regina and set her a place in the living room in front of the television.

When he was satisfied that she was comfortable, Jason pointed up the stairs. "Are you sure you don't mind?"

She blew him a kiss and answered, "I'm sure."

"I won't be too long."

"You better not be too short either."

They both chuckled.

Regina felt at home and was able to calm down and let the disappointment of the evening drain out of her as she munched on reheated Chinese food. Being with friends who were so loving and so embracing was like being in a warm bubble bath. It felt relaxing. It felt good. And entertaining little Kyle had made her forget all of her troubles for a while.

She flipped through the channels but wasn't in the mood for television, so she put it on mute and curled up on the couch. It felt like home, but it was good to be away from home, too.

Her eyes were closed when Jason came back out. He had changed into a pair of old sweats.

"Are you asleep already?"

"No, just resting. What about the two little ones? Asleep?"

"Yes, both."

Jason pulled her legs up and placed them on his lap. "Elli had to be up before six this morning. Little thing was plumb tuckered out."

Regina smiled, but she was already dreading the moment when the spotlight would turn on her, which it did.

"And you? You've been owing me info for weeks. Who was he?"

Regina let out a breath. She didn't want to talk about it, but she needed to, and at least she was in a space she could trust.

"He's my ex-fiancé."

"Fiancé? You were engaged?"

"For over four years. I broke it off. I was pregnant and needed someone serious or no one at all. I never told him about the baby, and then I lost it."

"I'm so sorry, Regina." He started to rub her feet. It was soothing. "You've been keeping this under wraps, honey. You could have told me."

"I know. It's just something I don't tell anyone, really."

"What happened? Why did it fall through?"

"I don't know. I guess we were too young. We were sweethearts in high school our senior year. We decided to go to the same college and to get married right after graduation. Even that seemed too long to wait, but our parents liked it."

She was quiet for a moment, remembering the good days, when she was lost in his arms and his touch.

"So what happened?"

"By the time I was done with college, we were just in two different places. I knew I had to be serious if I wanted to survive as an artist. My parents wanted me to take a 'safe' job—become a lawyer or get a job in the government or something."

"Don't they all? When I said I was going into art history, mine had a fit."

"I guess so. By graduation, he was running behind. He had gotten caught up in the party life. He was skipping classes. He would have flunked out if he hadn't been so smart. He was spending more time with his buddies on the couch or at dorm parties than in school. And his parents kept sending him money. They didn't know."

Regina sat up, pulling her legs from his lap to tuck them under her but missing the soothing comfort of his hands.

"Sounds like he did have some growing up to do. But you were young, too."

"Yeah, well, that's when the arguments started. I wanted him to take things more seriously so we could start a life together and have a future. He thought I had turned into a bookworm or something, someone who wanted to make him old before his time, someone who didn't know how to have a good time. After a while, we stopped talking so much."

"That must have hurt."

He leaned over to rub her hair and run his fingers along her face down the lines where tears threatened to fall. But she wasn't going to let herself cry.

"It did. We were supposed to be married in four years, and the four-year mark was coming up. Then I found out that I was pregnant—not planned and not for lack of being safe."

"That's one hell of a wake-up call."

"It was for me, but I didn't tell him. I tried to get him to take things more seriously, but the harder I tried, the more it seemed to only make him want to be a kid even longer. That's when things got bad. He was skipping classes and running the streets with his boys even more. Nothing changed. But me, I knew I had to grow up or end up in my parents' house again, and I wasn't going to let that happen. When I realized I'd turned into a nag and when the arguing got bad enough, I called off the wedding and told him to leave. If he wasn't going to grow up, I didn't need him."

She shook her head to wake up from remembering the past and took one of the pillow cushions onto her lap, hugging it.

"How were you going to do it on your own?"

"I don't know, but I was going to try. I was already out to show my parents I could make a life as an artist. I figured I'd just have to show him, too. I planned to raise the baby on my own, and if he ever grew up, so be it. But I wasn't waiting to find out."

"That explains a lot about you. There's an edge to you. Always working hard. Always keeping a bit to yourself. Always determined to figure things out on your own, alone."

"Well, some of it I didn't have to. I lost the baby before I really told anyone and before I really started to show. My parents didn't even know. I thought I would tell everyone after the wedding or at the wedding or something like that."

Jason scooped his arms around her and pulled her between his legs and against his chest, resting his chin on top of her head. It wasn't a sexual gesture. It was a gesture between old friends when one needed solace, when one needed a shielded space from which to speak and in which to be heard. Regina put her arms over the ones that were wrapped around her waist.

"I was alone when it happened. I ended up calling an ambulance, and they took me to the hospital, but nothing could be done. They never knew what went wrong."

"Oh, honey, I'm so sorry."

Maybe it was because she had cried with Nigel, but she didn't cry now. She felt sad, but she could say it without the tears. It still hurt, but the hurt didn't consume her the way it had before, when she had first confessed.

"What about now? What does he want now? Why were you arguing?"

Regina sighed. In order to answer that question, she would have to figure a lot of things out.

"He wanted to take care of his children. He thought Kyle and Tenisha were ours."

"But you never told him. How did he know?"

"Apparently, my college roommate told her boyfriend. Nigel found out from him a few months ago that I was pregnant when I graduated. It's been over six years. How does he expect to waltz back up in here? But here he is, trying to be with me again."

Regina's anger made her restless, and she sat up and turned to face Jason. This might have been a mistake because he peered at her quietly until her anger settled, then he asked her a question.

"And you? How do you feel about him now?"

It was startling because it was a real question, one she was unprepared to answer.

"I don't know. He makes me so angry that I want to be over him. But I don't know."

"Has anything *happened* between you two recently?"

Regina rolled her head to ease her neck; she hadn't realized that she was so tense.

"Ugh. Do we have to go there?"

Jason's wry look said that she couldn't hide from him.

"I already know the answer. Look, it's been a long time since you've been with anyone. Right?"

"Yes."

"It could be him, or it could be that you're just lonely. Find out before you get caught up in something from the past that's not meant to be."

"I think I already know. I think it needs to be over. I just need to convince him of that."

"If it's really over, you'll convince him," Jason said.

"I think I have, and if not, I'm sure I will."

She'd had enough.

Regina woke up the next day before the house had stirred. It was eight in the morning on a Saturday, and her cell phone was ringing in her purse. That could only be one person.

"Hey, Mom."

She uncurled herself on Jason's couch. It was a pull-out, but she didn't need the room and was comfortable on the thick, velvety cushions. She and Jason had stayed up talking, and he had gotten her a pillow and sheets before heading up to Ellison. They were going to have brunch together at ten near the studio so that she could change and open up by noon.

"Hello, sweetheart. I hope you're not still down about that little shop of yours. It'll work out, honey. You'll see. Do you need any money, baby?"

"No, Mom, I'm fine. How are you doing?"

"My knees get to bothering me, but other than that, we're both just fine. Look, I'm calling because your father and I talked it over, and we're coming down to help you move your things into your new place."

Her parents had moved from South Carolina to New Jersey her second year in college.

"Mom, you just said that your knees were bothering you."

"I know, I won't be able to move the heavy things, but I can do some of the packing up while your father helps you."

"I actually have a few friends who are willing to help. I'll be okay."

Regina hated it when her parents treated her like an adolescent, but she also understood that this was their way of feeling involved.

"No, we've done made up our minds. Now, when are you planning on moving so we can figure out when to come down?"

To keep them happy, she would graciously accept their help with a few of the smaller things—not the heavy tile, finished boards, kilns or supplies. The movers would take care of the rest, and she and her parents would be able to spend most of their time enjoying one another. But she had to time it just right to make sure the heavy stuff was out of the way.

"Let me call you back when I get home. I'm over at Jason's now."

"So early?"

"I came by last night, and it got late, so I stayed over."

"That's good, sweetheart. I hate it when you're out late at night. How is little Kyle?"

"He's as adorable as ever. You'll see him when you get here."

"Here, say hello to your father."

"Hi, Dad. Mom's roped you into coming down."

Her father laughed. "Yep, she got her mind set on it. We're just gonna help you move some things. Won't be no trouble."

"It's no trouble having you visit, Dad."

"Good. We'll be seeing you soon. Goodbye, sweet pea."

"Bye, Daddy."

Regina stood and stretched her legs. The house was still quiet; it was two hours before brunch.

Talking with Jason had made her a little raw, and she wondered now about his question. What about her? How did she feel?

She did want it to be over, and she was still angry as all get-out. But she had given in to Nigel, had even let herself be in a playful mood around him. Was she still just getting over him? If so, she needed to do so quickly. She not only had to get on with her life, she had to put it back together again.

Chapter 8

"You okay back there, Andre?"

"Yup." His little cousin was engrossed in the video game that Nigel had gotten him for the ride and didn't look up. He'd been at it for almost an hour.

"Those games were genius." His cousin Michelle winked at him.

"I'm surprised he hasn't fallen asleep."

"If we were at home, he would have napped, but this is too exciting for him."

Nigel pressed the clutch, changed gears and stepped up the speed a notch as they cruised south on I-95. The car trip home was a chance to open up his two-month-old Lexus and see what she could do.

His cousin Michelle needed to get some of her things from home, and he hadn't seen his folks in a while. Rather than having her try to ship things, they had opted for a short trip home. They could pack up his trunk and most of the backseat to bring some of her things back up to DC.

"How much longer until we stop?"

They'd been on the road for four hours. It was an eight-and-half-hour drive to Charleston, but they had decided to make a real trip of it and spend the night in Raleigh.

"About forty-five minutes, maybe less given the time we've made."

"That gets us in at three."

"Here, I got the movie listings online. Find us an animated film we can take Andre to."

"Really?" Michelle seemed surprised.

"Yeah, why not?"

"I thought you might want some time to yourself by then. I didn't know you'd want go to a kids' movie with us."

"Yeah, it'll be fun."

Nigel had noticed that Michelle was always surprised by little things like that. Why wouldn't someone want to go with them to a children's movie? It made him wonder how bad her ex-husband had been and in what ways.

They'd talked for the first hour, and he'd gotten to know her a little better. After that, conversation popped up from time to time, but mainly they turned up the radio and just cruised.

Unfortunately, this part of the trek also made him think about Regina—how much he wished it was her that was riding with him to see his folks, how badly he'd messed up with her. His jealous tantrum had been childish. From her point of view, he'd probably regressed to the way he was before, when they were together in college. No wonder she didn't want him now. Who could blame her?

He had been a child then. And she had grown up. He'd loved her, but she wanted them to act like an old retired couple, and he was all for just having fun. He'd never cheated on her, but while she studied, he got too caught up with the party life at school, mooching off his parents and letting an education pass him by.

They'd been in her apartment when she'd confronted him for the last time. It started as an argument he'd gotten used to. Why wasn't he studying? When was he going to get serious? Then it turned into something else. If he wasn't going to grow up, then he needed to leave. The wedding was off. She was crying. He was hurt and stunned.

"I don't need you," she had said, "so get out—for good." And he had. Now he could see only too well what had driven her to that. He could also see what he had lost, what he wanted back.

If she had been with him in the car now, he could've pulled her over to his side of the seat, nestled her under his arm and rubbed her thigh while they enjoyed the ride.

They pulled into the Raleigh Marriot City Center just as they'd timed it and checked in.

"You guys freshen up, and meet me at my room whenever you're done," Nigel said.

"We won't be long. We just need a potty break. Sorry, I'm used to being around a little one."

"No need to apologize. Take your time."

Nigel took off his blazer, stretched from the hours of driving and lay back on his bed to wait for his cousins. If Regina was with him, they could have spent the whole afternoon making love in the hotel room—right on the bed he was lying on. They could have gone out to dinner when the sun went down and then taken a walk around downtown before it got late.

Back then, he had known they were arguing, but he didn't realize how bad it was or how much they were drifting apart until she'd called off the wedding and put him out. He didn't actually live with her, but he spent more time with her and her housemates at their apartment than he spent in his dorm room, so it felt like being put out. It broke his heart. Whatever was wrong, he had still assumed that they'd always be together.

He heard a knock at the door. "It's just us," Michelle said.

"Ready to head out?" he asked. "Did you pick a movie?"

"I think he'd like *Where's Wellington?* It's a new animated feature from Cypress. You don't have to go unless you really want to."

"I really want to. Is that okay with you, Andre?"

Andre nodded eagerly. Both of the adults chuckled. Nigel picked him up, anchored him on his hip and headed them down the hall to the elevator.

Where's Wellington? turned out to be the most fun he'd had in a long time. The movie was made to be amusing for adults as well as children, but Nigel was equally intrigued by interacting with Andre, who spent much of the movie on his lap, except when he got restless and climbed over to his mother.

Nigel made sure he could reach the popcorn, held the soda for him when he said he was thirsty and tried to keep him relatively quiet. It made him understand what it meant to be an adult responsible for the well-being of a child. It made him miss the child he never had. After the movie, he gave Michelle some money, pressing her to take it, and they went shopping at the stores around the Convention Center to get gifts for the family they were about to see. They had heavy shopping bags, so they headed back to the hotel and had dinner there.

By then, Andre was getting cranky.

"I better go put him down. What time do we meet in the morning?"

"I want to go to the fitness center and the pool before

we go. Why don't we meet at ten-thirty for breakfast and head out at eleven again?"

"Works for me. You heading up now?" Michelle asked.

He didn't want to admit that he would feel alone in his room—alone without a specific person.

"No, I think I'll have some coffee before I head up. I have some work to do tonight, and it'll keep me up for a while."

"Take care, then, cousin. And thank you for…the shopping."

"We're family. You don't have to thank me."

"Yes, I do." She gave him a hug.

While Michelle headed up to her room, Nigel went to the hotel bar. He didn't really want coffee, but it couldn't hurt, and he did have work to do that night. He took a seat at the long, curved counter and ordered his coffee.

It wasn't long before a woman came and sat next to him. She had on a revealing dress and high heels, and she leaned toward him, looking his way from one seat over. She had smooth, ebony skin and her neatly piled dreads were drawn up to the crown of head. She was actually a good-looking woman.

She slid over to the seat next to him. "I'm here for a wedding. Do you mind the company?" she asked.

"Help yourself. No bachelorette party to go to?"

"No. That's over. No naked men."

Nigel looked at her when she said it and found her staring at him. She had wanted to get a reaction out of him, to tell him something unexpected. He thought about a night of hot sex with a random stranger, no strings attached. He couldn't say he wasn't tempted.

"I'm sorry to hear that."

She turned toward him on her stool, letting her foot

come to rest on the back of his calf and looking directly into his eyes.

"I was sorry, too."

Her offer was direct and unmistakable. It was nice being the one who was getting chased for a change. Nevertheless, Nigel had a decision to make.

"Do you have any plans for the evening?" she asked and let her hand drop to his thigh.

He had a decision to make very soon.

Back in his room, Nigel pulled out his laptop and tried to get some work done, but his mind was wandering.

"Unfortunately, I have work to do," he'd said and taken his leave, paying for his coffee and her drink.

He had turned down an offer from an attractive woman, and why? Part of it was because he wasn't actually a player; in fact, it had been a very long time—high school—since he'd been that kind of player.

Mainly, though, he was invested in a woman who wanted nothing to do with him.

"How's that working for you?" he asked himself out loud.

But at the same time, Regina was the reason he had actually been tempted to have a tryst. He wanted to be wanted, needed—even by some random woman. He wanted Regina to know that he was desirable again—to someone.

It wasn't until she had actually put him out in college that he had realized how little she had come to think of him. And that had made him think little of himself. It had made him take a good look at where he was and what he was doing, and he hadn't liked what he saw.

After a couple of months of wallowing, though, he started to tally up the figures, calculate what had caused him to lose her respect, her love. That's when he figured out he was a year behind in school and would be even more behind if he flunked that semester. That's when he woke up.

He wouldn't settle for a partial transformation. He cut off his so-called friends, threw out his CDs, discarded most of his wardrobe, left behind his urban vernacular. He found his schoolbooks, saw his professors, started trying to salvage what was left of the semester. He needed to prove to her that he could make it, really make it. He started plotting for success and all its trappings.

Now, he had those things, and he desperately wanted to go forward with Regina. That's why it had been so stupid to get jealous and act so childishly with her the other night. He'd seen himself devolve into what he was before—an immature kid. When he'd put that person behind him, he'd thought it was for good. He desperately wanted to go forward with her. But he had no inroad now, no reason to call her. Or none that she would listen to. Whatever plan he thought he had was not working, and it had turned into one big up-and-down circus ride.

He was thinking himself in circles and decided to stop.

It was almost one o'clock, and he wanted to make it an early morning. He got undressed and got in bed—alone. He would be able to figure out the next step after a good night's sleep.

It took them less than four hours to make it the rest of the way to Charleston. Nigel dropped Michelle off at her mother's house before three, said hello to his aunt, who gushed over him because of the help he'd been to Michelle, and headed home.

His mother greeted him at the door with a big hug, pulling his head down to take his face in both of her palms.

"My baby. Oh, it's so good to have you home. Come see our son in his new suit," she called to his father.

He towered over his mother, who was barely five-three, so it was always odd to him when she called him her baby, but he loved it nonetheless. It let him know that though he had been away, he was home.

"It's not a new suit, Mom."

"It looks brand-new. Come say hello to your aunt Elizabeth and your cousins and some folks from the church."

Oh, lord. This meant that she'd invited people over to see him. In his "new" suit, no less.

"Where's the new suit?" his father asked, coming out of the kitchen.

"Hey, Pop. It's not a new suit."

His father gave him a brief hug, as was his way, and pulled him into the dining room, where people were eating and talking. Like his mother, his father was showing him off to the family and friends. He made sure he had a polite smile on his face and greeted everyone in turn. Secretly, he also wished that Regina was there so that she would be able to see that he wasn't the same mess-up he used to be.

"We were worried about you there for a while," one of his parents' church friends was saying.

"He just had to find his way," said another. "Each in his own time."

"Hey, cuz, you hungry? Come get a plate."

His cousin Jeremy was just a bit older than he was and could probably see how awkward Nigel felt with people fussing over him. Nigel was glad to have an out and slipped into the kitchen.

"Hey, Jeremy. Thanks."

"Don't mind them. They just want you—and everybody else they know—to know that you done good. You made it."

"I know. I know."

But the person he most wanted to know that he'd made it wasn't there. "You've done well for yourself, too."

"Thanks," Jeremy said. "But I was caught up in stuff, as well. I remember you went through it. It makes them even more grateful when you turn out okay."

The two men chuckled.

"If we'd known," Nigel said, "we could have planned it that way."

"Just remember," his cousin said, "it's about balance."

After he ate, he sat around with his folks and their friends until late into the evening, and after their guests left, he broke out the presents he'd gotten for his parents. His mother got a gold necklace with a heart on it, and his father got a watch for himself and a check for the both of them.

After helping his mother load the dishwasher and watching some baseball with his dad, he finally headed upstairs to change and get to bed. Going into his room had become something of a shock. His mother hadn't changed it since he left for college. It still had his sports trophies on the dresser, his old music posters on the walls, his football-themed bedspread on the bed.

He hung his suits in a closet that still held his high school football jersey and dropped his suitcase on a chest that still held some of his barely used books from his first four years in college.

He fingered the cover of his text for College Algebra, wondering how he had passed the course. Now numbers were a major part of his life. His transformation had taken him longer than he'd thought, longer than he'd wanted. He'd finished college in a year, but the rest—the professional degree, the bank account, the car, the move back to DC—all that had taken him the better part of the past five years.

Maybe if he hadn't waited so long things would be easier now. When his net worth tripled in the past twenty-four months, he had begun to put out feelers for relocation. Then he found out that Regina had been pregnant. It was the news that there was a child that propelled him into real action. The truth was that he didn't feel he'd made it yet—that he was worthy. He was waiting for that, but perhaps only having Regina would make him feel that way: unbroken.

Nigel sat down on his old twin bed and scanned the furnishings of his past.

He had become something very different than this room. He had become grown.

The next day Nigel took his parents, grandmother and aunt out to dinner and would have been content after that to stay home and catch up on some work. Instead, he was heading downtown to meet Jeremy and two of his other cousins and some of their friends at a club.

"They just want to be nice," his mother had said. "It can't hurt to go out for a little while so they know you're family."

He rolled his eyes as he pulled into the lot at the Cheshire Cat. Jeremy clapped his back when he got out of the car.

"Okay, brother, you need to loosen up—a lot. You ready?"

In the day, he'd have liked nothing more than partying with the boys, but now, to be honest, he just didn't know how to anymore. He didn't go to "occasions" unless business called for it, and now he found himself sitting at a table and watching drinks.

"Hey," Jeremy said over the music, "you're out of practice."

"Not in the mood."

If Regina was there, he would have had a reason to dance. It might all come back to him. As it was, he had little to celebrate.

"Aw, what did I expect?" Jeremy teased. "You turned into a nerdy bookworm right before our eyes."

"I think you might be right," his other cousin returned. "Man, you don't know how to get a life anymore. Come, let us school you."

Jeremy got him up and backed him into a woman, giving him a nod and wink. Since it looked like he'd interrupted her, Nigel had no real choice but to ask her to dance.

After two songs, he waved to her and headed back to the table. One of their group had disappeared, and Nigel asked where he'd gone.

"His girlfriend is here. We won't see him for the rest of the night," Jeremy said.

Lucky man.

Nigel got home late that night. He'd enjoyed the music, but he wouldn't be going to clubs with his cousins and friends again on this trip. What the night confirmed for him was that he really was through with the club scene, at least without Regina, and that he wanted her back very much.

His parents were already sleeping when he got home, because church was the next day. He only had until Tuesday afternoon to spend with them before picking up his cousin, packing her things in his car and making the eight-and-a-half-hour trek back to DC. Come to think of it, he should stop tomorrow and get some more games for Andre. This would be a very long trip for him.

He got in bed thinking about Regina. Her parents had lived nearby before they'd moved up to the northeast. She'd been in this house, this room; he'd kissed her on this bed. Now the twin box spring seemed small for him, but he'd love to have her there to try to fit them both in. She'd have to be wrapped in his arms for it to work.

She wanted to be left alone, but as long as there was a chance, he couldn't leave it alone. When he'd moved back up to the DC area to be near her—near them, he had thought—he'd outfitted everything so that she would see that he'd actually made it. Only now she wasn't trying to see his life.

Now they were cut off with no real reason for contacting each other, but he wanted contact.

He needed a new plan.

Chapter 9

Regina kicked off her flip-flops and slipped her feet into black pumps. She tossed the shoes into the backseat, straightened her skirt, grabbed her purse and pulled out her briefcase, the one on wheels. After she pulled up the handle, she checked her hair in the rearview mirror and was on her way.

She was going to the workshops on starting a small business that she'd found at the community center. In fact, a member of National Bank was supposed to be speaking and staying for consultations, so she and Amelie had decided to look the part. If they were close enough to being ready, they could make a contact.

She stopped at the registration desk to sign in and get an information packet. When she'd gotten a Danish and coffee from the breakfast table and had finished pinning on the name tag that they'd given her, she headed down the long hall to the banquet room. She found Amelie inside already, and the two hugged. She looked around nervously. It was a large space set up with rows of tables and chairs. And it was full. In a real way, this was their competition.

Amelie had on a blue linen pantsuit with a white shirt, and her braids were pulled back into a ponytail. She took a second look at Regina.

"Lord, girl, you look like a lawyer. You clean up well."

"I hope it works. Here—" she pulled Amelie down to their seats and opened her case "—let me show you what I've done so far."

She pulled out books and notes and several folders of paperwork. Then she began walking through the paperwork she'd brought, starting at the top.

"That's the proposal you emailed me," Amelie said. "I've read that."

"Yes. That's the three-page version, and this is the thirty-five-page version with your corrections. Here's the thing I couldn't scan. It's a new draft of the loan application. I've put sticky notes with my questions and problems on everything. The two main problems are a space and the financial statement. Oh, and there's collateral. With the old place, we were getting it at such a good price that it became a huge chunk of the collateral. Now, what do we use? All of the estimates we have are for the old space. That would work for a new space too, right? Or not."

Regina pulled out one of the books she'd been using. Then she stopped and put it back. "It doesn't make sense to look at that now."

"And we went over all of this on Saturday. Calm down. At worst, we're just here to get the 4-1-1."

Regina took a breath. "I know. I just feel like so much is riding on this." And it was. If they could get a small-business loan, they could start again. If not… But she felt prepared enough to face people and try to get answers to her questions. It was the first time things felt like they might actually work out since she'd had to move. All they needed was a new space and the loan. Right now, though, Amelie was right—she needed to calm down.

She took the pad of paper and pen out of the information folder, and readied herself for the first session.

"This is a totally professional setup," said Amelie as they looked around.

"I know. And it's free. All the speakers are working professionals in the business, and they're all doing it pro bono."

Amelie turned to her. "You've done an amazing job putting this application together."

"You've been helping, too."

"I know, but you've been leading the charge. I wouldn't have even attempted it on my own. You're the one who's put in the long hours on this. Relax. It'll work out for us. And thank you."

She looked at Amelie's face, and the sincerity there brought tears to her eyes. It had been a lot of work. If they could start again, though, it would be worth it.

"No problem."

She smiled at her friend.

The presenters started pulling down the screen on the platform at the front of the room, setting up AV for the morning sessions. That drew her eyes toward the front table.

And there stood Nigel. He was watching as the screen came down and talking to two of the other people at the head table. A young woman came up to him and handed him some papers. He gave her direction of some kind, and then went back to chatting. After a moment he stopped and went to the AV cart and started doing something with the laptop that was on it.

Regina couldn't believe her eyes. She pulled out the final seminar program from the information packet—the version with all the names of speakers and moderators. There it was. Nigel Johns. He was the moderator for the morning sessions and a speaker on both the morning and the afternoon panels. She flipped to the back. The investment and accounting firm of Hoffman, Johnson and Dowd was one of the contributors.

What was she going to do? He'd insulted her the last time she saw him, and she didn't feel like sitting under his watchful gaze as the absorbent pupil. She'd since decided that she was done with him for good. She didn't want to put herself through this.

She replaced the notepad, pen and program, closed the folder and stood to begin packing up the things she'd pulled out—everything but the paperwork. Amelie would need that.

"What are you doing?"

"I can't stay."

"Why? What's going on? Regina?"

"I'll explain later. I just can't stay."

She glanced up and found Nigel's eyes on her. She pressed her lips together, gritted her teeth and moved more hastily, turning from the table to get the hell out of there.

Amelie grabbed her arm. "You can't leave. We start in less than fifteen minutes."

"I'm not staying." She sat for a moment. "Look— everything is in the folders, and it's all labeled."

"Yes, but you're the one who knows what everything is. You know what questions to ask. I need you here."

"All you have to do is take good notes on what they say. I can't stay for this. I can't be here with him."

"Who?" She followed Regina's glance to Nigel. "Oh. That's the guy who came to see you the night you went out with what's-his-name. Did something happen between you two?"

There was a hint of innuendo in her voice, but Regina didn't have time to correct her or explain.

"Look, I can tell you about it later. For now, I need you to handle it. Just show them what we have so far, and write down whatever they say. I'll leave all the folders. You don't need the books. Can you get the folders in your bag? No, just hold on to the case. We can talk tonight."

She grabbed her purse and hurried out.

Nigel spotted Regina when he turned on the laptop to set up his slide-show presentation. He'd never really seen her in business attire. She was…breathtaking. She was always beautiful, but something about seeing her dressed in the fashion of his world made his manhood stir and begin to menace him something awful. He had to calm his body down.

She had on a navy blue skirt suit that hugged her body the way he wanted to. It was a traditional cut, except that the top tapered toward the waist right where his hands would go, and from there a ruffled hem flared out over her curves. A triangle of her camisole was visible under the jacket above the bust, just below a row of white pearls. Her hair spilled out over her head in neat curls parted on the side, and dangling pearls fell from her ears. He had to control himself or lose his composure, but he'd never wanted to touch and ravish a woman so badly.

He couldn't take his eyes off her, not even when she glanced in his direction and caught him staring. He didn't move until he realized that she was passing her things over to her business partner, as if she was about to leave. When she turned on her heels and hurried toward the back door, he called one of the office assistants to come check the slide show, and sprinted after her.

He stopped at Amelie's table.

"Hello, Ms. Richardson. Where's Regina going? Is she all right?"

"It's Richards—Amelie."

"Sorry. I almost had it."

"That's okay, and so is she. What's going on between you two?"

"I was an idiot is what. Let me go try to catch her. Can I speak with you later, about business? Can I reach you at the number on your card?"

"Yes, you can."

"Good, let me go try to catch her."

She made it out of the large banquet room and halfway down the hall before she heard an out-of-breath voice behind her, getting nearer.

"Wait. Reggie. Don't leave the seminar on account of me. We have good information. I can help you."

"Leave me alone," she said over her shoulder.

He caught her arm at the glass doors leading outside the building, but she didn't stop and pulled away.

"You don't have to leave, Reggie. It's good information."

"I know." She didn't break her stride. "And I have a good partner who can get it for us."

He followed her down the walkway outside, toward the parking lot, his tie flying over his shoulder as he jostled to keep up with her, get ahead of her, stop her.

"Regina, please don't go. I was an idiot when I came by your place. I was jealous and acting like a kid. Don't let it cheat you out of a good opportunity. Don't let my stupidity do that."

She was at her car and found her keys.

"I wouldn't. I'll get what I need to know."

She got in, closed the door and gunned the engine.

He slapped the back hood in frustration as she tore away.

When she got to the end of the row of cars, she slowed down, then stopped. She watched him in her rearview mirror as he headed back up the walk and into the building.

She had stopped at the end of the lot, and she hadn't started again. She just sat in her car with the blinker flashing, torn.

She shouldn't let his foolishness cheat her out of good information. But wasn't she doing just that? At least he had acknowledged that it was foolishness.

"I was jealous and acting like a kid."

Amelie could get the information, but Amelie was also right. Regina had done more of the background work and knew better what questions to ask.

"Don't let it cheat you out of a good opportunity. Don't let my stupidity do that."

She sighed. She needed to get a grip.

A car beeped for her to move and she had to decide. She switched her blinker, turned back into the lot and found another space. She would feel silly going back past the registration desk, but she'd get over it.

She found Nigel bending over her table talking to Amelie.

"You guys have done a lot already. You can walk through it with a lender this afternoon."

When he saw her, he straightened and stepped back for her to take her seat again.

"I'm so glad you came back, Regina."

She nodded noncommittally, and he headed toward the front. It was time to start.

"I'm glad you're here, too, girl," Amelie said. "I didn't know if I could make my way through all of this stuff."

Nigel took the podium to welcome the participants, thank the sponsors, go over the lineup for the day and introduce the first speaker. Seeing him in a business capacity was like seeing a new light. He was all about business, but he was also congenial, humorous, interesting. This was his world, and he was clearly a polished and professional master of it. He went over some statistics on new businesses to end his opening remarks: a third broke even; a third suffered a loss; more than half failed within ten years.

"We're here to arm you with information so that you can supersede those odds."

The morning session on business proposals didn't have as much new information as Regina expected. But it gave her a lot of ways to tweak what they already had to make it better. It also confirmed for her what she had known. They needed to get more information on competition, and they needed to fix their financial section.

It was Nigel who spoke about the financial statements and projections. He seemed at ease in this world, knowledgeable about how it worked. He opened his jacket and stuck one hand in his pocket as he flipped through a slideshow presentation of his major points.

It was all a lot to take in, but it was just as much to take in the professional bearing and acumen of Nigel Johns. At moments he seemed to be staring directly at her as she took notes and absorbed the points he was making. Other times, he panned the room or pointed to the graphs on the screen. He knew statistics off the top of his head. He held everyone's attention. During the question-and-answer session, he received the most queries and was comfortable interacting with the large audience.

"Actually, the financial portion of the business plan

is one of the reasons people hire or consult accountants, like me. Avail yourself of me while it's free." The audience laughed. "And don't be afraid to seek help with this."

He wasn't at all the boy she had known in college. He was sharp and handsome, professional and at ease.

During lunch he was busy making good on his word; people lined up at the speakers' table to ask him questions or have him go over their financial statements. When the line melted away, he brought his box lunch over to their table and turned around one of the seats in front of them.

"Can I sit down?"

"Sure," Amelie offered.

"If I don't eat somewhere else, I may not get to eat at all."

"We understand," said Amelie. "Help yourself."

Regina glared at her for a second, but the gesture went unnoticed.

"Can I check out your financial statements and projections while I'm here? If you don't mind me eating as I do it."

"That—"

This time Regina cut Amelie off. "That section of our plan needs a lot of work. We're not ready to have someone look at it yet."

Amelie's eyes widened, but she said nothing.

"I'm used to seeing partial drafts and that kind of thing. I don't mind taking a look—no judgment."

"If you insist," Amelie said. With some effort, she slipped the folder from under Regina's hands and handed it over to Nigel.

"So how have you ladies enjoyed the seminar so far?" he asked while reading the pages and flipping to the appendices.

Amelie was the first to respond. "It's great. We might

actually be able to get this done. But it's a whole lot to follow, as laypeople."

"I know. I'm for teaching business to everyone in high school and college. It impacts us all. People get to this stage, and it's like taking a crash college course with no intro to soften it."

He took a bite of his sandwich and finished perusing their pages.

"You guys," he said, but he was looking at Regina, "I can tell that you've done your research. This is great. There are some sections that aren't fully done, and it would be better if your business had been making more, but there are ways to pump it up, regardless."

"What's not finished?" Amelie asked.

"Several things. For one, the cash flow projections are presented monthly for the first year and quarterly after that. It's one of the most important parts of the proposal. You also—"

"We know," Regina said. It nettled her to have him critiquing her work. She didn't know why, but she wanted to stop it nonetheless.

"I know you do. I was only explaining to Ms. Richards." His reaction suggested that he could tell that he'd upset her, but he wasn't sure why. Regina had to admit that he wasn't being condescending or unkind. "Look, you've done a huge part of the work. Why not let me help you guys with some of this?"

"That would be great. Do you do private consultations?"

"All the time. And Regina, I would do anything for you. Please know that."

Amelie's eyebrows went up, but Regina remained aloof.

"Think about it, please." He was looking at Regina. "Let's talk more during the breakout sessions this afternoon. Is that okay?"

"You got it," Amelie said.

The afternoon sessions were starting, and even though Nigel wasn't moderating anymore, he was on the panel again, so he had to leave.

"He seems to want to help," Amelie said. "What's up?"

"It's a long story."

"Give it to me, girl."

"We don't have time. This is the session we need most."

Amelie looked at her with skepticism.

"Look," Regina said, "without an address, we don't even know if what we have is useful or if we need to go to a startup loan. In short, we don't know what we're doing anymore."

Amelie finally turned her attention to the moderator, and Regina followed suit.

The afternoon session was more intense than the morning's had been.

Regina listened carefully and took notes. Like the first session, it only confirmed for her how far they had to go. Her determination wasn't wavering, but her confidence was. If they hadn't lost the site, they might be okay, but now...she didn't know.

After the afternoon sessions, the speakers were placed at tables around the room so that people could go to them with questions.

They got a few minutes with the representative of National Bank, who suggested, in short, that they had to find another location before they could finalize the application. After that, they wandered to the other tables with their less pressing questions, and Regina was glad that she'd stayed, because she did know better what to ask. Amelie even pulled her to Nigel's table, where he looked over the drafts of their financial sections and made suggestions.

Nigel had been at his table for the duration of the breakout session but came over to them as the participants were beginning to leave. Amelie and Regina were packing up things at their table, and after a day of taking notes on things that needed to be done, fixed or changed, Regina's spirits weren't very high.

"I'm glad you stayed, Regina."

She nodded her head, not in the mood for chipper conversation.

"Thank you for all your help," Amelie said.

"No problem. Hey, would you guys like to grab dinner and talk more about the business plan and the application needs? We can even set up some consultations. I can help you get the financial sections in order and help you find people to look over the other sections."

Regina could tell that Amelie saw what a resource he could be and was grateful for his offer. "That would be great, and I'm hungry."

"I need to head home," Regina replied. "And if what the lender said is right, the application isn't going anywhere until we have another location."

Nigel didn't back down. "That doesn't mean we can't put the application in order, and Regina, I can help you with the location. I've been looking into the studio site ever since you came to see me, and—"

"Nigel, you've been more than helpful. Thank you." She was clearly shutting him down.

Amelie glared at her but didn't say anything.

"Then why don't we set up a consultation?"

"Yes, Regina, let's. He has so much of the information we need," Amelie said.

"Fine," she agreed, to appease Amelie and to get the conversation over with. "We'll set up a time by phone when *both* of us can come in for a consultation."

"Just call my office—" he handed Amelie his card "—and tell them you'll need a couple of hours."

"It's been a long day. I'm going home," Regina said.

"I can walk you both out," Nigel offered.

He and Amelie followed Regina out to the parking lot.

"What about you, Ms. Richards? Would you be up for an early dinner? We can talk more about the application process."

Regina gave Amelie a look, but Amelie clearly wasn't paying her any mind.

"Yes, that would be great. Regina, are you sure you won't come?"

"I'm sure."

"We'll set up a consultation time over dinner and let you know," Nigel said. "I'll just be a few more minutes, Ms. Richards, if you can wait. I have to make sure that the speakers have gotten off and that the cleanup is just about over."

"My car is over there."

"I'll be right back."

Regina headed toward her car. Nigel turned to her as she opened her door and put his hand on the small of her back.

"It'll be all right, Reggie. I know it's a lot, but you've already done most of it."

From the tone of his voice, she could tell that the hand on her back was meant to console her. It also sent a shiver up her spine. Heat flooded her middle. She hoped he couldn't tell and tried to figure out how to get him to remove his hand.

"I know. I'm just tired."

"I'm only going out with Ms. Richards to give her more information, Reggie. She doesn't know as much as you do. You're the one who's been doing the work. We'll set up a consultation time."

"I'm not worried about you going out with Amelie. I have no claim on you."

"But you do. You just don't know it." He shook his head and seemed to clear his thoughts. "But I didn't mean to say that. I just want to help you."

"You've been helpful already. I have to go."

She almost expected him to kiss her, but he didn't.

"Reggie, have a good night."

As Regina backed out of her space, she saw Nigel heading back into the building. She wasn't pleased that Nigel and Amelie were going out to dinner. He could say things about her past that she didn't necessarily want her friend to know—things that should come from her, if at all. But there was nothing she could do about that, so she might as well not worry. She didn't like the idea of involving Nigel even more in their affairs, but she had agreed to the consultation, and in all likelihood, they needed it.

She needed to stick to her real priorities and focus on the future. The next thing they needed was a new studio space.

Regina exhaled and let her shoulders droop. She hadn't realized she'd been holding her breath and steeling her back and shoulders. The slump gave her relief from the stress of the day. But she could still feel the tingling at the small of her back where Nigel's hand had been, and heat still flowed to the pit of her stomach from that brief touch. It had always been that way for them.

Chapter 10

Nigel stood in his office going over the copies he'd marked up. He'd gotten Amelie to give him her set of paperwork after dinner, which turned out to be just what he needed to get his plans under way. As before, she was full of information that Regina refused to give him, and as he had seen at the seminar, she was more than willing to take up his offer of assistance, especially once he explained that he was in love with Regina and that no strings were attached. He just wanted to help her.

The women were coming at four-thirty, and they were his last clients for that day, so he could take as much time as he needed with them. They'd need at least two hours, but whenever they finished, he could call it an early day and take them to dinner.

His secretary buzzed him at four-twenty to let him know that they had arrived. Perfect timing. He had just finished reviewing the notes he had for them. He went to call them from the waiting area himself and found Regina beautiful as ever, wearing a light yellow mid-thigh-length sundress. Something about the dress and the way it allowed the air access to her body made her seem vulnerable, fragile. He longed to touch all the places the dress would allow and had to pull his thoughts back to the work at hand.

Amelie was standing next to her in an African-print pantsuit with her braids coiled in a crown at the top of her head. Nigel nodded to her as he pulled his mind out of the gutter and motioned both women into his office and toward a small conference table.

"Welcome, both of you. Come sit over here. I set the chairs up over here so that we can all go over the draft I've marked up at the same time. It'll take a little while, but when it's over, you'll know exactly what to do to have a draft that we can send around for more commentary and then submit."

He looked at Regina to see if her spirits were still down, but her features were neutral. He put a hand on her shoulder.

"Reggie, when we're done, this will work."

"Okay."

"Let's do it," Amelie said, more enthused.

"One thing before we start the walk-through. Can we change the figure of the money you have to put up? I know you don't have a lot because you were putting a lot into renovations at the old place, but this figure is fairly low. Have you thought about outside investors? Individuals? Corporate?"

The women looked at one another and shook their heads no.

"How about me? I can put up—"

"No." Regina cut him off. "No way, no how. That just leaves us with two bills to pay instead of one."

"But I—"

"No."

Regina was adamant. Amelie just shook her head, conceding.

"Okay, but know that I'm here if you change your mind."

Nigel didn't like it, but he let it go. "You have a few other accounting calculations that need to be done. Is it all right if I do those?"

"Hallelujah," Amelie sang out loud.

Regina chuckled at that. She probably echoed the sentiment but wouldn't let herself say it out loud. Her suppressed laugh said it all. Then she caught herself and glanced at Nigel, seeming to feel awkward, as though her weakness had been found out.

Nigel had noticed. "It's okay, really. It's one of the reasons people hire accountants for this stuff, and I have all the software to do the layout." He made his voice as comforting as possible. He was trying to make sure that she didn't feel foolish.

"That done, let's walk through the marked copy," he said. Regina took out a pad and pencil. "You don't need to take separate notes. I'll give you this copy so that you can make changes. Write any clarification you need right on this so that all the notes are in one place."

Regina looked at him. They would all be looking over the same pages, and it meant that she would have to lean closer to him to take notes. He saw her weighing the threat of being closer to him in her mind.

"Okay," she said softly, and they looked at one another, a charge between them.

But Amelie was there. He ignored the electricity he felt and stifled the desire to pull her against his chest so that they could read the pages as one body. He continued on.

"A lot of my notes on the plan have to do with wording, but one of the new things you need is a section on risks."

They spent the next couple of hours walking through his copious notes and comments, and when he was done, the women had a good bit of work to do, but they knew what was needed.

"If you can do another draft of this with those changes, we'll be in business. If you'll do that and send it to me electronically, I can add the changes to the financials and go over it one more time before we hand it off to some of my colleagues for commentary. By the time you submit it, it'll be airtight."

"Except for a location," Regina said.

She looked wistful for a moment and then sighed. Nigel and Amelie exchanged glances.

"That will come," Nigel said finally. "How long do you think it will take you to get the new info, add the new sections and make changes?"

Amelie looked at Regina since it was clear that Regina would lead the brigade.

Regina looked at him, uncertain.

"At two to three hours a day, how long should it take me?"

He didn't want to underestimate and make her feel inadequate. "Two or three weeks, I'd think."

"This isn't my field, so let's say three."

He fished in his pocket and gave her another card. "Email it to me as soon as you're done, and then the three of us can meet again. Oh, one last thing. Your website. I took a look at it, and it seems dated. It doesn't show all the things that you had in the studio. I don't recall seeing mention of your classes or your credentials either."

"I know," Regina said. "We planned to update it."

"And change the name," Amelie added.

"But now we need a new address and class schedule, as well."

"Get it updated now," Nigel suggested. "Leave the old address for now, and add a projected class schedule for the fall. You can always change the address later. Even shopping the proposal around, people will want to see the website, so pretend that you're still at the old location, and update. Change the name, remove the old picture of the location, add more pictures of the pieces, a photo of a class in progress, all of that. Can you afford it, or—"

"Yes. Don't ask," Regina said.

Nigel hung his head, caught offering to help again.

"How about dinner together?" he ventured.

"It's after eight. I have to get home," Regina said quickly.

"Unfortunately, so do I." Amelie had real regret in her voice.

He hadn't noticed the time, only the electric pull he felt toward Regina. He had been close enough to smell her perfume, and his whole body had reoriented toward her center. Lost in the prospect of her future, the hours had skipped by.

The next few weeks couldn't go by quickly enough and didn't go by quickly at all. He had no real reason to contact Regina, but he called anyway, just to ask how things were going. She was polite but didn't engage him in anything other than brief talk about the paperwork.

The three were set to meet on a Friday evening three weeks later, and he'd gotten the electronic version of the updated draft that Regina had emailed. He pored over it for two evenings, correcting new issues that arose in revision, finding things that had gone unnoted the first time around and playing with the layout using his software so that it would look professionally done.

When he opened the door to his office to invite the women in, he found Regina by herself. She wore a lavender peasant blouse made of lace, and the matching crinkle peasant skirt was trimmed with lace at the hem. Her one-inch silver sandals made her seem ready for an evening out, and the whole composition seemed designed to inundate him. Simple as it was, it made him want to take her in his arms.

Focus, he told himself.

He motioned Regina in and looked about for Amelie.

"Restroom?"

"Restless is more like it."

"What?"

"She had a date—of all things—and flaked out at the last minute. This is our future we're talking about. That woman can be one hot mess. She says he's a 'visitor' from out of town and is only here until tomorrow morning. But I know it's a booty call."

Nigel chuckled.

Regina continued, "She begged off, and I let her get away with it because she really chipped in with this leg of the work."

"She knows that you're the one who really knows what's going on. She can afford to be absent."

She dismissed his statement and walked toward the conference table. Her step was hesitant. Without Amelie, she had no buffer, and she was clearly less at ease. He hated that and set about to change it.

"Well, it's the same process as last time, but it won't take as long. I'm sorry about the late hour. I didn't have an opening before five, and since this is pro bono, I didn't want to cut in too much on the company's time."

"Oh, no. No problem. We understand."

"I won't have you here as late as last time, and there are still a bunch of people here. Many of our clients need to come after business hours."

"I could see that. I'm not being skittish."

"Good, have a seat. I have few changes for the proposal. Most of what I have is for the loan-application packet. Amelie gave me all of her copies, so I was able to look through everything."

He flipped opened the first folder and then had a thought.

"Hey, let's just make changes now right on the computer, at least for all of the items that aren't scanned. We can start here with things that will need to be changed at home and then move to my desk."

"Okay."

He started going through the changes, and they drew together, Regina bending toward him to make additional notes for her own clarification.

Her hand was inches from his on the table, and he absentmindedly found himself touching her fingers as he flipped through pages and folders. He didn't notice it until a strong shiver ran through her body.

"Are you cold? Should I turn down the AC?"

"No," she said, pulling her hand away.

That's when he noticed what he'd been doing. And knowing that her body had reacted to it sent heat into the pit of his stomach, made him want to do it more. But he took hold of himself and tried to control his mind. It was his lack of self-control that had widened the rift between them before, and he knew that if he chased her off again, she would walk out now and never come back—not even with Amelie.

When they were done with the scanned items, they

stacked up the folders and moved to his desk, chairs together behind his computer, with her at the keyboard. He continued walking her through suggestions and changes, as both bent toward the screen.

"No," he said at one point, catching an error. "These figures should match the ones in Exhibit G, the equipment or non-real-estate assets to be purchased. And I don't recall them being..."

As he leaned over her to reach the file with the exhibits, Nigel brushed against Regina's breast. Her chest leapt forward, and a heavy shudder ran over her body. She sucked in a trembling breath, and her eyes fluttered. Good God, she was so responsive tonight.

Nigel couldn't help himself. He forgot the folder, bent toward her, and brought her lips to his, moving his hand back to her chest, which heaved against it. Her mouth opened and he moved his tongue into her moist heat, opening his palm to rake her nipples with his fingertips. And he couldn't stop.

Every tremor of her body made his manhood rage. When her hand came up to his nearest shoulder, he spun around in his seat to better position himself in front of her, all the while rubbing her rigid nipples through the thin lace of her blouse.

He moved his tongue farther into Regina's mouth, wanting more. She grabbed his neck and pulled his face closer to hers, her chest still leaping. She moaned softly into his mouth, and his manhood leapt in response.

He finally stood, pulling her up with him and into his arms where he could press her body into his, into the parts of him that had been longing to feel her. Her arms came around his neck, and his hand moved up and down her back.

He tugged her skirt upward until he could put his foot

between her feet, settling his thigh between her legs. He
kneaded her buttocks with one of his hands until he felt
her hips tilt forward, grinding the center of her womanhood against his thigh. She moaned again.

He had never had such strong desire to take a woman,
and he might have ripped off her clothes and lifted her
onto his body right there had he not been aware that the
door was unlocked and had he not been certain that the
gesture would send her bolting.

He pulled his head up, separating his mouth from hers.

"Reggie, come home with me. Let me make love to you.
I want you so badly."

Before she could respond, his mouth found hers again.
They began to kiss again, but then her hand came up between them, and she stepped back, shaking her head and
taking deep breaths.

"I can't. I didn't come here to—"

Nigel inhaled slowly and exhaled.

"I'm sorry, Reggie. I don't know what hit me. It was
just that you seemed so… You seemed to respond. I won't
do anything like this if it means I can't help you. I'm not
doing this to seduce you into being with me or anything
like that. Here, sit. Let's finish."

She sat down, still breathing heavily. "Okay. Let's finish."

Nigel sat back down as well, trying to force his pulse to
calm and his body to quiet. After the heat of the exchange
between them, he wanted nothing more than to gather
up their things and take her home. His disappointment
was matched only by his determination to be of real help.
That's what allowed him to regain his focus and apply it
to the work at hand.

They went through the rest of the changes quickly and
quietly.

"These are finished," he said when they were done.

"What about the address? I haven't changed it."

"Leave the address. There will be one there, so let's leave this one where it is for now. Oh, what about the website?"

"It will be finished next week."

"Good."

He hadn't expected it to be done that quickly, but the timing was perfect for his plans. He printed them both copies.

"Here. This draft is good. Sign these."

"They're still drafts. Amelie isn't here."

"We want them to be as complete as possible, even to show around. But we can get Amelie's signature later."

"Okay," she said, and picked up a pen from his desk.

"Once you scan the rest of the pages and get them to me, I'll make a couple of copies and hand them around. A few items will change when the location changes, but this is enough to get more feedback before the final submission. Just so you know, it can take a few weeks to get feedback. Industry people are pretty busy, and I'm not just getting this to my friends. I'll get it to the right people, not the ones who'll get it back in a couple days as a favor."

"You do that, and I'll work on the space."

Regina started packing up.

"Nigel."

"Yes, Reggie."

"I've had a few minutes to think."

She turned to him, and he could see that she had gotten serious. She had a determined look on her face, and her fist tightened around the handle of her satchel. She met his eyes with a fixed regard.

"After what just happened, I don't think we should see each other anymore," she said. "If we need to meet once more when you get the commentary back, it can be with Amelie."

"Reggie, I told you. I won't do anything to jeopardize helping you. There aren't any strings attached here. This is part of what I do. Let me help."

"I just don't want to keep sending you mixed signals."

Her signal wasn't mixed at all. He knew that she wanted him. Right from the top of her head to her little pinky toe, she wanted him. But her mind didn't want him.

And right now, it was more important to help her with this than to pursue anything else that might chase her away. She was right. This was her future that they were talking about. She wanted to do this; it was her dream. And he wanted to help her have her dream.

He decided to let it go.

"Okay. Send me the other files. When I get those, I'll send them around. We can decide later who I meet with, and it will be all three of us or just me and Amelie."

"It can be just—"

"If there are changes she won't understand, then the three of us can meet in a bright public space. If there are only minor revisions, I'll convey them to you through her. You'll be making them. That I know."

"I'm sorry for the confusion, Nigel. That's why it's better this way."

Dinner was out of the question, of course. He walked her to the elevator and watched as she got on.

The elevator closed. It closed with him not knowing when he would see her again, when he could touch her again. But he wouldn't worry about that now. He would have a long time to worry about that in the coming weeks.

Nigel went back to his office. First things first. First he had to get her business back. Then he had to try to get her back.

Chapter 11

It was some weeks later that Regina, glancing up from her plate of smoked salmon at a restaurant, saw Nigel again.

He was wearing a gray pinstriped three-piece suit and looked as professionally manicured as ever. Next to him was a tall woman, almost as tall as he was, wearing a form-fitting purple evening gown with sequins over the top. It was sleeveless and had a low cut in the front, coming down to the cusps of her ample breasts. She had her hands wrapped around Nigel's arm, and he was guiding her down the steps to the main dining floor.

Given her proportions, she was a perfect Black Barbie and probably as brainless, too—a fitting match for a successful young accountant-investor. But why was Regina being critical of the woman? She was glad that Nigel was getting on with his life the same way she was finally getting on with hers.

It was the opening night of a new jazz restaurant in

downtown DC called The Jay Birds, and Regina had finally kept her promise to herself to get a life. She was out
on the town.

Nigel caught her gaze as he looked over the dining floor
and held it long enough to notice the date seated across
from her. Regina's face flushed, and she turned back to
her dinner partner. But the intrigue made her glance back
in time to see the couple be seated, with Nigel getting a
chair that gave him a plain view of her.

She watched as the woman said something, palming Nigel's chest and shoulder before settling back in her chair.
When he looked up and caught her watching, Regina
turned her attention back to her date. He was a medical
technician at the George Washington University Hospital. He was also some distant relation of Ellison, who had
set them up.

The evening was young, but she and her date had already exhausted the topics they seemed to have in common. They inspected their plates quietly. Of course, now
that the seven-piece jazz band had started up, it wasn't
really possible to talk on the main dining floor. It was better to watch as people on the lower level, a dance floor,
moved to the band.

The music was good, and Regina couldn't help swaying to it now and again. So far, it was the best part of the
evening. If she got no other pleasure out of the night, she
would at least have the joy of listening to the band—The
Jay Birds, she assumed—do classic jazz and do it the right
way.

Whenever she dared glance his way, the woman's hands
were somewhere on Nigel, and Nigel's eyes were on Regina. He was probably wondering if he should say hello.
He could spare himself the worry.

She made sure not to look over very often but couldn't

help having her attention drawn that way when three bois-
terous men and a woman stopped at Nigel's table, greeting him and his guest in loud voices and carrying on a
conversation above the music. Once again, she found his
eyes shift to her.

When they were finished with dinner, Regina and her
date turned their chairs toward the band and enjoyed the
music. He wasn't much for dancing—didn't know how to
dance to jazz, he said—so they sat and watched the danc-
ers. The music was energetic, but it didn't seem to move
him. His stillness and his plastic features made him seem
unreal to Regina.

Now that he was out of sight, she had no reason to think
about Nigel Johns, but she couldn't help wondering if he
was still glancing her way, couldn't help remembering
what had happened between them in his office. She shook
her head to free her mind of the image, then let herself become immersed in the music.

She tried not to think about Nigel again, but then he
appeared at her side, motioning toward the dance floor.
She wouldn't have given it a second thought, but the band
was playing New Orleans–style jazz, and she loved that.
She would never get a chance to dance with her date, so
she leaned over to him and shouted in his ear.

"Do you mind if I dance for a while?"

He shrugged, and she got up, moving to the dance floor
with Nigel and then kicking back to the sound.

It was pretty clear that Nigel didn't know how to move
to this music either. His awkward jerks made her laugh
out loud, but at least he was willing to try.

After a couple of songs, he found his groove and began
matching her step for step. He put one of his hands on her
hip and brought her closer, never losing a beat. A soft smile
came onto his face, and for a moment, she thought that he

might do more, but he didn't. He just moved with her, his eyes trained on her face.

If he wanted to say something, he had no chance. The music was just too loud. When the set was over, they both turned, heading back to their tables. She figured that he needed to get back to his date, and she might as well get back to hers. Her date didn't seem to be enjoying too much of this, so it was about time for them to go—either somewhere else or home, she didn't know. If she had her vote, it would be home.

Nigel couldn't keep his eyes off Regina.

When his date, Laurie, started talking with the owners, he slipped over and asked her to dance. Laurie was a networker and would spend a while working the bar area where the owners were stationed for opening night. She was the sister of one of his coworkers and only needed someone well dressed to show off for opening night. He was there because he'd helped the owner get the loan to start the place and was his accountant; he was expected. But after he'd shown his face, he planned to leave.

Regina had on a simple dress rather than an evening gown, but she looked stunning. The top part of the bodice was pleated around her torso with two little straps over her shoulders, and when she got up to dance with him, the skirt of her dress fell around the curves of her hips.

He was surprised when Regina actually agreed to dance with him, and downright shocked when she actually looked back at him—not wanting him, but not hating him. It made his heart skip a beat, made him hope that he might have a chance.

After that dance, he made sure the owner would put Laurie in a cab, made sure she knew the change in plans, and hurried to his car so that he could catch Regina leaving. He didn't personally know her date, but he had recognized him and remembered hearing that he was something of a ladies' man from mutual friends. He had to make sure that Regina got home safely. He felt like a thief or a stalker, but when they came out just as he pulled up, he followed them to their car and followed them to wherever they were going, hoping that it was her place and not his.

He was relieved to see the guy leave Regina at the curb and to see her walk up to the third story of a three-story house. Still acting on impulse, he followed her, not sure what he would say or how she would react.

Regina kicked her shoes off as soon as she hit the living room. When she heard the knock on the door, she thought that maybe her date had forgotten something. Or maybe he thought they might be continuing the evening in her apartment. If so, he was terribly mistaken.

She paused at the door, wondering what her date might be thinking and if she might have to fight off any advances. Outside of tonight, she didn't know him at all. In fact, tonight had given her no real clue either.

It was late, but she picked up her phone and dialed Amelie's number.

"Hey. If I don't call you back in ten minutes, come get me."

She opened the door with the phone in her hand and was surprised to see Nigel, not her date. "Oh."

"Disappointed?"

"Relieved. Don't ask," she said. If it had been her date, it would have been awkward, at the very least.

Actually, this should be awkward, too, but it wasn't. Somewhere in the back of her mind, she had imagined the knock on the door might be Nigel. Something about dancing with him, even in a crowded club on opening night, had made them seem like friends again. It had surprised her that he hadn't tried to talk. Maybe she had even been a little disappointed. But then, he had been on a date, as had she.

"First, once again, you should check the peephole before you open the door."

"The landing light is out. I can't see a thing out the peephole. And it's too high for me—I have to get that fixed. By the way, there is a buzzer. But you can't see it, can you?"

After the lack of conversation with her date that evening, she now felt rather chatty. She was breaking her own rules, but it was a relief to have someone around who could hold a conversation.

"And second," Nigel said, "I thought we could have a cup of coffee or…"

"Or?"

"I don't know. That's as far as I got. I only know that I had to see you."

"I'm sure—" she almost said Black Barbie "—your girlfriend wouldn't appreciate you saying that."

"She's not my girlfriend. She's my coworker's sister, who will be put in a cab by the owner, and he's the only reason I went. Business."

"I guess that doesn't let me off the hook."

She reluctantly stepped back, letting Nigel in. Part of her knew she should send him away, but the larger part of her wanted to decompress after the long night and have a real conversation with a real person.

"Okay," Regina said, "let's clear the air. I'm not putting those shoes on again, so you'll have to take whatever's in my kitchen, which is decaf, I think."

"So this is where you're living now?"

"You didn't know? My new address is on the application."

"No, I didn't get it from the application. I followed you home."

Regina made an exaggerated face, looking at Nigel like he might be a crazy stalker. He got her meaning and cracked up.

"I know. I'm a bit out there right now," he said, not wanting to tell her what he'd heard about her date. "But seeing you again… Seeing you in that dress. I don't know. Maybe it *is* time to clear the air."

"I'm in a strange mood, too. It was just one of those nights. Anyway. Clearing the air." She turned serious. "We can't go back there."

He got quiet, too. "I know. I know. But who you are now, who I am now—"

"We're different people now," she said.

"Who you are now is interesting, too. Where's your artwork?"

"I found a dealer in the art district who took pity on me and took about a third of my finished pieces on consignment. The rest is in there."

Nigel headed into the room she had pointed to.

"It's not pity. Your work is beautiful. I saw a little at the studio—I'm sorry again that you lost it. What about Amelie?"

"Oh. Amelie."

Regina still had the phone in her hand and hit Redial.

"No, you're not coming for me. It was just Nigel…. He didn't say anything about that, so I assume not." She turned to him. "Did we get any commentary back yet?" He shook his head no. "No, but I'll let you know….Oh, hush. Bye-bye." She clicked the phone shut. "Sorry about that."

"Protection?"

"Yes. That was Amelie. We have a booth on weekends in the open market at Eastern Market. Have you been there?"

"Not yet." He was walking slowly through the room, looking at the pieces she had out front, sometimes stopping to tip a board forward and see the one behind it.

"We share a booth, but she's doing well there. Sharing it takes the pressure off the need to be there all weekend, which is nice. She has a show coming up, as well."

"She's beginning to be recognized."

"Yes. We're still trying for a place of our own."

"You'll be recognized soon, too."

They were in what would usually have been the second bedroom of her two-bedroom place. For her, it served as an art studio. His attention to her pieces drew her eyes to them, as well. She didn't realize he had moved behind her until he wrapped his arm around her.

"It's getting muddy again," she said, but she didn't pull away.

"I know," he answered.

They were quiet for a long moment.

Perhaps she just wanted to break the mood, but she had a playful thought. "You know, when you asked me to dance, you didn't say that you couldn't dance a lick to New Orleans jazz."

"Or any other jazz," he added.

They both chuckled.

"Thank you for trying. You caught on quickly."

"Yeah, your boyfriend didn't look like he was about to."

"Like I said, don't go there."

They chuckled again.

"Hey," he said, "where did you learn to dance to New Orleans jazz?" He said it like he should know everything about her.

"My older cousin Willie, from the Big Easy. He used to come visit us about once a year when I was little."

Regina moved to break the spell between them and return them to reality, but he held on to her. From behind her, he crossed his arms over her chest and rubbed her arms. The movement dragged his forearms gently over her breasts, and her body started to tingle. His mouth was near her ear, close enough that his warm breath sent shivers through her.

"You dance well. I don't dance anymore at all."

"You? The eternal partier? You're just out of practice."

"That I am."

He pointed to one of her pieces. "What do you call that one?"

She stirred slightly at his question, but he gently held her back to his chest, and rubbed her arms again. The name that had been on the tip of her tongue slipped out of her mind.

"Um. Oh, it's called *The Overlook*. See the way the figure is overlooking the horizon?"

"Yes," he said into her loose hair. He drew one of his hands around her waist and drew the other to her breast, gently caressing it through the pleats of her dress. Her body tensed, and goose bumps ran up her spine.

"Tell me about that one."

"That one is called *The Crucible*. It's a Georgia O'Keefe–type theme. Women's sexuality."

Nigel lifted his head. "Where?"

"See, there are the lips, the V for the hair. It's abstract."

"I see it now. It's beautiful. I wouldn't have gotten it if you hadn't told me."

He moved the hand on her waist down to her thighs and drew his palm up toward her V. Her buttocks contracted involuntarily, and her thighs clenched, tilting her hips. She sucked in a breath.

"Your body wants me. I want you, too."

She stopped, exhaled.

"Let's be clear. I can't go back there. This is…" She didn't know how to finish.

"Let's just say it is what it is and leave it at that."

Nigel moved his palm down Regina's thighs again and then back up. He loved the way her body bucked against his when he did it, making him stiffen.

"You know. I haven't—" she said.

"You haven't what?"

"I haven't been with anyone other than you since high school."

Nigel was floored and broke out in a grin, which she turned her head in time to catch. She playfully elbowed him in the side.

"I'm sorry," he said. "But the truth is that I haven't been with anyone other than you all this time either. Not that I haven't had offers."

"I'm sure you have."

"And clearly you have, as well."

He still held her breast in his palm, and he ran his thumb over her nipple, feeling it stiffen, feeling her whole body sway.

"It's getting murky again, Nigel."

"No, it's not. Not really. Let's just say that we're two people who've been starved for affection and who are used to each other."

"I'm not used to you," she protested. "I'm not used to anyone."

"Well, we're more used to each other than anyone else."

"And it is what it is," she said, as if to make certain that they were on the same page.

"It is what it is," he confirmed.

"But let's not make it a habit. That's when things get murky again."

He was too busy smelling her hair to respond. When he opened his eyes and dipped his head down, she looked like she was wondering what the hell she was doing. But when he ran his hand over her breasts again, her eyes fluttered shut, and a shiver ran through her whole body.

He took her and drew into the hall, looking for her bedroom.

They went inside and faced one another next to her bed. She looked at him for a long moment and then stepped into the radius of his embrace, pressing her hands against his chest, finding his nipples and closing her fingers around them, weakening his knees.

It was his grin. It seemed to turn back time in his face, making him into the boy she had known and loved before he became the man who stood in front of her now.

And it was his touch—the way he moved his fingers over her chest and the way he moved his palm up her legs, making heat and moisture flood into her body.

Still, she had to wonder what on earth she was doing with the man who had once left her. But thinking about that didn't answer her real question. Why was her body still lit on fire by his touch? Though she hedged, in the end she knew that she wanted this as much as he did, and as long as they were both clear...

But she couldn't be clear with his fingers moving over her, his hand exploring her body. She moved her hands along his chest and let herself be lost in the sensations.

When she heard the zipper of her dress, she opened her

eyes. When she felt his fingers fluttering down her back, her body arched into his, and she began to throb. She got her hands between them and undid the buttons of his shirt, wanting to feel the warmth of his skin against hers. Then she felt her dress sliding down between them, and his head dipped down to her neck and then her breasts, as the material fell to the floor.

His mouth was hot through the fabric of her bra, turning her nipples into hard peaks. He sucked one into his mouth and wetness flooded her. Her body shivered from the touch, and she couldn't hold in the murmur that escaped her. Then his fingers moved between her legs, finding her heat. Her body jerked and a soft moan poured from her throat. She had to hold his shoulder to stop from sinking to the floor as a heavy throbbing overtook her.

She slipped his blazer and shirt from his shoulders at the same time, and he straightened, letting her undress him. The passion she saw in his face made her flush. She brought the jacket over to her chair and turned to find him stripping off his pants, along with his shoes. When he saw her undo the clip of her bra and let it slip from her torso, he stopped and stared, his manhood tugging against his shorts.

She held out her hand for his pants and laid them over the seat. Then she moved into his open arms.

His mouth covered hers, and his hard chest dragged across her breasts, making her moan again. He slipped the panties down her legs and took off his shorts before lifting her onto the bed. He stopped to put on a condom he must have taken from his clothes while undressing, and then he covered her with his body.

When his manhood grazed her center, her back arched and she murmured. But instead of moving inside her, he slid his body down the length of hers, suckling her nipples before moving lower. When his mouth found her, when the heat of it covered her, Regina moaned out loud and thrust her hips. Sensations flooded her. She clung to the bedspread and thrust against his teasing lips. And he didn't stop.

She was moaning and thrusting when his fingers found her breasts, pushing her over the edge as a wave of release shattered through her body. She cried out as the pleasure ripped through her body.

She was breathing heavily as he slid upward next to her, letting her run her hands along his body—its hardness, its curves, its thick peak. She pulled him toward her, and he followed her tug, landing between her legs.

He entered her in one slow movement, building the pressure inside of her all over again. His slow thrusts filled her. His lips captured her breath. His moan filled her mouth.

His movements spread fire through her, made her body grip on to his. But he was taking his time, making her moan, making her thrust, making her build toward the edge.

When his movements became short, hard jerks, her back arched, bringing her chest to stroke along his. She moaned and he moaned as they both tumbled over the boundary.

Chapter 12

A week later, Nigel couldn't wait to see Regina again. In fact, he wasn't going to wait. And he wasn't going to follow the little rules she'd laid out for them; she could never be just a warm body to him. He had already decided to drop in on her and see what she was up to. Where it went from there, well, that was up to her.

Nigel knocked on Regina's door for the second time. When he still didn't get an answer, he remembered that there was a buzzer and decided to try it before giving up.

He heard a chain sliding, and then the door opened.

"Yes. I did look out the peephole this time, thank you."

"I didn't say a thing."

She eyed him. "You were thinking it."

He gave her an innocent face and shook his head. She laughed.

"What are you doing here? And don't you know that I

have a phone? You can call ahead. You know, I'm usually at our booth in Eastern Market by now."

"I figured, but I thought I would take a chance."

He followed her into the living room and took a seat. She was wearing jeans with a tank top and had sneakers in her hand. He loved seeing her in casual clothes almost as much as he had loved seeing her in business attire. The tank top left her shoulders out, and already his lips were itching to kiss them. In fact, he wanted to play with all of her curves.

She sat down to put on her sneakers.

"I actually do have quite a bit to get done," she said. "I can't stop and play."

"So what are we doing today?"

"Nothing in those clothes."

He wasn't ready for her to say that. He imagined that she might turn him down altogether, not that she would have an issue with his clothes.

"Don't you have any casual wear? Jeans?"

Nigel looked down at himself, perturbed.

"I think I have some jeans at home. I know I have sweat pants."

"Jeans are better," she said. "Sweat pants will do."

"Why? What are we doing today?"

"Errands."

"Errands?"

"You'll see."

At least she was amenable to the company.

They headed out as if they were used to being together. They left his car on her street, and she followed his directions to his place so he could change. Nigel liked the new feeling of being out with her, doing things, but she had never been to his place, and now he wasn't sure what she would make of it.

He let her go in ahead of him and watched her as she took it all in: a winding black leather sectional, a fully stocked cherry wood entertainment center with a six-foot coffee table and matching chest, a deep-piled eggshell carpet.

"Damn," she said.

"I actually had a decorator do it. I wanted to impress you."

"You're kidding, right?"

He sighed, realizing too late that he had perhaps admitted too much. "No, I wanted to show you that I'd made it after all."

She walked to the end of the living room and back, then turned into the hallway and found his equally decked-out bedroom. He liked the idea of having her in his room and followed her in.

"This isn't necessarily what I think of when I think of making it." She'd found his closet.

"I know. I— You seemed so certain that I would waste my life. I wanted to—"

"I wasn't certain of any such thing. I was waiting for you to…just take things a little more seriously, not ditch all the casual clothes you own." She'd been rifling in his closet, then his drawers. "Here. Let's have you try these on."

She handed him a pair of unworn jeans that still had the tags on them and a similarly new Janet Jackson T-shirt. He laughed at the tee but started stripping anyway.

"See, I do have casual clothes."

"Yes, but you've never worn them. How come?"

"I thought I needed to get rid of my old life." He shook his head, remembering the days he refused to wear anything that didn't look gangsta. "I needed to change my life around—finish school, make it in the world, prove that I could be what you needed. I guess I went to the other extreme, but it got me here. It got me to change, and I haven't looked back."

"It doesn't have to be one or the other."

"At that time, for me, it did. Now, maybe not."

When he was finished, she sized him up and apparently approved.

"Okay, let's get to it."

The first stop turned out to be a huge hardware store out in Maryland. This was Regina's element, and he followed her around while she handed him things to put in their cart—dusty ceramic tiles, powdery grout bags, tubs of mastic, cylinders of sealant, cans of paint, tubes of epoxy. Now he knew why casual clothes were needed.

"I miss teaching my classes," she mused.

"Were they adults or children?"

"Adults or teens mostly for the found-object mosaics. I can do clay work with littler ones, but the other stuff is too sharp and dangerous for them."

"You'll have a classroom back again soon."

"I know. And I'm looking for other places I can teach in the meantime."

She spent a while in the molding aisle and then pointed at a bunch of eight-foot-long molding pieces and at the cart with the handsaw.

"Make yourself useful," she said, then smiled.

"You want me to?"

"Cut them in half so they'll fit in the car. Here, I'll start them for you." She brought him over to the cart, laughing. He pulled a few pieces of the molding from the shelf and joined her.

He never knew the sight of a woman with a handsaw could be so sexy. She laid two of the pieces on the cart and measured to find the center. He didn't need to, but he got behind her to see what she was doing, fitting his thumbs into the belt loops of her jeans. He couldn't resist pulling her against him and running his cheek over her hair.

She laughed and tried to wiggle away.

"You're not looking at what I'm doing," she said, but as she turned toward him, he caught her lips with his.

They parted for him, and he turned her body toward him, pulling her into his embrace. He had to tear himself from her before he got lost in the moment.

"Okay, I got distracted. Show me again," he said.

She pursed her lips at him, turned back to the cart and started a notch in the molding. He finished them up in no time but not without a naughty picture in his mind.

A question occurred to him as they continued shopping. These supplies were going to cost a bit.

"Do you have enough coming in from Eastern Market and the art dealer?"

"That's a very private question. Actually, you've seen all my financials. You know I have a morning job, right?"

"Oh, yeah. Does it help you out enough?"

"It pays okay. I don't do a lot of hours, though. For now it gives me rent and health insurance."

"What is it?"

"It's just office work with an architectural firm in downtown DC. Nothing special. But it helps with the bills."

Next was the plywood section. This time she had the store cut down sections of large boards for her, the sawdust flying from the circular saw.

"What about you? Do you like your work?"

He was surprised by the question.

"Yes, I do. I think I started it just for the money. But I really love what I do. Some things are a little tedious—crunching numbers sometimes—but most of it I love."

"Like what?"

"Like helping people get a business going. You and Amelie, for example. Or seeing it grow. Being able to teach people more about business rather than just adding up numbers for them. Being able to guide people through the process rather than just handing them balance sheets. Helping people figure out how to save and grow money."

He stopped. It seemed to him that he'd started rambling.

"Don't stop. I like to hear you get passionate."

He hoped she did, because he wanted to get passionate with her. He dragged his mind from the gutter.

After the hardware store, they went to a tile shop. After that it was an art supply store, where Regina needed clay and slip.

"I tried the non-firing clay. It wasn't strong enough."

"Where's your kiln now?"

"It's in the workroom in my apartment. Didn't you notice it when you were in there?"

"No, I was looking at your art and at you." He dipped his head down and kissed her. Then he wrapped his arm around her as they continued through the store. The clay and slip were both incredibly heavy.

"How do you get this by yourself?"

"I'm not by myself."

"But when you are?"

"One case at a time."

Since they were in the area, they stopped at the pet store. He was thinking of a dog. They played with the puppies, looked at the fish and petted the hamsters. It was a riot.

In fact, Nigel found himself laughing on and off all day, something he didn't do a lot of anymore. As they unloaded her hatchback later that afternoon, Nigel paused and looked at her for a long moment.

"I haven't had this much fun in years."

"And you're not in a business suit. See? Success doesn't mean being all business all the time."

"And it doesn't mean that you have to do everything on your own all the time either."

Regina stopped for a minute and put her hand up to disagree but then seemed to think the better of it.

"Okay. Maybe. In fact, here."

She handed him two boxes of clay, and he started laughing.

"I don't just mean the heavy stuff. You know, I might be able to help you as well, help fund your art…"

She had already started shaking her head.

"…or help you find a new place or help you get the down payment. You don't have to be all business all the time either."

"I don't need that kind of help, but thank you."

They got everything up the stairs to her apartment and had to sit down for a minute.

"You know," he said, "you're probably exceeding the weight limit for that room."

"Hopefully it's a sturdy house. I took this place because it had the two large rooms, and that one can handle the wattage of the kiln. I have to pay for it, but I can still do my work. Luckily, I have another big installation I'm working on."

He could see how much it mattered to her.

"Come to me," he said.

"What?"

"Come here."

"Why?" she asked, but she came to him anyway.

Nigel pulled Regina onto his lap and settled back onto the sofa, massaging her back.

"That's nice."

Moments later, she started to giggle and squirm, making him laugh. This woman lit up his world.

"Not there," she squealed.

"Oh, you're ticklish here. What if..."

He did it again and she tried to get away, but he held her. He had to kiss that spot, and he lifted her tank top before toppling her forward on the couch. He kissed her back until he found the spot again. He could tell when she squirmed. Only this time when her body arched, she also murmured.

Regina's response to the touch of his lips set Nigel's body on fire. He could finally touch her without worrying that he might drive her away. She was finally his to have, to please. He opened his mouth and ran his tongue along the spot he'd found, and he was rewarded by the heavy shudder of her body and a soft moan. He lowered his torso on her thighs and continued the pressure, reaching underneath her to find a full, firm breast. Regina's breathing quickened, and her hips swirled beneath him.

It was early in the evening, but he was going to make it a long night.

Chapter 13

Regina pulled her eyelet camisole over her head, stepped into her leggings, brushed her hair into a ponytail and slipped into her sandals. She didn't have time for anything else.

The times she'd been with Nigel were all impromptu—him stopping by to see her. She'd helped to make it that way—keeping things casual so that he wouldn't get the wrong idea, keeping the pressure off so that things between them wouldn't escalate. This was a little different. They had spoken by phone in advance. They were going to look at possible new locations for the studio. Since he was closer to the first stop, she would meet him at his place. Yes, this was different.

She was implying that it was okay for them to hang out together. Maybe it was, as long as things were clear between them. The times they'd been together had felt good. And she had to admit that it felt great having some attention to her…well, womanly needs. As long as that was all it was; as long as they both knew that it was what it was.

She rang his buzzer, and he let her into his building.

The door to his apartment was open, and he called to her from the bedroom.

"Sorry I'm a bit late. Damn, it's early in the morning."

"I have seven places to see and one day to do it."

"I know. I'll be right there."

Nigel came out of his room wearing only his boxers. She could see the muscular ridges of his chest and the rugged curves of his arms. He looked like a chocolate statue— good enough to eat. He put a cup of coffee in the kitchen and came back to kiss her, a light peck on the lips. She pulled him back and ran her fingers over his chest, kissing him again. Definitely good enough to eat.

As long as everything was clear between them.

He stayed beneath her touch and looked at her.

"You know, we could see places another day. And if you keep touching me this way, we might have to."

She slipped her arms around him. "I'm just a bit randy today."

"Oh, hell."

She laughed when he picked her up and strode into his bedroom.

"No, no. We don't have time for this. I have to see the places."

He gave her a crestfallen look, placed her on the bed and pulled his shirt off the hanger.

What had gotten into her? She took a breath and tried to focus on the property search.

The first location was in DC but too far from down-town to be inviting and more broken-down than their old place was. There was no place for a classroom setting, and there was peeling woodwork, rodent droppings and little visibility from the street. They could afford the rent, but it would drive them into bankruptcy.

"Let's go. We can't attract clients from here. It would take more than we can get to fix it up."

"They'll get better, Reggie. Don't worry."

The next location was actually in the art district. It had recently been vacated by a silversmith and still had the jewelry display cases. It didn't have a separate class space, but it was big enough to improvise, with large storefront windows and the jeweler's shelving. It was clean and white and looked new. It was also out of their price range—way out. The jeweler had probably gone out of business trying to make the rent.

"I couldn't price my work high enough to keep this place."

They went on to the next two locations, then the next three. It was the same story. They were either crap that was affordable or nice but too expensive to keep up. The whole day was wasted.

"We'll keep looking, Reggie. There'll be something soon."

Regina looked through her papers at the listings she'd found and all the leads the real estate agent had given her to try to find something else they might go see. Nothing. She threw them all into a garbage can on the way back to the car. What next? They were looking in DC, Maryland and Virginia. Maybe they were in the wrong states. She could widen her search. Damn it. How did other businesses make it?

"What are you thinking?" Nigel asked as they sat together in the car.

It shook her out of her reverie. "I'm just wondering what to do next."

"You're letting it get you down. It could take a while to find the right place. Give it time."

"Right now, time is income. I've—"

She had started to say that she'd asked for more hours at her morning job, and she'd gotten them, but it meant less time to work on her art. It meant she was losing her dream. But she didn't want to say this out loud, and not to Nigel, sitting there staring at her in his designer suit. It was some reversal, wasn't it? Tears moistened her eyes, but she didn't want to cry.

"I'll keep looking," she said. "If it's meant to be, we'll find something fairly soon. If it's not, I'll take a break and start some other path."

"Reggie, trust me, please. It will be okay. And if you need anything in the meantime, I'm here."

"I know," she said. But she would never turn to him for that kind of assistance. "You know, this is why I was so serious in school."

"What?" Nigel turned to her.

"I knew it would be this hard. Or at least that it was likely to be."

"You couldn't have known that we'd have a major economic recession."

"No, but even without that, I knew that trying to live as an artist would be hard. I knew it, so I should be ready for it. Let's hope I am."

Regina started the car and headed back to his place, still down.

"Can you come in for a while?" he asked. "I'll make us something to eat."

"No, you go ahead. I have to get ready for my housewarming party tonight. You still coming?"

"I'll be there, tot in tow."

She started to pull off.

"Reggie," he called out. She slowed down and turned back to look at him. "I promise you that things will be okay. Don't let it get you down."

"I know. I won't."

But it seemed like a promise that he couldn't make.

When she got home, Regina didn't go into the kitchen to start getting ready for the evening. She got on the computer. She had to find other options, or she wouldn't be able to make it through the evening. In an hour, she had the information for another commercial real estate broker-age company in the DC area and two more sites on which to do searches. She picked an afternoon to drive around and look for open locations near the Torpedo Factory; if she'd learned anything today, it was that location was in-deed everything.

She also had the name of a photographer who could take pictures of a few of her mosaics—the ones she made the tiles for herself and had soldered templates for. Those she could reproduce. Maybe she could get a Black catalogue company to advertise them or could put ads in a magazine herself. It was all worth trying.

That would have to be it for now. She was having a housewarming party that night, and she did have to get ready.

Regina had changed into an African-print summer dress and had finished preparing the food.

Jason and Ellison, along with little Kyle, were the first to arrive and brought a platter of home-broiled chicken. Nigel was the next to arrive, and as soon as he entered, he bent down and gave her a warm hello kiss.

Nigel had a little boy in one arm and a bag in the other.

She took the bag from him. She didn't know he had planned to, but he'd brought homemade pasta salad. The bag also had a wrapped present for her that turned out be a sweetgrass basket from South Carolina. "It's beautiful. And expensive. You didn't have to."

"I wanted to. I thought you'd like it."

"Oh, I love it."

Regina knew that Jason was all eyes and would want more information later. So be it. She drew Nigel into the living room and introduced him around.

"Nigel, this is Jason."

They shook hands. "I remember you from the studio. Hey," Nigel said.

"This is his partner, Ellison, and their son, Kyle."

Regina watched his response to her gay friends, but he didn't seem surprised and didn't miss a beat.

"I remember you from the studio, too," he said to Kyle, then shook Ellison's hand. He turned to the little one in his arm.

"You remember Andre from my office."

"Hello, Andre," Regina said.

Surrounded mainly by adults who were peering at him, Andre twisted on Nigel's shoulder and hid his face against it.

"He's a little shy sometimes," said Nigel. "I'm babysitting for my cousin Michelle. Say hello." Andre continued to hide his face and shook his head no. "Okay. Maybe later. Here, meet Kyle. He's little like you." Andre turned around and looked over at Kyle, held on Ellison's hip. "Maybe he wants to watch your movie with you. You want to ask him? Yeah, let's ask him."

Nigel pulled the movie out of his blazer.

"Can I put on a movie for them? I promised Andre he could see it."

He handed the DVD to Jason.

"Looks good."

"They can watch it in the corner. I'll set up a little table for them as well so that they can eat."

"Does that sound good? You hungry?" Nigel asked Andre and rubbed his tummy. Andre giggled. "I'll take that as a yes."

Regina set the kids up in front of the movie with plates and went to set things out in the kitchen now that people were starting to arrive. When she got back, the kids were glued to an animated film about robots, and the three men were engaged in a lively debate over old-school dance music. Regina didn't know much of what they were talking about, but it had Ellison off his seat, and before she knew it, the three men were doing some step from back in the day, clapping each other's backs and laughing out loud.

She raised an eyebrow in question, and the men broke out laughing again.

Nigel slid his arm around her back as she neared, still laughing. She saw Jason taking mental notes, but there was nothing she could do.

"Actually, should I put on some music?" Jason asked.

"Funkadelic," Ellison said.

"Hush, now," Jason said. "That's before your time."

"Technically, it's before all of our times," Nigel said. "It was the sampling that turned us on to all the older stuff."

"Ice Cube," they said in unison.

"You have no idea what we're talking about, do you, sweetie?" Nigel teased.

"I know Parliament Funkadelic—kind of."

The three men laughed, and she didn't mind that it was at her expense. She was glad that they were all getting on so well. She got up, put on some music and checked on the kids. When she sat down, the conversation had turned to money, finances and the economy. Knowing Jason and

Nigel, she guessed this would be another heated topic. She was glad she had to leave them to get the door.

Guests had started coming. Amelie brought a date. Little Tenisha was there, along with her parents, and she joined the boys for the movie. A couple of her coworkers from her morning job came. Several of her college friends who where still in the area stopped in. One even remembered Nigel.

"No, it isn't Nigel Johns!" Simone yelled.

The two hugged enthusiastically. Simone had been one of Regina's closest friends and knew Nigel well.

"Simone. You were my big sister. Man, I was a pain in your butt, wasn't I?"

They both laughed.

"Not all the time."

The two stepped aside to catch up.

When the movie was done, Nigel went to amuse the kids for a while, but little Andre was cranky and started to cry. Nigel gathered Andre up and placed him on his shoulder, and then came to Regina.

"I'm not an expert, but I think this one is tuckered out. I better head home."

"You can put him down in my room."

"Actually," Nigel said, "let me call his mother so she knows we're still here. Can she pick him up from here?"

"Sure."

Regina spent parts of the night next to Nigel and other parts with her other friends. Toward eleven o'clock, though, the gathering had gotten thin, and by midnight, it was as it had begun: Jason, Ellison, Nigel and Regina.

Regina got up to start loading the dishwasher when the buzzer rang.

"That'll be Michelle."

"I got it," Regina said on her way.

Regina welcomed Michelle in, got her something to eat and kept her company in the kitchen while doing some cleaning up.

"Why don't I know you from Charleston? I lived not too far from Nigel," Regina said.

"Our families weren't that close. We saw each other for weddings and funerals—that kind of thing," Michelle explained. "I was also a bit wild."

"I know what you mean."

When she was done, Michelle started helping Regina pick things up.

"Stop. You don't have to do that."

"I don't mind. Nigel really likes you. That makes you like family. You're lucky, Regina. He's a good guy."

Regina didn't know what to do with the comment, so she simply smiled.

After Michelle left with Andre, Jason and Ellison got ready to leave with Kyle. At the door, Jason bent down and whispered to her.

"We need to talk, honey. I need a major update."

He nodded toward Nigel, who was saying good-night to Ellison, and winked at her. "Overnight guest?"

Regina waved him away but smiled as Nigel and Ellison approached them.

"Nice to meet you," Nigel said to Jason, shaking his hand.

"You, too," said Jason.

When the door closed, Regina was left standing alone with Nigel.

She looked up at him.

"You want help with the rest of the cleanup?"

"Okay."

"I was worried about you after today," Nigel said.

She was doing some of the dishes in the sink, and he was wrapping up the leftovers.

"I'm over it, for now at least."

"Good. It'll be okay. Hey, we're almost done. You up for a late-night movie?"

"Like?"

"I still have the one the kids watched."

She laughed. "That sounds fun. And thank you for bringing the pasta and for the sweetgrass basket. It's perfect. You didn't have to."

"I wanted to. And I had a great time tonight."

She knew he had. He had laughed a lot, and the serious man he had become had slipped away for the night.

They curled up together on the couch and started the movie. It was strange to her—the way they were getting along. She needed to process it, figure it out, but right then, it simply felt comfortable.

"Oh, no. The robots' children are being reprogrammed," Nigel cried, and they both laughed. "What do they make for kids these days?"

"Stop. It's cute."

He rubbed her head. "Aww."

Regina found herself looking at him more than the movie, and finally she turned to simply stare. She stopped and turned her head back to the television as she reached up and ran her fingers down his face. She repositioned herself on the couch and bent toward him until her mouth was next to his ear. But she didn't say anything. She kissed his lobe and ran her tongue along the inside of his ear.

Nigel got still for a moment, but as she continued, he brought his hands to rest around her back. She wanted to turn him on. She had never wanted to turn a man on so much in her life.

"What are you doing?"

"Do you want me to stop?"

"No. Hell, no."

Regina moved down from his ear to his neck, moving her hand up to his chest. Frustrated, she pulled his shirt out of his pants and slid her hands underneath, playing with his nipples.

He moaned softly, and she felt her womanhood inflame. Turning him on was making her hot and wet, and she didn't want to stop.

She shifted herself onto him, straddling his thighs, and brought her mouth to his, gently running her lips over his before opening her mouth to him. He dragged her up his lap to sit flush against his body, but she didn't want him to be the one in control, not just yet.

When she started rocking her hips over his thighs, Nigel moaned and squeezed her waist.

"Can you feel that?" she asked.

"Yes, yes."

She unbuttoned his shirt to have freer access to his chest. Then she pulled her dress over her head and took off her bra. She ran her breasts over his chest, rocking her hips over him until the center of her heat undulated over his manhood. Then she couldn't help moaning.

Nigel moved his hand over one of her breasts, but she took it away and pressed herself back against his chest. Then Nigel moved his hand between them, using his thumb to caress her. She knew that he must feel her wetness through the thin mesh of her panties. But at that moment, such exquisite anguish filled her body that she could only cry out and oscillate against him.

She hadn't meant it to happen this way, but as his finger moved over her, it filled her body with an excruciating ache. She pulled back from him and gripped his shoulders as pleasure tore through her center. His finger continued to move over her, and she couldn't stop herself from rocking over it, from riding along his body. She couldn't stop, even knowing that he was watching her shameless gyration. As her womanhood convulsed, she cried out, shuddering as waves of contractions flowed through her center.

When her body had started to calm, she felt naked and embarrassed and looked at him to see what he was thinking. His eyes were glazed over with passion, but he must have seen her hesitation.

"That was the most erotic thing I've ever experienced," he said, looking directly in her eyes.

She smiled and kissed him, grateful.

Then she felt down between them.

"It's not over yet."

She got up from his lap and pulled him up with her. Then she took his hand and led him to the bedroom. It was late, but she was going to have her way the rest of the night.

Chapter 14

Nigel switched the phone from one ear to the other.

"I can't tonight," Regina said on the other line. "I just found out that my father's having surgery. They didn't tell me because they didn't want to worry me with all that I have on my plate right now. But it's major surgery, and it's tomorrow. My aunt, his sister, has already flown in from Charleston to New Jersey. I can't take my car, and the last Amtrak train leaves at ten o'clock, which I can't make. Maybe I should just take my car."

"Slow down. What's going on?"

Regina took a breath that was audible over the line. "I'm sorry. I didn't mean to unload on you. I'm just a bit frantic right now."

"Why can't you drive?"

"I've been having minor trouble with my car. A pinging sound that comes and goes, trouble starting sometimes. I don't trust it before the next tune-up."

"I'll drive you."

"You have to work tomorrow."

"I can get back in time. I'm checking driving times on-line right now. What time do you want to leave?"

"It's almost nine now. How about ten, when the train leaves? I can't make it to the station, but I can be ready by then."

"Have you eaten?"

"Yes."

"I'll get a snack for myself on the way and see you at ten. It takes three and a half hours to get to Trenton. It's a straight shot on I-95. We'll make it fine, and I'll be back in time for work."

"You'll be up all night."

"I'll be fine. I'll see you at ten."

Nigel changed out of his good suit, stopped for a sandwich at a convenience store and headed over to Regina's early. He ate on the couch while she called her mom, started packing, called work and left a message, emailed her boss, called Amelie about the booth at Eastern Market over the weekend, finished packing and changed. It was nine forty-five when she was done with everything and sat down to fidget. He ate his late dinner knowing that his main job was to simply be there and to stay out of the way.

"If you're ready, let's leave early so you can get some sleep when you get there," he said.

"I don't think I'll be able to sleep, but we might as well go."

"Don't worry." He rubbed her shoulder. "You'll be there soon."

Along the way Nigel learned that they'd found a growth in her father's liver. Tests couldn't tell if it was malignant or benign, but the goal was to go in and get it out regardless.

Regina was nervous, and he did his best to ease her tension, but all he could really do was listen and be an arm for her to rest on.

They got to Trenton just after one and to her parents' house before one-thirty. Regina's parents were asleep, but her aunt let them in. He stayed long enough to use the restroom, make sure Regina had her cell phone and say good-night.

She walked him to the door, worry written over her features.

"Try not to stress, Reggie," he said.

He pulled her into his arms, and she clung to him for a moment. He tightened his embrace and just held her.

They didn't stir until she took a deep breath and let go.

"Thank you, Nigel. This means—"

He found her mouth with his and muffled her words. He felt her open to his kiss, and when he pulled away, her arms remained wrapped around his neck.

"I'll be there for you, Reggie," he said. "I'll never let you down again."

"Thank you."

They didn't step apart until they heard Regina's aunt rustling in the kitchen. They lingered for a moment and moved together into one final hug.

"He's in good hands," Nigel said. "Don't worry."

Regina nodded, and he turned to go.

He was home in time to grab a couple hours of sleep before heading to the office.

He spoke to her a couple of times that week. The surgery had gone well, and the tumor was benign. It was relatively small, and her father would be home recovering by the end of the week.

"When should I come pick you up?"

"I can take the train back. It's not a panic like it was coming here."

"I can come pick you up. That way, I get to see you, spend a little time with you. Just tell me when."

She hesitated for a minute.

"With my aunt here and my dad doing well, I don't need to stay too long. Why don't you come on Saturday, stay over and we can leave on Sunday?"

"Do your parents have room for me, or should I find a hotel? I don't mind staying in a hotel. In fact, it would be best, with your father just home recovering."

"No. There's a den with a pullout sofa. It won't be a problem."

Now it was his turn to hesitate. "Sure?"

"Sure."

"Okay. I'll be there at noon on Saturday," he said. "That gives us time to run errands."

"See you then."

"Bye, baby."

He spent a good part of the week working on the designs he had for her application and getting more information from Amelie for his plans. As the weekend approached, he was more than ready to see her again, though he was nervous about meeting her parents after all that had happened between them. And he was right to be nervous, at least in part.

He called her just before he got there to let her know he was close. She met him at the door of her parents' home in Trenton's West Ward. They greeted each other with a brief hug, but he gritted his teeth as she led him inside.

"Mom, Aunt April, you remember Nigel."

Her mother was the one to speak.

"I don't have to think too hard after how he broke your heart."

"I know, Mom. That was a while ago."

Nigel finally found his voice. "Hello, Mrs. Gibson."

He stood near the door with his backpack, looking into the living room where the two older women were seated. Behind them was a dining set and a doorway leading to the kitchen, and off to his left were stairs leading up to the second story.

As he took in their home, Regina's mother was eyeing him up and down, making it clear that "a while ago" didn't matter. He had broken her baby's heart.

"Well, come in. Put your things down in here."

"How is Mr. Gibson doing, ma'am?"

She sighed and softened a bit. "We brought him home yesterday. Still has pain but has medication to take. They just rush folks out of the hospital these days. Soon as he could walk down the hall, they let him go. But the good thing is that the surgery went well, so he's out. Sleeping now."

"This is for him."

Nigel handed her a gift bag that held a housecoat and a toiletry set. She looked inside but didn't take anything out.

"That's thoughtful of you. We'll wait 'til he wakes before giving it to him.

"Well, Nigel Johns." She turned to face him and looked at him hard. "I ain't forgot how you tore this one to pieces." She gestured at Regina, and he swallowed hard. "But I thank you for bringing her up here Monday night and for coming to get her."

He could tell that he was being placed on warning. He'd done it once. He better not do it again, not even if he was being nice about bringing her home.

"It's no problem at all, Mrs. Gibson."

"You look like you made out okay for yourself. How're your folks? They still in the old neighborhood?"

"Yes, ma'am. They're still in Charleston in the same place. They're doing fine."

Thankfully, Regina stepped in.

"Nigel, I have some errands for us to run."

"And I need to check on your father," her mother said.

After Regina's mother went upstairs, her aunt April came out of the kitchen and offered them some iced tea.

"I remember you, too, son. You turned out good. Don't worry about Maretha too much. She'll come around."

"Thank you, ma'am."

It was thanks for both the tea and the welcoming words.

Nigel exhaled and turned to Regina. "Errands sound good."

They both chuckled.

"I'm sorry about my mom."

"Don't be. She's right to be protective of you."

"I know, but I'm still sorry."

Nigel put down his empty glass. "Let's get to those errands."

"Aunt April, when we come back, we're taking you out to dinner. Okay?"

"That'll be nice. Y'all be careful."

They picked up a few movies in the department store—a couple of Westerns for her father, a couple for them to watch that night.

"You know this city pretty well for a South Carolinian," Nigel commented.

"My parents moved here when I was in college, remember?"

"Yeah, I do now. I noticed how strong your mom's accent sounds. We don't notice it until we're somewhere up north."

Regina smiled. "I know. And notice how we've lost ours? Assimilationism."

They both chuckled.

"I hope my mom didn't put you off."

"No, don't worry about it. She has every right to be angry with me after all that happened. Did she know about...the pregnancy?"

A sternness came into Regina's face, and he almost wished he hadn't asked. "No."

The severe look on her face made him let it go, even though he wanted to say more.

"I'm sorry," she said. "It's a sore spot. But don't take my parents too much to heart. It was a bad time for me."

"I thought I knew that, but now I understand even more."

She didn't say anything else, so he let it go, and they started on their last errand.

Regina knew the city, but she didn't know the grocery store. It took them a while to complete the list, but they liked feeling that they were helping out. They also threw in a few extra items: some meats, a selection of gourmet cookies, some nutrition-boosting drinks for her father.

When they got back to her parents' house, her father was awake, and Regina went up to sit with him for a little while. After an hour or so, she called down to Nigel.

"Yes. What can I do?"

"Come up and say hello to my dad."

Nigel took a breath and climbed the steps to Regina.

"Knock and go in," she whispered.

He did. Mr. Gibson was propped up in bed with his eyes closed. He opened them to look at Nigel when he entered but then spoke with them closed.

"Come in, Nigel. Sit for a moment."

Nigel went in and took the seat next to the bed.

"Good evening, Mr. Gibson. How are you feeling?"

"I've had better days. Still sore from the surgery, but it

looks like they got everything. Took some pain medicine when I got up about two hours ago."

"I hope you feel better soon, Mr. Gibson."

"Now, what are you doing with my daughter again?"

He hadn't even tried to soften the blow. Nigel wasn't prepared for the question, but he knew he had to answer with the truth.

"I love your daughter, Mr. Gibson. She's the only woman in the world I want to be with—if she'll have me. I don't know that yet. But I want to find out."

He opened his eyes to look at Nigel for a moment and then closed them again.

"You cracked her heart open before, boy. You know what it's like to see your own child cry, and you can't do nothing about it?"

Nigel's mind went to the child that hadn't come to be, and it made the question real.

"No, sir."

"I won't let you hurt her again. Know that."

"I won't, sir. I promise."

"Good. Keep that word. A man is his word."

"Yes, sir." Mr. Gibson was quiet after that. "I'll let you rest, sir. Let me know if you need anything."

"Good night, boy."

Nigel headed downstairs. He felt like he'd been grilled again, but he also understood why. In fact, he understood why even more now. When Regina called off their wedding, to him, it was like being put out. But to her? Even though she was the one to call it off, it had hurt her in ways he hadn't understood then, and then the baby… Being here only emphasized to him the real extent of her pain.

He looked at Regina, who was sitting on the couch talking to her mother and aunt. She smiled at him as he neared. He wanted to talk to her, but it would have to wait.

They took Aunt April to dinner and then to do a little shopping downtown before the stores closed. She didn't need anything, but she wanted to get out a little bit while she was visiting her brother up north. After that they sat and talked with her mother, watched one of the movies they'd gotten and turned in.

It toyed with his urges to be sleeping in the same house with Regina when he couldn't hold her, but he also understood what it meant that she had let him come see her family and stay overnight.

The next day they let Nigel sleep in until after ten o'clock.

"You needed to get your rest, son, all this driving," Mrs. Gibson said.

"I'm usually up early. I guess I did need it."

"Here, take this up to Mr. Gibson before you head out."

"Head out?"

"We're going to get everybody brunch," Regina said.

"Hold his head while he drinks it. Then leave it on the table."

Nigel took the cup of nutritional supplement upstairs and knocked on the door before entering.

"I have a drink for you, Mr. Gibson."

"Come in."

"I'm supposed to hold your head while you drink," he said, propping the older man's head up with his hand and holding the cup to his mouth. It was a little awkward, especially after the talk they'd had the day before, but being asked to do it made him feel that they'd started to forgive him—both Regina's mother, who had asked him to do it, and her father, who allowed him to do it. "Just let me know when you've had enough."

"There. That's good. Thank you, son."

"I'll leave it here for you. Do you need anything else?"

"Find me something on the television."

Nigel sat down, found the remote and started flipping through channels, not sure where to stop.

"Here's *Law and Order*. Do you like that?"

"Not right now."

"Here's a Western. How about that?"

"That's good. Leave it there. Thank you."

"We'll be back soon, sir."

"Good."

Nigel went back downstairs to find Regina smiling at him again, and they headed out to the restaurant in his car.

"What's the smile for?" he asked.

"I'm just glad to see that my parents have mellowed out about you."

"Yeah, I guess they have. I wonder why?"

"I don't care why," she said, "as long as they stop the cold-shoulder routine."

"It's understandable."

"They should get over it."

He turned to her, seriously.

"Can *you* get over it?"

She waved the question away, but he couldn't let it go.

It came up again when they stopped for lunch on the three-and-a-half-hour ride home.

"Reggie, can we talk?"

"Yeah. What?"

He reached across the table and took her hand.

"I tried to say this before at your parent's house, but we were busy, and we couldn't just sit down and talk. I hurt you. I hurt you more than I realized. I guess I thought that because you had been the one to call things off, you couldn't be as devastated as I was. And I didn't know about losing the baby. I didn't know that I wasn't there when you were going through that. And your parents didn't know, so they weren't there. You were alone."

She sighed. "I was."

"That's why you can't forgive me. But I'm sorry. I never meant to hurt you that way. I never meant not to be there."

"I know."

"I'd do anything to make those things up to you, if I could. I just need you to know that."

"Okay," she said.

"Okay."

They finished their lunch in silence and then got back on the road.

Could she forgive him? It was the question that would determine his future, but he couldn't bring himself to ask it out loud. He couldn't face all the possible answers, especially because underneath that question was another. Could he forgive himself?

As they drove, Nigel drew her closer to his side and took her hand in his. They were quiet. With her warm body near his, all he could think was how much he loved this woman, how glad he was that she was next to him, how much he wanted to have her in his life.

Chapter 15

Regina had just finished teaching a mosaics class at the school of one of her friends, an art teacher, and she got home to find that she'd missed another call from Nigel.

Regina was beginning to worry. She had been wrong about Nigel; or rather, she had been right. She had always thought that he was smart and that he had potential. But now she was starting to get used to seeing him, starting to want to see him, and that bothered her. After their past, she had to be the stupidest person in the world for even still talking to him. She remembered his question. Could she get over it?

It was one thing when it was only physical. Now he had met her friends, had visited her folks, was getting along with everyone. And worse, she liked it that he did. It was getting muddier and muddier. She'd been ignoring his calls for a few days and was determined to put a bit of distance between them. She picked up the phone and called him back. It was time to put on the brakes.

"Hey. Can you talk, or are you still at work?"

"I'm between clients. I can talk. I need to know why you've been avoiding me, not returning my calls. What's going on? Wait, do you want to have dinner tonight and talk in person?"

"I can't. I'm seeing Jason and Elli tonight."

It wasn't an excuse. She did already have plans.

"Then tell me now. Why are you avoiding me?"

"I'm not avoiding you. I just don't want to get too dependent, too serious."

"Too serious?"

She heard the surprise in his voice.

"Yes. We've been seeing a lot of each other. I don't want it to become…"

"To become?"

She couldn't find other words at the moment, so she repeated herself.

"Too serious."

He paused for a second and then sought clarification.

"You think we've been getting too close, talking too often, seeing each other too much?"

"Yes."

He was silent. When he spoke again, his voice was softer.

"Don't you enjoy our time together?"

"Yes, maybe too much."

She regretted the words as they came out of her mouth. She had given away her own state of ambivalence and confusion. She hurriedly tried to cover her tracks.

"I don't want us to get too attached. I can't go back there, remember? I need to put on the brakes."

She heard him sigh.

"I guess things have been going pretty quickly recently. We can slow it down. Let's go out next week. How about

Thursday? I'll call you on Wednesday, and I won't nag you by phone until then. How's that?"

She didn't have a reason handy to say no.

"Okay."

"I'll get us tickets for something, and we'll have dinner. Sound good?"

"Okay."

"Reggie."

"Yes?"

"I'll have some news on the application by then. I just got one response. The news is good so far. The one we really need, though, the one who works at a bank—he needs more time. It's taking longer than I thought."

"I know. Has Amelie gotten you the last pieces of information you said you needed to update her personal finances?"

"No, she hasn't. But with this delay, it doesn't really matter."

"And with no space as yet. I'm still looking."

"I know. We can talk more next week."

"Okay."

Nigel hung up the phone. When he'd called her name, he'd wanted to say "I love you."

He'd been worried about her. Now, he was glad that she was all right, but he had to deal with her putting on "the brakes" when his body ached for her.

"Too much," she'd said. She enjoyed their time together too much. This woman loved him and didn't want to love him. Maybe he should understand it after how much she'd been hurt, but he wanted them to have passed that already. It *felt* like they were past that already.

He'd wanted to tell her again that he loved her, but instead he'd diverted their attention to the business proposals and loan application. He needed to give her an update about that anyway, before she started asking. But he didn't want that to become the only reason they saw each other.

He wanted to talk about it more.

He would see her next Thursday. Until then, he would just have to wait.

Regina met Jason, Ellison and Kyle at a children's restaurant out in Maryland where they had planned to have dinner and play with Kyle. She got lost on the way there and was late, so Kyle and Ellison had already eaten, and Kyle was already playing in a ball pit by the time she got there. Ellison was at the side watching him and waved at her when she came in.

"Have you eaten, too?"

"No," Jason said. "I've been waiting for you."

"Sorry I'm late."

They ordered burgers when the waitress came around, and then Jason got down to the real talk.

"So?"

Regina sighed. She knew what he was quizzing her about.

"So we decided to be friends."

"With benefits?" He raised a brow. He already knew the answer.

"Well, yes."

He swallowed his bite and leaned across the table. "What I saw wasn't just friends."

"I know. It's way out of hand. I don't actually know what to do."

"What about what happened before? Are you over that?"

She shrugged. "I don't know."

"Do you like being with him now?"

Regina didn't want to admit it but had to. "Yes. But I

don't want it to get serious. I don't want to get back in a relationship with him."

"What I saw was already a relationship."

"I'd been ignoring his calls for a few days. It is like we're dating, but that's not what I want."

Jason was very matter-of-fact. "You want to be friends with benefits."

She shrugged. "I guess."

"And if he wants more?"

"That's the problem."

He eyed her closely. "You seem to like it when it's more."

"That's a problem, too."

Jason laughed. "Girl, you're confused."

"That's a problem, too."

They both laughed.

Then Jason got more serious. "You may not be able to have it both ways, sweetie. It sounds like you need to make a decision."

Regina sighed and toyed with her French fries. She knew that Jason was right.

Chapter 16

Nigel picked Regina up on Thursday at seven. He'd gotten them tickets for an eight o'clock show at the Arena Stage, and he'd found an all-night diner on Connecticut Avenue where they could have a late supper afterwards.

It would have been better if they could start with dinner so she wouldn't get hungry during the show, but he had to work a bit late doing the books for two companies that were merging. Regina didn't seem to mind.

She was dressed for a night at the theater when he got to her door, and she smiled at him. She seemed delighted to be going out. It wasn't what he had expected after her talk about them needing to slow down, but then, she had always been the type to get excited for a night out. He hoped she was delighted to be going out *with him*.

She had on a strapless white cocktail dress. The top was crinkled and hugged her body down to her hips. From there it flared out into a wide skirt that was covered in organza and ended above the knee. Along with that she had on a matching organza shawl and high-heeled strappy silver shoes. Her hair was piled in newly set curls on the crown of her head, with a studded barrette holding it in place. She was nothing short of a vision.

There was a slight reserve about her at first, but when she found him staring at her, speechless, she opened the shawl out behind her and twirled slowly on her heels, grinning, all reservation gone.

"You like?"

"You're gorgeous."

She laughed, made a hop. Then she just smiled.

He was still frustrated over the moratorium she'd put on their seeing one another, but in the face of her playfulness and obvious cheer, he started to forget all their troubles.

"We haven't really been out before, have we?" he asked.

She looked puzzled.

"I mean just out to have a good time, not to do something else."

She thought about it. "I guess not."

"Well, this will be good for us then. I hope you like the show."

"I will. What is it?"

He chuckled.

"You can't say you'll like it if you don't know what it is. It's called *Shooting Star*. It's a musical about a Black woman who's struggling to become a singer. I guess it's in line with *Dreamgirls*."

"Sounds good. Let's go."

He was proud to have her on his arm when they entered the theater and pleased that despite what she'd said the other day, she seemed happy to be with him. Throughout the show, he kept his arm around her, and she leaned over in her chair to nestle against him. During one of the musical numbers, they were bobbing together in unison, their heads almost touching. They looked at each other and broke out laughing. He kissed her forehead and pulled her closer.

After the show, they headed to the diner.

"I'm sorry to bring you to a diner in such a lovely gown. Most places are closed already."

"I love diners."

"Still, it doesn't fit."

"It suits me fine."

They ordered and talked about her business proposal and loan application while they were waiting for their dinners to arrive. He updated her on the feedback he was supposed to be collecting, repeating what he'd said on the phone in more detail.

Then they talked about how her search for a location was going. It hadn't gotten anywhere yet, but she hadn't given up hope. He found out that her father was recovering a little more each day and that she had taught an art class last week for a friend working at a private high school.

They talked about everything except what they most needed to talk about. He thought about broaching the subject of their relationship a dozen times. But each time, he put it aside, not wanting to disturb the warmth between them.

When they were finished, he wrapped his arm around her again, squeezed her thigh and said, "Come home with me."

"Okay."

He hadn't expected her to say yes but was elated when she did.

"But I have to be home early in the morning," she said. "I have to be at work by eight."

"Me, too."

They drove back to his apartment and settled into the living room together. He'd never spent time with her at his place before, and despite the unanswered questions that hung between them, he was thrilled to see her curled up on his sectional, her shoes discarded on the floor, her white dress standing out against the black leather, her bare shoulders calling to his lips.

He took off his jacket and slid over on the couch, positioning himself so that he could kiss her, and then he stopped.

"Can I get you something more comfortable to sleep in?"

He would love to see her lounging about his place covered only in one of his big white dress shirts, giving him access to all the curves of her body. The image excited him almost as much as the reality of her before him.

"Maybe later. Do I have to sleep in anything?" She said it with a saucy gleam in her eye.

He still needed to know how they were really going to proceed. Yet, with the beauty of her beckoning him, he put the question from his mind and brought his lips to her shoulder.

In response, she giggled and kicked out her feet in front of her.

He did it again. She giggled again. Another sensitive spot.

When they had been together in college, he had never really taken the time to explore her body like he was doing now. He was learning her secret places for the first time, and he liked being the one who really knew her that way.

He brought his lips back to her shoulder and felt her body tense for another tickle, but instead of kissing it with his lips, he drew his tongue lightly over the spot that made her giggle. Her chest arched forward, and a shiver ran through her body.

He did it again. She brought her arms around him and pressed her lips to his ear and murmured, sending goose bumps down his back and heat into his groin.

He lifted her from the couch, careful not to tear the organza mesh over the skirt of her dress. She wrapped her arms about him and let him carry her into the bedroom. This time, there were no errands to run, no locations to see, no places they had to rush off to.

He pulled down the spread and top sheet and laid her in the middle of his bed. Then he kicked off his shoes and climbed in next to her where he could continue to play with her shoulders.

As he ran his tongue along her shoulder, he smoothed his fingers over the crinkled fabric covering her chest, making her arch toward him. In response, she moved her hand over the front of his pants, teasing him mercilessly.

But he was going to get back at her. He slipped his hand under the wide skirt of her dress and ran it up along her thighs until her body convulsed under his touch. His tongue still played over her shoulder. He wanted to taste every inch of her body, and tonight he would take his time.

Nigel was up before the alarm went off at six. He extricated his limbs from around Regina's sleeping body, shut off the alarm, slipped on his briefs and headed into the kitchen to make them breakfast. He woke her up with a tray of eggs, toast, cereal, milk, juice and coffee.

Regina rubbed her eyes and pulled the covers up over her naked body, but he handed her his shirt from the previous night.

She smiled and slipped into it as he settled into bed beside her with the tray.

"What time is it?"

"It's just after six. That gives us time for breakfast before I get you home."

"Okay." She smiled and dug into the eggs.

"So when can I call you?"

He could no longer avoid the questions of the previous day. He had to know how to proceed from there.

She looked at him. "What?"

"You said I call too much, and I don't want to cramp you. When can I call?"

"I don't know," she said, pouring milk into both of their cereal bowls. "Play it by ear."

"Reggie, our ears are different on this. I was happy with how we were going. You were the one who thought it was getting to be too much."

"It was just starting to seem to get too heavy."

Too much like dating, he thought. The irony wasn't lost on him, them having just been on a real date and all the night before.

"I don't mean to push too hard."

He wasn't saying what he really wanted to say, but he didn't want to chase her away.

"I know," she said. "Eat your cereal before it gets soft."

They ate quietly for a little while.

"I just enjoy spending time with you," he said. "I don't—"

"I do, too. Let's just leave it at that."

He nodded his head. She had shut him down again. There was no way around the blockade. He settled back on the bed, and they turned to their breakfast again. But he had questions that needed to be answered.

When they finished, he put the tray on his nightstand and drew her under his arm.

"I just need to know how to go on from here. I don't

want you avoiding my calls because you think it's getting too heavy."

"Look, Nigel. We're not going to agree on this. Let's let it go and just…"

"Just what? I can't even play it by ear if I don't know what you're thinking."

"I'm thinking that I just want to be friends, enjoy time with you, without it getting too serious."

"Define *too serious*."

"Look," she said. She was agitated and rustled under his arm. "I just can't go back there."

"What about us now? What about me now?"

"I like now, just as it is."

He lifted the arm he had around her to play with the strands of hair that had fallen to her temples.

"Okay, but tell me this. What's so wrong with getting a little serious? The times we've been intimate, didn't you feel anything?"

She backed away from him, clearly flustered. "I just enjoyed it, that's all."

"You seemed to feel something for me last night."

"Nigel, stop pushing for something that's not there."

He was pushing, and he knew he should stop, but something in him wanted her to admit that she had feelings for him, that it was more than physical. They had both gotten to their feet. She had snatched up her things and was pulling her dress up under the shirt he'd given her to wear.

"Wasn't last night real? Didn't you want me? Not sex in general, but me."

"It was what it was. Remember? Nothing more."

He could tell that she was getting more agitated and was ready to go, and he was just as upset. He pulled on his socks and pants and took his shirt from the bed where she'd tossed it. He put it on so that he would be ready to drive her home. No use suggesting a shower together now.

"Are you ready to go?" he asked.

"Yes, but wait." She seemed to have calmed down slightly. She came and sat on the bed next to him and looked at him. "If you're going to get serious, then maybe we should call this off."

He looked at her; she was serious. It made him angry that she could suggest tossing everything aside so easily, as if it didn't really mean anything to her, especially after the night they'd spent together.

"If that's how you see it."

As he said it, matching her nonchalance, he wondered what he was doing. But it was out. And if she could dismiss him so easily, maybe it was for the best.

"Okay," she said and walked into the living room.

Okay, if that's the way she wanted it.

He drove her home in silence and watched her trek up to the third-story landing and go inside. Then he headed back to his place to shower and get to work.

His world had been turned upside down overnight by Regina Gibson. Once she had ended their relationship because he wasn't serious enough. Now she was ending their relationship because he was too serious.

"If you're going to get serious, then maybe we should call this off."

So be it. She wanted a break. She would have a break.

Chapter 17

Regina pulled up the bottom of her overalls and squatted in front of one of her pieces in the spare bedroom that she used as a studio. She'd already carried the bulk of them over to the gallery, leaving anything that had a flaw or that hadn't come out quite right. These she was double-checking. It was her last chance to get things there before the showing, and she wanted as much of her work on display as possible.

She hadn't seen or heard from Nigel in several weeks, and her mind went to him now because he'd been in this room with her. It was here that he'd touched her that time, driving her crazy. She missed having his arms around her, his fingers touching her. She missed knowing that they would be together again.

She'd gotten used to him. That was the problem. Maybe she shouldn't have said they should call it off, but it was the wise thing to do. Between her getting used to him and him turning serious on her, things had gotten muddled beyond clarification.

She turned a tiled sculpture around on the table. Why hadn't she taken this one? The grout color hadn't turned out as she'd wanted it, but she couldn't find anything else wrong, so it went on the table near the door. She'd get one more load of pieces to carry to the gallery tonight, and that would be it. She'd be there late setting up for tomorrow evening.

She'd thought about inviting him to her gallery showing, but that wouldn't make sense. She didn't know if he would even agree to come after she'd called it quits. If he did, that would just start things up again. It would open the door to the same unanswerable questions. Can't we just be friends? Isn't there more going on here?

She lifted a large board to the table and turned the light toward it. What was wrong with this piece? Ah, the grout had pulled away from the tile in one area. It would have to stay.

It didn't make sense thinking about him. She had been the one to call it off. She should just stick to what she'd said and remember why she'd said it: she wasn't going back there.

She got the car loaded, grabbed a sandwich and headed to the Spring View Art Gallery in Silver Spring. Her work would be there for a month, and she hoped that there would be enough sales to boost her depleted savings account. She was putting several ads in the *Washington Post* and had fliers made up to hand out. It was an extra effort, but she needed it to pay off.

She got finished setting up in time to get home, sleep for a few hours and get to work. After that, she came back to change into something suitable for that night. She decided on the gown she'd worn two summers before to a girlfriend's wedding—the turquoise satin one with spaghetti straps that was cut close to her body and that had a matching bolero jacket made out of lace. She finished the outfit with black pumps and a black pocketbook. It was an important night, and she wanted to dress for the occasion.

Once she arrived at the gallery, she saw that most of the people there were people she knew, with a few gallery-goers mixed into the gathering. Then she saw Nigel. He was with Lillith, the manager of the gallery, who was putting a sold sticker on a piece that he was pointing to.

Lillith saw her looking and beckoned her over. "Regina, we've sold our first three pieces—three of the larger ones. This is—"

"Nigel Johns. I know him."

Lillith must have caught the look that passed between them because she excused herself. "Let me go see if I can help some of our other patrons while you catch up. Thank you, Mr. Johns. You can pick these up after the showing. Here's my card."

As she passed by Regina, she pointed discreetly at Nigel, mouthed "hottie" and gave Regina a wink. Lillith was such a prim matron that the gestures made Regina laugh.

Once Lillith was gone, Regina found herself smiling up at Nigel. She couldn't help feeling glad to see him.

"Hello, Nigel. I'm surprised to see you here. I thought about giving you a call to let you know about the show, but then, we weren't really…in touch."

"I found out from Amelie and saw one of your announcements in the *Post*."

"Did Amelie get you her info for the application?"

"Not yet, but she's been in contact to let me know that she's pulling it together."

"Oh, good," Regina said. "We're going out this week together to look at more locations."

"Let me know how it goes. I think that's all you need now."

"I know."

He backed up to point at one of the mosaics he'd purchased.

"I came early to get the pick of the litter. I'm sending a few of my clients along to take a look as well, and one's a new restaurant owner. I had to get mine before they came in and took the best ones. This is one of the ones I'm getting."

"Nigel, you don't have to buy anything. Just coming out to show your support is more than enough."

"No, I actually needed at least three pieces—one to add color to the living room, one for the bedroom and one to show off in my office."

"You didn't have to get them here. You got large ones, and these are gallery prices. I could have—"

"It's worth paying them, especially when one day I'll own the work of a famous artist."

Regina couldn't help smiling.

"Thank you. Now let me tell you how to take care of them."

"How about over a late supper? What time do you get through here?"

"We close at eight tonight, but I don't know if it's a good idea for us to…get together."

"I've missed you terribly, Reggie. Come to dinner with me."

Before she could answer, he stepped toward her, pulled her into his arms and bent down to claim her lips. His kiss was so sudden, so passionate, that it knocked the breath out of her and started a throbbing in her center. He pulled away just as quickly.

"I won't take no as an answer."

When they stepped apart, she glanced around in time to see Jason giving her a naughty look. She laughed out loud. Being with this man made her act silly.

Nigel looked over and saw Jason and nodded to him and Ellison before waving to Kyle, who waved back from his place on Ellison's hip. He struggled to get down, and when Ellison relented, he ran over to Nigel.

Nigel picked him up and gave him a hug.

"Here, give Auntie Regina a kiss."

Nigel held Kyle like an airplane and the little one giggled as he landed on Regina and gave her a kiss.

"Okay," said Nigel. "That's enough. Those lips are spoken for."

Regina raised her finger to protest but thought the better of it. There was such a simple pleasure in the moment that she didn't want to spoil it.

"Were you going out with friends after to celebrate the opening?"

"A few of us were going to go to dinner. You can join us if you'd like."

"That would be nice.

"And can I see you after dinner, as well?"

"I'm not sure we should...hang out."

"There's no getting out of it, Reggie. I've missed you too much."

Kyle started struggling to get down. Nigel put him on his feet, and they watched him until he'd returned to his parents, who were talking with Amelie now.

Nigel pulled Regina into his arms again.

"Haven't you missed me, too?"

"Well…I guess." She was trying to deny it but couldn't. They both broke out laughing.

"If you don't admit it, I'll have to use unorthodox means to get you to confess."

He turned his fingers into spiders and ran them up her stomach. She giggled and tried to shoo him away.

"Okay, yes."

"I'm sorry," he said. "I'm just in a funny mood tonight. It's seeing you and seeing that you're glad to see me."

Lillith came up to them.

"We have another purchase. Come meet the buyers."

"Clients of yours?" she asked Nigel.

"No, they're not." He kissed her temple. "I'll go say hello to your friends while you go do your thing."

He walked over to her group of friends standing next to the wine and cheese table, and she gave her attention to Lillith and the customers. After that, Lillith drew her around the exhibit to talk to visitors. It was delightful to hear their comments on her work and to answer questions. Not many were buying, but she hoped that at least a few would come back another time.

Whenever she glanced over, she found Nigel talking to Jason, Ellison and Amelie. From the looks of it, they were having a good time together; they all seemed jovial.

When it was almost eight, she turned from the guest she'd been talking to and found Lillith, who was writing a receipt out for the last purchase of the night.

"We sold over a dozen pieces. For a relatively unknown artist, that's great. It bodes well for the rest of the show. We also had a great turnout."

"Well, I had a lot of my friends come in tonight."

"Keep them coming."

"I will. I made cards to send out to everyone I know and everyone I've ever worked with and everyone I've ever taken classes from. If there are any left over, I'll hand them out to strangers on the street."

"That's great. Wait. Let me dim the lights so people know it's time to go."

Lillith dimmed the lights and then brought them all the way up. The remaining guests started meandering toward the door, so Regina went to say good-night and hand out her business cards to them as they left. It was just after eight when she sought out the little group that had been waiting for her.

"We're going to have to cut out," said Jason.

"No, but you waited all this time," she responded.

"I know, but this one's getting tired. He's been getting a bit antsy."

She pursed her lips and fingered Kyle's little tummy. "Is the little one tired?"

"We're gonna stop for some fast food and get him home."

"Okay." She hugged Kyle, then Ellison, then Jason. "Thank you so much for coming tonight."

"I'm going, too," said Amelie. "I have to be at Eastern Market tomorrow morning for setup."

She hugged Amelie. "Everybody's going?"

"Not me," said Nigel, coming to place a hand on her back.

"Did you do this? Did you chase my friends away?"

He raised his hands in innocence.

"Don't look at me. Eight o'clock on a Friday. Folks are tired."

She smacked his shoulder playfully, not fully believing his story.

Lillith came out and started wrapping up the cheese and crackers.

"Can I stay to do anything?" asked Regina.

"Nope. You've done your part. Head home. I'll see you next week."

"Okay," she said and hugged Lillith. "Thank you for everything."

"Good night, Regina. Good night, Mr. Johns."

They waved and headed to their cars.

Nigel pressed his palm on the small of Regina's back as they walked to her car. She was radiant in her shimmering gown, and it fit her body in a way that teased him with her every curve. It was her special night, and she looked it.

But it was his night, too. His reentry into her life had gone much better than he had dared to hope. He had been ready to dispute, debate and rebut, but he didn't have to. The bond between them had just been there.

As beautiful as she looked tonight, he just wanted to take her out so that the world could see that she was with him. And as sexy as she looked tonight, he just wanted to take her home where she would be only his.

"How do we do this?" she asked. "Should I follow you? Where are we going?"

"We're in Silver Spring. Let's go park in the lot for the mall. They have restaurants over there."

"Okay. We'll meet there."

They stayed close to one another on the road and parked next to each other in the lot.

They decided on Italian food and entered the restaurant together.

Over dinner, he kept smiling at her. She couldn't help smiling back.

"What?" she asked.

"You missed me."

She swatted at him across the table, but he knew that she couldn't rightly deny it. After this, they both knew that she was going home with him to make love. It wasn't because he insisted; it was because she wanted him, too, even if she wouldn't say it out loud.

"And you love me," he added.

She raised her hand, and he could tell that she was about to tell him a thing or two about the assumptions he was making, but he cut in.

"Don't get all in a huff." He smiled at her. "It's okay if you don't know it yet. And it's okay if you want to pretend it's not serious. I won't rush you."

"Your smug, know-it-all attitude is starting to piss me off," she said, but she couldn't hold her angry tone and broke out in a smile. "I'll correct you later. Right now, let's enjoy our food and tonight."

He touched her arm. "Tonight." He looked into her eyes, and the passion he saw there made him take a breath.

"I want you, Reggie."

He took her hand.

"Let's finish eating first," she said. She took a deep breath, and he could tell she was trying not to give herself away.

He smiled. "Okay. So how did the show go?"

"It went well. We sold over a dozen pieces."

"Congratulations, honey."

The rest of dinner was light conversation. Then they followed each other to his apartment.

They started kissing before the elevator door closed, and by the time they reached his floor, they were wrapped in each other's arms. Nigel closed the door to his apartment and pressed her against it with his body. Regina could feel the full length of him.

One of his hands came between them to cup her breast, and the other traveled up her thigh to grip her buttocks.

She murmured against his lips, and in response, he parted her lips, and his low groan filled her mouth.

She felt one of his legs come between hers and spread her thighs apart, and she opened for him, feeling his fingers begin to explore her through her clothes. She began to throb as his knuckles gently grazed the front of her gown, finding her center and sending tingles spreading throughout her body.

She lifted herself onto her toes to try to feel more of him, and he lifted her from her feet against his body, her back pressed to the door. Heat filled her center as it pressed onto his, and she couldn't help the moan that filled her throat and passed into his mouth.

He let her down and drew her to the bedroom.

She took off his suit jacket and hung it on the back of his chair. He unzipped her gown and sat on the edge of his bed, drawing her between his knees so that he could run his mouth over the fabric of her bra, licking her nipples into hard peaks while she gasped for air. When he ran his hand between her thighs and began to knead the wet slip of her panties, she bucked against his fingers and moaned.

Regina wanted to play, as well. She pushed Nigel back onto the bed, unbuttoned his shirt and brought her lips to one of his nipples. Her soft bites made him writhe, but not enough, so she ran her hand along the front of his pants until his body was jerking with her every touch and his groan filled her ears.

They stood to remove the rest of their clothes, and Nigel dug in his dresser for a condom. She took it from him. She sat on the edge of his bed and pulled him before her. She ran her hand over the hard ripples of his chest and down the firm line of his belly before opening the packet and taking out the slick disc. Then she rolled it onto him, and her mouth followed the path it had taken.

He moaned and called her name, spreading his fingers into her hair. When he stepped back from her, his eyes were glazed with passion, and he exhaled deeply. He moved onto the bed, covering her body.

"I want you, Reggie."

"I want you, too, Nigel."

She clung to his shoulders as he moved inside of her, finding her mouth again and filling her with his heat and his presence. He began to thrust against her, making her womanhood throb as his chest dragged along her breasts.

Then he found the place that made her lunge against him, and his long prods became short thrusts, making her cry out and gasp, making pressure begin to build in her center because he was pushing her toward the edge.

"Do you love me, Reggie?" he asked.

She heard him as from afar.

"Do you love me, Reggie?"

At first she couldn't answer; the pleasure mounting inside her blocked out rational thought, comprehensible language.

"Do you love me?"

Her body clenched.

"Yes."

"Do you love me?"

She felt the first wave of her explosion moving through her.

She cried out. "Yes."

"Do you love me?"

She moved along him as she was pushed over the edge.

"Yes, Nigel, yes."

Her sex began to quiver, and she pressed it against his length.

"Yes, yes."

* * *

Nigel felt Regina's body grip his even tighter. Her hands pressed into his back. Her hips tilted upward to meet his. Her thrusts matched his.

"Yes, Nigel."

Her answer was music to his ears, driving him toward the precipice. And once her voice was unleashed, she couldn't seem to stop it; it had become a mantra.

"Yes," she said and cried out.

Her legs began to shake at his hips, and her breath became short and labored.

"I do. I need you. Please."

He felt her body grip on to his again.

"Please what? I'll do anything."

"Don't stop."

"I won't."

Her womanhood clamped around him, causing him to buck. He felt the waves of her contraction as it pulsed through her and along his manhood.

"Yes," she called out, "yes."

Nigel could only groan as he plunged within her, driven over the edge.

They lay together as their breathing slowed. A broad smile spread across Nigel's face. She had said yes.

As their bodies cooled, she turned in his arms and raised herself on her elbows to see his face, which wore a silly grin.

"I knew you did," he said.

She slapped his arm. "No. I can't be held accountable for what I say in the throes of lovemaking."

"When you're not censoring yourself?"

"When I'm not thinking at all."

"I don't believe you. Or rather, I do."

She ran her hand down his face to try to get rid of his satisfied grin. "Stop smiling like that. I didn't know what I was saying."

She settled back down next to him, concern filling her. Soon they would start to make love again. Only, this time, it was making love and not just having sex. She was in love again—in love with Nigel Johns.

Chapter 18

Nigel picked his way through the crowd inside Eastern Market. The meat looked plump and fresh. If he wasn't hoping to get Regina to go to a movie with him, he would get some lamb shanks and some pork chops. In fact, as good as they looked, he still might.

He'd never been to Eastern Market before, much less on a cool weekend day near the end of summer. The place was packed. Inside, the shoppers filled the central aisle and formed packed lines in front of every counter. They were two or three deep in front of the produce bins, and as fresh as it looked, Nigel could understand why. He'd gotten some peaches from one of the farmers out front under the outdoor tent.

"Excuse me." He stopped an older woman. "Where would I find the jewelry and art?"

"That's at the flea market outside. Go through that door over there, and you'll see the booths."

"Thank you, ma'am."

"You're welcome."

He followed her directions to an area outside that was bigger than the indoor food market and separate from the farmer's market out front. Here, he started making his way through aisles of booths that had just about anything you could name. Furniture, crafts, housewares, art, jewelry, clothes, books, imports—more than he could have imagined.

He saw Amelie's jewelry first.

"Hey," she said as they hugged. "What are you doing here?"

"I'm looking for your partner."

"She just went to get us some drinks. She'll be back in a minute. Let me just help this lady, and then we can chat."

Amelie turned back to her customer, and he turned around to find some of Regina's mosaics on the opposite side of the table. They were mostly smaller pieces, ones that could be moved more easily. They were piled and stacked, with some out front as accents. This setting didn't allow them to be displayed properly.

The booth in front of them was an importer of African clothing—the kind Amelie and Regina wore often. Now he knew where they got them. Next to them was a glassworker's booth with everything from vases to plates. On the other side were exotic wooden pieces, some furniture but mostly light fixtures and ornaments. Behind them was a textile booth; he wasn't sure what was being sold there, perhaps tablecloths or wall hangings, maybe just material. Every direction had something unique.

"Can I help you?"

He turned around to find that it was Regina. She handed a bottle of juice to Amelie and turned back to him.

"Nigel, I didn't recognize you from behind without a suit on."

He stepped back and turned around with his arms out. He had on a white T-shirt, a blue sweat suit, striped sneakers and a baseball cap. He was showing her that he could do casual.

She smiled at him, but only for a moment. She wasn't as cheerful today.

"Actually, you *can* help me," he said. "I need something smallish that I can send to my mom. Her birthday's coming up. I was thinking about one of your mosaic African sculptures."

"Mosaics are heavy. It's pricey to mail them."

She didn't have many sculptures out, but he saw one that was what he had in mind. "How about this piece?"

"Why not some perfume? A nice dress?"

"Is she trying to talk you out of a sale, Nigel?" asked Amelie, smiling.

"Yes, she is."

"He's done too much already, Amelie. He got three pieces at the gallery—larger ones. That's more than enough."

Luckily, Amelie paid her no mind.

"Which one do you like, Nigel?"

"I was thinking about this one for my mom."

"Oh, I like that one, too."

Amelie picked it up and looked at the bottom. "It's $185, but for you, we can do $150. How's that?"

"I'll do the $185. Do you take checks?"

"From you we do. Make it out to Beads and Tiles."

"I like your new name better."

Amelie doubled a shopping bag, wrapped the sculpture in newspaper and placed it carefully into the bottom of the bag. "So do I. We think African-American Beadwork and Mosaic Arts works better for us now. I'm sorry we don't have a gift box, but if you go to The Wrap Store, you'll find something."

Regina had been quiet while he made the purchase. Now she turned to Amelie. "Do you mind if I steal Nigel away for a few minutes? I need to talk to him. Can I walk you to your car?"

"No, I'm still looking for another present for my mom, and this is my first time around the market. Walk around with me. Here." He handed Amelie the bag of peaches. "These can be for you guys."

He hugged Regina when she stepped around the booth and tugged her toward the booths he hadn't seen yet.

She went along with him without saying anything, not even when he pointed out an African dress that his mom might like. He tugged her hand.

"Hey, what's wrong?"

"Nigel, I can't see you anymore."

"What? Why?"

"I can't say. I can only say that I can't see you anymore."

"Not again. We just went through this. I told you, I won't rush you. If you just want to call us friends, that's fine. Whatever you want."

She pulled her hand out of his.

"It's not any of that. I just can't see you anymore—for good this time."

"Why?"

She looked around. They were between two booths, and other shoppers were skirting around them. He could see her distraction.

"This is not the best place to talk," he said. "What time are you through tonight?"

"There isn't anything to talk about. I just can't continue to see you."

Her eyes were misty. He could tell that she was serious this time, but he wasn't about to let her go—not without a real reason and not without a fight.

"What time do you close down?"

She sighed. "We shut down at six. I'm home by seven."

"Do you need help breaking things down?"

"No, no. But—"

"I'll be at your place waiting."

He walked her back to the booth and hugged Amelie.

He had several hours. He had thought that today he would be doing some window-shopping and getting movie tickets, maybe helping them break things down at the booth.

Instead, he was again fretting over the newest incarnation of Regina Gibson—the newest ultimatum.

He doubled back to the indoor market, stopping to get some more peaches on the way in. He went inside and got some lamb shanks and pork chops, some pasta and sauce, some bread and some fresh flowers.

He got home, cooked the lamb shanks and the pasta, showered and changed. He still had time to kill before going to wait for Regina, so while he packed up the meal to take with him, he called his mother to ask her what she wanted for her birthday.

"Oh, honey, I don't need a thing."

He knew she would say that. She always did. Regina's suggestion of perfume wasn't a bad idea, and maybe an African dress to round it out. He would get an extra box from the department store for the statue and put everything in one large box to mail.

He talked to his mom for a little bit, just finding out how things were at home. It helped to calm him down when he was riled up, even if she didn't know there was anything going on with him.

He got to Regina's apartment early, toted dinner up to the third floor landing and waited for her on the bottom step. It wasn't too long before she came home, and he got up to meet her at her car.

"Can I help you unload things?"

"No, everything for Eastern Market stays in Amelie's car. Look, Nigel, I don't think there's anything to talk about."

"Yes, Reggie, there is."

He followed her up the steps, where she found the bag he'd placed at her door.

"That's dinner, but these are for you."

He took out the bouquet he'd gotten from the market— Birds of Paradise and other exotic long-stemmed flowers. They drew her in for a second look.

"They're beautiful. Thank you. But—"

"They don't change your mind. I know. That's not why I got them."

She was clearly hesitant about letting them into her apartment, but she did.

"Are you hungry now, or should we talk first?"

She didn't seem to want to do either, so he nudged. "Why don't we eat now, while the food is warm and the wine is cold? Then we can talk without rushing."

She rolled her eyes but pointed to the cabinet for him to get out plates. Reluctantly, she followed suit and took out the silverware, napkins, two water glasses and two wineglasses. She pulled two place mats from the corner of the table and set places for them.

"I hope it turned out all right. I don't make lamb shanks often."

"That sounds fancy."

"No, my parents made them at home every now and then. I got six at Eastern Market, so dig in."

"This is a lot of food. I think one will be enough for me."

"Not if you don't fill up on pasta," he said and chuckled.

"Nigel, we're just delaying the inevitable."

"Just until after dinner. Let's catch up on other things for a while."

He passed her the bread, and they began eating. Over dinner they talked about everything that wasn't the real issue at hand: how her father was doing, how the search for a new location was going, how her art show was doing, how his work was going, what he invested in, how his cousin Michelle was doing.

They seemed like a regular couple, but they both knew that the difficult part was still coming. While Regina cleared the plates, he refreshed their wineglasses. She came back to the table and sat across from him.

"If I'd known we were eating in, I'd have gotten dessert," she said.

"I'm stuffed, no dessert for me."

"Me, too. Thank you for dinner."

Nigel leaned over the table and took Regina's hand. He exhaled slowly and launched in.

"You don't want to see me anymore."

"No."

He waited for more.

She shook her head. "I just don't think we should continue. I can't continue. It's been… I've enjoyed our time. I just can't let it go on."

"Why? What's changed?"

"I've been ambivalent about this all along. But it keeps getting muddled."

"What's changed in the last week?"

"I—"

She started, but she stopped. He could tell that there

was something that she wasn't telling him, something that he needed to know.

"Tell me."

"I can't say. Just take my word for it."

"If you expect me to stay away from you, I need to know why."

She turned to him with tears in her eyes. "Because I think I'm in love with you. I can't—"

Nigel whooped out loud, broke out in a grin, lifted her from her chair and spun her around. He let her down against his chest, caressing her loose hair.

"It's about time you figured that out."

He laughed, rubbing her back. It was a weight lifted off him, a weight lifted off the evening. He couldn't stop smiling.

She put her hand up to his chest, shaking her head. It was then that he realized she was crying.

"Reggie, what's wrong? This is great. I love you so much."

He wrapped his arm around her and stroked her back until she broke free.

"No, stop. I can't do this."

"You love me. I love you. Where's the problem?"

He was mystified. He needed her to make sense of this for him. She went into the living room, and he followed. She paced a few times and then turned to him.

"I look at you, and sometimes I remember the baby I lost. I remember the nights I cried my eyes out because my marriage never happened. I remember…"

It made sense to him now, but he couldn't accept it. He wouldn't accept it as the end of their relationship.

"Why not just see me? See where we are now. See who I am now. It's not about going back there. It's about being here."

He sat on her sofa and pulled her down with him onto his lap.

"I love you. I can't change the past, but I can make us a present and a future."

He kissed the tracks of her tears, and then he took her lips with his. He kissed her until she was kissing him back.

"It's always been that way with us," he said.

"I just don't know. I don't know if I can do it…again."

"Let's just see where it goes."

He kissed her again, and she curled against his chest.

"Is it okay if we just see where it goes with us being in love?"

Her head was against his neck, and he felt her move slightly. She was nodding.

Chapter 19

Regina shifted under Nigel's arm and put her head on his shoulder.

It had been a couple of months since she had given in to her feelings for Nigel, since they had started really seeing one another, but it still felt new to her.

"If I'm supposed to be giving directions, why am I in the backseat?" asked Jason.

The group laughed.

"Because you wanted to sit next to your love thing," Amelie replied. "Here, give me the directions."

"Oh, no," Regina said. "Amelie got us lost going to Prince George's Plaza."

The group laughed again.

"How is the little one?" Nigel asked.

Ellison looked at Kyle, who was in the backseat with them in a child safety seat.

"After all the food and rides today at the amusement

park, he's out like a light again. We'll have to wake him for dinner."

They'd rented a minivan for the drive back from Ocean City, where they'd spent the Labor Day weekend. Jason, Ellison and Kyle were in the third row; Amelie was stretched out by herself in the middle; and Regina was up front with Nigel, who was behind the wheel.

They'd driven up on Thursday afternoon and walked the boardwalk that evening. Friday and Saturday they'd hit the beach and done some shopping—at least Regina and Amelie had. Kyle had gone with them, and the men had played miniature golf. Both nights they had gone to the movies and to dinner.

Sunday they had slept in, hit the beach and gone to a nightclub (except for Amelie, who stayed to watch Kyle). Monday was the amusement park, and it was all about little Kyle. They were driving back late that afternoon, early enough to get rested for work the next day.

Regina's body was still vibrating from all of the love she and Nigel had made. Even after last night, they still stole an hour to be with each other again when they were supposed to be packing to leave. Everyone was waiting for them in the lobby and teased them when they got down.

They stopped for lunch halfway to DC and finished the last leg of the three-hour drive in one straight shot.

"Hey, whose idea was this trip?" Ellison asked.

"Nigel's," Regina said.

"Props. It was a blast. We have to do it again."

"I'm in," Amelie said.

"Me, too," Regina echoed.

"Hey, put on some of that old school you had on during the drive up."

Nigel plugged his MP3 player in, and the guys started talking about the song, singing with it and telling its history. Regina started to pull away because Nigel's body had become animated, bouncing her head, but he pulled her back and settled down a bit.

"Sorry." He glanced over his shoulder. "Did we wake Kyle?"

"Nope," Jason said, "he yawned and kept on sleeping."

The group laughed.

"I think I need some sleep, as well," Regina said.

"I know why," Amelie said. "Something's keeping you up nights."

"Hush," Regina said.

"Too late," Ellison said. "I heard it, and I concur."

Regina turned into Nigel's shoulder for a moment. Nigel, perhaps to save her further embarrassment, steered the conversation elsewhere.

"You know, it's a good thing we're in DC already so I don't actually need directions."

Everyone laughed again.

"I told you," Jason said. "I shouldn't be in the back."

"Look," Amelie said. "It's our old place. It's all changed. Can we stop and look?"

Regina lifted her head to see. Her spirits fell at the same time.

"What kind of business is it now, a restaurant?" she asked.

The structure itself was different. The building had been entirely redone. There was a larger first floor with wide windows and a raised ceiling, and there were two regular stories on top.

"Yeah, let's stop," Jason said.

"You okay with this?" Nigel asked her.

"Sure."

Looking at the old place without a new one in sight

brought her down, but she didn't want to spoil it for the others.

They parked out back and walked around to the front, Nigel leading the way.

"Hey, it's open," he said.

"Let's go inside," Amelie said.

Inside, Jason found the lights.

Regina looked about, feeling like a thief. Then she got confused. Along one wall was a station that would be perfect for beads: a counter of inset bowls, a wall of pegs for strings of beads. The front was set up for displays.

Regina took another step inside and stopped. A long display case in the middle of the room was already stocked. Regina's eyes flew open. She recognized Amelie's jewelry right away, and next to those pieces were her own mosaics—pieces that Amelie was supposed to have in storage for their booth at Eastern Market.

Regina's head was spinning as she tried to make sense of it all. These were her things. Somehow, they'd gotten back the space. Somehow her dream for this place, for her art, had come true. Her heart was filling up with hope. It was too good to be real. Had they really gotten the space? How?

"What have you done, Nigel?"

Amelie linked arms with her and pulled her farther inside, almost squealing. "Come look."

"You're in on this, too?"

Amelie couldn't stop talking. "Look, there are windows for display cases big enough to be spotted from the street, brand-new counters and workstations, two large classrooms."

"What have you guys done?"

"Look." Amelie pulled her toward the back. "There's even a small separate room for your ceramic kilns and my

pewter kiln. There are boxes of supplies piled in the classrooms. All you have to do is say yes."

"Look at your new sign," Jason said.

She gave him a look. "Why would all of you gang up
on me?"

Ellison held a still-sleeping Kyle on his shoulder. "Consider it an intervention, honey," he said. "Go with the flow."

She turned toward the front of the store and read the
huge sign that hadn't yet been hung out front—African-
American Beadwork and Mosaic Arts.

Tears came to her eyes.

She turned to Amelie. "Our paperwork isn't even in
yet. Even with full drafts, we still need…"

"A location. Here it is."

"You'd been procrastinating so long getting the info
to Nigel that I was worried that you might be thinking of
backing out."

"Back out nothing! We found a private lender, honey.
Look at it. There's even an extra floor upstairs; you can
have a real home now. Or we can rent it out."

"I bet I know who the private lender is."

She turned to Nigel.

"I said that I wanted to help. I've wanted to tell you so
many times so that you'd stop worrying about finding another location."

"We made sure we were with you in case we needed to
talk you out of a good place," Amelie said, "but one never
materialized."

"How did this happen?"

Nigel stepped toward her and put his arm around her
shoulder.

"We were able to get it back from the person Mr. Lundstrum sold it to before any remodeling was done. Then we

got an architect who could get all the paperwork done and redo the place the way you wanted it."

"I told him what we talked about and helped with the plans," Amelie said. "The whole place had to be demolished. I hope we got it right, Regina. We couldn't ask you exactly what you wanted."

"Why didn't you tell me?"

"We couldn't," Amelie said.

"Every time I tried to bring it up, you got defensive, Reggie. In the end, I thought I should just pursue it on my own. At worst, it would be an improved property to put back on the market, and you'd hate me for trying. But at best, you'd have a good location that you can afford in the condition that you need it to be in."

Nigel was still trying to gauge her reaction. Amelie was almost giddy. Jason and Ellison were hanging back, looking around. She was still trying to take it all in and get her bearings so that she knew what her reaction should be.

"It's beautiful. But I don't know if I want to owe you money, Nigel."

"It's him or the banks, honey," Amelie said. "Guess which one is more likely to pull a fast one. Actually, it's him *and* the banks." She turned to Nigel. "Can I tell her?"

"Tell me what?"

"Our paperwork is in to the bank. It went in a long time ago, and we have an angel investor." Regina caught Nigel giving Amelie the head-chopping signal about the last part; Amelie wasn't supposed to have said that.

"I know what an angel investor is," Regina said.

"What is it?" Ellison asked.

"It's someone who provides capital for a business just starting out," Jason answered, "or who agrees to pay on a loan if you default."

"Look, we have an agreement from National Bank,"

Amelie said. "That's not even included in this." She opened her arms to indicate the location.

"Reggie," Nigel said, "new companies are less likely to fail if they have angel investors."

"You can use it for advertising," Ellison said.

"And if you sign these," Nigel said, taking papers out of the cash register, "you won't be a renter here, you'll be the *owner*. The bank loan has to be paid on once you sign for it, but you'll have as much time as you want to make good on this place. No strings attached—to anything."

"Please, Regina," Amelie said. "We have our dream back. We're not going to find another location like this that we can afford."

She walked around and ended up in front of Jason. He drew her in for a hug, and then she stepped back to look up at him.

"It's up to you, kiddo," he said, "but it's a good opportunity."

She went back to Amelie and Nigel.

"It's just what we wanted," she said to Amelie. She looked at Amelie and then at Nigel. "I'll do it."

Amelie squealed and hugged her, and they started bouncing up and down, and soon both of them were crying. Linked arm in arm, they started circling the room again, seeing what it was now that it was theirs.

In the end, she stood before Nigel.

"Nigel, could you really afford to do all this? Didn't it empty your bank account?"

"Yes, I could, and no, it didn't."

"Thank you so much, Nigel. I'll pay you back every penny."

"It was my pleasure, Reggie."

She put her arms around him and hugged him. In response, he dipped his head down and kissed her.

"I just want to see you happy, Reggie. And I want your talent to get recognized."

"I can't thank you enough."

"You don't have to thank me. Just get to work," he said and chuckled.

Gratitude filled Regina's heart and filled her eyes with tears. Nigel was kidding, but what he had done—this gift—would change her life. She didn't know what to say. She reached up to his cheek and ran her fingers along its curve while tears ran down her face. He took her hand and put her fingers to his lips then pulled her into an embrace.

She looked up at him, and he leaned down and kissed her again, first soft then strong. Their lips spelled out the tenderness that had grown between them.

"Ahem," said Ellison. "Shall we see the apartment upstairs?"

Everyone else laughed, and they broke the kiss.

"Yes," Nigel said, "let's."

They locked up downstairs and headed out back, where Ellison handed Kyle to Jason for the climb upstairs. The apartment was fully new and partially furnished. Now it opened into the living room with the kitchen off to the left.

There were brand-new appliances, a dinette set, a sectional sofa and matching end tables, an entertainment center. It was all clean and empty.

Regina tapped Nigel on the arm. "You had your designer pick stuff out, didn't you?"

He chuckled. "No, Amelie and I did this all on our own."

"There's a small bedroom on this floor," Amelie said, "but the master bedroom, master bath and studio space are upstairs. Come see."

"I'll wait here," Nigel said. "I have this thing about seeing Reggie in bedrooms."

Regina blushed as the group broke out laughing.

"Here," Nigel said, "I'll hold Kyle."

Jason handed the little one over.

Amelie led the group upstairs. There was a four-poster in the master suite, with a dresser and nightstand. There were two walk-in closets and a huge bath. The studio space had its own small bathroom, as well.

Regina led them back down and took a seat next to Nigel on the sofa.

"When did you start all this? How did you get it done so quickly?"

"I started looking into it the day you came to my office thinking that I was the one who'd purchased the place."

"And our paperwork went to the bank the day after I ditched you two for our meeting."

"Are you going to move back in here?" Ellison asked.

"I don't know. I feel like I just moved. Would it be better to rent it out and put that down as business income? It would be far more than I'm paying."

"It would be your income," Amelie said. "Right?" she asked Nigel.

"Yes, downstairs is equally owned by both of you. Up here we drew up as yours, like a condo. And where you live doesn't matter as long as the business gets off its feet. It's up to you, but yes, while you're still working to establish yourself, it's better to have the income from this place."

"We have to go over all the papers so I'll know what we're doing," Regina said. She turned toward Amelie. "There's so much to talk about."

"We can do that," Nigel said.

"I'm in," Amelie said.

"Is it too early for dinner?" Ellison asked.

The group cracked up.

This time, the laughter woke up Kyle, who was lying

next to Nigel on the sofa. Nigel picked him up and set him into a sitting position.

"We'll let you decide," Nigel said to Kyle. "You hungry?"

The little one thought about it then shook his head yes.

"How about I fill them in another day and we just go to eat?"

"Word," Ellison said.

At the car, Amelie and Regina stopped to do a happy dance and ended up bouncing up and down and yelling.

"That's all the repayment I need," Nigel said to Jason.

Chapter 20

Nigel spooned a second helping of pasta onto their plates while Regina poured more water into their goblets.

"When are you going to come home with me and see my parents again?" Nigel asked. "They haven't seen you in years."

Regina smiled. "That would be nice. I still have friends there."

"So you'll come?" He smiled at her, thinking about holding her on the long ride home.

"Sure. The weekend flea market at Eastern Market ends soon. But the studio opens again in a couple of weeks, and our classes start again not long after that." She was excited about the reopening and about her teaching. "We already have people enrolled in classes for Thursday and Saturday, and we haven't even opened yet. Your advice on advertising has really paid off. Thank you."

"You never have to thank me, Reggie." He pulled her

hand to him and kissed it. "Maybe we should go home after you guys get going. Maybe for Thanksgiving."

"My parents will die if I'm not there for Thanksgiving. You coming?"

"Am I invited?"

She smiled at him. "Yes, but you'll have to stay in the den."

"I can live with that. Okay, a compromise. Take off an extra day for Columbus Day, and we go home to South Carolina. Then we go to New Jersey for Thanksgiving."

"Okay. What about Christmas?" she asked.

"Why don't we do Christmas here together, just the two of us?"

She thought of them wrapped in each other's arms in front of his fireplace with glasses of cider.

"That sounds nice. My parents won't be happy, but hopefully we'll be doing a lot of business, and I'll need to stay anyway. I'm doing a series of mosaic crosses for Christmas. They're easy to do, and they sell well. I'm also making one for my aunt. I can go up for New Year's."

"If we keep it up," he said, "we'll have parceled out every holiday through Easter before dinner is over."

They chuckled.

Regina finished first and folded her napkin. She got up and rounded Nigel's chair and bent over to wrap her arms around his neck. She hummed.

"Finish up."

Nigel cut his pork chop, added a forkful of pasta and brought it to his mouth.

As he took the bite, Regina pressed her lips to his neck, and as he savored the mouthful, she rubbed her hands along his chest, undoing his buttons as she went along.

"What are you doing?"

"Nothing. Go ahead and eat."

By the time Nigel took another mouthful, Regina had his shirt partway down his back. She moved her lips from his neck down to the back of one of his shoulder blades and bit down gently. She ran her tongue over the surface, and then she moved a piece of ice she'd been sucking on between her lips and drew it along the surface.

Nigel's chest heaved outward, and his shoulders flexed backward.

"Finish your dinner, honey," she prodded.

Nigel eyed her over his shoulder and found a mischievous grin on her face. She wanted to play, and he loved when she wanted to play.

As he brought another forkful of pasta to his mouth, Regina pressed her warm tongue to the back of his neck. As he swallowed, she pressed the ice to the spot, feeling his torso straighten.

As he cut another slice of his pork chop, she picked the ice out of her mouth and brought her lips to his ear. She licked the inside of the lobe as she brought the ice to one of his nipples. His chest clenched inward, and he swallowed hard.

"Do you like that?"

"Yes."

"I want proof."

She ran her hand along the crease in his pants, and when she found what she was looking for, his thighs flexed, and he sucked in a breath.

"You're not eating."

"I think I'm finished."

"Aw." Regina straightened up. "I don't want to stop you from finishing your dinner."

As she stepped away, Nigel scooted back his chair and pulled her onto his lap, making her laugh.

"I'm finished. Look." She found his plate nearly empty. "And you don't get away that easily."

His first touch tickled her and set Regina to laughing again. But when his mouth found her neck and his hand found her breast, Regina murmured. He toyed with her body until she twisted on his lap.

"Do you like that?" he asked.

"Yes."

"I want proof."

Nigel slipped his hand under her dress and moved them up her thighs. Regina laughed again, making Nigel laugh. She got up briefly and repositioned herself over his legs, straddling him as she covered his lips with her own.

"Let me feel you," she said, scooting closer to his chest.

He gripped her buttocks and pulled her onto his body. She tilted her hips to meet him and settled along his body. She pulled the straps of her dress from over her shoulders, put her arms around his neck and rubbed her breasts across his chest.

The heat that ran through her body made her murmur against his ear. She licked the lobe of his ear and felt his body tense.

He drew his fingers over her bra, kneading her nipples into peaks. At the same time, he took over her mouth. Regina's body started pulsing, and she rocked along his thighs.

Feeling her oscillate over his manhood drove Nigel to distraction, and he groaned, glaring at her for wreaking such havoc on him. He wanted to make her feel that way also.

"I still want proof," he said, slipping his hand between them and running his fingers over her slick panties.

"You're so wet."

Regina tensed, self-conscious, and started to pull back.

"No, don't go. I love you wet."

He pressed his thumb over her womanhood and began to knead her, and Regina moaned, gripping onto his shoulders.

When Nigel stood, Regina linked her legs around his waist and held on to his neck. He let them down in the middle of his bed, running his body up and down along hers so that she could feel how ready he was to be inside of her. He felt her tilt toward him and pull down on his hips, wanting to feel more. He continued until she moaned and cried out, clinging to him.

When he lifted himself away from her, she grumbled and held on to him.

"Don't stop."

"I'll be right back. I want to be inside of you, baby."

He rifled in his drawer for a condom, removed his clothes and came back to relieve her of the dress that was knotted about her waist and the panties beneath them, as well as her bra and sandals.

She grasped his sheathed member and drew him to her.

"I want you, Nigel."

His body leapt in her hand, and he climbed onto the bed, positioning himself above her. Regina surprised him. She pushed him down instead, and straddled his thighs.

"Is this okay?" she asked once she had him pinned.

He could tell that she was unsure in this position. They had never done this before. "Yes. I love seeing you this way. You look beautiful."

Regina moved her hips, drawing herself over his rigid member and making them both moan. She reached the end and moved back the other way, teasing them both.

Nigel groaned and thrust his hips upward.

"If you keep doing that..."

She moved up along him again.

"If I keep doing this?"

The naughty glint had returned to her eyes.

"Yes, that."

She reached the end and moved back the other way, making him arch his back off the bed and thrust upward.

"Then what?"

He couldn't think to reply to her question. But he gripped her hips and pulled her toward him. She murmured as she slid along his body. This time when she reached the end, he lifted her slightly and moved his leaping manhood just inside of her.

She cried out as the pleasure of him pierced her and made her throb. She couldn't help rotating her hips to tease herself on his body.

This time, his upward thrust brought him deeper inside her body. She held his shoulders and pressed back, driving him home.

They began to move together.

Nigel bit off a groan and then gritted his teeth, needing to keep control. The sight of Regina's naked beauty, the feel of her honeyed warmth, the vision of her trembling breasts, the scent of her perfumed body, the sound of her muted cries of pleasure, the movement of her body as she rode along his—it all filled him with an aching for release.

Nigel reached up and spread his palm across both of her breasts, feeling both of her nipples with his fingers. Regina moaned and bucked on top of him, feeling heat spread through her breast to her center. Her throbbing became heavy and filled her entire body with unleashed longing.

She bent downward, tilting her hips so that her womanhood grazed along his rippled abdomen and her breasts along his chest, and the pleasure made her cry out.

"Nigel," she called, agonized by the need building inside of her.

"Yes, Reggie," he said, and captured her lips.

They moved as one, her body grating over his chest, his lower stomach, his manhood. The sensations singed her. She pulled her mouth away.

"Nigel, Nigel."

"Yes, Reggie, yes."

Their foreheads pressed together, he drove inside her faster and harder, responding to her call, heady with the urgency he heard in her voice.

"Nigel," she cried, "please, please."

"Reggie."

Nigel groaned. Her desire held him at the precipice, but he wanted to fulfill her need.

"Take it, Reggie. Take your pleasure from me."

Regina cried out as her muscles contracted around Nigel's thrusting member. She moaned as wave after wave of pleasure ripped through her body, blinding her to anything but the feeling of rhapsody.

Nigel felt her clench, felt her contract about him like fingers in massage. His body buckled, sending him into her in uncontrollable pulses as he felt his own release.

They wrapped their arms around each other as she collapsed on him. Nigel lowered her to his side, unsheathed himself and returned to Regina's arms.

"Everything you do drives me crazy," he said. "If I'm not careful, I'll end up in the loony bin."

He chuckled, and she elbowed him playfully.

Then Nigel got serious.

"Reggie, has it been okay being with me, us being in love? Do you still look at me and think about…what happened before?"

She reached out and touched his cheek, looking into his face.

"No. I love being with you. I don't think about what happened before."

He leaned over and kissed her mouth.

"I'm so glad. I have another question. Have you forgiven me?"

"What? Where is this coming from?"

"Have you forgiven me—for being a kid and for leaving when I should have stayed and for not being there when you lost the baby and for...everything?"

Regina sighed and thought about it so that she could answer truthfully. "Yes. Yes, I have." She hesitated, and then she added, "I need to know something, too."

"Anything."

She took a breath and looked up at the ceiling.

"Have you forgiven me for losing our child?" Tears spilled down her face.

"What?"

"I felt so ashamed that I couldn't— I wanted to tell you before, to find out before, but I couldn't. We weren't... close enough then."

"Oh, Reggie." Nigel turned to her, wrapping his arms around her. "There's nothing to forgive. It wasn't your fault. It happens."

He kissed her temples and her eyes.

"I know. I know. I guess I just had to get that off my chest. I've been holding it in for so long. I just felt...so ashamed."

"There was nothing for you to feel ashamed about. You did everything you were supposed to do."

"I know. I just couldn't help it. I couldn't help thinking it was me." Regina exhaled and shook her head to clear her mind. "I'm okay."

Nigel got up, pulling something from inside the dresser

and coming to her side of the bed, where he knelt. Regina leaned up on her elbow to meet him.

"There was a reason I needed to know the answer to those questions."

"What is it?"

"I love you with all of my heart. I'm only happy in life when I'm with you." He opened the box he'd taken from the dresser. It was his grandmother's wedding ring. "Marry me because you love me, and never think of paying me back again."

Regina sat up, bringing the covers with her. Her hand flew to her chest, and tears streamed down her face.

She took the ring from the box. It was an antique with a large diamond in the middle of a circular crest and smaller diamonds all around it. She looked at Nigel and then slipped it onto her ring finger.

She turned to face Nigel again.

"Yes. I will."

She wiped at the tears.

"But we're going to pay you back anyway—Amelie and me."

Nigel laughed, which made Regina laugh, too.

"I knew you would say that."

"Good," she said.

"I'm so happy, Reggie. I love you."

"I love you, too, Nigel."

They reached for each other at the same time, the fire reigniting between them. It had always been that way for them. She opened her arms for him, and he climbed into bed and into her embrace, their bodies coming together.

"Reggie," he said, breaking their kiss.

"Yes."

"I know that your business is just getting started, and

this might not be the best time, but when can we try for another baby, or do you still want children?"

In response, she captured his mouth with her lips, reached between them to grip him and guided him inside of her.

Nigel moaned as the wet warmth of her body surrounded his unsheathed manhood, making it spring and swell inside of her.

"Reggie, Reggie," he said, while he still had the presence of mind.

"Yes, Nigel."

"Are you sure? Are you sure you want this now?"

The answer came from her body, which clamped around him and twisted, bringing him home.

Nigel winced in exquisite anguish as Regina's heat flooded his body. He covered her mouth again, giving himself to the electricity between them.

Then Regina stopped, shaking her head to wake herself and slowing down to pull him from his reverie.

"You, what about you? Do you want this now?" she asked.

Nigel pressed his grinning face against Regina's cheek, pulled one of her nipples taut and gyrated inside of her until her hips rocked upward to ride her along his tumid crest.

"Yes, I do. Yes, I'm sure."

He drew himself out, stopping at the point he knew she liked, and made short thrusts against her until she moaned and careened her hips. But she paused again.

"You know," she said, "we're doing it backwards again—baby, marriage."

Nigel leaned up and chuckled, at least until Regina's mouth found one of his nipples and sent a quiver up his back.

When he could talk, he said, "First, this time, it's a de-

liberate choice. And second, I hope to be married long before it's a question in anybody's mind."

Regina turned Nigel on his side and started to get up,
but he held her back.

"Where are you going?"

"I have to start planning a wedding."

Nigel laughed, and then she did, too.

"We can start that tomorrow."

"We better, at the rate we're going."

His was still wedged deep inside her body and turned
her onto her back again. He put his hands beneath her
shoulders and slowly dove deeper inside of her. She pressed
her fingers into his back and pivoted along his thrust. Their
lips found one another, and their bodies moved together.

They were going to make it a long night.

* * * * *

LET'S TALK
Romance

For exclusive extracts, competitions and special offers, find us online:

f MillsandBoon

𝕏 @MillsandBoon

◎ @MillsandBoonUK

♪ @MillsandBoonUK

Get in touch on 01413 063 232

MILLS & BOON

THE HEART OF ROMANCE

A ROMANCE FOR EVERY READER

MODERN
Prepare to be swept off your feet by sophisticated, sexy and seductive heroes, in some of the world's most glamourous and romantic locations, where power and passion collide.

HISTORICAL
Escape with historical heroes from time gone by. Whether your passion is for wicked Regency Rakes, muscled Vikings or rugged Highlanders, awaken the romance of the past.

MEDICAL
Set your pulse racing with dedicated, delectable doctors in the high-pressure world of medicine, where emotions run high and passion, comfort and love are the best medicine.

True Love
Celebrate true love with tender stories of heartfelt romance, from the rush of falling in love to the joy a new baby can bring, and a focus on the emotional heart of a relationship.

Desire
Indulge in secrets and scandal, intense drama and sizzling hot action with heroes who have it all: wealth, status, good looks…everything but the right woman.

HEROES
The excitement of a gripping thriller, with intense romance at its heart. Resourceful, true-to-life women and strong, fearless men face danger and desire - a killer combination!

To see which titles are coming soon, please visit

millsandboon.co.uk/nextmonth

GET YOUR ROMANCE FIX!

Get the latest romance news, exclusive author interviews, story extracts and much more!

blog.millsandboon.co.uk